BIG *Date* ENERGY

BETHANY RUTTER

HarperCollins*Publishers*

HarperCollins*Publishers* Ltd
1 London Bridge Street,
London SE1 9GF
www.harpercollins.co.uk

HarperCollins*Publishers*
Macken House,
39/40 Mayor Street Upper,
Dublin 1
D01 C9W8

First published by HarperCollins*Publishers* 2024
1

A catalogue record for this book is available from the British Library

ISBN: 978-0-00-847003-6

Typeset in Bembo by Palimpsest Book Production Ltd, Falkirk, Stirlingshire

Printed and bound in the UK using
100% Renewable Electricity by CPI Group (UK) Ltd

For anyone who specifically identifies as a greedy bisexual

APPLICATION FORM TO SUBMIT A FRIEND OR FAMILY MEMBER TO NEW TV SHOW *The Meet-Cute* FROM RED ROOSTER PRODUCTIONS

Who's your mate?
Fran Baker.

How do you know them?
I'm her mother.

Why do you want your mate to take part in *The Meet-Cute?*
I recently heard my daughter use the phrase 'slag era' to describe her current dating habits. That just isn't her. Fran unfortunately experienced a break-up recently and hasn't been herself ever since. She needs to find someone to settle down with but instead she's been dating everyone – and I mean everyone.

Describe your mate in 3 words?
Optimistic, loving, confident.

What is your mate's type?
Tall, fun, attractive.

If your mate was a dog what breed would they be?
A poodle, no question. Very showy.

What kind of person should they not go on a date with?
Anyone that likes getting a word in edgeways.

What would you be looking for in a partner for your mate?
Fran is good fun, so someone who doesn't take themselves too seriously, however she can sometimes be too much fun (if you get what I mean) so maybe someone who is a calming influence on her. (And she likes tall people.)

What would be their dream date?
She tells me about all the dates she's going on at the moment and all they ever seem to do is go to the pub! Where's the romance? My daughter deserves to be swept off her feet and have some glamour in her life.

What dating advice would you give them?
I'm not exactly famous for my long/successful relationships – can I skip this question?

What are their relationship weaknesses?
The main bloody weakness is that she now doesn't seem very interested in a relationship! But I know if she met the right person she could change her mind.

What's their relationship history?
Well, that's the thing – she's always been in a relationship! And I mean always. Ever since she was at school. That's why it's so strange for her to be single! She's just not a single kind of girl. Everyone knows that. She's recently broken up with her girlfriend Miranda – I liked her but she was a bit boring, wasn't right for Franny, too sensible, and I think her and Fran had different ideas about life. That's how Fran put

it to me, anyway. It's a shame they broke up, but I have to say I don't think they were a perfect match. Still, it was nice for her to be with someone calm and kind. She was a librarian, I think. Loved a cardigan. Or was she an archivist? You'll have to ask Fran. Either way, they were together for four years so there must have been something there. Before Miranda, there was Daniel. God, he was handsome! He was big and blond, Polish surname, maybe? Lemansky, I think it was. Anyway, he was very good-looking and they were together for years. Seven years, in all. Lots of fighting, though. She never seemed that happy with him, like she could never just relax and enjoy it because there was always some drama to distract her. I think she liked him because he was very handsome – I know I've mentioned that before ha ha. I could never get it out of her whether he cheated on her or not, she never seemed to want to talk about it. Anyway, about a week after they had finally broken up she met Miranda so she's really never been single! Oh and I think she met Daniel straight after another break-up . . . I suppose that would be from her girlfriend in secondary school. Now her, that was a fucking awful bad break-up, lots of tears and moping but it was so long ago I can't tell you too much about the relationship. God, I've really gone on, haven't I? You probably didn't need to know any of this, did you!

How is your mate going to react to being set up on *The Meet-Cute*?
She'll be furious but it's for her own good. And if this truly is her 'slag era' as she so delicately puts it then she won't object too much.

1

As far back as I can remember, I always wanted to be single.

Purely by chance I ended up being a serial monogamist. Fate handed me Big Loves. First there was Ivy (ages 16–18), quickly followed by Daniel (18–25) and then straight into Miranda (25— literally *just now*). Who was I to complain? Big Loves are what we all want, right? But to me, there was something so glamorous about being single. I don't know, blame *Sex and the City* or something. I would fall in love with pretty waitresses, men on the tube, people who sold me coffee, girls I met in pub toilets and not be able to act on it. But then I got dumped by Miranda and finally the world was my oyster. No more Big Loves – it was time for some fun and adventures . . .

'Birthday girl's awake,' says the guy next to me in bed, rubbing his eye with one hand as he scrolls through Instagram with the other. James? Joe?

'It's me! I'm the birthday girl!' I say brightly, sitting up and hoping that a change of perspective will help dislodge his name from my brain. 'Oh, God . . .' I lie back down again. Not feeling *quite* so bright, as it turns out.

'I know, you kept telling me that last night in the bar.'

'That sounds like me . . .' I say, the foggy remembrances of the night before slowly unfurling themselves. 'Now I remember! I was trying to steal your baseball cap, wasn't I?'

'You said it would look better on you.' He turns onto his side and the sight of the blond hair on his chest *stirs* something in me.

'I bet I was right,' I say, smiling, wondering if I can ask him his name. It's in there somewhere. My head spins and my stomach lurches. 'Oh my God, I'm going to die.'

'You mean those 2 a.m. negronis were a mistake? The drink that is *pure alcohol*?'

'Ah, yes, in the words of Celine Dion, it's all coming back to me now. My last friend wanted to go home and I'd been alternately spying on and harassing you for your baseball cap for some time, and for some reason you bought me a drink.'

'Correct.'

'Well, thank you,' I say. 'Can you rummage around in my bag for my phone, please? I feel like if I bend over I might actually die.'

He does what he's told and produces my phone, which, to my great surprise, is all in one piece. Battery low, but screen uncracked. He yanks a T-shirt on over his head and tosses me the phone. 'Want a coffee?'

As he stands there in his pants and a T-shirt, I can definitely see why I would have been drawn to him like a moth to a sexy flame in a state of inebriation. Messy blond hair, soft brown eyes, a nice beard situation, kinda chunky. Dad bod without the dad part. Well, I assume not, anyway.

'Yes, please,' I say, a little sheepishly.

'Milk? Sugar?' he asks. He is not a man of many words.
'Milk please, but not sugar. Thanks.'

I hear him pad downstairs and check my phone. Amid the happy birthday messages rolling in, there are a couple I actually have to reply to. First up, from my best friend Marie, who was the last gal standing last night (except for me, of course).

Can you please confirm that this George character didn't murder you last night? He seemed normal but you never know.

Oooh, a name! I told you it was something like Joe, didn't I? I reassure her I am not murdered, and as soon as I send the message I can see the little dots of her replying already.

THANK GOD! At first I was like, oooh fun good for her, love this new slutty Fran, and then overnight I got convinced he was a murderer and I was going to have to call the police but I didn't know anything about him except for his name which might not even really be his name. Happy Birthday btw. Do you feel as rough as me?

I open the camera on my phone and switch it to front-facing so I can take a proof-of-life selfie for Marie. Urgh! No! Hideous! My mascara is smeared around my eyes like a raccoon and my skin looks *deathly* pale. In the spirit of friendship, I overcome my natural vanity and duly take a photo and send it to her.

You're alive . . . but at what cost!

And a text from Vic:

7

Sorry I could only pop in last night! Can I take you for dinner this week? I heard they've got deep-fried cheese at Cafe Deco???

You had me at deep-fried cheese xx I reply. That gives me a reason to survive this hangover.

George nudges the bedroom door open with his hip and reappears with two large mugs of coffee.

I sit up in bed and we sip them in silence. I could probably do with about a litre of water at the same time, possibly delivered intravenously. Once I'm sitting up and my dehydrated brain is correctly oriented, I find that a lot of last night has not, in fact, evaporated from my memory. I remember drinking negronis with George after my friends left and his friends left, and then I remember taking an Uber here, and I remember we had sex and I *definitely* remember we used a condom (safety first), and then I remember we fell asleep. See? Not a complete mess after all!

'I thought you were, like, gay,' George says from between sips of boiling hot coffee. 'That's why I was surprised you were hitting on me. I was sure I saw you making out with that girl with the red hair.'

'I was,' I say, shrugging. 'That's Jessie. A little birthday kiss with Jessie.' I wouldn't have minded going home with Jessie, but she had to work and besides, variety is the spice of life, isn't it?

He nods.

'But she's not my girlfriend. I am very much not doing that right now. No girlfriends for me. Or boyfriends. Or people who are neither boys nor girls.'

'Wise,' he says.

'Anyway, where *exactly* do you live? I'm sensing . . . Peckham? Maybe?' And by *sensing* I mean *dredging my brain for specific geographical markers from the Uber journey.*

'Close. Camberwell.'

'Nice,' I say, extremely relieved that I am this side of the river and not too far away from my current abode. My birthday was yesterday, the festivities are now decidedly *over* and today I have to see my mother for professional purposes. I certainly *cannot* see her in my present state. A pit stop is required. A refresh. A cleansing. A nap. 'Don't worry, I'm not going to stay here all day. I just need to gather my strength.' I close my eyes and breathe deeply, the thought of entering the loud and busy world extremely hostile to my fragile self. But the coffee is incredibly delicious and seems to be doing a pretty decent job of reviving me.

'My flatmates are out at five-a-side so if you want to use the shower or anything that's cool.'

'Ye-e-e-es,' I say, deciding a shower will definitely aid the hangover.

George jumps out of bed and opens a wardrobe, pulling a towel down from the top shelf. Oooh, a man who owns more than one towel? A luxury prince!

'There'll be a spare toothbrush in the medicine cabinet, I think. Maybe a green one? I think I used the blue one. You'll figure it out,' he says, getting back into bed.

I nod. 'I'm smart like that.' I drain my coffee, pull my party dress on so I'm not walking around naked even though I know there's no one else home, and head into the bathroom. I sit on the toilet and lean my head against the cool wall tile.

Nice. Nice. Nice. Nice feeling. Maybe I can stay here for a little nap.

No! I have things to do! I spring to my feet and try to figure out how to work the shower before shakily making my way under the jets, careful to not let it get on my hair because I'm sure as hell not washing my troublesome mane here. Washing my hair is not so much a ritual as an ordeal. I have too much of it and I don't know what to do with it, but the one thing I *do* know is that I can't let it come into contact with whatever two-in-one situation is lurking on the side of the bath.

Once I feel sufficiently cleansed, I make my slightly-less-shaky way out of the shower and wrap myself in the towel that George provided me with. Oh, look, it's too small and barely covers my bits. What a surprise! Newsflash: people have got bigger in the last twenty years, so why haven't towels? Hmm? When I run for prime minister as a member of the Improving Quality of Life for Hot Fat Babes Party, my first policy will be making bath towels 50 per cent larger.

'Thanks for that,' I say.

'Feeling more alive?' George is hanging some clothes in his wardrobe.

'Yep, I think I will live to see another day,' I say, handing the towel back to him and wondering if there's a bus that'll take me all the way home or if it's going to be a Sunday transport hell. But when he takes the towel from me, there's a *look* in his nice brown eyes. Oh.

'I was thinking . . .' he says, maintaining eye contact. Maybe he's into the smeary-mascara racoon look that I couldn't over-come on my bathroom sojourn since there is no make-up

10

remover in the medicine cabinet. 'It seems like a bit of a waste to have sex we don't really remember . . .'

I smile. 'Yeah. I guess it does.'

'Maybe we should . . . ?' He glances over at the unmade bed.

'Maybe we should.'

And off comes the birthday dress and the inside-out knickers and the bra that I should probably replace but honestly who can afford to replace their bras, and then it's me and George aggressively making out on his bed as I pull his T-shirt off and he wriggles off his boxers and my freshly showered body is ready and I can only conclude that this is actually a really good hangover cure because when my sleekly manicured hands are wrapped around the metal poles of his bed frame as he fucks me, I start to feel close to fully human again. And when he goes down on me I forget *all* my hangover woes.

Before I leave, I give him my number and he texts me so I have his. 'You know, if you want to do this again,' he says. He's cute. I would probably do this again. And besides, he makes good coffee. And is skilled at going down on me. What more could a girl want from one person of many people that they are sleeping with at one particular point in time?

Aged twenty-nine and one day, I stride forth from the block of flats in Camberwell where this George fellow lives, and as he closes the door behind me, I breathe in the lovely late September air and wish just a little bit that I had anticipated staying out last night and worn a jacket. But never mind! All is well in the world! I am infused with the good birthday vibes!

Mercifully, despite copious selfie-taking last night, my phone has 20 per cent battery, which is more than enough to get

11

me home and entertain me. While I *could* walk home in half an hour, there's a bus that would get me there in fifteen minutes, and, well, who am I to argue with simple maths?

Ah, wonderful, just my luck, there's the bus cruising past me. Am I going to run for it? Absolutely not. I resist the urge to squander my phone's battery life, knowing I'll appreciate the internet time-wasting time more on the bus. Instead I take in my surroundings: the guy cycling past with his hands off the handlebars, blasting music from a boombox, the fancy cafe I'm waiting outside, the pigeons nibbling at a discarded chip on the pavement, and then I realize that a woman pushing a pram in my direction is Laura, an old colleague from the women's magazine I used to work at. I feel like I'm always bumping into people, even though I live in a city with a population of more than nine million. Maybe I've just met most of them.

'Fran!' She grins.

'Hello!' I greet her jubilantly, the hangover ebbing away with the unexpected joy of seeing an old friend. 'And who's this?' I lean down to examine the serenely dozing baby in the expensive pram.

'This is Elodie,' Laura says, gently stroking the baby's cheek with the side of her finger.

'Hello, Elodie,' I whisper. The baby is beautiful, perfect, adorable. Soft and warm and sweet and chubby. I wait for the maternal stirrings to emerge. They do not. They never do. 'She's so lovely, congratulations. I don't think I even knew you were pregnant!'

'I guess I'd left the mag before then so why would you? Anyway, are you still there?'

'Uh, no, I'm not. Redundant.'

'Oh! I'm sorry! Are you still in Leyton with . . . Miranda, right?'

'No, and no,' I say with a tight smile. 'Lots of changes!'

But before I can explain them all, my bus slides into the stop. 'Is this you?' Laura asks.

'Yeah, it was nice to see you!'

When the doors open I head for the top deck where the 'king seat' (front, on top of the driver) is unoccupied, therefore vindicating my decision to take the bus. But then we immediately get stuck in traffic which rather undermines my decision to take the bus home. Oh well, there are worse places to be than in the king seat of the 136 bus on a Sunday morning, worse places to be than some road between Camberwell and Elephant and Castle, worse lives to live than the life of Fran Baker aged twenty-nine, single for the first time in many years with the promise of deep-fried belated birthday cheese on her horizon and an excuse to see her beloved mother later.

As I gaze out of the window, I catch sight of a little Italian restaurant I went to with Miranda on one of our early dates and feel my nose wrinkle involuntarily at the memory. That's the problem with doing all your life, love, sex, break-ups and heartbreaks in one city: many, many ghosts.

I use my remaining 18 per cent of battery to distract myself by moseying around the internet, namely to check that my birthday outfit photo with the caption *29 and feeling fine* did good numbers, which I am happy to say it did. I check my email for the first time since Friday in the hope that some brand whose newsletter I signed up to in pursuit of free stuff on my birthday has actually come through with the aforementioned free stuff. Result! I absolutely *will* be claiming that free burger, thank you very much. But when I scroll back through the emails, there's something else. Sent on Friday afternoon, late in the day.

From: Tilly@redroosterproductions.com

Subject: HELLO FROM RED ROOSTER PRODUCTIONS – The Meet-Cute

Hi Frances!

I hope this email finds you well! I'm Tilly and I'm a producer working on a new show called *The Meet-Cute*. I'm not sure if you know, but you've been put forward by one of your friends and/or family to go on a date on the show. You sound like a really good candidate! The nature of the show means you get submitted by someone else but obviously we don't actually force you to participate against your will! The basic premise is that we pair you up with someone and you go on a date which we film (in a completely non-obtrusive way, of course!) and hopefully you find true love, to the great pleasure of whoever submitted you! So before we get too involved, I wanted to check: are you up for it? If so, we can talk more about what it will involve and when you're available. I've checked out your Insta and I just love your confidence and your look and I think you'll be a great participant! Please let me know ASAP!

Tilly

I burst out laughing so abruptly that the beautifully turned-out old lady in the 'queen seat' (front, but *not* on top of the driver) flashes me a frightened look before going back to surveying the road ahead. One thing's for sure: this has got Janice Baker written *all* over it. I would be willing to bet all the money in my bank account (which, let's be real, is not very much) that my darling mother has put me forward for this ludicrous escapade. I contemplate giving her a ring to ask her precisely what she's playing at, but the shop is open on Sundays so there's no way she'll answer, and besides I'm seeing her later anyway.

Well, well, well, my mother is so keen to see me paired up again that she's literally offering me up to the TV gods. I knew I shouldn't have told her about 'slag era'.

The Meet-Cute – what even is that? It's new so I can't even watch an episode of it to decide if I want to do it or not. But who am I kidding . . . being on TV might be fun. And I'm in a Dynamic New Phase of my life. I'll think about it. It's Sunday, so no point replying today. I can't stop laughing at the idea of my mum submitting me for a TV dating programme. It's simply *too* her.

I'm down to about 6 per cent battery when I notice my best friend Marie is attempting to FaceTime me. When I swipe my finger across the screen to answer, a decidedly badly lit and grey-faced version of the Marie I know and love appears on the screen. It's clear she's very much still in bed.

'Hello the love of my life!' I say brightly.

'How the fuck are you like . . . out in the world?' she croaks.

'I had STD. Shit To Do.'

'Mate, I woke up earlier, texted you to check you were alive, ordered McDonalds on Deliveroo then fell asleep again before the dude even got here with my "share box" of twenty chicken nuggets.' She puts weak air quotes around 'share box' to indicate she had no intention of sharing these now-lost nuggets with anyone. 'Did you have fun though?'

'I loved it, honestly. And very refreshing to know it's still possible to meet people on a night out rather than on the apps . . .'

'Yes, I figured that was what was going on when I turned around for one second and the next thing I know you're aggressively making out with that baseball cap guy.'

'Get used to it, mi amor.'

'I don't even really know why I called you . . .' she says, furrowing her brow. 'I think I was just bored and lonely.'

'Craving human contact.'

'Yeah . . . that.'

'No Carly?'

'She left your party earlier than I did to go to another birthday. She seemed kind of annoyed I didn't go with her – *as if* I was going to leave my best friend's birthday for some rando?'

'Not happening, mate.'

'Where are you, anyway?'

'Bus home before going to my mum's shop for photos.'

'You're telling me you're doing your pretty girl bride cosplay photos? Today? On a hangover?'

'Needs must,' I shrug. 'You know me, I'm good at keeping appointments. Can't let Janice down.'

'Do you want to come over after and we can get two share boxes?'

'And the biggest vat of Coke that money can buy.'

16

'And that.'

'Go on then,' I grin. 'See you as soon as humanly possible.'

When I get off the bus on Heygate Street, a guy at the bus stop opposite whistles at me to get my attention. 'Walk of shame, is it?' he shouts, with a leering grin.

'Stride of pride, mate. You want to get with the times!' I call back before heading off towards the house.

I've been bedroom-surfing since Miranda and I broke up. First a friend of a friend was moving out a month before the end of their tenancy and wanted someone to cover the last month's rent. And then when *that* ended, I spent two weeks house-sitting for a photographer friend who was on assignment, and now I'm doing a short-term sublet with Daria and Cherie until one of Daria's friends moves in when she comes over from Italy. An imperfect system but right now I don't have anything more perfect. So I never think of anywhere I'm staying as *my house* because I know it's very temporary, but as I put my key in the door, I'm glad to have a place to come back to. Somewhere I can be alone in my room, even if Daria and Cherie are milling around somewhere.

Speak of the devil!

'Hey,' Daria calls from the kitchen, surveying me in my profoundly hungover state through her kindly Italian eyeballs. 'There was this post for you, maybe you didn't see.' She puts down the wooden spoon she was using to stir something inevitably delicious and picks up a package from the work surface.

'Oh, thanks,' I say.

'Maybe it is a birthday present?'

I smile. 'I don't think so, I don't know who would know my address here. It's probably—'

She cuts me off, holding up a hand. 'Homely . . . trinkets?' she offers, raising her eyebrows.

'Exactly! Homely trinkets!' I had to explain the concept to Daria, who was unfamiliar with the word *trinket* but was delighted to learn a new expression straight from the dictionary of Fran Baker. 'Apologies for my appearance, I feel like I'm about to die.'

'Cheeky nap?' she suggests, using another phrase of imparted linguistic wisdom.

I take her advice and head up to my room. I open the packaging to reveal the framed embroidery of wildflowers I bought on eBay the week before. You know, an early birthday present-to-self sort of thing. I rest it against the wall on the top of the cheap landlord-special MDF chest of drawers that came with the room, and everything about the space feels a little bit better.

Dress and underwear get thrown unceremoniously into my big suitcase, which I'm using as a laundry bag now the clothes have a wardrobe to live in (clothes and general life stuff and Homely Trinkets get packed in the big suitcase, duvet and duvet cover and towels get expertly vacuum-packed in the small suitcase that lives under the bed. See? I've got a system!). Temporary living is kind of shitty, but I'm rolling with it. I have a place to live that I can afford, and I know I'll have to move again and find somewhere else in a few weeks' time.

My last break-up happened very slowly and then all at once. I had to move out. It wasn't my idea to break up so I'm not sure how I ended up being the one who moved out, but c'est la vie. I didn't want to commit long-term to a new place, to new people, so right now I'm . . . riding the wave of short-term London housing.

I put on my pyjamas and plug my phone into the charger, setting an alarm for an hour before I told my mum I would meet her, and curl up under the duvet. Sunday's the day for hungover naps, especially when it's your birthday. It's the rules!

2

'Twenty-nine doesn't suit you, darling.'

My darling mother is holding court from behind the counter at Beckenham's premier destination for size-inclusive wedding dresses. Clearly the hangover is still visible in my overall aura.

'You're meant to look fresh-faced, not bloody *grey*!'

'Thanks, Mum,' I say, considering my reflection in one of the full-length mirrors used to framing glowing brides-to-be. I don't think I look *that* bad. 'I think you're exaggerating just a little bit,' I tell her, which is true, because I did my make-up on the train and I literally get paid to do people's make-up (sometimes) and I have definitely concealed hangovers more obvious than mine.

In fact, that's down to Mum. I know most girls' first memories of make-up will be watching their mothers get ready, but mine left a real impression on me. The appearance of her illuminated mirror on her dressing table followed by a plume of loose powder, the way she would open her mouth while she did her mascara, the creamy, sweet smell of Lancôme lipstick and the way all her lipsticks ended up being worn down into the same shape, the loyalty of that. How could I not become fascinated by beauty? 'So . . . which one's first?'

'The blush one,' she says, gesturing at the rail. 'You brought your strapless bra, didn't you?'

'This isn't my first rodeo,' I say, rolling my eyes. 'I brought my strapless bra, yes.'

I take the dress out the back to change while Mum sets up the lights and when I re-emerge and hold my arms up so she can zip me in, she looks me over. 'Beautiful.' It's possible that hearing such a thing out of my mum's mouth for my whole life left me with such a sense of peace about my fat body. I'll always be grateful for it.

'I thought you said I was grey.'

'The dress *illuminates* you, darling.'

I look at myself in the mirror. I do look rather delicious in this blush-coloured strapless lacy wedding dress. Mum finds posting photos on Instagram of *actual plus-size women* in the *actual plus-size wedding dresses* that she sells in the shop leads to more people booking fittings with her and, consequently, buying their wedding dresses from her little boutique. And since I am, in her words, 'a perfect size 22', every few weeks I do my make-up in a decidedly bridal fashion, the subtlest smoky eye, that Bobbi Brown shade of pinky brown that looks good on everyone, a matte finish foundation so it doesn't look shiny in the photos.

I pretend I don't enjoy playing dress-up, but secretly I do. I have absolutely no problem having my photo taken (self-consciousness? Never heard of her. Body hang-ups? Unfamiliar with the concept), and I'm happy to help Mum. The only downside is that it means the idea of me as a bride is never far from her mind. I, on the other hand, am not remotely invested in marriage.

'This style was absolutely *made* for you. Such a shame I've never got to see you in one of these for proper,' she says, shaking her head.

'Oh yeah,' I say. 'About that.'

'Hmmm?' Mum says, looking up from my image on the screen of the SLR camera.

'I got an email.' I fold my arms across my chest and narrow my eyes at her.

'What kind of email?'

'Does the name Tilly ring a bell with you, by any chance?'

'Oh, Tilly!' Her face lights up. 'What a sweet girl, she was in here a couple of weeks ago.'

'And you somehow got round to offering up your only daughter *and* favourite child to a TV dating show?'

'Can you stop calling yourself my favourite child? You know it annoys your brother.'

'What *doesn't* annoy Andrew? Anyway, what possessed you to put me forward for this?'

'Well, it sounded like the nicest programme! *The Meet-Cute*, how lovely. And she's a producer! She kept telling me it was about finding true love, not some silly entertainment thing, you know?'

'But what if I'm not looking for true love?' I say with absolute conviction.

'Stop that! There's someone out there for you, I know it!'

I sigh but I don't want to go down *this specific path* again with her. It's beyond her comprehension that I am not remotely concerned whether there is 'someone out there' for me or not. In fact, I'm well aware that there is! There are tons of people! And that's precisely why I'm enjoying my time as a single woman rather than inadvertently leaping from one relationship to the next like a chubby frog on a lily pad, as was my way for the last ten years. Clearly, Mum thinks I'm secretly suffering and need to be lifted out of my tragic singledom at the first possible opportunity, even if that requires intervention from a film crew.

'So?'

'So what?'

'Are you going to do it?' she asks eagerly. 'Tilly said I couldn't, sort of, *force you*, you know? Apparently me signing you up and filling in the form didn't mean you had to do it, alas. So, are you going to?'

'I'll talk to this Tilly.'

'Good girl!'

'No promises! I'll see what it sounds like,' I say, before pausing, because I know Mum will object so I have to take a deep breath and get it all out in one go. 'But I'm pretty positive it's a no from me. It seems like a waste of time if I'm not looking for, you know, *romance*? Which I most definitely am not, however disappointing that may be for you.'

'Well maybe romance is looking for you! You never know! Go on, just give it a go. Ooh, that tea's gone right through me, you get into the next dress while I'm gone and I'll zip you up.'

I change into the second outfit, which is a bias-cut silk number that I can already tell will be very unpopular with her clientele because of the way it hugs the body. Though maybe they'll feel more inspired after seeing it on an Actual Fat Person.

Mum puts a veil on me and then fusses about where my crown is, taking the veil out and putting it back in about a hundred times until it's finally in the right place, which looks basically the same as her first attempt but who am I to judge? She takes some photos of me looking serene and demure, doing those downward Princess Diana eyes, and then some photos of me beaming with bridal joy.

'Done?' I ask her as she's flicking through the photos on the camera.

'Done,' she says.

To my great relief, I am allowed to change back into my own clothes.

She claps her hands. 'Oh! I meant to tell you, I think I've found you another bridal make-up client! Aren't I good?'

'Offering me up to reality TV shows notwithstanding, yes.' I can't help smiling. My mum's been looking out for me my whole life. 'Text me their details and I'll get in touch! I don't think I'm doing a very good job at the cafe, I think Jamie's regretting giving me the job.' Jamie, the lovely, gorgeous bear of a man I briefly dated before he met someone else and decided to Get Serious, had the good grace to offer me a job at his popular neighbourhood cafe as a sort of consolation prize for not sleeping together anymore. I'm hoping I get more e-commerce clients soon so I'm not relying so much on my mum referring her brides to me *or* relying on Jamie to tolerate the ways in which I am an inadequate barista, but needs must.

'I suppose at some point I'll have to come by and pick up my make-up kit,' I tell her as she's locking up the shop. I've been stowing my suitcase full of immaculately clean brushes, lipsticks melted down into palettes, foundations in every colour, sterilized tweezers and a whole lot more in my old bedroom at her house.

'How about the rest of your stuff? Or am I not allowed to ask?'

'In the fullness of time,' I say, sighing.

Mum can't understand why I wouldn't just move back home if I don't have a permanent place to live, and I don't have the heart to tell her that it's because we would simply kill each other within days, and more to the point, I don't want to. Not in my slag era, anyway. I moved back home briefly when me and Miranda broke up, but as soon as something became available, however short-term, I was out again.

'Surely it's not *that* hard to find a room in a house share?'

'But I don't want to live *anywhere*. I don't know where I want to live or who I want to live with, and I don't want to commit to something too soon.'

'There it is, that word again!'

'Look, once I figure out what I'm doing I'll come and pick my stuff up. Is it getting in your way there?'

'Well, when the girls come and stay over it would be nice if they weren't having to pick their way around moving boxes.'

'I'm working on it,' I say, although I'm not particularly inclined to rush finding a flat to accommodate the needs of The Girls, aka my brother's children, and collective apples of my mother's eye.

Mum slips me the £100 she insists on giving me for taking my photo. A little cash in hand never hurt anyone, right?

'And a bit extra in there,' she says, handing me a birthday card. 'And . . .' She crouches under the counter and I can hear a repetitive clicking sound and my mum huffing about something clearly not going right, until she reappears with a red velvet cupcake with a little candle in it.

26

We share the cupcake in comfortable silence. Before I leave I draw her into a tight hug and breathe in her powdery perfume and the scent of her hairspray. 'Thanks, Mummy.'

I head out of the shop and in the direction of Marie's so we can eat chicken nuggets on her sofa and watch TV, the prospect filling me with an enormous sense of calm and well-being. Maybe she'll even talk me into going on *The Meet-Cute*.

3

Two days later I'm sitting in a pub in Brixton waiting for my date, Katie, to arrive.

I click through her app photos and look and ask myself: *Am I, by my nature, drawn to Katie?* Well, she's hot in a severe way, very angular, edgy haircut and those thick-rimmed round tiny glasses that I very specifically associate with middle-aged male architects. No, I would not say I *am* drawn to her. But if prolific dating has taught me anything it's that vibes count for more than instant attraction. A lot more.

And that is what this 'slag era' is for me. I suppose it could be described, more delicately, as an *exploratory phase*. What is time spent swiping the apps if not a little anthropological explorating?

Katie walks into the pub. She still looks quite *severe*. But as ever, I'm going in with a positive attitude, albeit curious.

Her edgy glasses are even more intense in person, *and* she's dyed her fringe a juicy lime green since the app photos were taken. It contrasts with the rest of her peroxide blond hair. When I spot her across the pub, it strikes me that we would be a funnier match than any of the people I've been seeing recently.

But she's undoubtedly hot, and so am I, so maybe not such a funny match after all.

When she's about two feet away from the table I've commandeered, I'm seized with the fear that she's going to be hard to talk to (aka my worst first date fear, *much* worse than not fancying them), but as soon as she catches sight of me, her face breaks into a wide smile and I stand up for a hug.

'What can I get you?' she asks.

'A glass of rosé, please,' I say, trying to elegantly squeeze myself back into the booth. (Why so small, booth? Why must you be this way?)

'You got it,' she says before heading for the bar.

We fall into easy conversation, me telling her about my newly single lifestyle, the occasional make-up jobs, the temping, the carousel of homes, her telling me about her work, the studio she works from in Bethnal Green.

'I mostly sell stuff through Instagram but once in a while I get a commission, so I know I'm going to get paid,' she says, taking a sip of the pint she brought back from the bar, now on to our third round. 'And I teach sometimes. OK, I teach quite a lot. I wish the portrait work was my money-maker, but needs must.'

'So it's portraits you paint?'

'Yeah, mostly. But not so formal. I think of them less as portraits and more as paintings of people. Do you know what I mean?'

'Yeah, I think so,' I say. Maybe I do, maybe I don't, maybe three glasses of wine is where my ability to consider artistic concepts leaves my brain. 'Do you find painting people means you look at people differently?'

30

'I guess so . . .' she says, furrowing her heavy, dark brow that contrasts with the pale brightness of her hair. 'I guess it makes you more interested in difference. What makes someone look the way they look. What is their face composed of, what tones, what is the thing you would have to get right in portraying them to capture what they actually look like rather than depicting someone of their gender or with their hairstyle — you know what I mean?'

'This time I actually do,' I say. I'm glad I said yes to meeting her tonight.

'Like with you,' she says, gesturing loosely in that third–pint way. 'The important things about your face are how bright your eyes are, getting that shade of blue right. And the shape of your lips is really distinctive. So perfect, sort of like a heart.'

'Thank you,' I say, bowing my head graciously. 'I grew them all by myself.'

'And your hair colour is beautiful . . . is it natural?' she asks, which is not the first time I've had to answer this question about this precise shade of deep, rich strawberry blond.

I run my hand through my hair. 'Yeah, once again, I grew it all by myself. I'm kind of over it, though. I've had long hair all my life. Since I was a child. I'm thinking about getting rid of it.'

'Do it!' she says enthusiastically. 'I love a bold move!'

'That's pretty clear,' I say, nodding at the green fringe. 'But yeah . . . I think it's time for a change.'

'To change!' she says, clinking her glass against mine.

She smiles down at her drink and I feel sure enough that she's interested in me that a second date is on the cards. 'This is good, right?' I ask her.

'Yeah,' she says, her cheeks flushing a little. 'I knew it would be. I could tell from your profile I would probably like you.'

'I wasn't sure about you,' I say with a cheeky grin.

'Oh?'

'You look quite serious, it made me wonder if you were going to think I was an idiot.'

'No way!' she says, frowning. 'You're hot. And interesting.'

'I would definitely do this—' I begin, but she cuts me off.

'Do you want to come back to mine?'

I like it! It's usually me asking this! I'm usually the only one of two people sitting at a table in a pub brave enough to actually make the move!

When we're lying together in her bed, a little cold on top of the covers, and I'm wondering if she wants me to go home or if it would be rude for me to go home (an age-old dilemma!), I look at our bodies next to each other, and am struck by how different they are. Hers so much smaller than mine, a scar on her stomach from surgery as a child, the contours of her body less exaggerated, less defined than mine. She runs her hands over my body, from my breastbone down to my belly button and then down the side of my hip, the fingers that have felt inside me now exploring the outside.

'You should do life modelling. Have you ever done it before?'

'No, I haven't,' I say, smiling.

'Why are you smiling like that?' she says, her gentle hand now poking my side. 'I'm serious!'

'Is it, like, *fully* naked?'

'Are you scared?'

'No! It's just . . . you don't often get naked around people who aren't enthusiastic enough about you to be having sex with you, you know?'

'The students always say they prefer the bigger models to the skinny ones,' she says, shrugging. 'You should think about it.'

'I'll think about it. Don't they get cold?'

'We put a heater nearby so your bits don't freeze.'

'Well good, because I don't know what I'd do without my bits,' I say.

'It would be a horrible loss to the world,' she says, a little smirk of amusement dancing across her face.

'Now I'm wondering if you actually fancy me or this is some kind of recruitment drive for life models,' I say, narrowing my eyes at her suspiciously.

'Of course I fancy you,' she says, kissing me and climbing on top of me again, and I decide it's not time to go home yet. By the time Miranda and I broke up, things were severely lacking in the bed department so half the joy of being single really is the pleasure of sex with new people.

When I leave, my face feeling warm and flushed from sex, I go to tie up my hair so it's not sticking to the back of my neck in the still-warm September heat. Twisting the hairband that's always on my wrist around my mane, I feel the sharp twang of the elastic breaking against my fingers. Fuck! That's it, it's got to go. Tomorrow.

4

'You're *sure*,' Zoe the hairdresser asks me when I'm sitting in her chair the next afternoon.

'Yes.'

'Really, you promise, you're sure you're sure?'

I chose her based on a combination of Google reviews and the fact she had an appointment in Soho at the precise time after work at the cafe that I had free before meeting my pal Vic for dinner. It's not the first time she's asked me whether I'm sure.

'I'm sure,' I say, the strain of frustration evident in my voice. 'I've been thinking about it and it's definitely time. Please? Just do it like the photo?'

'But you know . . .' she says, looking at the photo on my phone over my shoulder. 'She has a different . . . face shape to you?'

I try not to sigh too loudly. Yes, I am *aware* I have a *different face shape* to this very famous and thin actress whose photo I am using as a reference image for my haircut! I am fat! She is not! I still want the haircut! 'Yes, I know,' I say politely. 'I think it'll look good on me anyway.' I am *slightly* nervous about this haircut as financial constraints mean I can't go to the very fanciest of fancy salons for my Big Chop. But, now I'm here, this salon meets my twin requirements of being not too expensive and having a promising vibe.

She studies me sceptically in the reflection of the mirror in front of us. 'OK, if you're sure.'

'I'm sure! I'm not going to sue you for giving me a haircut. I promise.'

'You don't want me to take it shorter, like a bob, so you can see how you feel about it? You know, before you commit properly?'

'No, absolutely not,' I say resolutely. 'Off with it.'

'All right . . .' she says, gesturing for me to stand up and go to the sink, and as she's washing my hair, it strikes me that I won't have to go through the whole tedious hours-long ritual of washing and drying my hair *ever again* and I nearly start crying with joy right then and there. What a time to be alive!

The phone rings once she's ushered me back to the chair and the receptionist is away from the desk so Zoe huffs and dashes over to pick it up. While she's gone I check my emails in case there's some lucrative offer of work, but instead there's a nudging email from the producer Tilly.

Hi lovely! Don't want to be a bother but just wanted to follow up on my email from the other week! If you're not interested in taking part in *The Meet-Cute*, please let me know! Your mum thought you would be keen for it and her application form was great so I hope you're still interested as I would love to have you on board, and if you've got any questions please ask! The thing is, we were originally hoping to cast you in the next round of filming but someone has dropped out so we need someone like you a bit more urgently! Hope you're able to help.

A twinge of guilt pricks at me for neglecting to reply. I don't know exactly why I'm dragging my heels over the whole thing, it's most unlike me. I'll reply later. For now, I want to watch the transformation take place.

And what a transformation it is! With every snip of the scissors I feel more and more excited, more and more sure that this was definitely what I wanted. It's strange to see myself looking so fundamentally different and yet still so very *me*.

By the time she finishes, long tendrils of hair are snaking around the floor beneath the chair, and I am a whole new Fran.

As she takes off the cape and shows me the back in the hand mirror, she nervously asks, 'Happy?'

I nod, too overcome with delight to say anything, but as soon as I'm out the door, I go into full selfie monster mode and faithfully document my Extreme Makeover: Hair Edition for Instagram.

'*Wow,*' says Vic when I walk into the restaurant to meet her. 'Just wow.'

'Is that a good wow?' I ask her.

'I honestly can't believe it,' she says, pulling me into a tight hug. 'I've *never* known you with short hair! Ever!' And Vic has known me for quite a while – not as long as Marie but still, several years of professional acquaintance-turned-close-friends after meeting at one of my old magazine jobs.

37

'I haven't either,' I say, smiling and touching the pixie cut that now sits on top of my head. 'I can't stop looking at myself in shop windows. My head feels light! I'm absolutely obsessed!'

'Let's be honest, you never stopped looking at yourself in shop windows *before* you got your hair cut.'

'True,' I concede. 'I always get the urge to do something big this time of year . . . it feels like a time for fresh starts, that back-to-school feeling, you know?'

'God,' says Vic. 'It really brings out your eyes, doesn't it?'

I put my hands around my face in an angelic pose worthy of Shirley Temple. 'So, how are you?'

'Bleurgh, boring boring boring at work,' she says, dismissing the question with a wave and keeping her eyes on the menu. She's now some big deal at a PR agency that specializes in beauty clients and works her absolute butt off.

'I was *shocked* you booked for dinner on a weekday evening, I have to say.'

She looks up at me through her subtly expensive glasses, her straight blond hair in a sensible mid-length style to her collarbone. 'I'm sick of staying late every night, and for what? For nothing! I decided a few weeks ago to have *one* night a week where I leave bang on time and see if anyone mentions it, and then slowly slowly add more and more days.'

'I love this for you! My most workaholic friend, finally seeing the light!'

'It was my appraisal that totally pushed me over the edge. I was listening to their feedback and felt, like . . . . I don't actually care about any of this, I'm only here because I'm good at this job, but on some *deeper level* I realized I don't actually care at all? I feel like at one time I felt like it was something intrinsic to my life or my personality and now I'm . . . trying to *not* feel that.'

'Yes!' I say, slamming my hand down on the table emphatically.

'Like the old saying goes, it's PR not ER.'

'So true,' I say, looking at the menu. 'I'm extremely hyped for this, by the way.'

'Same! Your birthday was a bit mad and raucous for me to really be able to chat to you.'

'Mad and raucous? Moi?' I bat my eyelashes at her.

'You know it, Baker. Right, let the fried cheese roll . . .'

Once we've ordered and are sipping on our wine like demure professional ladies, Vic surveys me with her razor-sharp gaze.

'So, I'm going to assume this haircut isn't part of some post-break-up meltdown, since it seems like you're actually having the time of your fucking life.'

'I'm also having the time of my life fucking.'

'Please, tell me all? Let me live vicariously through you?'

'It's all a bit weird,' I say, wrinkling my nose. 'I mean, sure, I'm really making the most of being single, but I didn't, like . . . see it coming?'

'I feel like I haven't seen you properly since then,' she says with a wince. 'Trying to sort the flat out to sell and summer holidays and time ran away with me a bit. How are you doing?'

'I am honestly, genuinely A-OK. It was a bit of a shock that we actually broke up. I thought everything was, you know, same old us, and then . . . we started fighting more and more. Or rather' – I furrow my brow, trying to remember how it actually happened – 'she wanted to have big conversations more and more, which turned into arguments.'

'I'm sorry, Franny.' She squeezes my hand affectionately from across the table. 'And I'm sorry I haven't been around much. *You* know what an absolute nightmare moving house is.'

I laugh, 'As someone who has to do it on a semi-regular basis, I know that pain well, my friend. But I'm OK, I promise.'

'I suppose it's a bit easier when the break-up is mutual,' she says, shrugging.

I swallow hard. Hearing Vic repeat my little white lie back to me is weirdly jarring. It's possible I *slightly* massaged the truth about our break-up to some people. Of course, I couldn't lie to Marie, my BFF, my oldest friend, my closest ally, the person who has known me since we were at school: *she* knows I got unceremoniously dumped out of nowhere. But to other pals? *It was a very mature mutual break-up, darling.*

I really should have seen the break-up coming. There I was, thinking everything was fine and dandy, and then we started fighting more and more. Big, contentious conversations about marriage and babies and where we should live. In brief, as far as marriage was concerned, she was pro and I was anti. Babies? She was pro and I was anti. Where we should live? Would it shock you to learn she would like to live in The Middle Of Fucking Nowhere and I would rather die than live more than five minutes' walk from a Little Tesco? More than anything it felt like she was trying to provoke me. Like she'd want us to have these conversations because she wanted a fight. But I didn't realize it at the time, I thought maybe we were in a weird patch. Then one evening I came home and she was sitting on the sofa looking very serious and said we needed to talk and that was . . . sort of that. And *not* seeing it coming made me feel stupid, and it was bad enough that I *felt* stupid,

I didn't need various esteemed friends like Vic to *think* I'm stupid, to think I'm the kind of gal who gets dumped out of the blue.

'It's rubbish but . . . I suppose those *are* the reasons people break up at our age, aren't they? Knowing that the way you see your futures don't really line up?'

'*Quite* true, Vic. I assume your vision of the future lines up very well with Greg's?' I smile, knowing that they are a Genuinely Functional Couple.

'So far so good! Though he unpacked the kitchen and his choice of cutlery drawer distance from kettle is sociopathic. Anyway, I'm not finished talking about your single life. Is it *very* thrilling? What happened with the guy you met at your party? I feel like you never give the juicy details over WhatsApp!'

'This is why we need to remember to schedule more actual hangouts! Especially now you're de-prioritizing work,' I say with a devilish eyebrow-raise. 'Anyway, as far as George goes, we have each other's numbers, but I probably won't see him again. Which is a shame because he's, like, *extremely* good in bed. But I'm certainly not struggling to get dates at the moment so it's no great loss.'

'What about the red-haired girl who was at your birthday?'

'Jessie? I see her every couple of weeks . . .'

'She was hot.'

'And there's this girl Katie who I met last night . . . she's trying to get me to be a life-drawing model,' I say, knowing Vic will absolutely love the idea of this.

'Oh what fun!' Vic exclaims, her eyes lighting up.

'If you want fun, let me tell you about what my mum's trying to get me involved in.'

'Go on . . .'

'She's put me forward for this dating show,' I begin, but her enthusiasm is so total that I don't even need to explain more.

'Oh my God, you have to do it!'

'I might, you know,' I say, because I've been thinking about it and it sounds fun and I'm in the mood to say yes to things, as evidenced by me not *yet* telling Tilly to stop asking me to fill out the *The Meet-Cute* application form.

'What's stopping you?' Vic asks, sensing that I'm not totally on board.

'It feels a bit rude to go on a dating show when I don't really want a relationship, you know?'

'Who cares! That's up to them to sort out! It sounds fun and I would do it in a heartbeat.'

'You're right, I know you are. And it's so extremely my kind of thing, you know, a silly little escapade. I just don't want anyone to be shocked that I'm not in the market for a spouse or something. I'm enjoying the single gal lifestyle too much.'

'You've really got that BDE,' she says, raising her eyebrows at me over the top of her glass. 'Big Date Energy.'

'Ha!' I laugh jubilantly. 'That's so deeply accurate I can't believe I didn't think of it myself.'

'I'm actually shocked that you've managed to stay single this long,' she says. 'I thought maybe you'd decide you'd change your mind about dating and you're now in a relationship with this George guy or something.'

'I know! It's a record,' I say, setting the wine glass down. 'I never managed more than a week before.'

'*Really?*' she asks incredulously. 'I knew it was quick, but I didn't know it was *that* quick. How long was it between Daniel and Miranda?'

'I literally met Miranda a few days after I broke up with Daniel. Marie lured me out to a gay girl club night in the hope that I would return to dating women. I don't think even *she* suspected my next relationship was going to begin that actual night,' I say, smiling.

'And what about when you met Daniel?'

'Picture the scene: I was a mere eighteen years old and completely discombobulated after experiencing *the* worst break-up in the history of the world, not only by eighteen-year-old standards but also in general. I was temping at the construction company off Oxford Street where my brother used to work. That is, instead of being at university because I didn't get the grades to go where I wanted to go,' I begin.

'I'm learning so much about you tonight!'

'The life and times of Fran Baker. Anyway, on my second day temping there, I was on the tube with my back to those windows between compartments and a huge gust of wind blew through the carriage and the very cool beret I was wearing got swept off my head and into the carriage behind, where it hit some guy in the face. That guy was Daniel, and that's how we met. It's a bit grim to think about now, to be honest. I was eighteen and he was twenty-five and he was so hot and had all the power and more money than me and . . .' I shudder involuntarily. 'It was a weird time for me. I was very unhappy because I was meant to be at university in Edinburgh with my high school girlfriend Ivy and we were meant to be together forever and we weren't because she broke up with me on

A-level results day and here I am more than ten years later still thinking about it!' I laugh, but Vic can sense it's not a happy laugh.

She smiles, she can tell by my shifty as hell vibe not to press for more information about *that* break-up. 'Well, thank you for sharing your rebounds with me!'

'Queen of the rebound, that's me.' I wink at her, wanting to shake off the thoughts of Ivy. Better to focus on the fun of the now than dwell too much in the sad corners of my brain where my unsuccessful relationships live. 'But not anymore! I'm going to be gloriously single for as long as humanly possible. I've *done* big relationships. I'm done with big relationships. I want to date as much as I can and have all the fun you're not allowed to have when you're with someone.'

'Well, I salute you,' she says with a sigh. 'You do make being single look fun.'

'It *is* very fun.'

'Oooh, do you think I've got time for a wee before our food comes?'

'Go!' I urge her. And then I'm alone with my thoughts. Horrible.

It's funny how someone I haven't seen in more than ten years still rattles around my brain. I guess you never forget your first love.

This too shall pass, Mum reassured me as I cried hysterically when it happened. She was right. It did pass, and I met Daniel a week later. But no one's ever been quite like Ivy.

Mercifully for my maudlin thoughts, Vic returns to the table as our food arrives and we fall upon it like we haven't eaten in weeks, pausing only to emit sounds of the most profound enjoyment.

'Has freelance stuff picked up?' Vic asks when our plates are cleared.

'It's stable now, at least. Some mornings at Jamie's cafe, then some make-up work, mostly bridal stuff,' I tell her, my pride preventing me from mentioning that a lot of my make-up work comes through my mum. 'At least I'm not, like, crying in the toilets anymore!'

'I still can't believe those fuckers,' she says, shaking her head.

'Yeah, well, it's the way of print media, isn't it? It was always going to happen, I'm only surprised I lasted this long. And at least I got to meet you.'

I had known for some time that being a beauty journalist at a women's weekly print magazine wasn't working for me. But the thing about having a job like that – a desirable, supposedly glamorous job – is that you internalize all these messages about how *lucky* you are to be there. How there's a long line of girls outside the office desperate to take your place. So it makes you scared to leave.

'That's always a plus,' she says, smiling. 'I'm really glad you got into the make-up stuff at the right time.'

If I wasn't going to be a beauty journalist, I knew I wanted to be a make-up artist, so even before I got made redundant I was doing a qualification at a beauty college off Oxford Street.

'I'll keep an ear out for any make-up jobs for you,' she says. One of the many benefits of having a friend who's a beauty PR.

'Thanks, dude,' I say. 'You're a real one. Anyway, enough about my messy, messy life. I want to hear all about Argentina.'

'God, it was *amazing*, honestly so beautiful. And me and Greg didn't argue once!'

'Now *that's* a holiday.'

'Who knew that couples therapy actually works, right?'

'I think it only works if you're actually committed to the relationship, which you guys obviously are.'

'Yeah,' she says, smiling. 'We are. But if we ever did break up, heaven forbid, I feel like you're making it look a bit less scary to be single.'

'Well, I don't think you should break up but . . . I'm really having a good time, you know?'

'I guess at least I had my . . . what do you call it? My *slag era* at uni,' she says.

'I've had to wait *so* long for mine,' I say, shaking my head. 'And my mum is already trying to fix me up with someone else with this TV show!'

'So will you do it?'

I shrug. 'I don't know. Probably not? I mean, what's the point?'

'For the adventure?'

'I suppose I could do it *for the adventure*,' I say, narrowing my eyes at her.

'And best-case scenario,' Vic says, eyeing me over the top of her glasses, 'you don't meet the love of your life but you *do* meet a hottie.'

'I suppose you're right,' I say, and I do feel inspired by the idea of doing it for the adventure. 'So . . . you think I should say yes?'

'I have made that abundantly clear. Do it now.'

'Fine,' I say, taking my phone out and sending a quick reply to Tilly saying I'm up for it.

A look of inspiration passes over Vic's face, a veritable *eureka* moment. 'Hey, not to sound too much like your mum trying to matchmake you, but . . . you know who's single? And might be the love of your life or might be a fun fling?' She bites her bottom lip in eagerness, like the words are about to spill out of her mouth.

'Pray tell.'

'Doug.'

'Doug who?' I ask, furrowing my brow, diving into the depths of my brain to pull up a Doug. Oh! I gasp with anticipatory delight. 'Not . . . Doug ManHoney?'

'The very same,' Vic says. 'The stars have finally aligned. We thought it couldn't be done! You and Doug, single at the same time!'

'Oh no, this is too much,' I say, shaking my head. 'Me and ManHoney were never meant to be single simultaneously. It defies nature.'

His name isn't actually ManHoney. It's Mahoney, but, well, he's very cute! If you're going to have a silly nickname it might as well be based on how good-looking you are, right? Anyway, he's a friend of Vic's boyfriend Greg, one of those vague acquaintances that you run into every now and then.

'God, I remember when you first met! You two really hit it off!' We didn't have much choice, stuck on the end of a table at a birthday dinner, but the seating turned out to be quite fortuitous. 'Weren't you still with Daniel then?'

'Yeah, fuck, it was *that* long ago.'

'And then you and Daniel broke up and by then Doug was with that girl who needed a fringe, you know the one . . .'

'Oh, I know the one,' I say, recalling a woman who was otherwise very attractive but had an unusually large forehead, leading Vic to ask me whether it was in any way acceptable to give unsolicited advice recommending she get a fringe. I told her it was not. 'He sent me a happy birthday message the other week and I felt a fluttering in my swimsuit area.'

'And you didn't even have to feel guilty about it now you're single!'

'Guilt-free flutters. Maybe I should . . .' I twitch my nose in contemplation.

'Send him a flirty little DM?'

'Precisely.'

Vic shrugs nonchalantly. 'Maybe you should.' She takes a sip of her wine and looks at me expectantly.

'What, now?' I ask, taken aback.

'Strike while the iron's hot.'

'Nah, I've got to play the long game. Got to start commenting on his photos and replying to his Insta stories every so often, to put myself back on his radar, then we'll get into a little chat one day and somehow one thing turns into another and then it's all dick pics and sex media.'

'You've got this all worked out, haven't you?'

'I was born for this moment.'

5

After dinner, we go for one drink in a pub nearby. I smile in acknowledgement at a model I recognize from a photoshoot I did recently at the table opposite. She smiles back and raises a hand in a friendly wave. I can't resist checking my Instagram while Vic is at the bar, and the likes are truly rolling in on my new hair photo. Amid the many enthusiastic comments, I notice I've been tagged in a photo. It's a repost of my selfie from outside the hair salon, posted by @ZoeHairSoho with the caption *Just look at my gorgeous client Fran! Proves that pixie cuts can work on ALL shapes and sizes.*

'Ha,' I say bitterly, to no one in particular. Thanks, Zoe, for stealing my photo and posting it with a vaguely patronizing caption after putting considerable effort into trying to discourage me from getting this specific haircut because I'm too fat for it. *Thanks.*

I'm politely putting my phone away as Vic returns with the drinks, when a text pops up from George, the guy from my birthday party . . . and the morning *after* my birthday party. Actually, there are *two* texts.

49

Here's that article about dog shows I was telling you about –
[link]

Which is weird because I have no memory of discussing this with him whatsoever. But then two minutes later—

Oh, sorry, wrong Fran, meant to send that to someone else.
How's it going though?

'What are you reading? You look unusually serious,' Vic says, presenting me with my pint.

'Just a text from that guy I slept with after my party and then another text saying he didn't mean to text me but asking how I am anyway? I dunno.'

'Show me,' she says, holding out her hand for my phone.

She surveys the message and lets out a 'ha!' before saying, 'It's obvious. He wanted to text you but didn't want you to know that he wanted to text you so created this silly *ruse* to allow him to text you in a way that made him feel less keen, because you're not allowed to be keen, right?'

'How . . . elaborate,' I say, frowning at my screen.

'If that's not what's going on here, then I'll eat my hat,' Vic says, taking a big gulp of her pint. 'Do people still say that?'

'Huh. So he *does* want to see me again?'

'One hundred per cent.'

She's proved right when I text him back and say I'm fine and out with a friend and he replies asking if I want to come over later. He could have just gone ahead and *asked* me that. I would have still said yes!

'See?' Vic says when I report this to her.

'You were right!' I say, shrugging and holding my hands up. 'Are you going to?'

'Yeah, and you would too if you knew how good he was at . . . tongue stuff.'

She salutes me. 'A noble endeavour.'

And swing by I do, because who can resist such oral charms? That's one of the many advantages of dating around. You can be seeing the most average guy in the world and as long as he presents *some* benefit, some asset, some goodness to your life – like extremely strong head – then it doesn't matter that in every other way he's . . . fine. It's not the focus of all your romantic and sexual attention. It's just one piece of the puzzle.

There's something exciting about the feeling of his hands in my hair as I'm sucking his dick, knowing he's not touching those flowing mermaid locks I was too scared to cut for so long, that I clung to out of comfort and familiarity until I realized it wasn't right for me anymore. There's so little for him to hold onto when he comes that it's almost thrilling.

When we're chilling in his bed afterwards, I can't help but ask him, 'Was this . . . a ruse?'

He looks confused. 'What do you mean, a ruse?'

'Well, I was out for dinner with my friend, and when you texted me and then said you meant to text someone else, she said it was some kind of *ploy* to get my attention without looking like you wanted to get my attention, and now we've somehow ended up having sex as a result . . . her theory is looking like it stands up to scrrrrutiny,' I say, rolling the r obnoxiously.

George looks a bit embarrassed. 'Well . . .'

'You know . . . you could just be . . . normal? If you'd

texted me and been like . . . wanna fuck? I'd have been like, yeah.'

'I know, I know . . .' he says, rolling his eyes, but mostly looking relieved.

'All I'm saying is that doesn't have to be so hard. I won't, like, respect you less for wanting to sleep with me.'

'Yeah, well, not everyone is as *direct* as you.'

'I like getting what I want and knowing that I'm not going to get what I want if that happens to be the case.'

'No, it's good!' he says. 'I guess it would make life easier if everyone was a bit more like that. But . . . they're mostly not.'

'It's a defensive position. We do it because we're scared of being the one who's going to get rejected when actually, most of the time, we don't end up getting rejected. I think maybe being less scared of getting knocked back is actually the answer to this whole thing?'

'Yeah but . . . that's horrible, so maybe I'll stick to my *ruses*.'

'Well, you don't have to do that with me,' I say, throwing my hands up defensively. 'I'm *direct*, remember?'

'All right, I'll bear that in mind.'

I decide not to stay over, and when he's leading me out of the house, we pass the kitchen where one of his flatmates is washing up. He looks at us over his shoulder.

'Hey!' he nods in our direction, a lanky Black guy in a striped T-shirt.

'Hi!' I trill, although I get the feeling I am not meant to form bonds with his flatmates.

'Aren't you going to introduce us?' he says, turning the taps off.

George sighs. 'Jameel, this is Fran, Fran this is Jameel.'

'Nice to meet you,' we say simultaneously.

'I like your hair . . .' Jameel says, surveying me. 'Very cool.'

'Thanks,' I say, running my hands through it. 'I just did it, actually, like today!'

'I thought you looked different!' George says with incredulity.

I burst out laughing. 'You didn't notice? Like, at all?'

'Well,' he says, in a high-pitched tone. 'I noticed *something* was different . . . but I didn't know exactly what it was.'

'It was nearly waist length last time you saw me!' I say in absolute disbelief.

'Yeah, well . . .' he mumbles.

'Oh so this is, like, an ongoing thing is it?' Jameel looks between us.

I shrug, but George interjects quickly: 'Fran was about to leave, weren't you?'

'Yes,' I say, 'maybe I'll see you again, Jameel, nice to meet—' But George is already bundling me out the door.

'Well, bye then,' he says, quickly kissing me on the cheek.

'Bye,' I say to the sound of the door closing. 'You big weirdo . . .'

My phone rings as I'm walking to the bus stop and at first I wonder if it's George and I've left something behind, but then I see MUM flashing across the screen. She's usually text only so the fact she's calling me strikes fear into my heart. As I go to answer, I realize it's a FaceTime. Even weirder.

I hold the phone up to my face and stand under a streetlight near the bus stop. 'Hello?'

'Oh my God! Franny! What have you done?!' She's covering

her mouth with one hand and holding the phone with the other.

'What?' I ask, wondering what she knows that I don't.

'Your *hair*,' she says. 'I thought it was a joke at first when Andrew sent me the photo from your Instagram! I can't believe it! Why would you do that?!' Honestly, she sounds absolutely bereft. It's only hair! And it's not even her hair!

'I wanted a change!'

'It looks *horrible*!' she cries. 'God! I am so cross with you, Fran!'

'Why?!' I protest. 'It's my hair!'

'You had the most beautiful hair! Ever since you were little! And now it's gone!'

'I don't know what to tell you other than that I like it and besides, I am twenty-nine years old and there's nothing you can do about it.'

I resent the fact that at my age my mum is treating me like I'm a teenager and, consequently, she's making me talk like one.

'Well, I certainly can't be taking any more photos of you in the dresses now, can I?'

'Why not?'

'Because you won't look like a bride! Will you?!'

'Mum, that's the most ridiculous thing I've ever heard. People with short hair get married all the time and some of them even wear dresses.'

'But it doesn't look *pretty* and *feminine*, does it?'

'I think it does! It looks pretty and feminine because *I'm* pretty and feminine! And I think it's silly to stop doing dress photos because I've cut my hair!'

'Well, you should have thought of that before.'

I sigh, and spot the shiny double-decker with the right number on the front approaching. 'My bus is coming. I've got to go now,' I say, knowing that there's no reasoning with her at this point.

'All right,' she says, shaking her head furiously. 'Oh, before you go,' she says as if we were having a perfectly normal conversation, 'Tilly emailed me thanking me for getting you on board which I *assume* means you've agreed to do the show?'

'Yes, I thought if I'm going to betray you by cutting my hair off maybe I can redeem myself by trying to find true love?' I venture.

'It's a start,' she says huffily. 'Tilly said something about someone dropping out so maybe you'll get to go on the show soon!'

'How exciting,' I say with a grimace.

'Bye, darling. And I'm not happy with you! So don't think I am!'

I open my emails on the bus home. There's already one from Tilly the producer, who's frankly overjoyed that I've agreed to take part in the show, and has responded to my acceptance with what can only be described as a *very* thorough application form. I'll do it in the morning . . .

6

See? I wasn't lying when I said I would do the application. I did the application. And within about half an hour of emailing it I got a breathless call from Tilly begging me to come along for filming in about ten days' time because someone who had previously agreed to be filmed for the show had chickened out (my words, not hers). So now I'm here. *Actually* here. Yes, friends, today is the day of *The Meet-Cute!* And I am bringing that Fran Baker BDE. Big Date Energy.

The sun is shining out of a bright blue October sky, I have a spring in my step, and I am ready for my Big TV Escapade. Who knew it was such a long bloody day, though? Well, to be honest, I did. Doing make-up has given me a pretty good understanding of the fact that any kind of photos or filming or anything like that takes about a thousand times longer than you would expect. So even though my date is actually around lunchtime, I have to go and do various . . . business ahead of time. My last contact from the effusive Tilly told me that I had to bring two different outfits as they film an interview before the date that gets spliced into it, and that I should arrive at a nearby restaurant at 10 a.m. where they've got some kind of base for the crew.

I do my make-up *real* nice, paying extra attention to how it'll look on camera, and making sure I bring some powder with me to retouch with. I go for a neutral eye with a red lip because, well, it's a classic date look, isn't it? I check and double-check that my bronzer and blusher is blended nicely because can you imagine the embarrassment if I show up on TV with stripes on my face? Mortifying! The worst! I would never get another make-up job again! And I deliberately went for a lipstick shade that doesn't require lip liner and will fade evenly, because, likewise, the cringe of having a huge dark ring around my lips while the middle has faded off? I would simply expire. I check my face in my little hand mirror when I arrive at the appointed location and decide, yep, I am looking cute as hell.

My outfit, you may be wondering? For the date itself, a square-necked, rather *busty* midi dress in a chic light blue that looks positively angelic with my strawberry-blond hair, but not so very busty that I'll be showing my boobs to the TV-watching nation. And for the interview, a short-sleeve jumpsuit in black and white windowpane check. I am dressed for success, and my phone is a hotbed of activity, with Vic and Marie wishing me luck and demanding details at the earliest possible moment, and Katie confirming my first life-drawing engagement in a week's time.

The restaurant, the secondary location where Tilly has told me to go, appears . . . dark? Like, no one is there? I check my email from her and confirm it's the right time and the right place. It is. Hmmm. What's going on? I find Tilly's number on her email signature and call her.

'Hello?' she answers, sounding stressed.

'Hi, is that Tilly?'

'Speaking?'

'This is Fran . . . I'm here for my date . . . or like . . . the bit before the date? But I can't figure out how to get in?'

'Oh! You're here!' She hangs up. Thirty seconds later, she emerges, ushering me inside.

Tilly has a sharp, dark, glossy bob with a sleek fringe, which is often considered quite a bold move for a fat girl (due to years of women's mags telling you that if you're fat you shouldn't have a fringe because it'll make your round face look round) and instantly enhances her in my estimation.

'It's nice to meet you,' I say, extremely politely, as if it'll increase my chances of being paired up with a peak date.

'You too! Sorry, the restaurant we're using as a base isn't open to the public so we had to keep the door locked! Good job you called me!' she says, while striding towards the back of the restaurant. She's actually pretty stylish, now I meet her in real life – a nice, long-sleeve Breton top tucked into mom jeans and some expensive-looking trainers. I don't know what I was expecting, though. I suppose she was so keen and bouncy via email that I'd started to hold her in some sort of contempt.

'How are you feeling?' she asks.

'I'm feeling great, actually!'

'Normally people tell me they're absolutely shitting themselves.'

'I thought the show was new?'

'It is, but I've been in TV a while so I've dealt with a fair few nervous participants in my time.'

'Well, I'm happy to say I'm not one of them!'

'Your mum told me you'd be a great person to have on!'

'Did she now?'

'She's such a darling, isn't she? She's been absolutely amazing at helping me find the perfect dress.'

'That's one of her many talents.'

'And she was a natural in the taped interview!'

'She didn't mention she'd done that?'

'Of course! We had to get a little segment with the person who put you forward!'

'I dread to think what she said!' We've reached the doorway of a private dining area that's been designated as the green room, but instead of going in, we're standing outside chatting.

'Don't worry about that,' she says, waving away my concerns. 'It's clear she wants you to find love!'

'Now *that* is where we diverge.'

'Yeah, yeah,' Tilly says, rolling her eyes with a level of familiarity I might find grating if she wasn't so generally likeable. 'You're here for a good time, not a long time. Well, hopefully we've found you someone who can give you at least *one* of those!'

'I look forward to it.'

'Right,' she says, opening the door to the green room.

'They're not in there, are they?'

'No! Some of you are in here, and your dates are in another green room.'

'And are all the dates in a restaurant?'

'No,' she says, leaning against the doorframe, her glossy hair falling away from her face in a pleasingly thick, straight slice. 'Other dates are doing stuff like rock climbing, adventure golf, wild swimming. Each episode will have a mix. That's why we wanted to get filming done in the autumn

60

– can't imagine too many people agreeing to wild swimming in the depths of winter.'

'But because I'm not remotely outdoorsy . . .'

'Exactly. So here we are!' She ushers me into the green room, where a few other people are sitting already. 'Helena?' she says, and a woman with curly blond hair looks up from her phone and smiles. 'Let's do your interview now. Are you wearing your date outfit or your interview outfit?'

'Interview,' Helena says.

'Great, then let's go! Fran,' she puts her hand on my arm reassuringly. 'Take a seat, chat to the others or play on your phone or whatever, and I'll be back to get you in a bit.'

'All right,' I say, realizing that my nerves are maybe setting in. 'See you in a bit!'

I take a seat in a chair opposite a guy in a white T-shirt. It's me and him, plus a terrified-looking middle-aged woman who keeps touching her hair.

'Are you nervous?' I ask her.

'Who me?' she says, looking up suddenly, like she's been caught doing something naughty. 'Yes, I suppose I am. The thought of going on TV hadn't really hit me until now.'

I turn the chair to face her. 'Who put you forward for it?'

'My son,' she says, shaking her head, but smiling. 'He really wants me to meet someone. So he can stop worrying about me, I suppose.'

'That's nice of him,' I say gently, hoping to reassure her that everything is going to be fine.

'Yeah,' the white T-shirt guy says. 'My mates put me forward because if I've got a missus then they won't be so sick of me getting with all the fit birds on a night out.'

'Slightly less wholesome,' I say flatly. 'I'm Fran.'

'Stuart,' says white T-shirt man, who's nibbling on one of his fingernails.

'Judy,' says nervous lady.

'So, Stuart,' I say, looking across at him, fixing him with a narrow-eyed stare. 'Are you really looking for love?'

He throws his hands up. 'I dunno, mate, I'm not sure about all of this but I thought it would be a laugh once I found out the boys had put my name down.'

'But if they set you up with the most beautiful woman in the world who you thought was the best thing since sliced bread, you'd maybe consider abandoning your wicked ways?' I ask, because I'm not actually sure if I would. I'm here to have fun and meet someone nice, but, to my mother's great chagrin, I'm not actually hoping to find my next great romance. In fact, the thought of being trapped into another commitment situation makes me feel a bit sick. That hot, dizzy feeling I used to experience towards the end of my relationship with Miranda whenever the subject of The Future came up.

'Course I would!' he says, laughing. 'Gotta have someone to spend those duvet days with, haven't you?'

'That sounds nice,' says Judy. For the briefest second I contemplate suggesting that Stuart and Judy are clearly looking for the same thing so why not pair off and save the production crew a day's work, but I resist the urge.

The three of us chat for a while, trading stories about our lives, our families, our dating experiences, which means I'm feeling quite warmed up by the time Tilly comes through and tells me it's time for my interview. I go and change into my check jumpsuit in the bathroom (no way was I letting my sweet blue midi dress get all scrunched up in my bag!), and when I emerge, a very good-looking man with a thick head of black hair and soft, dark eyes is holding the door open for me.

'Thank you,' I say, feeling myself blush and wondering if he's my date. Because if he is, then, well, thank you, Tilly.

'So!' Tilly says, ushering me into a brightly lit space that's been set up with a backdrop and a chair. She introduces me to Steve, the camera operator, and a serious-looking woman called Dawn who's in charge of sound. I have to sit down on the chair while they all fuss around me, asking me what I had for breakfast so they can check the sound levels.

'Um . . .' I say, furrowing my brow, trying to cast my mind back to breakfast. 'I think it was . . . Crunchy Nut Cornflakes?' I hope I'm able to answer any further questions with greater precision and fluency.

'Can you say that again for me, please?' Dawn asks.

'Crunchy Nut Cornflakes.'

'And once more.'

'Crunchy Nut Cornflakes.'

'Could you say it one last time, not shouting but a bit louder, like you're excited.'

'Crunchy Nut Cornflakes!'

'Great, we're good to go!'

'Are you going to be interrogating me?' I ask Tilly.

'It's nothing too scary, I promise!' she says, looking up at me from her notepad. 'Shall we get going?'

'Sure,' I say, drawing myself up to a more confident posture, crossing my legs at the ankles.

'Tell us a little about your romantic history?' I've already filled in her survey and I feel self-conscious about going over

63

it all again, like I'll be boring her, but obviously it's because *this is for the public* which is a weird thought, like any answers I give her, anything I say now is for the benefit of random people I've never met. Strange.

'Well, I basically spent ages sixteen to twenty-eight in back-to-back monogamous relationships. And when I say back-to-back, I mean it. Really, there was only ever a week or so between relationships. There was my high school girlfriend and our break-up really messed me up . . . then I was with this guy for a long time and he wasn't a very good person . . . and then I was with my ex for a few years but we had quite different ideas about the future.'

'So you're a serial monogamist?' Tilly asks.

'I used to be, but not anymore.'

'Could you say that again so that it's a full sentence? Anything I say or ask you will be edited out, so can you say, *I used to be a serial monogamist?* Does that make sense?'

'Erm, yeah, sure, I guess,' I say, before clearing my throat. 'I used to be a serial monogamist, but . . . not so much these days. Now I'm in my slag era—'

'Let me stop you. Don't get me wrong, I love slag era, it's a great attitude, but is there some other way we can put it that won't need to be bleeped. You know, a little more pre-watershed.'

'OK, well . . .' I say, composing myself. 'Exploratory phase?'

'Perfect! So if you take it from "Now I'm in my exploratory phase".'

'Now I'm in my exploratory phase . . . that's a euphemism for sleeping around. I guess you could say I'm just sleeping around right now.'

'Would you say you're looking for love?'

'I think my mum really wants me to find love. But I'm not so sure about it myself. I'm kind of enjoying doing my own thing at the moment, being carefree and all that. But my mum runs a wedding dress shop and the idea of me getting married is, like, *super* important to her.'

'Can you maybe describe your dream date? What kind of person would you like to meet today?'

I think for a moment, because this is one of those questions that seems easy but is actually really hard. 'I don't know if there is a particular person I'd like to meet today. I'm pretty open, you know? That's what's been good about doing all this dating lately. Being able to kind of . . . try everything. Experience lots of different things and people and not have to choose between them. So maybe that's why I find it hard to imagine one perfect person. Sorry, I know that's not a very good answer . . .' I say, looking at Tilly.

'That's OK!' she says brightly. 'And is there anything you're *not* looking for in a partner?'

'I'm open-minded. Extremely open,' I say decisively.

'That's good news for me, then! Means you'll probably like whoever we match you up with!'

'I said open-minded, not easy!' I laugh, and I realize it's purely good luck that I often end up really fancying the people I meet up with and then I'm suddenly scared that they'll manage to pair me with the first person in the history of the world that I haven't fancied.

Tilly asks me a few more questions before declaring that I've done a great job of giving her lots of good material. 'And, last thing,' she says, producing a few sheets of paper and attaching them to a clipboard. 'I just need you to sign this.' She hands me the clipboard and a pen and my eyes scan over the paper. Blah blah blah, contributor, rights, transmission, additional content, blah blah, yes yes fine. I sign it and return it to Tilly, who tells me I can go back to the green room now. 'It's nearly your turn, so get changed into your date outfit!'

I feel my stomach lurch. It's happening! I'm never nervous about dates and I didn't think I was nervous about this one, but now it's nearly upon me I'm equal measures nervous and excited. I do what Tilly says and change into my blue dress, admiring myself in the full-length mirror in the bathroom. Definitely Big Date ready.

When I get back to the green room, Stuart and Judy have been replaced by a very pretty young woman with closely shaved Afro hair and a black jumpsuit.

'Nice dress,' she says, looking me over.

'Thanks,' I say, sitting back down in my original seat. 'Nice jumpsuit.'

She smiles. 'Thanks. I feel like the world would be a better place if we said stuff like this more often. Like, not only when you're getting ready to go on TV.'

'You're right,' I say, resolving to give more compliments to random strangers. Yeah! Positivity! Everything's gonna be good! I'm gonna meet someone nice today! Maybe not! But we're gonna have a good time and the world is beautiful and what a time to be alive and all that!

Before I can ask my new green-room-mate any pressing questions about her life, Tilly reappears.

'Fran, you're up!'

I grimace at my companion. 'Wish me luck!' I say, getting to my feet.

'Good luck!' she says.

Tilly grabs my arm as we walk. 'So I won't be there for your date – my colleagues Lucas and Megan will be in the restaurant while it's actually happening, but I have to stay here and do all the prep and the pre-date interviews and all that, but I wanted to say . . .' Tilly leans in to whisper, 'and I know I shouldn't really let this slip but I think we've done a really good job!' She squeezes my arm and gives me a wink.

'I hope so!' I say with a smile.

'So from when you step into the restaurant, you're being filmed, which means we need to put a lapel mic on you now before you go over there. We won't have someone hovering around you with a boom, it's all done remotely.'

In the bar area of the holding restaurant, a sound guy is waiting for me with a lapel microphone that I have to clip inside my dress. 'Better you do it than me,' he says flatly. He tests the levels and then Tilly smiles broadly at me.

'Right,' she says, leading us out of the holding restaurant. She points across the pedestrianized square to another restaurant called Gianluca's. 'That's where we're headed to, but I'll leave you at the door so the cameras don't pick me up. You'll go in first, so you'll be seated at your table and then your date will join you. I really hope you have a great time! Now it's up to you! You're on your own! It's your time to shine!'

At which point Tilly pushes me – literally gives me a shove – not in an aggressive way but enough of a jolt to make me realize this is it: it's really happening.

It does look like a normal restaurant, when you only look in the middle of the room. But when you look on either side, every wall is a row of cameras, keeping their beady eyes on you from every angle. There are no actual camera operators in here, but it's clear I'm under close surveillance on all sides. I notice Judy from the green room is deep in conversation with a bald man in a suit, and I must say, it looks like it's going very well indeed in spite of her nerves.

The guy behind the counter in the entrance who is standing very stiffly, like he's not used to the idea that he's being filmed, asks me, 'Can I take your name, madam?'

'Fran,' I say confidently.

'Come with me,' he says, and shows me to the table where I've been told to wait for my date.

I take a seat, making sure I sit down in a very elegant and TV-friendly way, and try not to look around at the cameras too much even though I am obviously fascinated by them. I look down at the menu but find that I'm not actually reading the words on the page, they're swimming in front of my eyes. I can hear my heart beating. And then I can hear footsteps. But I don't look up yet.

'Fran?' A woman's voice. But not the gentle tone of someone asking if I am, indeed, her date. More like . . . a statement. 'Hello, stranger.'

I look up.

'What the fuck?' Are the only words that come out of my mouth.

7

'What the fuck?' is surely the natural and only response to seeing Ivy.

Ivy! Ivy? Ivy! How can it possibly be Ivy? No! No no no!

There are no more words. I can only look up at her with horror. All at the same time my chest is tight and my head feels full of static and the temperature of my face has increased by about a thousand degrees and my breathing feels shallow and oh God oh God how is this happening?

'This is . . . a surprise,' she says, sitting down opposite me. Her voice is still low and scratchy. Of course it is, it's her voice for fuck's sake, that's not going to change, is it?

'I would call it more of a shock,' I mumble.

'Wow,' she says, staring at me from across the table. She's shaking her head and smiling like this is actually something nice rather than something extremely horrible, but I suppose since she was the one who got to walk away from me, maybe her residual memories aren't quite so fucking horrendous. 'I never thought I would see you again.'

'Me neither,' I say, but it comes out as a hoarse whisper.

'Foxy,' she says, using her stupid old nickname for me. 'It's you, it's really you!' She really, truly seems . . . pleased to see me? Her face is a picture of delight at this happy little 'accident'.

And as I look at her, look at that face, I feel so flooded with memories and sadness and pain for the completely lost eighteen-year-old girl I was when she broke up with me and left me feeling so completely empty that I was *primed* to be picked up by Daniel only days later to fill the massive gap she'd left in my life. And I realize she's talking to me but I haven't been listening to her at all, I'm so deep in my own memories from all those years ago that I don't think about often, or even at all, but they're still there and I can't make them go away. How can this be the way I have to go over them again? How can this possibly be the way?

'Fuck this,' I say, not looking her in the eye, pushing my chair out and standing up from the table.

Without consciously telling my limbs to move, I transport myself into the toilets, which, to my great relief are empty, although I notice that there's at least one camera, over near the row of sinks. I lock myself in a cubicle, slumping down to sit on the closed toilet lid. I let my head flop down between my knees and sit there, trying to get my brain around the shock of seeing her again after so many years, so unexpectedly. She was my first *everything*. Before Ivy I had no real sense of myself as being *desirable*. I was the only fat girl in my friendship group and had no idea that someone could want me as much as she did. Once the idea was in my head, I couldn't help wondering what it would be like to try that desirability on the rest of the world. But I never did find out, because I knew there would be no one better for me than Ivy. And then she broke my heart.

There can't be cameras in *here*, surely. But I'm barely in there any time at all before I'm interrupted.

'Fran?' Comes a tentative voice, like they're not sure whether I'm in there or not. Not Ivy's, mercifully. 'Fran?'

'Yes?' I say wearily.

'It's Megan, at Red Rooster. I'm going to chat to you for a second if that's OK?'

'Yes,' I say, without getting up or unlocking the door.

'Do you want to come out for a minute?'

'No?'

'I would much rather talk to you face to face,' she says gently.

'I don't want everyone to know I'm crying.'

'But we're picking up audio of you, well, you know . . .'

'Of course you are,' I say. I can hide in the toilets all I want but it's too late to conceal my tears. How very mortifying all this is. At least it isn't live. Reluctantly, I slide open the cubicle door and step outside.

Megan is standing by the sink putting on make-up. Initially I think this is a bit weird, but of course . . . I realize she's pretending to be a diner at the restaurant. She cocks her head in a very sympathetic way. 'So, you two know each other, then?'

'Yeah. From a long time ago.'

'What are the odds, eh?' she says, shifting a piece of gum around in her mouth before moving on to the main event.

'Is this a set-up? Who told you about me and Ivy? Tell me it wasn't my mum? Because if it is, I will kill her.' I turn to one of the cameras on the wall: 'And I don't mind if you record that. I will kill you, Mum, because you know how I feel about Ivy.'

71

Even Megan looks a little freaked at this outburst. 'No! No one has set anybody up. We didn't know, I promise.'

'Really?'

'Really. So, was it a bad break-up? Did she break your heart?'

'Yes. And yes,' I say, feeling the lump in my throat form again. I have to be honest, I knew I didn't have warm fuzzy feelings for Ivy but I didn't know she, and the memories of our break-up, still had the power to make me feel quite like *this*.

'Do you think you'll want to talk about it with her? Today, I mean?'

'I would rather not!' I say, taken aback by the mere idea of it.

'But don't you think it would be good for you to really get into it with her? Talk it over? Try to hash it out?'

'In front of the cameras?'

'Well, yes, that's why we're here, right?' she says, and the thirst in her eyes is like a bloodhound looking for . . . well, blood. I'm good content. Me and Ivy are good content.

'I'm *here*,' I say impatiently, 'to have a fun sexy time. Not to come face to face with the first and last person to break my heart and ruin my life.'

'OK, yes, I get that . . . but fortune favours the brave!'

'I hope you know by now that I'm not staying. I'm not putting myself through a whole meal with her, not now,' I say, like it's the most obvious thing in the world. They're not holding me hostage. I can *leave*. Can't I?

'Wouldn't you rather stay? You know, get your story across. Because, well, we're obviously . . . we're obviously going to use what we have, whether you stay or not. It's just a question of whether you want to stick with it and put yourself across or have the narrative be that she turned up and you stormed out.'

'To be honest, at this point I don't really care. I just want to go. I assume you can't physically restrain me here,' I say, even though I have no idea whether they can or not.

Megan looks pained, panicked even. 'I'll give you five hundred pounds to stay,' she says quickly.

'Five hundred pounds?' I ask, adding a little note of disgust at how low the number is in the hope I could bargain her up.

'If you stay, I can give you five hundred pounds.'

That's certainly . . . tempting. But I can definitely get more money in exchange for my emotional humiliation.

'A thousand pounds,' she offers, without me even having to ask for it.

My mouth forms a little O of surprise; £1,000 would certainly take the pressure off. She sees me wavering and her eyes narrow at me, weighing her options. 'A grand, OK, deal?'

I stare at her, my breathing heavy. A thousand pounds is hard to turn down, but do I really want to do this? I have to get through the date and then I never have to see Ivy again. Plus, who knows, maybe I'll get 'closure' or something. 'Fine. I'll do it. But I'm not happy about it.'

The relief on her face is palpable. 'You're doing the right thing,' she says, as if it's terribly moral of me to stick around and continue to be horrified and embarrassed by coming face to face with Ivy.

When I finally make my way back to the table, past the other participants and what I assume are the production crew's mates pretending to be normal diners, I see the other producer, the guy, scuttling away from our table where Ivy's still sitting, looking bemused. I dread to think what the two of them have been talking about, how fucking gleeful the producers must be at having stumbled across such rich dramatic ground for their show. I just can't believe the rich dramatic ground is *me* and my bloody meltdown.

I take a deep breath and shakily sit down opposite her again.

Ivy smiles at me, hopefully. 'I . . . assume you didn't know who you were meeting either?' she ventures.

I shake my head. 'No.'

'What are the chances?' she says, smiling that fucking infuriatingly delightful smile.

'One in a million,' I say, still dazed.

'Probably more than that.'

'Mmm.'

'So . . .' she says, glancing down at the menu. 'Let me guess . . . you're going to have . . . the caprese salad because I *know* you must still like mozzarella, there's no way that's changed, and the chicken parmigiana because you never met a flattened chicken you didn't like.' The low buzz of her voice threatens to take my breath away. But I will not give in.

'Thank you so much for telling me how predictable I am,' I sigh, setting the menu down on the table.

'No, that's not . . . that's not what I meant,' Ivy says, frowning, her thick, dark eyebrows drawing themselves into a flat line. 'I just meant . . .'

'Fine,' I say, and we sit in uncomfortable silence until the waiter nervously comes over to take our order. 'I'll have the beef carpaccio and the sea bass. Please.' And as I say it I'm already mourning my lost caprese and chicken parmigiana that I specifically did not order because I didn't want to prove Ivy right. Congratulations, I played myself. Instantly, I feel stupid and petty, but somehow I couldn't stop myself. I had to *assert my dominance*.

'Thank you so much,' Ivy says, gazing up at the waiter as he turns to leave our table.

'So,' she says.

'So,' I say. Can I leave it at that? But no, knowing my hatred of bad chat on dates, I offer the rather feeble, 'How have you been?'

'Good,' she says, nodding her head enthusiastically so that her wild, frizzy, almost-black curls bob around her head. It's longer than it used to be. 'I mean, in general. I guess you can't really account for . . . what has it been? Ten years?'

'Eleven.'

'I guess you can't really account for all that time with one word, can you?'

'Mmm,' I say noncommittally.

'How about you?' she asks, looking me right in the eye, looking at me like she really wants to know. Really wants to know how I've been.

'I've been great!' I will not let her know the truth that, no, it hasn't all been great and that she really fucked me up.

'That's good,' she says gently. 'I'm glad.' She pauses, takes a breath. 'You look great, by the way. I really, really love the short hair on you.'

'Thanks,' I say, raking my hands through it. 'It's fairly recent.'

'It's funny . . .' she says. 'Even though I thought you would have your mermaid hair forever, when I saw you from across the restaurant, I just knew it was you. It felt like you.'

'You can't . . .' I say, and I already feel the hot tears pricking at the back of my eyeballs. 'Can you please not say things like that? It's taken a lot for me to stay. So can you not say stuff that makes it sound like you care about me.'

'But I do care . . .' she says, looking hurt. 'Or at least, am I allowed to say that I'm interested in what you've been up to all this time?'

'Fine, whatever,' I say, waving my hands defensively, while simultaneously hating myself.

I will be the first to admit: I don't understand why I'm being like this. Or rather, I do, and I don't like myself for acting this way, but I can't help myself. It's an impulse towards self-preservation, and what's more powerful than that? But I *really* don't want to look like a dick on TV! I guess I already look like a dick by running off to the toilets and crying, so really what do I even have to lose at this point? God! What a mess!

I take a deep breath and draw myself up in my seat as Stuart walks over to a table where a pretty blond woman is waiting for him, who, judging by the look of anxious anticipation on his face, I assume was *not* his first love. Good for Stuart.

'So, what do you . . . do?' I ask Ivy as I contemplate how entirely fucking unnatural this whole thing is. Not the TV thing, the cameras, the producers hovering, obviously all of that is unnatural, but what strikes me as the most unnatural thing of all is the idea that I do not know what Ivy's life has looked like for more than a decade. I have no clue. That doesn't make sense to me, to the eighteen-year-old I was when we last saw each other. But it's the way it went.

'For work, you mean?' she asks, looking relieved that I'm

capable of engaging with her in a vaguely normal way.

'Yeah,' I say, shrugging.

'I'm a lecturer now. At King's. In the Classics department.'

'Oh!' I say, feeling something like pride bubble up in my chest, *entirely* against my will. 'That's . . . amazing. And . . . makes sense. You were always so clever.'

Ivy blushes, her pale cheeks flooded with colour. 'Like you weren't!' she says, tilting her head in a *come on now* pose.

'Not clever enough,' I say, attempting breeziness and failing.

'Oh,' Ivy flinches, remembering why we broke up in the first place. 'No, it wasn't that . . . it was . . . bad luck.'

'Well,' I say, trying to think of something to get us off this subject, when Megan From The Toilet swoops upon us.

'Sorry, ladies, I think Fran's microphone has moved, let me reposition it for you. Can you come with me for a moment, please?' she asks, and with absolutely zero enthusiasm, I follow her over to a side corridor. She fiddles with my lapel mic for a moment, unclipping and clipping it back on again in what appears to be exactly the same spot, before saying, 'So, are you going to talk about what happened?'

'What?'

'You know – there's clearly something *there*, what you just alluded to. You know, when you said *not clever enough* and Ivy reacted and said it was bad luck?'

'I don't want to go into it . . .'

'One thousand pounds,' Megan says, fixing me with a meaningful stare. 'Might I add, you're the only person that's being paid to be here.'

'Fine,' I sigh. 'I'll pick up where we left off.'

'Good girl,' she says, which makes me miss Tilly. I wonder

how she would be dealing with this. And then I wonder if she knew all along that me and Ivy knew each other. It's all too . . . random, too coincidental . . . there has to be an explanation for it.

Megan returns me to the table. 'Sorry for interrupting!' she says. 'I'll leave you to it now.'

'Thank you,' Ivy says, polite as ever.

'Just bad luck,' I repeat, trying to stay true to my promise to Megan.

'Yeah,' Ivy says. 'Bad timing. They were marking particularly harshly that year, remember?'

I clear my throat, trying to think of how to communicate the full story of what actually happened in a way that will seem natural enough for Megan to award me my money. 'Yeah . . .' I begin. 'Which meant when the A-level results came out, I didn't get the grades I needed to get into Edinburgh. And Edinburgh is really far away from London, especially when you're eighteen and have basically no autonomy and no real money of your own. So you decided that since you got in and I didn't, it was . . .' I swallow, remembering how incredibly painful it was to hear those words coming out of her mouth even though it was such a long time ago. 'It was for the best that we broke up then rather than trying to do a long-distance thing.'

Ivy's shoulders slump. 'That was a hard decision for me.'

'That's a shame,' I say, unable to keep the bitterness out of my voice. 'I hope you didn't suffer too much.'

'Come on,' Ivy says. 'It was something that happened when we were teenagers. It's in the very distant past. Maybe it wasn't the right thing for me to do. And it was bad timing—'

'Kicking me when I was down? Yeah, I'll say it was.'

Ivy opens her mouth to reply, but we're interrupted by the waiter bringing our starters, and I stare at my carpaccio, wishing it was mozzarella.

'I never thought it would mean *literally never seeing you again* until now, though,' she says when the waiter has backed away from the table, sensing the absolute madness happening here.

'You thought we were going to be friends?' I ask, taken aback.

'I suppose I did, yes,' Ivy says, frowning again. 'Because we were so close. We were *so* close.'

'That's precisely why we *couldn't* be friends!' I say, throwing my hands up. 'Because I loved you so much, and not in a teenage crush sort of way, I really, really loved you in a way that maybe I never loved either of my other partners. And then you took it all away and left me alone when everyone was going off to university and posting all their freshers' week photos on Facebook and I didn't get in and I was stuck in my boring life doing temp jobs, telling myself I would apply again next year. But then life moves on and before you know it everything has moved on. Except me.'

'Were things really that bad for you?' Ivy asks, sounding worried.

'No,' I say, shaking my head. 'I've had a really fun life. But it doesn't mean I'm happy about how things went for us, and how you left things, and how vulnerable that left me.'

Ivy nods. 'I understand.' She pauses for a moment. 'When you deleted me off Facebook and all of that, and stopped replying to my texts and emails, I think I knew then that I had really hurt you.'

'I just couldn't,' I say. 'I couldn't have you around, buzzing around my brain. Because I knew that if I kept seeing you, seeing pictures of you, seeing you having fun, looking at every fucking idiot you were hanging out with in Edinburgh that wasn't me, I would be looking at them and thinking *Is she with them? Is that my replacement?* Because I wasn't naive enough to believe that you would, like, never love again. So I knew it was inevitable that you would move on and forget about me and I didn't want to see it happening before my eyes.'

I am not used to being this honest. Or rather, there are not many things in my life that I feel compelled to gloss over. But my feelings about Ivy and the tailspin she sent me into were the source of so much pain that I don't really like to talk about it. I don't even like to talk about it now, but after bottling it up for so long, for so many years, pushing it all down, now I've started I don't know how to stop. It's like water pouring out of a burst dam. 'Out of sight, out of mind.' Maybe I took that mantra too seriously. Maybe if I'd let myself think a bit more about Ivy over the intervening years then I wouldn't be feeling so freshly wounded right now. Because it's embarrassing, isn't it? To be so hurt by something that happened to you so long ago. I should be over it by now. So why am I not?

'God, this is such a weird way to be meeting again,' Ivy says. 'Such a weird place to be trying to talk about any of this.' She shakes her head in disbelief.

'It doesn't feel real,' I say. 'It feels like a dream or something.' Because I do dream about her, every few years, and it always makes me feel hollowed out the next day. Empty. Wondering if I should look her up, see how she's doing. But I never do. And now the universe has intervened.

Ivy clears her throat and tosses her hair. 'Maybe we should talk about something a bit lighter,' she says.

I'm not sure how I'm supposed to reply to that, so I don't.

Ivy perseveres: 'What do you do now? For work, I mean.'

'I was a journalist. I used to write about beauty for a weekly magazine. And then I was made redundant. And now I've transitioned into being a make-up artist . . . so that's what I do. And I work in my friend's cafe.'

'That's great!' Ivy says enthusiastically, although I'm not sure which bit she thinks is great.

'Isn't it?' And I look at her with not contempt but certainly not affection, and I see in her eyes the desperation of someone who is drowning.

We leave the restaurant, and I'm mentally calculating my route to Mum's to vent all my frustrations, when we're intercepted by *another* producer.

'Hi, ladies, please come with me for your post-date interview. We just had to film you leaving but if you follow me we can get this wrapped up and take your mics off.'

Does it ever fucking end? Can't they give me my grand and let me leave? Maybe I live here now, somewhere between here and the other restaurant, bouncing between them for eternity talking to a never-ending parade of producers.

'Sure,' Ivy says politely. This whole thing has been fucking *classic*. Irrational, emotional Fran and calm, sensible-minded Ivy. Our whole relationship played out in miniature.

We're led back to the other restaurant, where only this morning I was so full of optimism and a sense of fun, imagining I'd be paired up with any random hottie for great conversation leading possibly to more but maybe not, whatever. And instead I got faced with the one person guaranteed to give me a breakdown on TV. Lucas chats breezily to Ivy and it's apparent he is thrilled that we're only now emerging from an incredibly uncomfortable experience.

'Right!' he says. 'We'll do Ivy first and then Fran, and then Ivy will come back in so we can talk to you together.'

They head into the room, with Ivy giving me a sympathetic, heavy-lidded glance over her shoulder. It feels apt that because she's so tall, she's always looking down on me.

I pace up and down the corridor waiting for Ivy to be done and for it to be my turn. I wonder if Tilly is around and if I can unleash my fury on her, because right now I'm feeling like I have nowhere in particular to direct my rage at being set up like this, either by the cosmos, Tilly, or my darling mother. Finally, the door opens and Ivy emerges, followed by Lucas.

I take a seat, suddenly conscious of how I look under the lights, suddenly worried about my make-up and the camera angles and things that I hadn't thought about when I was here earlier because I felt hopeful rather than bloody miserable.

'So!' Lucas says, pushing his glasses up his nose. 'How was your date?'

'Not pleasant,' I say, remembering I'm supposed to speak in full sentences but maybe if I don't then they won't be able to use this footage . . .

'But Ivy seems so nice?'

'Yeah—'

'Sorry, can you remember to answer in full sentences?'

Busted.

'Ivy is nice,' I say, grudgingly doing as instructed. 'But she broke my heart, so unsurprisingly I'm not that excited to see her again.'

'That's a shame,' he says, looking down at his clipboard.

'Yeah.'

'So she wasn't what you were hoping for today?'

'I thought this was going to be fun. That's basically why I agreed to come on. Fun. Maybe Ivy would have been what I was hoping for if we didn't already have so much history.'

'Wasn't it exciting to see her after so long?'

'No, it was horrible to see her after so long.'

'I guess you don't have much to say, do you?' he mumbles, casting his eye over the list of questions and predicting my answers to each one, deciding it's not worth it. 'Shall we get Ivy in here?'

'Whatever.'

He gets up and sticks his head out the door. 'Ivy?' he says, and even though I literally *know* in my brain that she's coming through the door this time, I still brace myself.

She smiles at me, hopefully (hopeful of what? Hopeful that I'm not going to start crying again? No bloody way am I going to start crying again, the least I can do is preserve what little dignity I have left), and sits down next to me.

'So! I only have one question for you both, really: Do you think you'll see each other again?' Lucas asks expectantly, although surely only someone who hadn't seen my horrified reaction with their own eyeballs could ask that. I suppose he has to ask.

'No,' I say, before Ivy can even open her mouth. 'This was enough.' I stand up and unclip the microphone from my collar and unthread it from inside my dress. I hand it to Lucas.

I make it to the door, where I pause, my head fizzing with every feeling from frustration to sadness to shame to anger, turn back to look at her, just once. I take a deep breath and say the thing I didn't get to say last time, because I couldn't believe I would ever have to say it.

'Goodbye, Ivy.'

8

'Mum!' I almost roar when I enter the bridal shop. I don't even remember the journey there, I feel like I was in some kind of fugue state brought on by extreme emotional distress.

'What on earth?' She looks up from pinning a bride-to-be into a dress.

'Excuse us,' I say to the bride-to-be, grabbing Mum by the arm and dragging her over to the counter, which stands alongside two changing cubicles next to each other. I look over my shoulder as I go, shouting cheerily at the customer. 'You look really nice, by the way – that shade of peach doesn't suit most people but it looks perfect on you! Lovely against your olive skin!' This poor woman looks completely bewildered by my sudden appearance in her dress fitting and who can blame her?

'Shelly?' Mum calls to her long-suffering employee who's currently out the back doing whatever mysterious business goes on in there. 'Can you come in here for a minute, please?'

I stand there, arms folded, steam possibly rising out of the top of my head. Shelly appears, looking like a deer in the headlights, wondering what she's done wrong. 'Could you please take care of Lucy for me while I see what my *rude* daughter is here for?' she says, turning to narrow her eyes at me for extra dramatic emphasis. Although, who am I kidding: I'm feeling pretty dramatic today myself. Shelly nods and trots over to the startled bride in her peach-toned dress.

Tucked away by the counter, Mum grabs the fleshy part of my upper arm so hard I can feel it through my jacket. 'What on earth is going on? You're scaring me!'

'Did you know?' I say, fixing her with a stare that I know is bordering somewhere near recently escaped axe murderer jumping out on you down a dark alley.

'Know what?'

'It was my date today.'

'What date? Aren't you on a different date every night of the week?'

'My stupid TV date,' I say, pressing my fingers into my eyeballs like I'm trying to block out the world, feeling like I'm going to cry with stress and anger and embarrassment while desperately trying not to. Then, when I take my hands away from my face, I catch my eye. What? Me? I catch my own eye? Yes, there I am above the counter, where my mum has had some of our dress photos printed and blown up in a banner to display the new styles and I can't quite reconcile the serene, smiling, Princess Diana-eyes-doing version of me with my flowing princess hair to the furious, emotionally distressed skinhead harpy that stands in the shop today. 'Gaaaah!' I wail, throwing my head back.

'Fran!' Mum says suddenly. 'What's that, behind you?'

And like an idiot I fall for it! Like I was literally born yesterday and I am but a tiny baby! I turn around in confusion and when I do my darling mother *shoves* me into one of the changing cubicles and pushes the door shut behind me. I am so taken aback by this that I stand there for a moment in shock, during which time she manages to whip out her key and lock me in from the outside. The audacity! My own darling mother!

I bang on the door for her to let me out, but instead her head appears over the top of the cubicle next door, where she's standing on the little stool.

'Fran Baker you are twenty-nine years old and this is my place of work and I am telling you that I will not let you out of there until you calm down. Got it?'

I look up at her, my eyeballs turned into daggers. 'Did you know?'

'Did! I! Know! What?' Mum hisses down at me from her overhead position.

'That they were going to pair me up with Ivy?'

'Ivy?' Mum's face is a picture of confusion. 'Who's Ivy? Ivy who?'

'My ex-girlfriend Ivy?'

'From when you were at school?' she says, the memory finally stirring.

'Yes! Who broke my heart and ruined my life!'

'Did she?'

Unsurprisingly this only enrages me further. 'You never took our relationship seriously anyway, so I'm not surprised that when she, like I said, broke my heart and ruined my life, you didn't think it was that important!'

'That's not fair! I take you seriously!'

'So you didn't know they were going to set me up with her?'

'Of course not! What do you think I am, some sort of evil bloody puppet master?'

'I thought maybe Tilly gave you her name or something . . .' I mumble.

'Absolutely not! How much do you think I bloody talk to Tilly anyway! I haven't had any contact with her since I had to film that little video about what kind of person I wanted them to pair you up with!'

'And what did you say?' I demand, wondering if she said *I would like you to dig around in my daughter's past to find the person who would be most likely to cause her to have a full-on meltdown on national TV.*

She looks thoughtful, like she's really trying to remember. 'All I said was that I thought you should be with someone who's confident, you know, to match you, and . . . calm to balance you out . . . and that I know you like people who are tall . . . um . . . and that I wanted to see you with someone who was kind and patient.'

'Well,' I say, reddening, and feeling decidedly chastened, if it's possible for me to become more flushed than I already am right now. 'That sounds . . . very nice.'

Mum folds her arms across the top of the cubicle and rests her chin on them, looking down at me. 'So it was horrible, was it?' she asks, and the sheer volume of love in that sentence makes me completely sure she had no idea they were pairing me up with Ivy, that it was a horrible, random accident and how could I have ever thought otherwise? Not least because clearly Ivy has loomed less large in *her* mind for the past eleven years than she has done in mine. But it being random is so . . . unfair?

'It was,' I sulk. 'It was so unexpected.'

'I can imagine, baba,' she says, reaching her hand down, expectantly and I reach mine up to meet it. She gives me a reassuring squeeze.

I slump down against the wall of the cubicle and come to rest on the stool. 'Shall I let you out now?' Mum asks.

'No,' I say. 'I'll stay here for a bit.'

'Bang on the door when you want to be let out,' she says, before blowing me a kiss and climbing down and away from sight. 'I've got work to do.'

As I sit there, I feel so completely stupid. Stupid for agreeing to do the show in the first place, stupid for having such a strong reaction to seeing Ivy, stupid for storming over here and trying to blame Mum for putting me forward for it. Of course she wouldn't know who they were going to match me with! I needed somewhere to direct all my pain. Which means now I also feel stupid for bursting into the shop.

In an attempt to distract myself from my own self-loathing, I check my phone.

There's a text from Tilly:

OMG Fran are you OK? I didn't know you two knew each other. Please get in touch when you can.

Oh, sure, Tilly, yeah, I can't wait to have a chat with you and revisit my meltdown in great detail. I had just come round to the idea that Tilly was quite cool and nice! And now she is the face of evil! All that is wrong with the world!

But there's also one from Marie, who's been extremely hyped and invested in this date:

Baby girl how was your date?! Were they a hottie? Guy or gal? Or neither? Tell me everything!

89

I decline to reply to Tilly. She can wait. But to Marie I write:

Literally the worst thing in the whole world ever, I am surprised I'm still alive and haven't fucking died of shame.

Wtf?

My date was IVY

IVY FROM SCHOOL ???? Comes her reply almost instantly.

Yes

COME TO MINE LATER!

If you insist . . . if I am still alive by 'later'

You're such a drama kween! But omg IVY! What a BLAST FROM THE PAST

One of the many good things about Marie is that she's known me so long that she was even around during the Ivy era so she knows how crazy this is without me having to spell it out for her.

If you think I'm a drama queen now just wait til I'll be there. And I will call upon ALL your legal skills to help block this show from ever getting broadcast later xx

I definitely need a friend right now and Marie is a lawyer, perhaps she can help me stop the show from airing.

'Mum!' I call in my sweetest, most gentle voice. 'I'm ready to come out now!'

A few seconds later I hear her key in the lock and she pulls the door open. 'You feeling better now, Franny?'

'Not really,' I tell her, at which point she brandishes the key, ready to sequester me again. '*But* I've calmed down. I'm sorry I was so angry when I got here.'

'It's all right,' she says, pulling me into a tight squeeze. 'Poor Lucy didn't know what hit her. At least you said her dress looked nice on her.'

'It does,' I shrug, and we make our way over to the door. 'Sorry I interrupted your fitting,' I say to the woman I assume is Lucy. 'It's been a bad day.'

'It happens,' she says, smiling, and I was right about the peach being the perfect match for her olive skin.

Shelly the assistant is glaring at me, and to be honest I don't really blame her. But give me a break! It's not like I storm in here every weekend demanding my mother account for her various crimes.

'Isn't that you?' Lucy asks, pointing at the banner above the till.

I turn to look even though I know that it is me. 'Yeah,' I say. 'You wouldn't guess, based on my absolute hag behaviour today, though, would you?'

'Oh, you're all right,' Mum says, ruffling my hair. 'And I was thinking . . .'

'Yes?'

'Your hair . . . well, it actually looks quite nice, doesn't it? I

91

mean, now I'm used to it and all. Do you want to do the photos again? Unless you don't want to or don't have time?'

I feel that warm rush of love and feel even more guilty for having a go at Mum. I shouldn't be such a little beast, especially not at my grand old age. 'Yeah, let's do it,' I say, squeezing her arm. 'Besides, no one else would stand about for so long being bossed around by you for so little money.'

'Cheeky!' she says, swatting at me. 'Where are you off to, baba?'

'Marie's,' I say with a heavy sigh.

'Well, look, take it easy the rest of the day. Get a takeaway or something. And don't worry about anything. I love you.'

'Love you too,' I say, because even though it will be impossible for me to opt out of worrying, I can't deny it's reassuring to hear that coming from Mum.

I hope I can cling onto this cringe little life until I see Marie later.

9

'It . . .' *sniff* 'was . . .' *sniff* 'so . . .' *sniff* 'HORRIBLE!' I gulp down a sob. I might have got it together at my mum's shop but in the safe space of Marie's flat, the floodgates are open again. 'I thought I would never see her again! I never *wanted* to see her again. I erased her from my life years ago!'

'My poor little pal,' Marie says, with the exact degree of comfort I need right now.

'It's fucking *mortifying* that someone could have this effect on me and that it should be *public!* What have I done to deserve this? Which god have I angered? I don't break mirrors! I don't step on cracks in the pavement! Have you ever seen me walk under a ladder?' I say, near hysterical at the injustice of my humiliation, wiping away what I hope are the final tears I will shed over this whole mess.

'I have not. And you don't deserve it.'

'Then help me! I'm serious,' I say, gulping down my rosé. 'What are best friends even *for* if not this? I am absolutely begging you to take me seriously this time. Just once! I need you to intervene.'

She sighs from the other end of the sofa, the picture of sympathy. 'But what do you want *me* to do?'

'You're a lawyer, aren't you?'

'Well, yes,' she says, kicking her comedically large fluffy slippers off and curling herself up on her sofa. Marie's flat is the location of many messy parties, *all* of which I have attended, and I have to say, I would rather endure a post–Marie's–party hangover than whatever emotional hangover I'm experiencing right now.

'Can't you get an injunction against the show ever being broadcast? Or, wait, what about a *super injunction*? That way no one can even talk about the *existence* of the show, right? Those exist, don't they?'

'I feel like this is very *you* – a mere injunction is not good enough, it simply has to be a super injunction.'

'Why aren't you taking me seriously in my hour of need?'

'OK, on what grounds do you reckon you could get a super injunction?'

'Shame. Humiliation. Bringing my good name into disrepute,' I offer her.

'And you're telling me you actually *cried*? You?'

I sigh. 'Yes! You see why this is so urgent!'

'But you never cry!'

'I know! I save it all up for when I'm in the cinema and no one can see me!' One of my many foibles but fortunately one I don't have to explain to Marie.

'And now you've cried on actual TV,' she says, shaking her head. And then she asks the question I've been asking myself for the past few hours. 'Why did you even go on it in the first place?'

'Oh, I don't know!' I say, burying my face in my hands. 'Can I blame it on Vic for making me feel like it would be fun?

I thought it would be an adventure, you know? I'm saying yes to stuff, trying something new, all of those things that are meant to make life interesting! Exploratory phase, remember! I would say yes to anything out of curiosity – blind dates, apps, speed dating, whatever, anything I used to think was awful now I'm like, oh, why not give it a go? But this is why! The universe has decided to smite me down! There I was naively thinking, *oh, how bad can it be? The worst that can happen is that we don't fancy each other and then we go our separate ways and I got a free meal out of it.* Well, I found out what the worst that can happen is! And I do not care for it!'

'I'm going to level with you, Franny,' Marie says sagely. 'I don't think you stand much chance of this super injunction situation working out . . .'

'But whyyyyy?' I moan, throwing my head back so it rests on the top of the sofa cushion. 'Surely there's a way?'

'I assume you signed a release form, right?'

'Yeah . . . I guess that was when my shitty fate was sealed . . .' I mumble. And there's no point telling Marie I literally agreed to be paid for my participation. Now I would pay a grand for them to not show it.

'I can look over the release form you signed but there is absolutely no way the production company will have put in a clause that says *if you are, with hindsight, embarrassed about anything you said or did on the show, you can ask us not to broadcast it, that's fine with us.*'

'Ugh! It's inhumane!'

'And was it *all* on camera?' She grimaces sympathetically.

'Yes! The restaurant was basically *made* of cameras! Nowhere to hide! And a bloody producer coming over every twenty minutes under the pretext of adjusting your microphone or something, but really they're trying to prod you to talk about the precise stuff you don't want to talk about!'

'Unfortunately, that's TV for you.' She shrugs, but she looks genuinely pained on my behalf. But then again, if she's so pained, why no super injunction, eh?

'Well, I hate TV,' I say, crossing my arms over my chest like a petulant schoolgirl.

Marie fixes me with a businesslike stare. 'Look,' she says, sitting up straight. 'All I'm going to say is, I bet it wasn't really *that* bad. I bet when you see it, you'll be surprised how bad it actually *wasn't*.'

'I don't think so, mate. You weren't there! You don't understand!' I realize I have to appeal to her own life experience. 'Think of it this way: imagine if you went on there and, without warning, they paired you up with Julia.'

I watch as her eyes widen and her nostrils flare at the mere mention of that name. I remember it well, Marie wailing into the phone that Julia had broken up with her, and me dashing over to Marie's flat with lots of tissues and cocktails in a can and the biggest box of crappy chocolate I could find in the supermarket. Marie wasn't just wailing about the loss of their relationship but the tedious reality of having to deal with the fact they'd bought this flat together and, as a solicitor, she was well aware of what a fucking headache it was all going to be. 'Well, firstly, I wouldn't be going on a TV dating show, but yeah, I would want to fucking die.'

'See!'

'But!' She holds her palm up to me. 'I would also *understand*,' she says very emphatically, 'that the whole thing was very much out of my control and that's one of the scary things about agreeing to do something like this.'

'So what you're saying is . . . you are not going to help me get this show blocked.'

'*What I'm saying* is there is literally no way anyone could do that. You know I would help you if I could! That's what friends are for!'

'I thought this was what lawyer friends are for.'

'Quick question, do you actually understand what I do?'

'Legal . . . things?' I offer, hopefully. 'You're a solicitor, I know that.'

'Yes indeed, I *am* a solicitor and I mostly sort out people's wills. Never in my life have I procured an injunction!'

'Can't you make an exception for me?'

'This is not going to happen!'

I sigh. 'Fine. I have to live with it, don't I?'

'Yes,' she says. 'I am very sorry. You have my deepest sympathies.'

'This is what I get for joyously pursuing fun and romance. Only deepest sympathies. Why does the universe not want me to thrive?'

'Well, you were thriving quite hard before all this. And you will thrive again.'

'Will I though? Because I feel like this is hanging over me like a huge black cloud and that maybe I will never know peace again in my one wild and precious life.'

'Try not to think about it.'

'Oh, yes, good, I'll do that,' I say sarcastically.

Marie laughs. 'I'm sorry! I wish I had something more helpful to offer you.'

'It wouldn't have been so bad if she was rattled too! But she wasn't! She was fucking cool like a cucumber or whatever. And there's me having a meltdown like . . . like a marshmallow over a fire. Why can't I be more cucumber?'

'Because you have big feelings! Because those feelings are often bubbling quite close to the surface! Because you are very passionate and sensitive and joyful and when something comes along and punctures that it's very confronting for you! Anyone that knows you knows that you are a marshmallow in cucumber's clothing. It's who you are! And that's fine!'

'I suppose so,' I say, although I definitely wish I was more cucumber. 'I hate that everyone is going to see me looking *weak*. It's off-brand. It's mortifying. It's un-chic.'

'Go on some more good dates, to take your mind off it.'

'But if I have bad luck once, I can have bad luck again!'

'Yes . . .' she says, thinking for a moment. 'That's . . . true. But the odds are, you won't. The fact is, lightning is probably not going to strike twice, so I think the best thing you can do now is to go about your merry little Franny business and get back to your plan of bonking your way around London and start enjoying yourself.'

'Sorry but at this point I literally want to retire from public life. Dating was fun while it lasted but I think I need to become a hermit, at least until after the show airs.' I'm pretty sure it's the only way through this. 'It's really thrown me off my game, is all. Robbed me of my good vibes.'

'No!' She claps her hands together decisively. 'You were so hyped about being single and you were having so much fun dating and sleeping around,' she says, which gives me a horrible, heart-in-throat flashback to me using that exact expression in my taped interview, which I know they'll definitely fucking use in the finished show, but what can I do about that now, eh? 'So we are *not* letting this throw you off. Get back on the horse, my friend.'

'I barely want to leave the house, let alone throw myself onto London's dating population.'

An impish expression passes over her face. 'Let's get the old Fran back. The joyous Fran who was so enjoying her single life. Your thirtieth is on the horizon—'

'I only just turned twenty-nine!'

'That was two whole weeks ago. My point is, instead of retiring from public life and doing the hermit thing, why don't you do the exact opposite? Get Ivy out of your system by increasing your, how shall we call it, *body count* as much as possible by your thirtieth birthday?'

'Make this the year of living . . . deliciously?'

'Precisely. The best way to get over somebody . . .'

'Is to get under somebody,' I say sagely.

'Quite bloody right. So, it's a good idea? You're up for it? You, Fran Baker, are up for aggressively living your best life in the face of emotional humiliation?'

'Oh, go on then.' I am unable to suppress a smile. God bless Marie. Maybe she couldn't do me a super injunction, but she can at least cheer me up.

'And now you never have to see Ivy again.'

'And now I never have to see Ivy again!'

'So, the future: have you got any nice little *prospects* going on?'

I think about it for a moment, trying to cast my mind back over the various hotties I was messaging pre-catastrophe. 'Yeah,'

I say, thinking of Doug ManHoney, among others. A smile creeps across my face. 'I got some prospects.'

'See! That's what we want, a nice happy Fran!'

'That's what I want too, I assure you!' I am not an unhappy person! I am an optimist! I live for fun! And never more so than in my present single life! This will not derail me! 'I *feel* so shit right now. I can be all motivated and up for dating new people and having fun, but it doesn't really change the fact that I feel so . . . embarrassed?'

'I know, baby,' she says, pawing at my hand. 'Let yourself feel it. Don't do the thing you do where you pretend everything is fine because you don't want people to think you're weak. If you don't have plans tomorrow then stay in bed all day and eat ice cream and watch TV. Kind of like what we're doing now but . . .' Marie raises her eyebrows. 'Alone.'

'Ugh, I hate alone.'

'You will get through this. It was a horrible shock and I totally get why it would feel very disruptive to you. But you will get through it.'

'I accept this,' I say, bringing my hands together in prayer. 'What's it they say? You know, Americans? Something something serenity to change the things I can change and the something to know the things I can't change and the something to know the difference.'

'Wow,' says Marie, smiling. 'That's *so* beautiful, what a moving and inspiring saying.'

'You know what I'm talking about!'

'Yeah, I do, I'm being a dick,' she says, leaning forward to pour us more wine before resettling on the sofa. 'Maybe I'm just feeling dickish today because I had a fight with Carly.'

'Ugh, I'm sorry! I'm the worst, I've just been pouring all my nonsense onto you and haven't so much as made a *polite enquiry* as to how you are.'

'It's fine,' she sighs. 'It's not like I have much to say about it anyway. I'm just sick of us fighting all the time.'

'It's one of those things,' I say, wondering how truthful to be. It's hard to know what to say when your friends are having trouble with their partners, because if it all blows over then they're going to remember you said something that cast some kind of negative light on their relationship, or said something that implied you didn't really like their partner. Oh well. 'People always talk about arguing like it's an *essential* ingredient for any relationship, but at a certain point you have to be like . . . is it?'

'Yeah,' Marie mumbles into her wine glass.

'This was what stuff with Miranda was like, by the end. We argued *all* the time. Like, something would flare up a few times a week – and I don't mean silly stuff like who was going to unload the dishwasher, I mean fundamental human connection stuff. And it got to the point where I was, like, this is actually dominating our relationship.'

'It's not like we argue *all* the time,' says Marie, and my cheeks flush as I realize I probably sounded as though I was telling her that the relationship was doomed. Look, it's not that I don't like Carly, it's more that I think they're a bad match! I want nothing but the best for my little mates, and I don't think Carly is the best for her!

'No, of course not. And it's probably nothing at all, nothing major anyway. But yeah, I feel like we're expected to have a lot more *room* for conflict in our relationships than maybe we should. What were you arguing about anyway?'

'She saw me texting my friend Olivia and she didn't like that I used the kissing emoji.'

I'm taking a sip of wine as she says this and my body is so ready to burst out the word '*What?!*' that I'm surprised I manage to swallow before I speak.

'Oh!' I say, trying to keep my tone neutral, even though it's quite evidently ridiculous.

'So, yeah, a little thing,' Marie says, shrugging.

Little's one word for it.

'Aaah, it's probably not working, is it?' she says, her whole body slumping down into the sofa.

'Only you know that, mate.' It's not that I want them to break up, I want Marie to know that that option is out there in the ether.

'Fuck it,' she says, uncurling her legs from underneath her, 'no more thinking about relationships and drama and stress, let's watch some nonsense. I bet there's an old episode of *Top Chef* on somewhere if I look hard enough.' She picks up the remote and turns the TV on, scrolling through the channels. There is no *Top Chef* to be found but there *is* an episode of *Man v Food* and we watch the guy eating what is allegedly Mississippi's biggest breakfast, which is as good a distraction as any from our relative anxieties.

At Marie's cosy flat with the wine and the comfy sofa, I feel my stress melt a little bit. It feels like I'm in a nice, safe cocoon. But I'm not about the cocoon lifestyle, I'm about regaining joie de vivre, I'm about forgetting Ivy ever happened!

10

OK I gave it a week. It turns out I cannot stop thinking about Ivy and public humiliation and that is very much the One Thing We Didn't Want To Happen so I am throwing myself back into the world of dating and, because I can no longer trust my own judgement, I chose to go on the most random date I've ever been on.

One dating rule that I have established: Never Be Late. I think it's rude. Whether it's a love-of-your-life or night-of-fun kind of date, it is a bad look to show up late. The nerves are too high to be dealing with 'I'll be there in 20' texts just as you arrive at the agreed time, as if that's, you know, completely normal behaviour.

Imagine my horror then when the Victoria Line train stopped. Like, *stopped*. Between stations in a zone where that beautiful subterranean 4G had yet to reach. I hated the thought of being That Person – and I got seriously stressed as I stood, stuck in that packed rush-hour traffic, thinking that . . . what was his name? Lee – that Lee might think I'd stood him up. Which, as we've already established, is ultimate villain behaviour. A single standing up deserves a lifetime dating ban IMHO.

Finally . . .

There is a collective sigh of relief as the train budges.

And then stops again.

Ah! But miracle . . . there is the flicker of reception. So tantalizingly close to the next station that the 4G reaches here like a ray of sunlight.

I fire a WhatsApp as fast as my fingers will allow and hit send.

One tick . . .

Come on, come on, come on, you little bastard – squeeze your way out and through to the other side of the digital ether.

Two ticks.

'Fuck me,' I say out loud.

'Ridiculous, isn't it?' says an aggrieved commuter.

'Oh yeah, sure,' I nod along, checking my phone to see if the ticks turn blue but the reception has dropped again.

At last I reach my destination: Tottenham Hale. And as I emerge from the underworld, a flurry of replies come through.

Hey, don't worry, I saw the Victoria Line was suspended. Hope you're good! I don't want to miss a minute of this show so I've gone ahead. I'll forward you the ticket.

Yeah, this was my first foray into an Activity Date. Usually a drink in a pub will suffice. I say *usually*, I mean . . . literally always. So I had my reservations but in the flurry of locking down the date Lee said he had two tickets for a show and . . . how bad could it be?

Two words: Immersive Theatre.

It was an 'experience' inspired by the film *Withnail & I*. Now, I've never been attracted to immersive theatre – I had a, shall we say, *traumatic experience* as a child at the London

Dungeon and I suppose I have associations with that. Secondly, I've never seen *Withnail & I*. It's not like I've been avoiding it, there are just some movies you never get around to watching, you know?

But hey ho, the train finally makes it to Tottenham Hale where I cross a bunch of traffic islands and pass through swathes of new builds under construction until I reach an industrial estate. Outside a warehouse are a cluster of people arriving in hippy costumes. Lee did not tell me it was fancy dress: that would have been *quite* the red flag. There is a performer with a sax miming to a rendition of 'Whiter Shade of Pale'.

This is fine.

Upon scanning my ticket, I am ushered into a holding room made up like an old-man boozer. A Doctor Who-looking man runs in and shrieks, 'We want the finest wines available to humanity! We want them here and we want them now!' He swigs a bottle of red and then disappears. This is our cue to get drinks. I'm in the mood for a glass of red and, once at the bar, I notice they are selling pork pies. And that everybody's buying them. Maybe this is an immersive experience I can get behind. Immerse me in pork pies, bitches.

I take my wine and pie and mill around. Lee is nowhere to be seen.

The lights dim and policemen arrive. Uproarious laughter. They pace around the room, inspecting us all and striking their palms with truncheons. The mood has changed and I suspect this is a serious show.

The policemen stop at me as I take a bite of pie. One offers a breathalyser kit.

'I want you to take one deep breath and fill this bag.'

What am I supposed to do?

'Are you refusing to fill this bag?'

Once again: what am I supposed to do?

Someone nudges me and then from over my shoulder says, 'I most certainly am!'

The policeman grabs my shoulder, 'I'm placing you under arrest.'

My geek in shining armour pushes them away and says, 'Don't be ridiculous, she hasn't done anything! Look here, her cousin is a QC.'

The other policeman suddenly speaks, or shrieks: 'Get in the back of the van!'

Huge laughter. The crowd, for some reason, love this. A doorway is then revealed to be a van door and we are ushered through. We sit inside the van for a while as there are engine sounds and 'Whiter Shade of Pale' returns. I feel hot and claustrophobic and more uncomfortable than being trapped on the Victoria Line. The prospect of a no-strings fuck seems very distant and I am questioning if immersive theatre is a price worth paying . . .

Eventually we are ushered out into a disgusting mess of a flat. There are pots and filth everywhere and Doctor Who-looking-man is running around with a cigarette.

From behind me, I feel a tap on my shoulder. Bloody hell, what nonsense is going to be behind me this time?

'Hello you!' Fortunately for me, it's only Lee, grinning from ear to ear as Doctor Who goes about the mess threatening to clean up. 'Isn't this wild? It's like being back in the sixties!' He shakes his head as he views the setting. Observing my glass of wine, he comments, 'Is that the finest wine known to humanity?'

I smile and nod. I only wish I'd bought a bottle.

'I really didn't think this would work but it's so cool the way they've mixed up the narrative, which makes sense because who doesn't know the story inside out?'

'Amen to that,' whispers another bro.

Doctor Who and another man jump about the kitchen all frightened. Eventually the police return and again scream, 'Get in the back of the van!' Is this a catchphrase? What is going on? And more to the point, why did I agree to this?

Next we enter a room that is like a drab and dowdy lounge. A hippy is spreadeagled on a couch rolling a joint. As he speaks, I notice that Lee is mouthing the words along with the hippy.

'The joint I'm about to roll requires a craftsman. It can utilize up to twelve skins. It is called a Camberwell Carrot.'

This elicits a huge laugh from the room. The Camberwell Carrot is lit and billowing clouds of dry ice fill the room.

The policeman then returns and screams again, 'Get in the back of the van!' and I don't know what is going on. What the story is. Is this what drugs are supposed to be like? Is it time travel? And will it ever end? Will Lee and I ever be allowed to leave, have a pint, an actual conversation leading possibly to a shag?

Ah, but Lee, my sweet summer child, this evening has been an absolute boner killer, and as the policeman ushers us through to another dimension I feign a cough – blame the Camberwell Carrot – and tell Lee, 'I'm so sorry, I'm feeling unwell.'

'No way?'

'I'm going to have to split but I want you to stay.'

'Oh no,' he says, but he doesn't look too bothered and is already leaving me for another dimension. I tell one of the actor stewards I need to leave and am secreted away through a fire exit.

I head to a nearby brewery for a stabilizing and restorative pint. I pretty much down it and make the decision that that was the last Activity Date I will ever go on. I don't blame Lee: he was having the time of his life and he in no way duped me into that experience. No date is a waste of time! It's all part of the process, man.

But henceforth my dates will be strictly results-oriented. Theatre, music, restaurants, escape rooms, table tennis bars — these all have their place on God's earth but they will not feature again in another first date.

11

I am naked in a room full of people. They are all wearing clothes and I am naked. They are all staring at me intently and I am naked. This is not a horrible dream, this is my life, thanks to Katie and her green fringe and mad ideas. Yes, dating is important and fun but I'm trying to let fun and joy and exploration into my life through other means, too. Hence saying yes to nude modelling.

'You doing all right?' Katie whispers in my ear. My ear, incidentally, is the only part of my body that's dressed, because I forgot to take out my earrings, which happen to be my *favourite* earrings. Cute little Georgian-inspired things, a hand-painted eye surrounded by seed pearls that Marie bought for me years ago. Many people have told me they're creepy, but I think they're cool as hell. And having short hair means an even better showcase for my cool creepy earrings.

'Yeah, fine,' I whisper back, which isn't strictly true because I didn't realize how much it would hurt to hold one fairly straightforward pose for twenty minutes. (Apparently in the world of life drawing, that's not even very long! I think I need to take up yoga.)

'Great! You're the best, I can tell they're really loving drawing you.'

I stare out at the sea of faces behind their easels and wonder if I even want to see what's on the other side of them. An involuntary shiver passes through my body, which Katie catches out of the corner of her eye and drags the space heater closer to me.

'You should have said!'

'I'm fine, I promise!' It is quite cold, what with it being literally November, but I don't want to complain. This is what I signed up for! I knew what I was getting into when I agreed to it!

Katie makes her way around the room, giving gentle advice to her students. I can't help but wonder what they make of me, and if it's somehow different to how they would perceive me on the street or on the bus. Most people are kind of weird about fatness, about other people taking up space. They'd probably huff and roll their eyes if they had to sit next to me on the bus. But here, they're taking pleasure in responding to my body, finding the things about it that they want to draw. And that is what I need right now – to feel exciting and delicious and magnetic, not a pathetic anxiety-riddled humiliated mess. I shiver again, and I realize it's because the back of my neck is exposed and my body is still not used to having lost that heavy, protective curtain of hair I was so used to.

'Great!' says Katie, looking at the clock and clapping her hands together. 'We'll take five so Fran can get warmed up and then we'll do a longer pose.' She throws me my sweater dress and I yank it on over my head without my underwear which feels weird and unnatural, but warm nonetheless. I know *real* life-drawing models wear *robes* or, as I call them, dressing gowns, but mine is buried in a laundry bag at my mum's house so I've had to go down the less professional route.

'I don't know if my body can withstand a longer pose,' I say to Katie as she sits down on my chair while I do a variety of stretches to regain feeling in my limbs.

'Of course you can,' she says, looking up at me through her round glasses. 'It's what you're getting paid for.'

'I keep forgetting I'm getting paid,' I say, clapping my hands together. In such a fancy part of town as Holland Park I bloody well *should* be getting paid. 'It feels like a weird experiment I'm doing, rather than, you know, actual work.'

'But it's not *too* horrible, is it? Being naked and all? It's weird, actually, you being naked and me having to keep touching you but in an extremely non-sexual way.'

'No, I'm actually fine with that bit. It's making me think about how people in general look at me, which is something I try to *avoid* thinking about.'

'I look at you like you're hot,' she says, nudging my calf with her paint-spattered canvas sneaker toe.

'I know *you* do. But I'm not naive about the fact the world hates fat bitches,' I shrug. 'And I am nothing if not a fat bitch.'

She nods, knowing this is probably something I'm more of an expert on than her.

'You ready for round two?' she asks at the end of the break.

'Let's go!' I say, although the thought of staying still for twice as long as I was already still for makes me want to run around screaming. I take off the sweater dress and she folds it neatly and puts it on one of the tables around the outside of the room for me. She bends my limbs into position, while repeatedly checking with me that I feel comfortable enough. It's gentle and intimate, and I can't help feeling affectionate towards her as she performs this highly unnatural ritual on my body.

She stands back and looks at me, then looks back at her students, and asks, 'Happy?' to which they murmur in assent.

This longer pose gives me time to zone out, which is nice, but when I do zone out, all I can think about is having to pack up and lug my shit across London in two days' time. Got to round up my homely trinkets and vacuum-pack my duvet aka the Most Satisfying Task. Oh, and find somewhere to live.

'Keep your eyes open!' Katie whispers to me, at which point I realize I'm dozing off.

'Oh, sorry,' I say, smiling serenely at the assembled class. 'I was trying to stay relaxed! Looks like I got too relaxed.' I wiggle my body around to try and wake myself up and then remember I'm only part way through my pose, which I attempt to recreate.

'I think your leg was straighter,' says a guy near the front. I hadn't really noticed him before but when I look to him for his approval after I extend my leg a bit further, I can't help but find him attractive in a dad way. Like, definite dad vibes. Maybe not an actual dad but definite dad vibes. 'That's great, thanks,' he says, pushing his glasses up and leaving a little smudge of graphite on the bridge of his nose. The dark shimmering grey of the smudge matches the dark grey of his hair, still holding onto its previous dark brown.

I try not to look at him too much over the rest of the hour, but I keep snatching little glimpses and every time I look at him he looks at me, which I know is precisely what he's meant to be doing and only makes me feel more silly for looking at *him* when there's a high chance he'll catch me. I look at Katie instead, observing her as she weaves slowly through the room, pointing to things on people's work, making gentle suggestions, issuing praise. It's hot to watch her be the expert, the teacher. I guess it makes me the teacher's pet. I fancy her even more now I've seen her art. I met her at her studio last week before we went for a drink and she showed me what she's working on at the moment: a big, bright canvas depicting a full male nude. I don't know how she does it, to be honest.

'We've got ten minutes until the end of the class,' Katie says. 'So make the most of having Fran here.'

The interjection of her voice in the quiet means I nearly leap up off my perch, forgetting that she's literally just said I have to stay still for another ten minutes. I make the effort to stay perfectly still and extremely awake for the last stretch. Stretch . . . I really want to stretch. But no! I am being paid to do this! I am a professional life-drawing model! I must stick with it for the next ten minutes!

'I think it's time to let Fran move around, don't you?' Katie says, to my great relief. 'Let's give her a round of applause for her hard work today.' They all clap and I blush because now it seems weird that I'm naked if they're not drawing me. Katie throws me my dress and I pull it on as she says, 'If you're happy for Fran to see your work, leave it out for her to look at while you tidy the rest of your stuff away.'

'I completely understand if not!' I say, although I'm desperate to get my eyeballs on all of them. I make my way through the room, surveying their estimations of me. I recognize my pose in all of them. I recognize the way I was sitting, with my arms behind my back, palms down on the table, holding myself up. My arms are still aching from being backwards for so long, but these pictures have captured the way the pose pushed my chest forward, the way the fat around my hips settled there as I sat. Some of Katie's students have exaggerated the way my body looks, some depicting it as bigger, more cartoonish, while others slimmed me down slightly. When I make my way back to the front of the room, I find myself hoping that the hot dad guy has left his out for my perusal.

'Wow,' I say involuntarily when I reach his station.

'Yeah?' he says, looking at me over his shoulder as he zips some nubby little pencils into a case.

'Yeah . . .' I say, transfixed by my own image like that Greek dude and his reflection. Narcissus? Yeah, him. The pencil drawing is so very me. So very much my body. It's completely mesmerizing. And I can even tell I'm wearing my favourite earrings. 'I love it.' I cover my mouth with my hand so he can't see how much I'm smiling.

'Do you . . . want it?' he asks tentatively.

'Would you sell it to me?'

'I don't want money for it . . . it's not . . . you know . . . it's just a sketch . . .' He blushes furiously, which is extremely cute and boyish.

'I can't take it from you for nothing.'

'A tenner?' he suggests.

'That's a bargain. I think I even have that in my purse . . . wait a second.' I stalk over to my bag and retrieve £10 from my battered leather purse overflowing with receipts and tickets I have absolutely zero need for but retain *in case*. 'Here,' I say, presenting him with the money.

114

'Sure?' he says. 'I feel like I'm scamming you.'

'I love it, honestly, I would have paid you a lot more for it!' I feel a tap on my shoulder and when I turn around, Katie has produced a tube for me to transport the picture in. 'Thank you!'

'My pleasure,' she says, smiling before disappearing in a very *I'll leave you to it* sort of way which only fans the flames of my attraction to this guy.

'Well . . .' I say.

'I'm Stephen, by the way,' he says, filling the heavy silence.

'Nice to meet you, I'm Fran.'

We look at each other for a moment, like we're waiting for the other one to make a move, neither of us quite sure enough of our footing to do it. I could. I easily could. But I decide not to. Sometimes it's nice to leave flirtations as just that: flirtations. I don't *need* to convert every flirtation into sex. Back in my serial monogamist days, even flirtation would have been too much, something I would have held myself back from. Now I don't have to.

As we're walking to the Japanese restaurant nearby, Katie says to me, 'Stephen's was my favourite, too. I try not to have favourites but . . . it's inevitable. And his *was* the best.'

Before I can reply, someone across the street catches my eye. A woman walking slowly, lazily, a curtain of inky curls falling over her face as she types on her phone, a backpack slung over one shoulder. I feel suddenly breathless. It can't be . . . *her?*

Not again. No, no, no. Is it? I look away from maybe-Ivy and back to Katie. I need to be present. I realize she's expecting me to say something. I shake off the thought of maybe-Ivy and bring back the warm enthusiasm I was feeling seconds ago. 'I never thought when I agreed to do this for you that someone would make something so fucking *cool*!'

'So it wasn't too horrible? Sorry, I thought you were about to tell me you'd hated it and found it extremely uncomfortable or something.'

'No!' I say enthusiastically, and when I flick my eyes back across the road maybe-Ivy is gone.

'Good! And you got a cool naked picture out of it,' she says, looking at me out of the corner of her eye.

'It felt kind of weird flirting with him with you there. The vibes were . . . very vibe-y . . . lots of eye contact and all that. Sorry if it was weird for you.'

'Don't worry about me!' she says, pushing the door to the restaurant open and fixing me with an earnest look over her shoulder. 'Neither of us are looking for a *formal relationship*, right?'

'Right,' I say with great relief.

We take a seat at a table in the corner. 'I like hanging out with you. I fancy you. I like seeing people. You clearly like seeing people too,' she says, shrugging her peacoat off and turning to hang it on the back of her chair.

'OK, good,' I say. 'I'm glad we're on the same page about this.'

'Why mess with a winning formula?'

She smiles at me from across the table, which is so intimate and knowing that I want to flip the table over and drag her out of there by her hand and dash home and sleep with her right this minute. But I don't. I wait until after dinner.

116

12

Do you know what's always a good idea? Spending time with a dog.

That's right, my friends, I am the temporary custodian of Billy the poodle while his parents are on holiday. I'm always casually putting out my feelers for anyone looking for a house-sitter while they're away, and the universe sent Billy my way. I didn't *necessarily* foresee me becoming a dog guardian, but Billy is pretty low maintenance, and it's sort of nice to have *something* around.

Joanne, a hairstylist I met on a recent shoot, had me come over the day before she and her boyfriend went on holiday, so I could acquaint myself with my new furry friend, and for her to go through the extremely exhaustive list of Things I Need to Know About Billy which is stuck on the fridge with a poodle magnet. Nothing if not on-brand. I've read the document several times and although I appreciate the hand-holding, it mostly boils down to *don't forget to feed him, he needs to go for a walk EVERY DAY and don't let him eat chocolate*. I got this.

'I know it's a lot,' she said, grimacing, as if I was doing her the favour of a lifetime. 'But please eat or drink anything in the fridge, have anyone over to stay . . . make yourself at home! No wild parties, though, obviously.'

'Obviously,' I said, while hoping she'd leave something interesting in the fridge. A truffle or something.

They live in a nice two-bedroom flat with a garden in Herne Hill, which is suboptimal for getting to the cafe, but I've got a few more make-up gigs recently so Jamie is going to have to live without me for a few shifts. Joanne is gone for a fortnight, and to be honest, this feels like a holiday for me too – nice decor, a garden, some (furry) company.

Once I've found the Wi-Fi password on the back of the router on a living room shelf cluttered with various techno junk, speakers and a record player, I lie on the nice dark velvet sofa and stroke Billy's puffy fur with one hand while I reply to some Tinder messages with the other hand. It would be nice to make the most of this place while I'm here, wouldn't it? Besides, Joanne *did* say I was very welcome to have people over, didn't she?

Amid the never-ending carousel of people I'm messaging, there's also one from someone I first met months and months ago, when I was pretty newly single. He was one of the first people I met in my initial flurry of dating, but we didn't sleep together and then ended up not seeing each other again because he travels for work so much, but we enjoy the occasional sext and he's possessed with the skills of taking the kind of dick pic that *doesn't* make you recoil in horror upon receipt.

Hey how's it going? I'm actually around this weekend if you want to get a drink (leading to . . . possibly more???)

118

I swipe through his photos, trying to re-familiarize myself with his face. It's a good face. A nice jawline. Black hair so shiny it almost doesn't look real. I'm in!

The pub is crowded, as pubs tend to be on a Saturday night, and me and Imran wander around trying to find a table.

'I don't think it's going to happen,' I say, shrugging. 'And I don't do standing.'

'We could always try somewhere else?' he suggests. 'Or . . . go back to mine?'

'I'm fine with that, since we were going to end up there anyway.'

'Oh were we?' he says playfully.

I roll my eyes. 'Oh! Shit! No, I can't!' I shake my head. 'I'm so stupid, I can't believe I nearly abandoned Billy for the night.'

'Who's . . . Billy?' Imran says, frowning at me. 'He's not your . . . boyfriend, is he?' It's clear that Imran does *not* want to get scammed out of his all-but-guaranteed sex.

'No!' I say, laughing. 'He's my dog. Well, not *my* dog, but a dog I'm looking after.'

'I *see*.' Imran looks relieved.

'I suppose I should check you're chill with dogs?'

'They're fine.' He shrugs. 'Better than a boyfriend who wants to kick my arse anyway.'

'Then to Billy we shall go,' I say, clapping my hands together decisively.

When I unlock the front door, Billy trots up to us with great enthusiasm. I crouch down and give him a kiss before introducing him to Imran. I hold out his paw for Imran to shake, which he does very dutifully. 'Nice to meet you, Bobby.'

'Billy!' I correct him, to which Billy lets out a short bark. 'He knows his name! He's so clever! You're so clever, aren't you?' I squeeze him to me affectionately, at which point he trots off towards his food. 'If he thinks he's going to be able to get me to feed him again, he is very wrong.' I get to my feet and show Imran into the living room. 'Can I get you a drink?'

'What are you having?'

'My friend left some fancy-looking wine she said I could have so I guess . . . fancy-looking wine?'

'Sounds good to me,' he says, before pacing over to Joanne's record collection and flicking through it.

I let Billy out of the back door so he can wee on a rose bush. He trots back in after me and curls up in his dog bed that is, for some reason, fine for him to chill in *now* but when it's time to actually sleep he'll decide is completely unacceptable and want to sleep in a human bed. I know his game. I learned this the hard way last night. I take a photo of him and send it to Joanne as proof of life. When I return to the living room with the drinks, Imran is expertly navigating the record player and putting on *Rumours* by Fleetwood Mac.

'Everyone likes *Rumours*,' he says, shrugging.

'Yeah, until there's one about *you*,' I reply, handing him a glass of wine.

'How very dad-joke of you.'

We sit on the sofa and drink together, catching each other up on the intervening months. Both of us meant to get in touch again but never did, and then because the other didn't, we both took it as a lack of interest. But, as becomes apparent quite quickly, there is no lack of interest.

'Um . . .' Imran says, his eyelashes fluttering. 'Is there anything you can do about . . . ?' He nods over my shoulder.

I turn around. Billy is sitting there like he's posing for a photo, straight-back and expectant like he wants me to give him a treat. 'Go away, Billy!' I urge him, but he keeps sitting there. I shrug and go back to making out with Imran.

'I'm sorry, I can't . . .' Imran says, pulling away. 'It's too creepy.'

I sigh and get up, smoothing down my dress with one hand as I usher Billy out into the kitchen with the other. I give him a squeeze and whisper at him that I'll let him out in the fullness of time, before making a quick exit and closing the door behind me.

'That's better,' I say, returning to my position on the sofa next to Imran.

'Sorry, it was just . . . the way he was looking at me was deeply off-putting.'

We return to the business of making out, which I know will not last much longer before we simply *have* to dash to the bedroom. I climb on top of him and feel how hard he is through his jeans and think how nice it would be to fuck here but I could *never* besmirch a friend's sofa like that. But before long we're interrupted. Again. This time by an unfamiliar sound. My phone ringing.

'Oh my God who is it?!' I leap up from Imran's lap. 'My phone only rings when the same number calls me three times, so clearly they're desperate!' I say, dashing over to where I'd plugged it in.

The screen says it's Joanne. 'Hello?' I answer, wondering what the hell is so urgent.

'Fran!' Joanne says breathlessly. 'There you are! I thought you were never going to answer!'

'What's the matter?'

'Oh I feel terrible,' she says. 'I forgot to tell you about the camera!'

'What camera?'

'It's on the mantelpiece near the router! It's just a little camera we use to watch Billy while we're out! But I forgot to turn it off before we left and I opened the app on my phone to see if I could disable it remotely and there you were! On top of a guy! I thought I was about ten seconds away from seeing a stranger's dick!'

'Oh my God I wasn't going to sleep with him there! Not on your sofa!'

'No, that's not what I mean! I told you to make yourself at home! I felt weird knowing you were literally being filmed and had no idea! I felt like a . . . a voyeur!'

'Well, look, can I turn it off here?' I ask, wanting to get back to business.

'Yes, yes, that's fine, look for the thing that looks like a speaker and switch it off! God, sorry, I'm so mortified, you coming over here and spending time looking after Billy and I'm spying on you from Greece!'

'Get off the phone, this'll be costing you a bomb. Me and Billy are alive and well, please enjoy your holiday and don't worry about us!'

'OK, OK,' she says. 'Sorry! Bye!'

I go back to the living room where Billy has escaped and is curled up in my space on the sofa next to Imran.

'Is everything all right?' Imran asks, stroking Billy absent-mindedly. Looks like they're friends now.

'Ye-e-e-s,' I say, scanning the mantelpiece for the camera that looks like a speaker. Bingo. I unplug it and *Rumours* keeps playing so definitely not an *actual* speaker. 'We were being spied on!'

'What?'

'Yeah, my friend didn't turn off the camera she uses to spy on Billy.'

'Kinky,' he says, raising his eyebrows.

'Quite. Now, if you don't mind leaving your new friend, I think we'd better, er, retire for the night because I can't take another interruption.'

'You don't have to ask me twice.' He leaps off the sofa. 'Sorry, mate,' he says, ruffling Billy's fur and leaving him curled up.

'Night, Billy!' I say, turning off the living room light and leading Imran into the bedroom.

'It feels like this has been a long time coming, right?'

'Right!' I say, enthusiastically removing my dress before putting my arms around him and kissing him.

We fall back onto the bed and, true to his word in his various sexts, he *is* very good at oral. It's a claim made by many men, yet few can live up to it. He produces a condom from his wallet, which is very welcome because mine are in my bag in the living room and the last thing I want to do is disturb Billy, and it turns out those dick pics weren't just flattering angles. This is the good shit.

We're mid-fuck when I catch a glimpse of someone crouching next to the bed.

'ARGH!' I scream and Imran recoils, shouting 'What? What?' but before I can answer our fuzzy interloper has jumped on the bed, trotted across it, masterfully navigating the two human bodies, and jumped down the other side. He then proceeds to loop back around the bottom of the bed and trot out again, panting enthusiastically.

'Fuck! I honestly thought he was a person,' I say, my hand against my chest, desperately trying to get my breath back.

'I suppose this was to be expected,' Imran says tightly, reaching down to the floor for his boxers. 'Game over?'

I bid Imran farewell and we mumble something about doing it again sometime, but I think we both understand that the universe is clearly very averse to the idea of us having sex. When I drag myself back into the bedroom alone, I overlook his crimes and let Billy curl up next to me in the bed. It's nice to know someone's there. Even if they're a poodle.

13

I feel like I've mostly got the Unfortunate TV Date Situation out of my system – Ivy is in the past! Where she belongs! I am in the present! Joyfully single! – by the time I see Marie for a coffee and a stroll the next weekend.

'Do you ever, like, talk to Miranda?' Marie asks as we walk. I have a feeling she has a reason for asking me this, but I don't want to know.

'No, not really,' I say with a shrug. 'It's not like we're Not Talking, but I find it's better to kind of . . . diverge after a break-up.'

'So you don't want to be friends or anything?' She wraps her scarf around her neck one more time with her free hand that isn't holding her coffee.

'Sure, but not yet. I still find the whole thing very jarring . . . but at least it's not like I want us to get back together anymore, you know? At first I thought that was going to happen, like I was *sure* of it. But then the dates started and I became less interested in the idea of getting back with her.'

'That makes sense,' she says, before shaking her head and laughing. 'Fuck, do you remember when me and Kim broke up and I would literally have a meltdown if I heard she was hanging out with any of our mutual friends?'

'I remember it well. Hey!' I say, a thought striking me. 'How can you ask me if I'm not interested in being friends with Miranda when you've literally not once ever managed to stay friends with one of *your* exes?'

'Because you're a more sensible person than I am. Less tempestuous.'

'You think everyone's sensible.'

'They are, though.'

'You're literally a solicitor?' I remind her. 'That's the most sensible job of them all.'

'No, that's an actuary,' she says, rolling her eyes.

My phone vibrates in my pocket. A call from Tilly. I slip it back into my coat pocket. It's not the first time she's called me since the filming, but I don't want to talk to her. I'm trying to pretend the whole thing *never fucking happened*. How am I meant to *comprehensively* move on rather than *mostly* move on from the Unfortunate TV Date Situation if Tilly's always looming?

'OK, fine. But regarding being friends with Miranda . . . I guess I'd like to achieve it one day? I never have before. Not with Ivy,' I say with an involuntary shudder. 'And not with Daniel. Not after . . . all *that*.'

'The cheating, you mean?' she ventures gently.

'Yeah. That really fucked me up,' I say, shaking my head. Another thing I've only really shared with Marie. The embarrassment of it was so overwhelming that I *couldn't* talk about it to anyone else. The shame, the feeling that I was so disposable, the fact I hadn't realized it was happening multiple times while we were together! While we were *living* together!

'I'm not surprised,' she says, wrapping an arm affectionately around my waist and squeezing. 'It's a fucked-up thing to do.'

I breathe out, a little dragon-stream of heat coming from my nostrils into the cool air. 'It's amazing I still had enough trust to get with Miranda so quickly after that.'

'Well, Miranda was trustworthy. You could tell.'

'But I thought I could tell with Daniel, too. That even though he was kind of . . . slippery . . . I thought deep down he did love me, really. That's why we were together as long as we were.'

'Do you think that's what it was?' she asks, and I know she wants me to say it.

'No,' I concede grudgingly. 'I didn't want to break up with him because he gave me a big self-esteem boost. Because he was hot and everyone kept saying how hot he was.'

'And what did we learn from that?' Marie prompts me.

'That it doesn't matter how hot someone is if they're fundamentally a worm of a person.'

'Right,' she says, knocking her coffee cup against mine.

When we go our separate ways, I hug her goodbye at the bus stop and watch her bus sail away.

Knowing I have nothing on my single shelf in the kitchen of my new flatshare, I pop into the Tesco outside the bus stop to pick up something for dinner. I let my eyes scan the aisles waiting for inspiration to strike, my brain buzzing and my cheeks warm with memories of Daniel and how he made me feel. How small and stupid and disposable until I decided enough had to be enough. I'm lost in the past when suddenly I realize I'm staring blankly at a row of pasta sauces. I snap out of it and pick up a jar of pesto – classic – and head for the till when who should emerge from around the corner of the aisle but . . . yes. Ivy. Again? Are you for real? Was I put on this earth solely to suffer? Is the sole cosmic plan for my one wild and precious life for me to keep bumping into Ivy? Yes, that is really Ivy in a chunky grey wool roll-neck under an oversized blazer reaching up to the top shelf to get a jar of something for a small, elderly lady who's gazing up at her with intense admiration. Ugh! She's so polite, so gallant. And more to the point, she's so fucking *everywhere*! More than ten years of zero contact, not one text, not one random encounter, and now? Non-stop!

I do a quick heel-turn so I can escape undetected and spin straight into the oncoming path of a Tesco employee pushing a trolley stacked with Pot Noodles, most of which immediately go flying, then roll in their plastic pots at great speed to all corners of the aisle. I scramble to pick up as many as I can while keeping my back strategically turned so Ivy can't see my face, and I thrust an armful back at the assistant while repeatedly muttering apologies. I abandon thoughts of pesto and dash out of the shop and onto my bus which is mercifully pulling into the stop. When I check my emails on the journey home, doing some deep breathing and trying to convince myself it wasn't *actually* Ivy I saw (when I know very well that it was, who else looks like her, is as tall as her and likes helping old ladies with their shopping as much as her?) there's one from Tilly, who simply Will Not Quit. I feel the rage returning!

Hi darling! Been trying to get a hold of you! As well as checking in with you, I was ringing about arranging to shoot some extra content we need for the show. We would have done it the other week after you finished your date but it seemed like you really wanted to get out of there so we left it! Please can you let me know your availability in the next week! We're on a bit of a tight deadline but we can work around you.

All the best,

Tilly

Will I ever know peace again?! Of course, I'm going to say no. It's a free country!

Hi Tilly,

No, thank you!

Fran

But mere seconds after I hit send on that short email, my phone rings. I sigh. It's Tilly. I have been avoiding her calls, but I suppose if I want to get this whole thing sorted, I should answer.

'Hi, Tilly,' I say, as brightly as I can manage.

'Hi, Fran. I thought it was easier if I called you.'

'Ye-e-e-s?' I want to get this over and done with.

'About the extra content.'

'I think I gave you good enough *content*, didn't I?'

Tilly pauses. 'The thing is, you *are* actually contractually obliged to do the extra content.'

This can't be right. 'What? I'm not *obliged* to do anything.'

'I get that you don't want to do it, that the date wasn't what you were expecting. I totally get that, and I'm really sorry that

129

things conspired against you. But the fact is, you signed a contract, which specifically stated that you were committed to creating extra content at the discretion of the producers.'

'Hmmm,' I say, my blood heating up. Contracts! The bane of my life!

'And . . . not to put too fine a point on it, but I understand you made an agreement with one of my colleagues about some payment?'

'I did.' And I would *very much* like that grand. I would *extremely much* like that grand.

'Well . . .'

'So you're holding it hostage,' I say flatly.

'Not in those exact terms.'

Look, I get it. Tilly is not a supervillain. She is just a cute fat babe doing her job. I relate to this! But still . . . this is very much *not* what I want to be doing. How am I meant to get past the extreme cringe of my performance on the show if I can never extricate myself from its clutches?!

I inhale deeply and close my eyes. 'Fine. I'll do it.'

'Thank you! Thank you! Thank you! I know you're probably busy but—'

'But I don't have a choice?' I interject.

'Well, yes, sort of . . . how's Thursday evening?'

I think for a moment, wondering if I have a good excuse to say no. I don't. 'Thursday is fine.' Ugh! I cannot believe I'm agreeing to this! Under duress!

'Thanks soooo much, Fran! You're the best! I'll email you the deets and I'll see you on Thursday!'

'See you then,' I say weakly.

This show was meant to be a bit of fun and now it's turned

into this bloody . . . *albatross* around my neck! That's an expression, right? Sounds weird but whatever. And just like that, I realize there's a question I didn't ask Tilly. Something that's only occurred to me now. Is Ivy going to be there? I feel the panic rise in my chest at the thought of it, the stress bubbling up. I feel my teeth reach for my lip to nibble the skin, the anxiety reflexes rearing up. God! How dare she smash into my life like this, invading my brain during my Big Sexy Time! She probably won't be there, will she? Tilly didn't mention it, anyway. So fine, it's going to be fine. Everything is going to be fine.

Cursed Thursday arrives and I grudgingly make my way to the Red Rooster offices, which are on an industrial estate in Hackney Wick. I've turned the corner into the estate when I see a gleaming penny on the floor. Ever a believer in fate, destiny and superstition, I pick it up and drop it in my pocket in the hope it will bring me at least a little bit of good luck.

'Hello, darling!' Tilly says enthusiastically when she picks me up from the reception.

'Hi, Tilly,' I say, feeling weirdly lifted by the sight of her. 'I'm sorry I was so . . . stressed out on the phone the other day.' I shake my head, embarrassed at the knowledge I probably came across quite rude.

She waves it away. 'Oh, that's all right. You hear a lot worse when you work in TV. Lots of big egos. I'm sorry to have to drag the whole thing out, but, like I said, you're all committed to extra filming.'

'Yeah, yeah, I get it,' I say, as she pushes open the double doors to the open-plan office. The first thing I see? A mass of dark curls. Ivy's sitting in an office chair and at the sound of the door opening she swivels around like a Bond villain.

A smile spreads across her face at the sight of me, but quickly disappears when she sees how distinctly un-amused I look.

She reminds me of all the ways I can feel hurt, all the ways I can be vulnerable, all the ways that it can come out of nowhere and fuck me up. Did I want her to be here? No. Did I accept it was a possibility? Yes. Her reappearance has been almost as jarring for me as her disappearance all those years ago. I like to feel on top of my shit and she very much reminds me that sometimes the universe likes to come along and knock me off the top of my shit.

'Hello, Foxy.' (What was that pet name?)

'Hello, Ivy,' I say drily.

She stands up from the chair as if she's going to give me a hug, before realizing that's absolutely not going to happen and sitting down awkwardly again. 'I thought I saw you the other day.'

'Really?'

'In Tesco on Peckham Rye.'

'Huh. Couldn't have been me,' I lie.

'So, we need you both to come into the little studio and we'll take some photos for promo.'

'Let's get it done,' I say decisively.

'I saw your mum the other day! For my last fitting!' Tilly says brightly. 'She was trying to convince me to use you as my make-up artist, but I had to let her down as I already have one sorted!'

'Your mum's still got her shop?' Ivy asks.

'Mmmhmmm,' I say.

132

'Oh, great,' says Ivy, shrugging off her oversized denim jacket. 'How is she doing?'

'She's fine,' I say tightly, and I realize that I'm deliberately angling myself so I don't have to look at her, don't have to look her in the eye when she's speaking. Well, maybe I am. Maybe I don't want to look at her dark eyes, the inky eyelashes even without mascara (of course she doesn't wear make-up, she never has), maybe I don't want to be *struck* by someone whose appearance was always described as *striking*, even when we were girls. I want to keep a safe distance from her. If I can't prevent myself from being forced into contact with her, at the very least I want to keep my guard up.

'Good,' Ivy says, nodding, sensing my caution.

'Well then,' says Tilly, now brandishing a camera. 'I've only got a bloody degree in photography, haven't I? So my boss makes me do all this stuff to keep costs down. Right, if you two stand against that backdrop . . .' With her free hand she manoeuvres me into a position in front of the *The Meet-Cute* logo, before returning to where Ivy is loitering nervously – not a natural model – and doing the same to her. We stand, awkwardly, side by side. 'Now,' Tilly stands back and holds the camera up to her face. 'Can you look, you know, *happy*? Like we did a good job of matching you up?'

'I can try,' I say as I fix a broad smile on my face.

We stand side by side, trying to *act natural* as Tilly photographs us, before producing a bunch of quite real-looking fake flowers from a cupboard. 'Can one of you give these to the other? You know, imagine you're showing up on the date and you're like *oooh, what a lovely date, I'd like to give her some flowers, so romantic,* something like that?'

We both stare at her, clearly both waiting for the other to hold their hand out and take the flowers from her. She thrusts them in my direction.

'Isn't this false advertising?' I ask, frowning. 'It makes us look like we had a good date. When we didn't.'

'We don't want people to *know* that from the promo,' Tilly says, rolling her eyes. 'We're not going to run Instagram ads of you looking like you want to burn the place down – it's a bit off-brand.'

'But not so off-brand that you won't show it?' I ask expectantly.

'I bet your meltdown makes for great TV.' Ivy nudges me playfully.

I'm not feeling *playful* so I exhale loudly and pretend to present her with the flowers. 'Glad to know you're taking my pain and suffering seriously,' I say.

'Can you do that again but, you know, not talking? Smiling, romantically?' Tilly asks hopefully, and I oblige so that I can get the hell out of there at some point in the near future. 'Great, that's better. And now Ivy, can you give them to Fran?' We repeat the charade, but apparently it's still not quite right. 'Can you, you know, look each other in the eyes? Maybe smile a little?'

'Sure!' Ivy says warmly. I used to be Tilly's little favourite and now Ivy's the one that's all sweet and compliant while I'm a sulky teenager. How embarrassing. 'Right,' Ivy says, before gallantly extending her arm towards me with the bunch of flowers at the end. The way that the sleeve of her scratchy jumper slightly moves and exposes her wrist, the raw physicality of the pale skin, muscle, bone, veins, has a weirdly erotic charge that makes my eyes snap away from her hand and up to her eyes. Watchful, curious, *irritatingly* beautiful.

It feels like when you think there's another stair and there's nothing. An unwelcome jolt. Uh oh. Can't be having that. I don't want to be her friend, I don't want to have her back in my life, I don't want to have any feelings about her other than *we used to be together, then she broke my heart, and now we're not, the end.*

'That's perfect!' Tilly says, snapping me out of my trance.

'Sorry, what?' I say.

'Whatever you were just doing, that's perfect! Can you do it again?'

'Oh,' I say, swallowing hard. 'No . . . I don't think I can . . .' I mumble, troubled by the stirrings of any kind of feelings towards Ivy.

'That's fine,' Tilly says, 'I think I got it anyway.'

'You sure?' says Ivy.

'I don't want to hold you two hostage any longer than I have to.'

'Great,' I grab my bag off the floor. 'Let you know if you need anything else – I mean, let *me* know if you need anything else,' I say, my brain working at about 20 per cent capacity. I've got to get out of there.

'Will do!' trills Tilly.

'See you,' I say, not turning to look at Ivy as I go.

'Maybe we can—' I hear her say as I head out of the door.

But I don't wait to catch the rest. No more Ivy. Christmas, New Year, good work, dates with people who haven't broken my heart, all I'm asking for is no more Ivy. Please, Universe, let this be the end of it? At least – and the thought truly makes me want to be sick – until the show airs.

14

I put it off as long as I could but this week I had to accept I was about to do the worst of all tasks: move house.

I turned to social media.

Hey! Anyone know anyone looking for a short-term tenant / house-sitter / pet-sitter / lodger / whatever? I'm mostly tidy and mostly normal, will consider living anywhere except West! DM me if you have any leads!

Which, fortunately for me, worked out. And here I am! In Stamford Hill! Much closer to the cafe than when I was in Elephant and Castle. Jamie even helped me move, which, for someone I am no longer sleeping with, seemed like a very nice thing to do. I'm now wishing I'd asked him to stay and help me put my duvet cover on, because I'm sitting on my unmade bed staring at the pile of bedding, hoping it will magically sort itself out.

I illegally Blu-tack the naked picture of me from life-drawing class to the wall. What a magnificent beast I am. I drag my magnificent beast self into the bathroom to brush my teeth, and then I get back into bed and pick up my phone again. What this room needs is a new homely trinket. A little something. A cute little nonsense thing. I open my laptop to search for 'ceramic figurine' on eBay because lord knows what I need is more breakable stuff to haul around London with me, and discover, of course, that I am not connected to the Wi-Fi. I had such grand intentions of starting work on my portfolio website! I was going to try to invent myself a business logo! What am I going to do all evening with no plans and no Wi-Fi? Burn through all my data watching Netflix on my phone?

I could . . . try and find someone to go on a date with tonight, couldn't I? That way I wouldn't have to be home alone and bored and at increased risk of thinking about Ivy. Let's see what the apps have to offer. I swipe for a while, deciding no one is quite right and, after all, I may be bored but I'm not desperate. But then, finally, someone catches my eye. Big, tall, dark hair, in London for work, seems sweet, profile says he's recently come out of a long relationship so not looking for anything serious, does not have serial killer vibes. I swipe right on Joshua and to my great satisfaction, it's a match. Now all I've got to do is get this show on the road.

> Hey! You like the look of me, I like the look of you, want to get a drink tonight?

It doesn't take long for him to reply:

> Sure! Faltering Fullback at eight?

A top-tier pub in a convenient location? Sign me the hell up!

I abandon my unpacking, do my make-up, throw on a cute little T-shirt dress and sneakers and head out to Finsbury Park to meet this cutie of the internet. When I get to the pub, it's predictably hopping because it's a Saturday night, but as I make my way through the labyrinthine pub and outside into the sprawling garden, my eyes settle on a big, gorgeous man who's just as big and just as gorgeous as his profile photos led me to believe.

A smile involuntarily passes over my face. 'Joshua?' I ask, taking a seat opposite him on the bench.

'That's me. Nice to meet you, Fran.' And there's something so easy and calm about him that I know we're going to have a good time. No awkward chat, no worries about whether he fancies me. We both know what we're here for, and we both know that you pretty much make your mind up about whether you fancy someone on first sight. And we definitely fancy each other.

'Let me get you a drink, what are you having?' he says, standing up, and wow he really is . . . big. Hot. A match made in heaven.

'A pint please, some kind of delicious pale ale or . . . whatever . . .' I tell him, feeling like a cartoon character with big hearts for eyes.

'You got it,' he says, smiling at me before disappearing to the bar.

He holds my gaze as we clink our glasses together. I take a sip. 'So, what are you doing in London?'

'I'm a web designer and the company I work for was having

a big conference last week. I stayed on another couple of days to see friends, do London things. I used to live near here, actually. It's just chance that work booked me into a Travelodge near the station.'

'And now you live . . . ?'

'Manchester. It's close to my parents and I felt like I was never going to be able to live on my own if I stayed here. Flat shares with no privacy, starts to get old fast, you know?'

'Oh, I know,' I say. 'I'm . . . kind of constantly on the move at the moment, after my last break-up. I don't want to commit to anything long-term. Which makes for a slightly chaotic existence.'

'A little chaos is nice once in a while. So, what do you do for work?'

'I'm a make-up artist and a barista.'

'Versatile.'

'I actually told myself I would work on my website tonight. I feel like having a good portfolio website will improve my life, you know? I had all these grand plans to invent myself a logo in Canva, research hosting sites or something. But then I couldn't find the router to get the Wi-Fi password so I gave up,' I shrug, grinning. 'And did some swiping instead.'

'And here we are,' Joshua says, rubbing his hand against the stubble on his jawline. 'With a web designer, of all people. It's almost like you planned it. Two birds with one stone.'

'Oh, I hadn't thought of that,' I laugh.

'It's really not even hard,' he says in an extremely reassuring tone of voice. 'As long as you know what you're doing, I mean. Which I do. Assuming all you want is nice big photos and some text? Nothing too crazy?'

'Well, I could go more avant-garde, I suppose?'

He holds up a big hand. 'Let me suggest you do not go more avant-garde with your website. Keep it simple. Let the content speak for itself. Assuming you're good at what you do.'

'You assume right.'

'It's good to invest in yourself. Show that you take yourself seriously.'

I nod. 'You're right. If I want more make-up work, I need to act like someone who deserves more make-up work.'

'Precisely.'

'So you're probably pretty expensive, right?'

'Right,' he says with a smile. 'But I'll do you mates' rates.'

'Are we mates?' I say, cocking an eyebrow in surprise.

'I hope not,' he says, and I feel his calf brush up and down against mine under the table. I stifle a gasp at the delicious intimacy of it. We look at each other across the table, his big brown eyes sparkling. 'We both know what this is, right?'

'You want me to buy you a drink or you want to get out of here?'

'I want to get out of here,' he says, standing up instantly.

We make it around the corner from the pub before we're making out against someone's wall.

'I really fancy you, you know?' I say, looking up at him.

'I'm glad my radar isn't broken. I've been out of the dating loop for a while.'

'I'm not particularly subtle,' I say, kissing him again, feeling the warmth of him against me, his hand running up the inside of my leg.

'It's hot,' he says, looking down at me. 'Someone saying what they want. No one ever says what they want.'

'Well,' I say, pulling him closer to me. 'I like getting what I want, so I know I have to ask for it.'

'Your place or mine?'

'You're the one in the hotel,' I tell him.

'Mine it is,' he says, and we start running towards the main road before stopping on the corner to make out again.

When we get south of the station and arrive at his hotel, I'm positively brimming with delight. And he does not disappoint. I can't stop touching his big, soft body, running my hands over the dark hair on his torso. The feeling of being on top of him and not even thinking for a second that I'm somehow crushing him or hurting him, letting myself be in the moment, feel how fucking amazing it feels to have sex with someone you really fancy, who makes it easy for you, who is asking nothing of you. This is *exactly* what I imagined being single would be like. And why on earth would I ever want to give it up?!

15

'I like Christmas music as much as the next person, but can we at least vary the playlist?' I beg Jamie. There are only a few days left until we close for the Christmas holidays and we're doing a roaring trade in hot chocolates and eggnog lattes.

'When you're the boss, you can choose the music,' Jamie winks at me.

'OK, I'm gonna stage a hostile takeover.'

'I'd like to see you try,' he says, smiling. 'Hey, I wonder if your fan is going to come in today.'

'I have many fans, who in particular are you referring to?'

'You know, the blond guy with the beard who always smiles at you but also sort of avoids ever making eye contact with you.'

'Ha! I can't believe you've noticed.'

'I'm observant, what can I say?'

'Jealous?' I ask, even though I know it's naughty of me to go there.

Jamie rolls his eyes. 'You wish. So, what are you going to do about it?'

I shrug. 'Nothing, going to wait and see what he does.'

'But you hold the power in this scenario, right?'

'How so?'

'You're the hot barista, he'll be intimidated to make a move on you.'

I think for a moment, before saying something extremely out of character. 'Do you know what? Objectively, I know he's cute. But I don't know if I fancy him. Does that make sense?'

Jamie looks thoughtful and shrugs. 'Sure, it's definitely a thing.'

'I mean, it's flattering that he fancies me but . . .' I wiggle my nose in deep thought. 'That doesn't mean I have to fancy him back, right?'

'Right! Sorry, I didn't mean to pressure you at all, it was just a bit of a laugh, you know?'

'No, no, of course not. We can cross that bridge if we come to it, I suppose. Let's see how things—'

I begin, but I'm cut off by the sound of the bell. A gust of cold air swoops through the cafe, accompanied by . . .

'You've got to be fucking kidding me,' I moan, spinning around and pretending to busy myself with the cups behind the counter.

'Friend of yours?' Jamie asks.

'She used to be the love of my life.'

'So nothing major?' He tries for a smile.

I take a deep breath and decide to turn around and face the music. It's my workplace, after all. Ivy catches my eye from across the room and seems genuinely surprised to see me there. She pauses for a moment, as if she might retreat and pretend she never came in. But then she shrugs off her thick wool coat and pulls off her beanie hat, shaking her curls out. She puts the beanie in the coat pocket and hangs the coat on a wall hook next to a table for two. My heart is in my throat, all the fun and frivolity disappears in an instant. Why is she here? To torment me?

Before I can figure out what my tactics will be, she's joined by a strikingly pretty woman whose bright green coat pops beautifully against her dark skin. A date? Here? Now? In front of my very eyes?

Ivy approaches the counter, grimacing. 'I had no idea you worked here. Do you want me to go somewhere else?' At least in this scenario it gives the impression that she was stalking me not me stalking her, which is an impression I would rather die than give Ivy.

'No,' I sigh, trying not to look at her too much. I want to forget her face, not be reminded of how much I used to love it. 'What can I get you?'

'Two flat whites, please.' She's shifting awkwardly from one foot to the other.

'Got it.' I start making them in the hope the noise of the machine will mean I'm not expected to talk to her. 'Ow!' I haven't burned myself on the coffee machine in ages! Why today! Why me!

'Are you all right?' Ivy frowns. Jamie looks up from where he's wiping down a table, but I gesture that it's fine. I run my hand under the cold tap for a moment. Fuck! Why!

'I'm fine!' I say over my shoulder, trying to keep everything chill.

'Look, I'm sorry, I didn't mean to stress you out . . .'

'I'm not stressed!' I protest, attempting a relaxed smile which probably ends up looking like the grimacing emoji. 'Just surprised!'

'I'm surprised too! I didn't know you worked here! Honestly! I'm meeting my friend who's visiting from America, her Airbnb is around the corner. I'm not stalking you, I promise.' She pushes her hair away from her face and the confident ease of the gesture makes me feel soft inside.

No! No soft! Tough! I am tough, I do not care! I am carefree and loving life! Hot, sexy, single gal!

I set the coffees in their chic handle-less ceramic cups down on the counter and lean with one hand on the surface. She's leaning on the other side of the counter, like we're in some kind of face-off. Part of me wants to freeze time so I can look at her like this as much as I want. The other part of me wants her to get out of here ASAP. I'm about to put the purchase through on the iPad when I decide on an effective way to show how much I do not care, how very chilled out I am.

'They're on the house,' I say brightly.

'Are you sure?' She looks down at me, eyebrows raised.

'Of course.'

When she reaches out to pick up the cups, her hand brushstrokes gently across the top of mine. How actually dare she? I'm fuming!

I watch Ivy and her companion chatting away while trying very much to look like I'm *not* watching them. Once in a while I see Ivy's eyes flick in my direction, at which point I avert mine. I chat to Jamie while we work and try to stay focused, but even he can tell my eyes want to wander in Ivy's direction. We're engaged in this silly cat-and-mouse game until the bell on the door rings and in walks The Regular Who Might Have A Crush On Me. Jamie gently elbows me in the side.

He's a good-looking bearded man with thick fair hair who is today wearing a quilted jacket that somehow doesn't make him look like he's about to go fox hunting.

'Hey, how are you?' he asks. He always asks.

'I'm fine, thank you, and you?' I try to suppress a little smile.

'I'm good.' He pauses for a moment, looking at me. 'Oh, could I get a black coffee, to go, please? I brought my own cup.' He hands me a chic reusable cup.

'Of course you did, you eco warrior!' Mortifying. I flick my eyes over and see that Ivy is watching me with interest. She's nodding along to what her friend is saying but she can't stop looking in our direction. Ha!

'Yes, an eco warrior, that's me!' he says, and for some reason I laugh really loud. Is it because I know Ivy is watching me? Who could possibly say?

'The Greta Thunberg of Seven Sisters,' I say, which is stupid, but it makes him laugh.

When I turn to make his coffee, I see Jamie chuckling to himself as he rearranges the pastries.

'So, any plans for Christmas?' he asks as I ring up his purchase on the machine. Me and the card reader are friends now, after my many false starts.

'I'm going to spend it with my family, nothing too exciting. How about you?'

I listen out for a *me and the Mrs* but it doesn't come. In spite of that, I'm still weighing up whether or not I'm actually attracted to him.

'Same, I always regress to childhood at Christmas and spend it with my parents and brother and sister. It seems like the right thing to do, somehow.' I hand him his coffee. 'I just realized, I've never asked — what's your name?'

'I'm Fran,' I say, cocking my head in a flirty manner.

'Luke.'

'Well, Luke, I hope you have a very productive day at work.' I flutter my eyelashes a little. Ivy better be watching this.

'This'll help,' he says, holding up the coffee cup. 'Well, bye then. Fran.'

I look over at Ivy but now she's got her eyes determinedly focused on her friend. They're deep in conversation until I hear the scrape of chairs, and all of a sudden my heart starts beating fast. I didn't want Ivy to come here, I didn't want to see her, but now I don't want her to leave, and I try to prepare myself for the level of breeziness I'll need to say goodbye to her, but—

The sound of the bell above the door. The feeling of cold air coming in. The sound of the door closing. And Ivy leaves without so much as a backwards glance.

16

A week later when I slide into a booth in the pub opposite Vic after my last make-up job before Christmas, I feel exhausted from the day's work. What is it about photo shoots that mean they *always* take twice as long as planned?

'Going somewhere?' she asks, eyeing my suitcase.

'Nope, I just came from a shoot,' I say, relief at sitting down flooding through my chunky bod.

'Oh that's so great! I've been keeping my ears open for stuff I could recommend you for, but everyone's got their fave make-up artists they always work with and it's hard to sneak someone new in.'

'Yeah, I mean, it's not the easiest thing to break into, even when you have contacts like we do, but . . . I'm kind of getting there?'

'Yeah?'

'Yeah,' I say, and it's true. I don't want to jinx it but . . . things are kind of picking up a bit on the work front. I feel like I'm now getting somewhere, maybe, a little bit? And Big Sexy Joshua has actually been true to his word and is working on a website for me, so maybe Dead Freelancer January could be a bit less dead for me! If I hadn't gone on a date to avoid Unwanted Ivy Thoughts I would never have met him!

'I love it,' she says, sliding one of the steaming glasses of mulled wine towards me. 'Cheers!'

'Cheers,' I answer. The frosty air outside, the cosy warmth of the pub, the twinkly lights, the spicy scent of mulled wine permeating every pub in London? Dreamy. 'Fuck, I feel like it's been ages since I've seen you.'

'You know how it is,' she shrugs, because I do know how it is. 'London.'

'What are your plans for Christmas?'

'Well,' she rolls her eyes. 'There's always this back and forth about where we're going to spend it, but I wanted to stay here on our own and have a quiet one, order some fancy food and expensive alcohol, you know, some cocktails in a glass bottle, and live the dream. But no. Greg's parents are insisting we go there because we went to my parents' last year and I don't know how to break us out of this cycle! It's never going to end!'

'My condolences, girl. Is it really that bad? Oh wait, is it Greg's parents who are weird about alcohol?'

'Yes!' she wails, taking a large gulp of her mulled wine. 'They have *one glass of wine* with dinner and then if you suggest even a drop more, or having one little drink at any other time of day, they're about ready to google the nearest AA meeting. It's horrible! Especially at Christmas!'

'For what is the meaning of Christmas without falling asleep on the sofa with a Bailey's in your hand?'

'Exactly!'

'You will take my Bailey's out of my cold, dead hand.'

'You going to your mum's this year?'

'How did you guess?' Even into adulthood, when I was with Daniel and then Miranda, I would never spend Christmas away from my mum and Andrew and The Girls.

'Aaah, that's nice!' she says, smiling. 'I'm actually jealous. It's so dead at Greg's parents'.'

'When I'm being jumped on by two extremely over-stimulated children on Christmas Day who are out of their fucking mind because they've already eaten all the chocolate from their stocking, I feel like I'll be wishing I was in a slightly more "dead" situation, and that's not even factoring in the sound of the baby crying,' I say, but secretly I do love the wild chaos of Christmas, spending it with my brother's cute kids and eating food that was bought by someone who isn't me.

I reach out to pick up my pint and knock over the salt cellar that's on the varnished tabletop. 'Shit!' I scrape the spilled salt off the table and throw it over my left shoulder before turning the cellar the right way up.

Vic laughs. 'You don't really believe in that, do you?'

'Maybe I do, maybe I don't,' I say mysteriously. 'But I won't take any chances with fate! I don't want to mess with destiny!'

'Destiny's been having *quite* a lot of fun recently,' Vic says, raising her eyebrows.

'I'll say. I didn't even tell you the latest thing – guess who graced my cafe with her presence last week?'

'No?' She gasps and looks appropriately horrified.

'Yep! The very same.'

'Maybe she's stalking you.'

'Maybe she bloody is! That's the only explanation! You

remember when we were in the pub after the fried cheese dinner and you said I always bump into people when I'm out?'

'I do.'

'Well, now I don't bump into *people*, I only ever bump into Ivy. It's absurd.'

'Or is it . . . destiny?' she ventures.

'Don't say it.'

'What? It's possible, isn't it?'

'I don't need any encouragement,' I mumble, rubbing at the condensation on the outside of the pint glass with my thumb. 'When she was in the cafe the other day I realized I was sort of . . . deliberately trying to make her jealous. I was flirting with this guy I don't really like and it was mostly for her. Like a performance.'

'At least you can admit you were doing it.' Vic shrugs.

'Well I need to *not*.'

'We're close to New Year and that's always a fresh start, right?'

'Speaking of which . . .' I raise my eyebrows meaningfully.

'Oh my God, yes! I had forgotten! Doug is definitely coming to Marie's party, so I feel like that's the perfect time to turn this into a *thing*.'

I've been laying the groundwork to swoop in on Doug ManHoney since Vic told me he was single a couple of months ago. What groundwork, you ask? A little comment here and there. Making sure I always reply to *his* replies to my Insta stories, which, incidentally, appear to be getting a little flirtier bit by bit. I even pretended I was listening to his football podcast, which is something I wouldn't do even if you paid me. Well, maybe if you paid me. I haven't quite plucked up the courage to ask him out, but I'll get there.

'We've been having a little flirty back and forth online that I feel either needs to move into the dick pic space, or needs to be taken offline and into the real world, and obviously I would prefer real world.'

'Too bloody right. And New Year's feels perfectly calibrated for romance.'

'Vic, you are so wise. I need to get through Christmas first . . .'

'Grandma? Grandma?' Erin asks Mum as soon as she's in the house. 'Why couldn't we stay here last night?'

Mum is busy helping Andrew and his wife Kelly get all their *stuff* through the door, not to mention baby Matilda who's sleeping surprisingly soundly in her portable cot thing in spite of the amount of noise her sisters are making. Erin gives up on trying to get Mum's attention and turns to me. 'Why couldn't we have a sleepover last night?'

I pick her up and kiss her on her round cheek. 'Because you only live around the corner, and I was sleeping in your bed!' I mean, really it's my bed but I understand what level the five-year-old brain operates on.

'Why?'

'Because I like waking up here on Christmas with Grandma!' I say, plonking her back on the floor.

'Is she your grandma?' asks Maisie, the middle child.

'No, she's my mummy!' I say, picking Maisie up for her kiss, which is considerably easier since she's only three. 'She's *your* grandma!'

'Why didn't you come to church with us last night, Auntie Fran?'

'Well, my little dumpling, me and Grandma don't go to church. That's something *your* mummy does, but mine doesn't!' I see her mouth setting itself to ask me another *why* but I honestly can't be bothered to get into the ins and outs of Kelly being a Catholic and the rest of us having frankly no interest in organized religion at all, so I pivot to a distraction. 'What's this you're wearing?'

'An Elsa costume,' she says.

'Ohhhh,' I say, in slight disbelief that a film that's a decade old still has such a stranglehold over the brains of girls who didn't even exist when it came out. 'Very pretty.'

'It was one of my Christmas presents,' she says.

'What else did you get?' I ask, and then she and Erin regale me with a list of about a thousand things that Andrew's going to be tripping over for the next year.

'Where are you living these days?' Andrew asks as we're peeling parsnips and chopping that weird bit off the end of some sprouts. Mum and Kelly are entertaining The Girls, which is definitely more work than this but at least they get to sit down.

'Hackney Wick, but I'll be moving again soon,' I say.

'So nowhere *permanent*?'

'No,' I say simply.

He pauses for a minute. Is it a great surprise to me that Andrew wants to engage me on my current lifestyle? No.

'Don't you find it depressing? That you had this nice life with Miranda and now you're living out of a suitcase?' Trust him to come out and say it! No sugar-coating required!

'Sometimes it's not *ideal* but I'm actually kind of enjoying the freedom. The lack of commitment and all that.' I glance sideways at Andrew and can see him roll his eyes.

'Really?'

'Yes! Why?'

'It doesn't seem like you.'

'Why not?'

'Because you've always been *stable* at the very least, that's why.'

'Well, maybe I don't want to be *stable* anymore,' I say, but he's not listening, he's off on his own little crusade.

'Even if you weren't doing the proper stuff,' he says, waving the knife in a way that verges on dangerous, 'you at least had that degree of stability.'

'What's proper stuff, in the mind of Andrew?' I ask, to torment myself by having to listen to the answer.

'You know what I mean,' he sighs impatiently. 'Going to uni, buying a home, getting married! At least you had a stable place to live, a stable job, a stable relationship.'

'Stop saying *stable*, for fuck's sake – I'm not a fucking horse!' I hiss at him.

'All right, all right!' he says, dropping the knife to the work surface and holding his hands up defensively. 'I don't get why you're going to such extremes right now, when you should probably be doing the opposite at your age.'

'My age! I'm literally in my twenties! What planet are you on?' I honestly sometimes wonder how we sprang from the same source!

'Well, Miranda's clearly doing all right. *She's* not living out of a suitcase.'

'How do you know what Miranda's doing?' I move on to peeling the potatoes. The potatoes are one of the best bits of a Christmas roast so I feel personally invested in their manufacture and success.

'I bumped into her near my office the other week. Is that allowed?'

'No.'

'She's getting married next year,' he says, scooping up all the sprouts and dumping them in a bowl. 'But you knew that, right?'

Before I can reply, Mum's head appears in the doorway. 'You two doing OK?'

'Yeah,' he says, 'We're nearly done.'

What?! It's so quick? It's . . . so incredibly quick? And to hear it from Andrew of all people!

Andrew shrugs. 'Miranda. She's getting married.'

'Fran's Miranda?' Mum asks.

'Not anymore,' I murmur. 'When did this happen?!'

'I didn't get all the details,' Andrew says. 'But apparently it was some whirlwind thing with some woman.'

'That's it? That's all you've got?' I ask, desperate for more intel.

'I didn't realize I was going to be grilled on it later,' he huffs impatiently.

'They can't have been together more than six months,' I say, shaking my head.

Mum swoops on me and wraps me up in a hug. 'Poor baby, I'm sorry,' she says.

'Mum, it's completely fine! I'm not sad about it!' And the truth is, I'm really not! I mean, it's a bit weird . . . and it's weird that I didn't know . . . and it's weird that my brother knew before me . . . but on a gut level, I'm . . . surprisingly OK?

'I can't believe you didn't know this!' Andrew says, shaking his head in disbelief.

'She's not on social media! And we don't really talk these days,' I say, shrugging. I wonder what kind of person she's marrying. I wonder if she's the complete opposite of me, or basically just like me except wants kids.

'Well,' says Mum, opening the wildly over-stuffed fridge and peering inside for whatever needs to go in the oven next from her Master List of Christmas Prep. 'It's a shame *you* didn't get paired up with someone nice.'

'Mum,' I say, rolling my eyes. 'That was never going to happen. I'm not Miranda, I'm not looking for Someone Nice in the same way, so even if I *had* met someone nice then I wouldn't be marrying them!'

'It was worth a try!' Mum slides the tray into the oven as a raging cry of *GRANDMA!* pierces the air from the living room. 'Coming!' she shouts back before disappearing back to The Girls.

'I can't believe you actually did it,' he says, shaking his head. 'As if you're going to meet someone good on a TV show. It's so idiotic.'

'I did it for fun. It's not that deep.'

'It's embarrassing! That's what it is!'

'Good job I am un-embarrassable, isn't it?' I say, even though thinking about the show makes me want to crawl in a hole and veritably die. 'Anyway, I thought you were keen for me to get some stability or something.'

'Yes, but in a *normal* way. You know, meet someone at work. I can't imagine what would possess someone to agree to go on TV for any reason, let alone to get a date.'

I hate that it's turned out that he's right, that his anti-fun attitude would have actually paid off in this instance.

A tiny stomping noise and shouts of 'Daddy!' announce Erin's arrival in the kitchen.

'Out!' says Mum, looming imperiously over her grand-daughter. 'I told you, missy! The kitchen is off limits today! Too many hot things and sharp things!'

'But I want to see Daddy,' she whines.

'Daddy's coming, baby,' he says. 'I need to finish sorting things out for lunch so we don't forget anything!'

'I'm not a baby! I'm a big girl!'

'I know,' Andrew grimaces. 'Sorry, big girl.'

'*Don't* forget the pigs in blankets,' she says, the expression on her face so serious that I have to do everything in my power not to laugh out loud.

'How could we!' I say, bending down to squeeze her. 'They're the most important bit!'

'All right, out with you,' Mum says, shepherding Erin back into the living room.

'It's a shame you have to spend your Christmas toiling away with me in here rather than in there,' I say.

'The peace and quiet is nice. It feels like a break, you know. I'm actually quite enjoying it in here,' he says, which strikes me as deeply tragic.

'You've got a funny way of showing it,' I say.

'Just because I'm not endorsing your every move, is it?'

I roll my eyes. 'I don't need you to *endorse* me, I need you to *support* me.'

'Well, I don't,' he says, like the disgruntled dad that he is. 'I didn't want you showing yourself up on TV – which, may I add, I think is perfectly reasonable – and you couldn't even do *that*.'

'Show myself up! Show myself up?!' I say indignantly, as if it's the most ridiculous idea I've ever heard when actually it's exactly what'll happen when it's broadcast. 'I did no such thing.'

'Good,' he says, and that's the end of that.

Our combined family endeavour means that Christmas dinner is served at not a completely unreasonable hour, and The Girls haven't had *too* much opportunity to raid the tin of Quality Street that me and Mum got started on in front of the TV last night (trying to get the worst ones like toffees out of the way first is only a good tactic if a child isn't going to come along and eat the good ones before you get to them in your elaborate system).

'So,' Kelly says, beaming, once the turkey has been consumed and Erin and Maisie have slunk away from the table to play with their Christmas presents and Matilda is snoozing in Mum's bedroom. She looks at Andrew furtively, and I know what's coming. We've been here before. Three times, in fact. 'We have some news!' I bet you do, Kelly old pal.

'Yes?' Mum says eagerly. As if she doesn't know what the *only* possible news is.

'We're having a baby!' Andrew grins.

I suppress the urge to burst out with *another one?!* and instead warmly congratulate them both on this new development.

'Oh, wonderful! Wonderful!' Mum sings.

'When will she be making her appearance? I say *she* because I can't imagine you'll be breaking the habit of a lifetime.'

'Early August,' says Kelly.

I frown and attempt to do the maths, which is not my

strong point. 'So . . . you're essentially telling us you two had unprotected sex a few weeks ago,' I say, unable to suppress a smile.

'Fran!' Mum whacks me with the back of her hand. 'Trust you to be casting a pall over this beautiful occasion.'

I hold my hands up in defeat. 'No, you're right, sorry for the pall-casting. I am the worst. Congratulations, I'm very excited to meet her.'

'Thanks, sis,' Andrew says drily. 'Anyway, your maths isn't even right. It was about eight weeks ago.'

'Ugh, Mum, make him stop talking about this at the dinner table!'

'Give over,' she says, rolling her eyes.

'It'll be your turn soon!' Kelly says to me, reassuringly, trying to dispel the bickering family vibes.

'Uh, I'm all right, thanks,' I say, frowning, wondering if she missed the part where my last relationship ended specifically because I did not want children.

'You say that now, but . . .' she says, shrugging and smiling smugly.

'Yeah. I do say that now.' I say it so flatly that Kelly knows to drop it.

'So, met anyone you like recently?'

'Oh yes, tons of people.'

'Anyone special?' she asks expectantly.

'They're all special. Are you trying to ask me if I've met my next long-term partner, Kel?' I say, fixing her with a weary expression I used to reserve for family but will now extend to her since she's been around for so long.

'Not *necessarily*,' she says, shrugging.

'Well, I haven't. I'm enjoying the s-e-x.' (This, for the benefit of The Girls.)

'Good for you,' she says, nudging me affectionately with her skinny arm.

'Are you not tempted to try it?' I ask naughtily.

'Fran!' Kelly gasps, horrified.

'I'm sorry, I'm infected with the Christmas spirit.'

'You mean Baileys, right?' Andrew says, overhearing. He and Mum are clearing the table around us.

'Like I said! The Christmas spirit!' I grin at him. 'I'll give you a hand with that.'

'No, it's fine, you stay here with Kelly and the girls, and you can do some washing-up in a bit.'

'Sounds like a fair deal to me,' I say, shrugging.

Once Andrew and Mum are out of the room and the children are distracted, Kelly says in a low voice, 'Andrew seems good this year, doesn't he?'

'He does,' I say, nodding. 'Time is a healer, I guess.'

'I think it all flared up when it was the first few Christmases with Erin. Like once he knew how it felt, he couldn't believe that anyone would choose to leave their family like that.'

I clear my throat. 'Mmm.' I can't believe it either, but I also don't really remember my dad that well anyway so it's not like there's a gaping hole in my life in the same way there seems to be for Andrew.

'But now . . . it's not so bad, I think.'

'That's good,' I say, nodding. I feel guilty that the absence of one of my parents hasn't had such a big impact on me, but I guess having Mum around more than compensated for it. It wasn't until I got older and realized everything that a parent has to do, all the sacrifices they have to make, all the inane chatter they have to listen to, all the boring school plays they have to sit through, that I really understood what Mum had done in going through it all by herself, and not by choice either.

I do my washing-up duty and then we all flop on the sofas and watch *Paddington 2*. A classic. I get up and go to the toilet halfway through and when I come back into the living room, I pick up Maisie, who's on the sofa next to Mum, and plonk her on my lap so I can sit there too. As we watch the film, I rest my head on Mum's shoulder and hope more than anything that she knows how much we appreciate her.

17

'Oh my God, can you stop moving, please?' I huff at Marie in a way I am absolutely unable to do with the actual models I have to make up. 'Keep still! Stop picking your phone up!'

'I'm just checking to make sure everyone isn't cancelling on me at the last minute!' she says, while trying to keep her head very still. She's the one who wanted me to do some very sharp graphic liquid liner to go with her space-age 1960s-inspired silver shift dress, and now she won't stop twitching like a nervous rabbit.

'No one is cancelling on you! It's New Year's Eve! Everyone's grateful to have a party to go to that's indoors and warm that they don't have to pay to get into!'

'All right, all right,' she says, taking a deep breath. 'But please, stop calling it a party, it's a *soirée*.'

'Your soirée is going to be excellent,' I reassure her.

'I thought I would have grown out of it by now, the fear that no one would come to my party, you know? Sorry, I mean, my *soirée*.'

'Some things never change,' I say slowly, as I try to keep my hand perfectly steady and match the left eye to the right.

I step back to admire my handiwork. 'Boom! Smashed it! Looking good, mate!'

She gropes on the desk in front of her for her hand mirror and holds it up to inspect. 'I *am* looking good! God, you're so clever, aren't you?! Thank you so much, babe, I really appreciate it.'

'Any time,' I say, taking a sip from my Prosecco.

'Any time?' she asks, her eyebrows arched expectantly.

'No, not actually any time.'

'Ugh!'

'Shit,' I say, checking the time on my phone. 'I've got to do my own make-up! Can't have people seeing me without my face on, can I?'

'What a nice face it is, though,' she says, pouring us more Prosecco.

'Nice it may be, but it's not yet soirée-ready. Especially not when there's a ManHoney about.'

Marie chatters to me about some argument she had with Carly about moving in together, while I get to work on my face, buffing the foundation into my skin, dabbing on the concealer, painting on bronzer and blusher in frighteningly bold stripes before blending and blending and blending until they look like they come from somewhere underneath my skin rather than on top of it. Now . . . how about the eye make-up?

'What are we thinking?' I ask Marie. 'Dramatic or subtle eyes?'

'Come on, mate, it's New Year's Eve.'

'You're right. If not glitter now . . . then glitter when?' I ask, rummaging around in my small make-up bag, hoping there's a pot of loose eye glitter in there somewhere. Times

164

like this I wish I carried my full kit with me all the time, not just for jobs . . . ah, bingo! A little pot of black pigment shot through with sparks of silver. Delicious. I draw it onto my eyelids in a graphic shape and tidy up the edges with a cotton bud dipped in micellar water.

'Hey,' I say, remembering I have business to discuss with her. 'Did you know Miranda was engaged?'

Marie grimaces. 'Yeah . . . I heard last month from Gobby Bobbie.'

'Of *course* you did,' I say, rolling my eyes at notorious gossip Bobbie Dyer. 'And you didn't think to tell me?'

'I didn't know if it was public knowledge!'

'If Gobby Bobbie knows then it automatically becomes public knowledge! You're meant to tell me these things!'

'I didn't want to upset you!'

'Did you really think I would be upset?'

She pauses for a second. 'No, not really. But you never know. You seem totally fine to me and doing your own thing and living the single dream, but you never actually know, do you? You might be well miserable and bonking around to keep the sads at bay.'

I roll my eyes. I fear this is a very common assumption. 'Well, I assure you, I'm not.'

'Sorry,' she says, grimacing again. 'I feel bad now!'

'Ugh, don't waste your time on *that*. Gimme deets. What do you know?'

'I know it's some older woman who's been married before. They're living in the woman's massive house in Highbury.'

'Fuck!' Envy veritably *washes* over me. Some people really do get all the luck.

'I know, right? But yeah, that's about all I have for you in the way of intelligence gathering. Sorry, pal.'

'Well, well, well,' I say, brushing my most dramatic, thickening mascara onto my lashes to finish things off. 'Good for her.'

'Cool!' Marie yells, clapping her hands together when she sees my finished look. 'So fucking cool! Look at us, we're so hot!'

'Carly is going to be the luckiest gal at the soirée.'

'And Doug is going to be the luckiest *dude* at the soirée!' she says with a grin.

'I wonder if he'll come or if he'll flake. I feel like the whole thing is too good to be true, you know?'

She sighs impatiently. 'He'll come, don't worry about it.'

'I really fancy him and want some of that New Year's magic in the atmosphere to glide us towards our natural conclusion.'

'God!' Marie wails, flicking through photos on her phone. 'Why can't I get a good selfie? I know I look cute! My make-up looks banging! So why is technology forsaking me?'

'My friend,' I say sagely, zipping my brushes back into my small make-up bag. 'Have you ever tried to take a photo of the moon? There you are, walking home after some drinks, and you look up and you see the biggest, brightest, most beautiful moon. So you get out your phone and you go to take a photo to put on your Insta story. And then you take the photo and you're like . . . what the fuck? This looks like absolute shit?'

'Ye-e-e-es?' Marie says slowly.

'And does that make you think, *oh, actually the moon looks like shit*? Or do you think, *well, maybe I couldn't take a good photo*

166

of that moon that looks so very beautiful as I am observing it with my own two eyes?'

'Yeah . . . the second one . . .' she concedes.

'You are the moon in this analogy. And you are also you, trying to take a photo of the moon.'

'I suppose that makes me feel a little bit better,' she says, still trying to get that perfect selfie.

'Also the lighting in here is shit, it's probably that. Go in the bathroom. But try not to get the toilet in the shot.'

'You're so wise.'

'I am, aren't I?' I say, to no one in particular.

Much as I expected, Marie had nothing to worry about in terms of numbers. By nine o'clock her living room and kitchen are full of friends and acquaintances, all milling around, some dancing, some sitting on the sofa, all drinking merrily and comparing notes on our various Christmases. Vic texts me that she, Greg and Doug ManHoney are about ten minutes away, so I decide it's high time for a refill. I'm bending over the fridge, trying to establish if I need to open a new bottle of wine or if there's something drinkable-looking already open, when I hear a voice behind me. Doug, could it be you?

'Is that you, Fran?' The plummy tones of Edward fill the kitchen.

'Hi, Edward,' I say with a sigh that I make sure is not audible outside the fridge, extracting a bottle of wine and turning around with a perky smile. 'It is indeed me.'

'I thought to myself, *that arse can only belong to one person,*' he says with what he probably believes to be a roguish smile. That's the problem with Edward. He thinks he's very charming but I do not think he's very charming. He's one of those people that the first time you meet him you think, *oh, how delightful! What good fun! And handsome, too!* And then after the next couple of encounters, especially if alcohol's involved, it's more like *oh God, there's Edward again*. And unfortunately, given he's one of Marie's old law degree friends, I'm now very far into *oh God, there's Edward again* territory. Edward is so good-looking that he is the reason I know that I am not shallow, because no amount of good looks can convince me to fancy him when I find his personality so annoying.

'That's me and my best feature!' I say, in a voice so jovial that it's obvious I'm taking the piss. 'What can I say!'

'How are you, darling?' he says, drawing me into a hug.

'I'm still here. How about you?' I'm pouring wine into my glass and wondering if I'll be allowed to leave the kitchen any time soon. At least Vic and the lads are imminent, that'll give me a good excuse to tear myself away.

'Not bad,' he drawls. 'Survived Christmas in Chamonix.'

'Was it positively hellish?' I ask in my best jolly hockey sticks voice.

'Wasn't my best skiing but mustn't grumble. Come, sit with me,' he says, noticing the sofa has freed up. There is no escaping it. I am trapped. I sit on the sofa and make myself comfortable in the knowledge I will probably be here for some time. 'I heard about you and Miranda. I'm very sorry.'

'Oh, it's OK,' I say, shrugging.

'You don't have to put on a brave face with me, you can tell me the truth,' he says, fixing me with a very serious look.

'No, really,' I protest. 'It's OK. I'm actually really happy!'

'Are you?' he says sceptically.

'Yes! I promise, Edward. You don't have to worry about me. I'm having a whale of a time,' I say, holding my wine glass up in a merry gesture. 'I'm dating loads, going out, seeing people, it's all good fun. It's what I've been wanting for ages, actually. A bit of freedom. A complete lack of accountability.'

Edward nods sagely. 'That's what you want?'

'Yeah! It's nice not to have to choose. To be able to have everything.'

'Aaah,' he says, his eyes twinkling with a *gotcha!* expression. 'A true greedy bisexual, are you?'

I smile. I can tell he wants me to protest, to disagree. 'That's me,' I say instead.

'And you're really OK with that?'

'I'm more than OK with it! I completely identify with it,' I say, and he looks a bit baffled and disappointed that I'm not playing his game. 'I know I'm meant to be like *oh no! That's not me!* And give you some elaborate reason why it's not greedy and it's actually morally correct or whatever, but I don't really think that being greedy is bad? Maybe that's my political platform: reclaiming greedy. I think it's OK to want things. And to want lots of things. And I do want lots of things. I mean . . . I don't see why I have to choose. There's literally no reason.' I clap my hands together decisively. 'I specifically identify as a greedy bisexual.'

'But . . .' Edward says, his brow furrowed. 'But surely you don't want to live like this forever? Gadding about and sleeping around?'

'Maybe. Maybe not. I don't know. I don't really know about forever, but I know that I'm quite enjoying myself for now. Why are you so bothered, eh? You want to lock me down?' I ask, trying to lighten the tone a bit.

'Oh, you're much too much for me,' he says, smiling weakly. Clearly I haven't converted him to the concept of joyful non-monogamy. But I won't have him trying to tell me there's something shameful about me wanting to live my life! Not on New Year's Eve!

'Come and dance!' Marie yelps, pulling me up from the sofa by my free hand. A little splash of wine leaps over the side of my glass.

'See you later, Edward!' I say, looking over my shoulder as Marie gets me dancing to 'Girls Just Wanna Have Fun'.

'I thought you found him tedious?' Marie asks.

'I do, but I'm still polite.'

'I thought maybe you'd had a change of heart.'

'No! He was interrogating me about my . . . lifestyle, or whatever; trying to tell me there was something good about not dating loads of people or something.'

'Maybe he's trying to get in there himself?'

'I don't think so,' I say, frowning. 'That would be weird. Much too weird.'

'He's hot, though?' she says, which is true.

'I cannot live on hot alone. I also need vibes. Edward's vibes are decidedly not my vibes. And I have Doug on the horizon. So it's a no from me.'

'Fair.' Marie spins me around and we laugh so much it makes me feel more tipsy than I am. Then the doorbell rings and she stumbles off to let in Vic and her entourage of Greg and Doug, and I feel my pulse quicken a little bit at the sight of him pulling off his coat and unwrapping his scarf. He winks at me from across the room and I feel my stomach turn into butterflies. ManHoney indeed.

170

I hug all three of them, and when I've got my arms around Vic she whispers in my ear, 'Is tonight going to be the night?!'

And I whisper back, 'I hope so!'

I feel a hand on my hip and I turn around to come face to gorgeous face with Doug. 'Drink?'

'I'll have what you're having,' I say, staring into his long-lashed eyes.

'I'll be right back,' he tells me, and when he's walking over to the kitchen he looks at me over his shoulder and smiles. All bodes well, I must say!

Doug returns with our drinks and we hover on the edge of the improvised dance floor in the middle of Marie's living room. 'Hey Ya!' by OutKast is playing, but Marie catches my eye from across the room and grins, hastily changing the music to something a little . . . sexier. She even dims the lights more as Aaliyah's 'More Than a Woman' plays from her Bluetooth speakers, presumably in the hope it will encourage us to start grinding on each other. As the lights dim, Doug and I both giggle at the enforced intimacy of it, but our bodies move closer together and while we don't exactly *grind* it does get a little hot and heavy. Just the way I like it.

We dance for a while, chatting and sipping our drinks, until we are abruptly interrupted.

'What time is it?' Marie grabs me as she stalks past us, wild-eyed.

I take my eyes off Doug for a moment and slide my phone out of my pocket. 'Eleven fifty-seven!'

'Shit!'

'I'm going to pop out for a quick smoke,' Doug says, leaping to his feet and feeling around in his pockets.

'Oh, OK,' I say, frowning a little. It's so close to midnight, I don't want to miss an excuse for a hot make-out sesh.

'You'll be all right without me, won't you?'

'You go,' I say, waving him off in the hope he's back quickly. He winks at me over his shoulder as he turns to go. Delicious.

Marie picks up a pen from the mantelpiece and taps it on the side of her glass. 'Hello? HELLO?! EVERYONE?' Finally the room quietens down. 'It's nearly MIDNIGHT? So make sure you've got a drink in your hand!'

This causes a mass exodus to the kitchen to refill drinks before the stroke of midnight. When I head back into the living room, Marie is squinting down at the TV remote, swaying gently on the spot.

'Gimme,' I say, holding my hand out.

She passes me the remote and I do the honours while she shouts, 'Carly?!!?' in search of her girlfriend. I turn the sound up on the scenes from the South Bank where people much colder than us with less ready access to toilets and refrigerated wine grin excitedly. I put the remote back on the TV as the countdown starts, and much like a football crowd is unable to resist a Mexican wave, the room finds itself powerless to resist raucously counting down from ten to start the new year. But still no Doug!

Ugh!

With every second we chant en masse my hope of a midnight kiss recedes further and further into the distance. But as it hits midnight, I feel a hand on my shoulder and my heart leaps! Doug! My handsome prince! I turn around to find myself face to face with . . . Edward. He is looking at me through an unfocused drunken haze. I understand what's going to happen

172

next and decide to let it happen, because he's kind of hot and I have no one else to kiss right now, and I'm annoyed about Doug. He crushes his lips against mine, which is curiously un-sexy for someone objectively sexy.

'Oh, Edward,' I say, shaking my head. 'I don't think you really meant that, did you?'

'I did!' He's got his hands on my shoulders and is looking at me with an expression of extreme seriousness.

'You're drunk!'

'In vino veritas, Fran!' he says, looking at me with the utmost sincerity, which makes me smile because it's such an extremely him thing to say.

I leave him swaying drunkenly on the spot, clinging onto the mantelpiece for dear life, and try to find Marie. She doesn't take much finding, because she's apparently been spying on me the whole time.

'I told you!' Marie says, pointing her finger in my face most jubilantly.

'He's drunk, it's nothing.'

'It may be nothing, but it proves me right! Anyway, what happened to Doug?' she says, suddenly remembering he was ever here.

'He went outside to smoke,' I say with a shrug that's transparently more nonchalant than I really feel.

'Oh, there he is!'

On the one hand, at least he wasn't around to see Edward's lunge, but on the other, if he had been here I would have been the one lunging at Doug so it wouldn't have happened anyway.

'I guess I missed it,' he says a little sheepishly, running his hands through his thick, soft-looking hair.

'I guess you did,' I shrug ruefully, trying not to let my disappointment show on my face. But when I feel him pull me towards him, the excitement is back and fizzier than ever . . . until our lips meet and my mouth is full of the taste of stale cigarettes and it takes all my erotic willpower not to pull away immediately. The funny thing is, the kiss itself isn't even that good. I don't feel the intimacy, the urgency that I felt when we were dancing together before. It's like the tobacco kiss has broken the spell.

But if it has, Doug hasn't noticed. 'Do you want to . . . come back to mine?' he suggests.

I think about it for a moment. The bad kiss was probably a one-off – I don't want to pass up the chance of sleeping with actual Doug ManHoney on the basis of one single stinky kiss. It was probably the bad taste, I bet the kiss itself was fine. 'Sure,' I purr in my most seductive tone, and I pull him towards me for another kiss. I really go for it this time, prepared for the stale cigarette taste, and – nothing. Still no erotic charge. Never mind, once we get into the bedroom everything will be better.

Doug pays New Year's Eve prices for an Uber to hurry us to his, and I go in for some hot make-out vibes in the back of the car, which as we all know can be a powerfully erotic space. Not tonight. The stale taste may be absent but so is the hot chemistry I was expecting. Nevertheless, I persist. I try to find the key that unlocks the vibes between Doug and me. Curiosity is driving me forward in this quest now, rather than erotic obsession.

When we get out of the Uber, we head into his chic flat on the ground floor of a new build. As the door closes behind us, he moves to kiss me again. This time, our teeth knock against each other's and we both pull back. 'Sorry!' I say, reflexively bringing my hand up to my mouth. 'Let's try that again . . .' I lean in once more and this time our noses bump against each other, but even so, we make it to the kiss. Still nothing. No stirrings in my swimsuit area.

Undeterred, we make it into the bedroom. Almost immediately he starts going down on me and I try to zone out and be in the moment rather than analysing what I'm feeling or what I'm not feeling. I wait for that spark, that sensation of melting into each other. I realize I'm holding my breath.

And then I feel him stop, and his head pops up from between my thighs. 'This isn't really working, is it?' he says, his brow furrowed.

I sigh. 'I don't think it is.'

'But it seemed like such a good idea, didn't it?'

'I guess sometimes the reality and the fantasy don't match up?' I suggest. 'I mean, I don't *regret* it or anything. But . . . yeah . . . let's chalk it up to an unsuccessful experiment?'

He slumps back against the end of the bed in defeat. 'I suppose so.'

'Maybe the fact we were never single at the same time was what fuelled the crush?' I say.

'And then once it was possible, we had to find out it wasn't actually that good?'

'Exactly.'

'Huh,' he says, returning to my end of the bed.

'Do you want me to go?' I ask, hoping against hope he doesn't. I can't face trekking across London at this hour on New Year's Eve.

'Nah, you might as well stay. Get a good night's sleep or something.'

'I have to say this is not remotely how I expected tonight panning out.'

'What can you do, eh?'

I plug my phone in to charge before I fall asleep under Doug's forest green linen sheets, all crisp and detergent-fresh. And there, amid the *Happy New Year* texts is one I'm not expecting.

Hey Foxy, on the off-chance you still have the same phone number from back in the day, I just wanted to say happy new year. I know it was a shock to be paired up like that – it was for me, too. But I was happy to see you again, and I hope you have a sweet year ahead. Ivy.

The sight of her name makes my head spin more than a kiss from Doug ever did. I breathe deeply. I type a reply. Happy new year xx. Then I delete the kisses. Then I put them back. Then I delete one kiss. Then I hit send. Call it New Year's optimism or something.

18

'Hello?' I croak out, blinking my eyes open on a Sunday morning blessed with the kind of sharp, bright light that makes cold January days bearable.

'Thank God you finally answered, are you busy today?' It's Vic, which is extremely random. She must have called enough times to bypass my Do Not Disturb function. What the hell is going on?

'Good morning to you too.'

'No time for that, babe. This is an emergency. Are you busy today?'

'No, not really,' I say, sitting up, trying to remember if I had plans today.

'Good, because this isn't any emergency, it's a wedding emergency! My friend Charlene is getting married *today* and her make-up artist has norovirus! Both ends!'

'And you want me to save the day?'

'No, I *need* you to save the day. She'll pay double whatever your usual rate is.'

'Well, in that case . . .' I stretch and try to get my brain out of snooze mode and into boss bitch mode. I only did a wedding last weekend (thanks, Mum!) and another paid at *double* my rate will help me feel chill for a little while. How can I say no to being someone's hero? 'I'm in.'

'God bless you, Fran Baker! It's at the Asylum Chapel in Peckham but they're getting ready at her house in Nunhead. It's a very chic winter wedding, an afternoon affair leading to an evening reception in a pub. I'll tell Charlene you'll be there by twelve?'

'Sure. How many people am I doing?'

'Her plus two bridesmaids. No big deal. She'll be so grateful and you'd be doing such a good deed.'

'Most importantly, for double bubble.'

'Exactly. So you'll do it?'

'Who am I to say no?'

'Great! I'll text you the address!'

Good job I was *very* on top of my shit with the last shoot and did all my brush cleaning, my disinfecting, my topping up of my lipstick palettes, all of that last week. So yes, I *am* there for twelve.

I press the doorbell and brace myself for the most stressed woman on the planet to answer the door. Instead, I am greeted by a serene and beautiful angel in a white dressing gown holding a midday glass of Prosecco.

'Charlene?'

'No, always a bridesmaid, never the bride.' She flashes me a fairly devastating smile. 'I'm Claudia. Come in.'

'She's here!' Claudia calls but before she can get the words out there is an almighty and protracted squeeeeeeeeeeeeeeeel as Charlene dashes down the stairs and collides with me.

'Thank God!' she wails. 'Thank you, thank you, thank you!'

Charlene promptly throws her arms around me. It's nice to be appreciated, I suppose. 'I couldn't believe it when she said she had norovirus.'

'Both ends,' says Claudia.

'I heard.'

'Can you do hair too?' pleads the bride-to-be. 'Please tell me you do hair?'

If I absolutely have to, yes. 'Of course,' I say confidently. 'So, tell me what you were thinking, show me photos, the lot. I'll start with you because obviously you are my number one priority. How long have we got?'

'The ceremony starts at four o'clock, so three and a half hours at the absolute limit, it can't be a second longer, not a second.' Charlene's expression is pure anxiety.

I try not to let my panic show on my face. I've got to work with what I've got.

'Right! Let's do this!'

The second bridesmaid emerges with a glass of Prosecco for me. 'Can you drink on the job?'

'Usually I wouldn't, but . . .'

'Needs must,' she says with a grimace, before lowering her voice.

I down half the glass of Prosecco. 'Here,' I say, unzipping the suitcase and retrieving three sheet masks. 'Put these on while I unpack. The panicking phase of the day is over, we are now in chill time. Everything is under control. Now, you relax with your sheet masks and, Charlene, get me a photo of your make-up from the trial you did with norovirus gal, and I can recreate it.'

Charlene still looks fit to explode. Somehow her stress radiates through the sheet mask. She shows me the photos of her trial and it's a classic: matte neutral eye with a slight smoke and a little hint of shimmer in the middle of the lid, a cool-toned pink blusher and what looks like Bobbi Brown Sandwash Pink lipstick and a slightly darker lip liner. Her sharp bob is styled into loose waves, which I'll be able to do with the tongs in fifteen minutes, tops.

I position the chair in front of the window. Let's go!

She's a ball of energy. 'I couldn't believe this was happening to me!'

'It's all under control now,' I try to reassure her, but she will not be reassured.

'It was like the universe was conspiring against me! Why me?!'

I open my mouth to suggest that maybe the universe wasn't thinking about her at all but instead I nod sympathetically as I unpack in a hurry, trying to eyeball what shade of foundation Charlene would wear, trying to figure out her skin type plus some extra hydration from the mask. I've got this. I am a pro.

'This is just not how I wanted today to go. I wanted to be happy and relaxed, not panicking, ringing Vic at half past six in the morning. But she really came through.' Finally, the bride-to-be manages a weak smile.

'I won't let you down. Promise. You're going to look absolutely stunning. What's your dress like?'

She describes it to me, and it does sound gorgeous. Plunging back, softly draped neckline, very sexy. As I progress through the skincare, on to the primer and into the make-up, I feel her stress melt away. Like she starts to believe everything will all work out. By the time I finish, with five minutes to spare in my self-imposed timeline, everything is back on track.

She looks at herself in the mirror. A proper smile breaks out across her face. 'I think this is actually . . . even better than what I had before?' She puts the mirror back on the side table. 'I honestly can't believe it. Thank you so much. Guys!' she calls to the bridesmaids who are upstairs putting their dresses on.

'Are we up?' Samantha calls back.

'Yep!'

'Exciting!' trills Claudia. 'I'm almost dressed!'

'I'm ready for you!' Samantha says, coming down the stairs in a beautiful forest green dress.

'Oh, Charlene!' She covers her mouth with her hands. 'You look so, so beautiful.' Samantha draws her into a hug. 'I honestly can't wait to see you in the dress, you're going to look incredible!'

'Fran really came through! Now it's you guys' turn while I finish getting ready!'

I check the clock on my phone. I can spend forty minutes on each of them, hair and make-up. I swallow down my anxiety and tell Samantha to take a seat.

It all begins well enough. I prep her skin, counteracting the dryness that comes from working in a heated office in the winter. I'm even making pretty good progress on the make-up, doing small talk about work. And then the chat turns, as it so often does on a wedding day, to love.

'Are you married?' I ask her.

'Engaged,' she smiles and holds up a hand with a sparkly ring.

'Oh, lovely! How long have you been together?'

'Two years,' she says serenely. 'People tell me it's quick but when you know, you know.'

181

'I guess you do,' I nod, feeling sick at the thought of committing THEORETICALLY, FOR LIFE to someone after only two years.

'Do you have a boyfriend?' she asks, before remembering the existence of LGBT people. 'Or a girlfriend?'

'I do not. I am very happily single and dating right now,' I say as I brush a tinted pomade through her eyebrows.

'God, dating is such a ball-ache, isn't it?'

I laugh. 'Not really! I actually find it quite fun.'

'Doesn't it depress you? Having to do all that to find love?'

'I don't particularly want to *find love*.'

'But you're single!' she says, aghast.

I smile, as sincerely as I can manage. 'Yes!' I positively brim with enthusiasm.

'And you don't want to . . . you know, meet someone? Settle down?'

I wonder how to put this delicately so as not to offend a client's bridesmaid on their wedding day. I can't very well say *I would rather eat my own foot* or *The idea of getting into another relationship makes me want to die a bit.* I settle on, 'It's not really my priority at the moment.'

'Are you a bit of a *career girl*, then?' she asks, as if it's a dirty word.

'Ha!' I laugh again, before realizing she's serious. 'No, it's not that . . . I mean, I am trying to build my freelance work at the moment, but it's not really about that. It's more that I quite like being single.'

'Why?!' she gasps, horrified.

'I was in romantic relationships for a long time and didn't

182

really have a breather between them. Sort of leapfrogged from one to the next. Being single always seemed . . . fun?'

'Fun's all right for when you're a teenager. When you're an adult, which you definitely are, don't you think you should be looking for something more than fun?' Samantha asks. 'Life is short, you don't want to look around one day and realize you've missed the boat!'

'What boat?'

'You know, *the boat*,' she says ominously. 'If you're not married by thirty, something is definitely wrong. I'd want to be on at least kid one before I reach three-oh. Yuck, I can't even say it.'

How was Charlene so normal and her bridesmaid such a freak? I dread to think what Claudia is going to be like, however hot she may be. Before I can think of a response to this insanity, Samantha pipes up again. 'It's different for men, they have all the time in the world. But women need to move quickly to lock down something proper.'

Unable to deal with whatever is going on here, I smile absent-mindedly as I reach for the eyelash glue and squeeze a little dot onto my Perspex palette before picking up individual clusters of false lashes with a pair of tweezers and dipping them in the glue. This is precision work. 'Close your eyes for me?'

Unfortunately, having your eyes closed doesn't mean your mouth has to be closed, too. 'I can't imagine not having Jack, you know? No one to come home to, no one to wake up with, no one to go on holiday with. Sad. No love in your life.'

'I have a lot of love in my life!' I say cheerfully, because I do. Great friends, close to my mum, I love my*self* too, which isn't easily won.

'But not this kind of love! You're a pretty girl, it can't be hard for you to meet someone nice?'

'I'm not *seeking* a relationship in that way,' I say, feeling myself getting frustrated. I don't know why it's so hard to make myself understood – it's like I'm speaking a different language that I *know* she can understand but is refusing to speak back to me.

'I can't imagine not having that security, knowing what things are going to be like for me from now until—' she shrugs. 'Forever!' Samantha says at the exact same moment as I say, 'You die!'

'Sorry,' I say, coughing to cover my awkward laughter. 'You know what I mean.'

'Wow!' She checks herself out in my mirror. 'You're a miracle worker!' Yes, Samantha, the miracle was that I didn't throw myself out the window at your chat.

'Thanks! Could you send Claudia down? I'm perfectly on schedule!'

I'm actually quite looking forward to doing Claudia's hair and make-up, unless she turns out to be the same flavour of weirdo as Samantha. She's so magnetically beautiful it'll be a pleasure to look at her face for forty minutes. Maybe you can get away with being a weirdo if you're that hot. When she descends the stairs and strolls confidently into the living room, her sage green dress is slightly hanging off one shoulder, her hair grazing the lazily draped strap.

She walks right up to me but doesn't sit down in the chair, instead turning around and gathering her hair in her hands. 'Could you zip me up, please?' she asks over her shoulder.

I blink, taken aback. Charlene or Samantha could have done

this, right? But I do it anyway, catching the warm, deep floral scent of her perfume.

'Do you like the dress?'

The question, again, catches me off guard.

'Yes . . .' I say, feeling a charge in the air. 'It really suits you.'

'I thought so, too.' She takes a seat in the chair.

Up close, her skin is even more radiant than I had previously thought. Of course it is. All full and glowing and magic, even through the winter chill. As I work the products into her skin, they seem to melt and merge with her.

'So, how do you know the bride?'

'We went to school together.' Her serenely closed eyelids flutter open. 'But we've stayed really close since then. Even now I live in Seoul, we Zoom every week without fail.'

'Seoul, wow, so you're only here for the wedding?'

'And to see my family and to drink Ribena and eat Jaffa Cakes and all of that good stuff.'

'I suppose the UK has to have *something* going for it,' I say, trying not to stare at her gorgeous wide mouth and gleaming, neat white teeth. I am a professional. I have work to do.

'I want a red lip,' she tells me. 'I brought my own.' She passes me a glossy black tube of Chanel Coromandel, a strange, difficult shade that looks awful on me but when I paint it onto her lips with a tiny brush, looks incredibly striking on her.

'Blot the lipstick on this,' I say, handing her a clean, white tissue from a new pack. 'It'll last longer.'

She holds my gaze as she presses the tissue to her lips in an open-mouthed kiss. When she's finished, she doesn't crumple the tissue in her hand the way most clients do. Instead, she neatly folds it backwards so it's a little square with the ghost

185

of her red lips at the centre. She places it deliberately on top of my kit like an offering.

Wow.

I focus on the job at hand, determined not to let Charlene down, determined to have all three of them ready and out the door on time, determined to earn my unexpected double pay.

'Close your eyes for me?' I trace a halo of eyeshadow around the outside of her eye. Something takes over me. 'I was thinking how beautiful your skin is.'

'Korea is the land of excellent skincare . . . but thank you. I suppose you see a lot of faces.'

Almost without thinking, it slips out. 'I do. But not many as beautiful as yours.'

She takes a deep breath, and a smile spreads across her face. Her eyelids remain closed, like I told her to. 'Are you saying that as a make-up artist or as a woman?'

'Which would you prefer?'

But before she can reply, Charlene and Samantha flit in, all nervous energy.

'How are you guys doing?' Charlene asks with a grimace and a glance at the wall clock.

'It's all under control,' I reassure her, my face feeling flushed from the turn of the conversation.

'Once we're done I just need to get my bag and put my shoes on!' Claudia promises her.

Charlene shakes her head at her own paranoia. 'I still can't quite believe that you saved the day like this, that it's actually all going to work out!'

'You're our hero,' says Claudia, looking up at me through her freshly mascaraed lashes.

There is simply no way I'm misreading: she is unquestion-ably flirting. *It's not against some professional code of conduct to ask for her number, is it?* I wonder as I backcomb her hair at the roots a little.

'Sorry if that hurts.'

'You can hurt me all you like,' she murmurs under her breath. Unquestionably.

I don't know what to say to that. I twist her glossy, shoulder-length hair into a sexy, tousled half-up half-down style that will wear well throughout the day. For all I was slightly un-certain about whether I could 'do hair' as Charlene asked me, today has shown me that it's well within my capabilities. I need to believe in myself more.

And then we're done.

'Taxi's here!' Charlene exclaims, picking her way carefully down the stairs in her wedding dress and heels as I see a shiny black car pull up outside. She must have been watching nerv-ously at the upstairs window. Samantha follows behind and Claudia rouses herself from her seat in front of me.

'Right in the nick of time!' I say, glancing at the clock before watching Claudia pick up a sleek vintage top-handle bag and slip her feet into silver cracked leather high heels. She'll be gone in a moment.

Charlene throws her arms around me again, but more cautiously this time so as not to disturb her look. 'All your stuff is still here – do you want to pack it up and follow in an Uber?'

'Follow?' I ask, my heart leaping at the thought of more time with Claudia.

'Yeah, to the venue – it's the Asylum Chapel. Can't be

looking shiny in the photos! I'll pay whatever extra you need if it's not usually included?'

'Right, of course,' I say. I don't generally hang around for touch-ups at weddings but whatever Charlene wants, she'll get. 'I'll be there ASAP!'

Charlene gathers the bottom of her dress and steps out the front door, followed by Samantha. Claudia turns to me before heading out of the door and winks at me over her shoulder, the heavy mascara on the outer lashes making her almost unbearably siren-esque.

I pack up my kit as fast as lightning, picking out all the products I used on Charlene and separating them into a make-up bag plus a couple of products I used on Samantha and Claudia, plus the Fenty blotting powder that's essential for de-shining in photos — God bless you, Rihanna.

I summon an Uber and arrive at the venue part way through the ceremony, so I stow my main kit and loiter on the steps outside until I hear the rapturous applause signalling that Charlene and . . . well, whoever, are man and wife.

When the crowd emerges, I'm ready to spring into action. I've clipped my brushes and bits around my waist so hopefully it is obvious to the other guests that I'm a make-up artist and not a mad interloper, and I hang back when everyone is throwing confetti on Charlene and her new husband, who is a very handsome Black man that I learn from eavesdropping is called Anthony. As soon as I spot Claudia again, resplendent in her sage satin dress, my stomach does a backflip at how hot she is. Her eyes are scanning the crowd and when she locks eyes with me instead of looking away, pretending she wasn't looking for me, a wolfish smile spreads across her face. But I am here to do business! Not eyeball and be eyeballed by hot bridesmaids! I am a serious businesswoman!

Amid the flurry of confetti, hugs, flowers, guests, Charlene catches my eye and gestures for me to come over.

'Congratulations!' I tell her.

'Thank you!' She is grinning from ear to ear, her eye make-up a little smudged with the emotion of the event. 'Fran, this is Anthony, Anthony, this is Fran.'

'So you're the one who saved the day,' he says warmly, pulling me into a hug.

'Honestly,' Charlene shakes her head. 'I can't believe the way you came through today. We're going to do photos while people move on to the reception venue for a drink, so do what you need to do.'

Even though hardly any time has passed, heavy make-up for photos requires quite a lot of maintenance, especially when the model, or in this case, the bride, has been weeping tears of joy at her good fortune to be marrying a kind man on a beautiful bright sunny day. I powder, conceal, touch up Charlene's mascara and her lipstick, and she's looking fresh as a daisy again.

'I can retouch the bridesmaids quickly for group shots while you and Anthony have some photos together,' I tell her.

'Great, thank you so much, you're the best. Will you come to the reception?'

'If you need me to, of course!'

'You can be my plus one,' says Claudia, who has materialized next to us along with Samantha.

'Classic Claudia,' Samantha rolls her eyes lovingly. Clearly Claudia's slag era is much more well-established than mine.

'So!' I say in a businesslike fashion because, like I said, I am nothing if not a business lady. 'I'll retouch your lipsticks and powder anywhere that needs it before the group photos.'

I start with Samantha as Claudia flits around, chatting to guests and greeting people she hasn't seen in a long time. I re-pin a section of Samantha's hair that isn't playing ball, and then declare her photo-ready. The whole time I'm basking in the hot sexy glow of Claudia. Being paid double my wedding rate was reward enough, but *this*? Truly a blessing. As I press colour into her lips and skim over her skin with a big, fluffy brush I feel that real thrill of the chase that I coveted so much when I was in a relationship. This is the good shit.

Charlene urges me to go on to the pub where the reception is being held, so I do as I'm told. I'm barely through the door with my kit to dump in the cloakroom when I feel someone throw their arms around me.

'Vic? What are *you* doing here?' I ask, delighted to see her.

'I was the one that rang you this morning to get you the job?' She squints at me in confusion. She looks gorgeous in a red silk dress with short, puffy sleeves that I know she bought on the Outnet after Christmas because she asked my opinion on it. It looks even lovelier on her than on the model.

I laugh and clap my hand to my forehead. 'Mate, that feels about two weeks ago. I had completely forgotten! Fuck, what a long day it's been.'

'But it's been all right? Charlene wasn't a nightmare?'

'Oh not at *all*.'

At that moment, Greg appears with two glasses of champagne. 'There you are! I hoped we'd get to see you after your good deed.'

I hug him and he offers me one of the champagne flutes and hands the other to Vic. 'Isn't this yours?' I ask.

He shrugs. 'I'll get another one.'

'Good lad,' I say, clinking my glass against Vic's. Greg strolls off in search of more champagne and I need some reassurance from Vic that I don't look a complete mess. 'I wasn't necessarily expecting to end up at the reception . . .' I grimace. 'I feel very under dressed.'

She takes a step back and surveys my outfit of a sleek navy blue jumpsuit with a sharp collar and brass buttons and a pair of shiny brogues. 'It's not necessarily classic wedding, but you look great,' she says, which is reassurance enough for me.

'Nice jumpsuit,' says a passing woman with a sharp, sleek fringe.

'Thank you,' I smile.

'Fran, meet Zara, Zara meet Fran,' Vic introduces us. 'Fran did Charlene's make-up today at the last minute.'

'God, I heard about that, what a nightmare – to lose your make-up artist *on the day*,' Zara shakes her head in horror. 'But you did a great job, the girls all looked amazing. Very harmonious.'

'Thanks! I appreciate it.'

She claps a hand to her mouth. 'Saying *on the day* reminded me of the most mortifying thing that happened to me at a wedding last year.'

'Do tell,' says Vic conspiratorially.

'I was chatting to this girl I just met who was super nice and friendly and I told her I'd heard from a friend about this wedding where all the guests and the groom were at the venue and ready to go and then the bride doesn't turn up! Word gets out that she's at a Harvester. Isn't going to show up!'

'And?' I ask expectantly.

'She *was* the bride! I only found out later, I couldn't figure out why she suddenly disappeared on me. Mortifying.'

'What are the odds, though?' I say. 'Anyway, you don't have to worry about that with me, I'm not a secret runaway bride.'

The reception is very informal, drinks, milling around, chatting, delicious food served family-style on long tables so it doesn't matter that I'm a last-minute addition, a guest in search of a place name. Claudia keeps catching my eye but we don't end up in each other's orbits until after the meal when the lights are dimmed and the DJ has started playing. The cover of darkness emboldens me, and I peel away from Vic, Greg and Zara. She's propping up the bar, waiting for a gin and tonic that the barman hands to her. She turns to me and sips seductively from the straw.

'Hello again,' she says.

'Are you having a good time?' I ask.

'I am, and it seems like Charlene and Anthony are too.' She glances over to the dance floor, where they're in the middle of a group of people enthusiastically getting down to 'Candy' by Cameo.

'So,' I say, smiling a little. 'Are we going to . . .' I begin, but she interrupts me.

'My Airbnb is around the corner. Let's go.'

'But you just got a drink?'

She looks me in the eye and downs the gin and tonic in about five seconds flat. She grabs me by the hand and drags me out of the pub. 'They won't even notice we're gone,' she says with a smile.

Her Airbnb really *is* around the corner and as soon as the door closes behind us we're all over each other. When she pulls me towards her I finally find out what those absurdly pillowy lips feel like. Fucking heaven. I do not hang about. I run my hand up the back of her dress, feeling for the zip. I pull it down and she shrugs it off her shoulders. For two people who are not drunk, our movements are feverish, intense. I unclasp her strapless bra as we collapse backwards over the arm of the sofa and I take her nipple between my teeth and reach into the ugly but strategically necessary flesh-coloured knickers she wore under the bridesmaid's dress. Her stomach is soft against the heel of my hand and as I slip my fingers inside her she bares her teeth against my lips.

'Yes . . . more . . .' she pants, and I just know she's someone that's always asking for more and usually gets it. I move my fingers inside her like I'm trying to pull her closer to me, like I'm trying to mesh her body with mine with only my thumb on her clit keeping us apart.

This was so completely inevitable: from the moment we saw each other earlier, it was always going to end up here. And after the let-down of Doug ManHoney, this was *exactly* what I needed to pep me up.

19

Hot Bridesmaid Claudia (now back in Seoul, neither of us under any illusions it was anything more than a very delightful big wedding fuck) was the precise kind of boost required to get me through gloomy January. February is upon us and we are marching inevitably towards the broadcast of *The Meet-Cute*.

I've actually been working so much recently at the cafe and on make-up jobs that I haven't had that much time for dating, not to mention the fact that I moved house again last weekend. It's only temporary but every time I open the door to the flat I'm hit so strongly with the smell of weed that I feel high almost instantly. Not great for the ol' productivity.

Obviously I'm grateful for Jamie's mate Steve letting me move into the small bedroom in his flat for a few weeks until his new flatmate moves in, but whoever they are, I hope they're a fan of the devil's lettuce.

It's Saturday afternoon and I'm faced with the glamorous task of cleaning my make-up brushes and sterilizing my various implements. I've resisted all temptation to go out or make a date this weekend, because I am a good and virtuous make-up artist and I take my job seriously. That's me. Serious. Professional.

Steve shuffles into the kitchen while I'm toiling away with my brush cleanser. 'Sup,' he says, his eyes bloodshot, nodding in my direction before opening one of the cupboards and extracting a multipack of Space Raiders crisps.

'Hi Steve,' I say brightly, but he shuffles back into his bedroom, where I can hear him playing computer games. Domestic harmony.

When I'm finally finished with the seemingly endless task and the brushes and sponges are drying on kitchen roll next to the sink, I dry my hands and check my phone. Oh, wonderful. I have a missed call from Andrew. And he's left a voicemail. Errgh, voicemails. That means it's serious. Extremely grudgingly, I listen to the message.

'Jesus Christ, Fran, can you ever just answer your phone? Why is it always on silent? What's even the point in having a phone if you never answer it? Call me as soon as you get this.'

OK, so clearly he's calling me in a great mood with good news, I can see that. Reluctantly I ring back.

'Hello?' he answers tersely, and I can hear the raucous noise of The Girls in the background, the indistinct aural assault of whatever mad game they're playing together.

'I got your voicemail. What were you ringing about?'

'I was ringing because I saw a trailer of . . . one second,' he says, and I can hear him getting up and stomping off somewhere before he seethes, 'A trailer of your *fucking television programme.*'

'Oh?' I say, my stomach dropping. 'I didn't know they were doing that . . .'

'Well, they are.'

'What am I doing? Am I crying?' My heart is racing thinking about that horrible experience.

'No, you're not. Why? Did you cry? On TV?' he asks without waiting for the reply. 'You're saying something stupid about how you're sleeping around. I think the exact phrase you use is, *I guess you could say I'm just sleeping around right now*.'

Weirdly, I am flooded with relief. 'Is that it? No meltdown?' Obviously they're saving the meltdown for the actual show, I'm not foolish enough to think that it's been cut altogether, but at least I get to delay the moment where everyone I know will see it.

'What do you mean *is that it*? It's fucking embarrassing, Fran!' he says impatiently. 'You're nearly thirty, for God's sake!'

'So there's no meltdown?'

'No, there's no meltdown! That's the only bit of you they use, so imagine how stupid you look!'

This may be, for some weird patriarchal reason, very embarrassing for Andrew, but for me it's the best possible outcome. For now, anyway. I've still got the actual show hanging over me like a big black raincloud. And now I know for sure that they're using my footage. Because of course they are. Why wouldn't they?

'Andrew, I need you to understand that I really don't care about this. The show was a mess and them using that clip is actually the least of my worries, as I thought you would understand by now. So please can you chill out about your sister looking like a slag? I am an adult! I am twenty-nine years old! It really has nothing to do with you! Got it?'

But I don't know whether he got it or not because he hung up on me. I didn't even have time to ask him when the show is being broadcast. I suppose I could email Tilly, couldn't I? But maybe I don't actually want to know.

And then, out of nowhere, a text from Ivy.

Apparently there's a TRAILER.

Clearly she's watching whatever my brother's watching. I can't pretend it doesn't feel weird to hear from her. It makes me want to exercise caution.

This is the first time I've heard from her since our strange little exchange of texts over the holidays and I can't help but feel silly that for an instant on New Year's Eve I let my mind wander around through time and space and wonder if we were going to end up knowing each other again, wondering how far I would test my limits of caution at letting her back into my life. But here she is again.

So I hear I reply. I don't ask a question, don't invite a response. But . . . part of me can't help myself. I send another. Already had a furious call from my brother about me bringing the family name into disrepute.

The three little dots hover on the screen as Ivy composes a reply. Then they disappear. Annoyingly, I feel disappointed by this. That little spark, that flash I felt when Tilly was taking our photos, the sheer surprise at hearing from Ivy again, the strangeness of thinking about her after all this time.

I sit on the sofa – permanently saturated with the smell of Steve's weed – and nibble at my nail, which is something I never do so I must be agitated. I stand up, then I change my mind and sit down again. I take a breath as if I'm about to say something even though no one's there, then stand up again and stomp upstairs to get my laptop.

When I'm back on the weed sofa, I check the phone again. Nothing. I wonder what she was going to say to me before she changed her mind. I open the laptop and search for the trailer. The production company has uploaded it to YouTube. Do I dare watch? I suppose if my brother says the only clip of me is talking about sleeping around, then maybe it's not so bad? I summon all my mental fortitude and press play.

It takes a moment for me to realize that I'm trying to watch it from behind my hands like it's a scene from a horror film. I take my hands away from my face and slide them under my thighs on the sofa. I'm only in it very briefly, a smash cut between a montage section of people gazing affectionately at each other on a climbing wall or a guy putting his hands over a woman's grip while playing mini golf and the pair of them giggling. 'The Meet-Cute: coming 20 March' flashes up on the screen at the end. I exhale loudly. Well, on the one hand, there's no clip of me running to the toilet crying. On the other hand, it's going to be broadcast in a few weeks. Two weeks until this black cloud gets pricked and all the rain falls out onto my pretty little head.

Unsurprisingly my family are unaware of my imminent TV debut, comes Ivy's reply.

I start typing: They never did like me anyway, before deleting it. Instead I take a deep breath and write Shall we watch it together?

Oh that would be nice!

I don't presently have a TV . . . that's the only thing

199

Me either but we could watch it on my laptop? An anxiety-filled night at Shifford Towers?

Sounds like a plan! I reply while wondering if this isn't all a huge mistake.

20

Ivy lives in a studio flat at the top of a big, converted house on a wide, tree-lined street in a far corner of Islington. Her flat is tiny and full of books, which are not just overflowing from the shelves but sitting in piles on the floor, some lying open and face-down, others littered with neon post-it notes or pages torn from notebooks.

'So, this is Shifford Towers, is it?' I ask while trying to conceal how breathless I am from the interminable climb up several flights of stairs.

'I guess you could call it that. It's tiny,' she says, raking her hands through her mass of hair. 'I know that.'

'Yeah but . . . you're the only person I know who lives on their own. Like, properly on their own. Not with a partner or any random housemates.'

She nods, her curls bouncing around her face. 'I pay a lot for the privilege. But I like it. My own little nest at the top of the house, in the attic.'

'How do you manage not to bump your head every day? I wouldn't have thought that an attic flat was particularly suitable for a basketball player.'

'I don't manage! I constantly forget about the sloping ceiling.' She laughs and holds out her hand. 'Give me your jacket.'

I shrug off my chic navy wool coat. She hangs it on the back of the door, where it seems like every item of outerwear she owns is piled up on hooks. I already feel weird about being in here. About knowing her again, in any capacity.

'Do you . . . still play basketball?' I ask, hovering awkwardly, unsure what to do with myself in her space, wondering if I should be here at all.

'Oh, yeah, of course. I trek all the way to bloody Holland Park for practice.'

I grimace. 'I can't tell you the last time I was in West London.' But then I realize . . . actually I can. Katie's life drawing, the first class I ever modelled for, when I thought I saw Ivy afterwards. So it *was* her.

'Right? It's unnatural! I have my little pocket of the world and that's where I like to stay. And yet the lure of my basketball league is enough to tempt me over there. It's fun. And it's nice to have something in my life that isn't work.'

'Mmm,' I say, as if I completely identify with this. Which I do not. I have never fallen into the category of *workaholic*. 'So you work at a university?'

She nods enthusiastically. 'King's, on the Strand. I feel very lucky. Academia is a fucking bloodbath. And it feels like no one takes the humanities seriously, let alone *properly dead* humanities. Every day of my life I feel like I'm so fucking *grateful* to get to do this, when actually it's a ton of work and admin and stress and fighting tooth and nail for absolute scraps. But hey ho. I have to do something, don't I?'

'I suppose you do.' I lean awkwardly against the arm of

her sofa, wondering what we're meant to do. We're standing around, deeply unsure of ourselves.

'What did you do at university in the end?' she asks, breaking the tentative silence.

I smile, a little taken aback by the question and the realization that she really doesn't know anything about what I've been doing all this time. 'I never went,' I say, feeling myself stiffening a little.

'Oh . . . I wondered if you deferred for a year or something.'

I shake my head. 'Nope. Never did. Not getting the grades to . . . well, to go with you, that all threw me off a bit,' I say, removing from the equation my complete emotional devastation at her breaking up with me, which left me in no state to make any decisions and instead left me very much open to life carrying me off on its long meandering river of people, places and things. 'I don't regret it. I temped for a while and then my . . . well, my boyfriend at the time, his sister knew someone who worked at a magazine and so I interned there and then that turned into a job and I was a beauty journalist.'

'You had a boyfriend?' she asks, and I'm quietly entertained that of all the information I gave her, that was the bit that stuck out.

'Yeah, we were together for . . . well, a really long time. My longest relationship, actually. Which I still find hard to believe, because he's basically left no impression on my life at all,' I say. 'How about you?'

'No,' she says, shaking her head. 'I tried to make myself be interested in men, but it only proved . . . that I really . . . was . . . gay.' We both laugh, and it feels like the ice is broken a little.

'Please, take a seat,' she says, gesturing to the sofa. 'God, how formal! I don't know why I said that.' She puts her palm against her face. It's clear she feels nervous too. I'm wondering if she's regretting this.

Ivy's flat is essentially an open-plan studio flat with a kitchen off the living area, a bed boxed in by two of those Ikea Kallax shelf things that she's using as a room divider, and one other door that presumably leads to the bathroom.

I do what she tells me and sit down on the sofa, which is threadbare but still comfortable, a crochet blanket draped neatly across the back.

'This is nice,' I say, stroking the small, bright squares of the blanket, so many of them so even and neat, and wondering how many hours of labour and love went into it by whoever made it.

'Thanks,' says Ivy, 'I've got to have *something* to occupy myself on those lonely winter nights, haven't I?'

'Huh,' I say, entertained. 'I would never have had you down as a crafty bitch. I assumed some nice girlfriend of yours had made it.'

'What nice girlfriend would that be? I've not been out with anyone else since you,' she says plainly. 'Wine?'

'Always,' I murmur, reflecting on the weirdness of Ivy being single for the past decade. Maybe she's exaggerating. 'I thought maybe the woman you were in the cafe with was your girlfriend.'

'Aminah? No, she was my favourite colleague at Kings and then she got snapped up by some clever Americans.'

From the sofa, I watch as she opens the fridge door and extracts a bottle gleaming with condensation. 'I bought white . . . I assume red is still, you know, *off limits*?'

I mime gagging. 'Never red. Never, ever red. Never again. I said it at the time and I stuck to that promise!'

'I feel like most people when they say *never again* about a certain drink don't really mean it . . . especially when they're, you know . . . seventeen. But you've really stuck to your guns!'

'That's me,' I shrug. 'I'm a gun-sticker. Honestly the *smell* of red wine makes me want to die. Even now.'

Ivy opens a drawer to extract a corkscrew. 'Whose party was it?'

'Chloe's, her eighteenth.'

'Oh yeah,' Ivy says, disappearing into her memories as she yanks the cork out. 'Her family lived in that cute bungalow with the flowers outside.'

'I think I was drinking the red wine because I was upset about something.'

'You were. You didn't like that that girl was . . . well, you thought she was coming on to me.'

'Chloe's sister's friend, right?' I say, dredging up the memory from so long ago.

'How do you remember all this stuff?' Ivy pours the wine into two little tumblers and comes and joins me. 'Cheers.'

We're sitting slightly stiffly at opposite ends of the sofa, which is not particularly big, but it's clear we're very consciously keeping our distance. This is still new, we're still figuring out how to be friends, how to know each other. Cautious.

She looks thoughtful for a moment as I sip my wine from the glass. 'That was kind of weird, right?' she says eventually. 'That whole dynamic. That whole thing.'

'What in particular?'

'You know, the way we were the only girls at school who were *out* and so anyone who wanted to, you know *experiment*,' she says, rolling her eyes, 'would come to us, even though everyone knew we were together.'

I laugh, because it's true. 'I hadn't thought about that in ages. You're right.'

'It was like we were public property.'

I nod.

'Anyway! God, why did I go so deep so quickly? What's wrong with me?' she says, shaking off the cloud of memories. 'I feel like we need a bit of a do-over of . . . you know, our reunion.' I notice she's careful not to use the word *date*.

'It's funny that Marie wasn't out at school, now that she's like, extremely gay.'

'Marie! Are you two still friends?'

'Best friends,' I say with a smile.

'Cute.'

We drink our wine in silence for a while, and I wonder if she's wondering what to say to me, or if it's that I'm wondering what to say to her and she's not thinking about it at all. But every so often I glance to the side and she's glancing my way too and then she looks away and down at her glass like it's very interesting.

'I was going to say,' she says, a little embarrassed. 'I love your eyeshadow.'

'Thank you,' I say, blushing furiously and very much against my will.

'Very pretty on your blue eyes.'

'It's sort of my job to know about these things.'

'From being a beauty journalist?'

206

'Well, yes, but also from being a make-up artist now.'

'Oh, that's what you do, isn't it?' she says, shaking her head like it's the most obvious thing in the world.

'Yes, sorry, I thought I told you that last time,' I say, feeling embarrassed at the idea of re-treading the same ground.

'Sorry, I found it really hard to take stuff in that day. It was such a weird, unexpected thing. I had no idea that was what I was walking into and then to have to see you again like that, with no warning, and then with all those producers trying to drag me off to tell me to ask you very personal questions and all the cameras everywhere . . .' she says, basically saying word-for-word exactly what my experience was, and making me feel weird because I'd assumed she felt fine about the whole thing, all chill and breezy.

'I know what you mean,' I say. I want to lighten the mood. 'I also have another job. Well, I have two other jobs but one is working in my mate's cafe. And then on top of that, I have a very infrequent but still actually paying job as a life model.'

'The kind who does not wear clothes?' Her face is animated with an expression of gentle amusement.

'Is there any other kind?' I say, grinning. 'I consider it a public service. Arts education or something.'

'Very noble. Are any of them any good?' she asks.

'Well, there was one I really loved the first time I ever did it. I actually bought it off the artist. Since then, they're all pretty good but I try not to look at them in case I want to take home another picture of myself and then my home will be filled with naked portraits of me.'

'I don't know why but it completely makes sense that you would do this. You were always . . .' she says, before stopping herself.

'Always what?' I ask cautiously, curiously.

'What I was going to say was that you were always very unselfconscious about taking your clothes off,' she says, blushing furiously. 'But I forgot that's not . . . really . . . you know, maybe the right thing to say right now. Maybe that would be a weird thing to say. But now I've said it, so I've probably made everything even more weird and awkward.'

'It's OK,' I reassure her, glad to be the one reassuring rather than the one receiving the reassurance. 'It's funny to think of the things you remember about me. What things have stayed in your mind. I never thought my, er, relaxed attitude to getting naked would be one of them.'

Neither of us know what to say at this point, and we lapse back into a heavy silence.

Ivy clears her throat. 'So . . . what did you do today?'

'I was at the cafe, which was same old same old, but then I got an email about another make-up job in a couple of weeks so that should be fun.'

'That's great,' she says. 'Is it a . . . fashion shoot?'

'Yeah, an e-commerce shoot.'

'What does that mean?'

'So you know if you're buying clothes online, the models that are wearing the clothes in the photos,' I explain.

'Oh, OK,' Ivy says. 'That's cool! Congratulations.'

'Thanks,' I say, smiling, because I can tell that Ivy doesn't buy clothes online very often and I find her slightly ramshackle assemblage of outfits annoyingly charming. My eyes flick down over her outfit and I see a veritable blast from the past. 'Is that . . . ?' I ask, narrowing my eyes at her T-shirt.

'Oh, you mean this old thing?' she says, her dark eyes dancing with glee, as she gestures with a magician's flourish and leaps to her feet.

I sigh, grudgingly charmed and amused. It's a My Chemical Romance T-shirt, identical to one she used to wear Back In The Day.

'It's not the same one, is it?'

'It *literally* is!' she says, clapping her hands in delight. 'I thought you would enjoy a little blast from the past.'

'I feel like I've had quite a lot of those recently,' I say, which comes out more flatly than I had intended.

Ivy blinks her inky eyelashes at me like she's not sure what to say to that, then glances up at a clock on the wall, one of those cat clocks with the big eyes and the tail that ticks left and right with every second. 'So, if it's on at nine, maybe we should eat soonish?'

'Sure,' I say brightly, to compensate for sounding unhappy.

'I was thinking a roasted vegetable tart,' she says, rising to her feet and taking the few steps over to the kitchen. 'If that's OK with you?' She pulls a few things out of the fridge and plonks them on the small work surface before rummaging in cupboards for the other ingredients.

'That's great with me,' I say cheerfully. 'I'll come and help you.'

'No, please, you chill.'

'No way,' I say, standing up. 'Give me an easy job.'

'If you insist,' she says, sliding some carrots down the work surface. There's barely room for two people in this little kitchen area but I'm determined to make myself useful.

Ivy glances over at me as I pick up a knife and lay my hand on the carrot to steady it. She places her hand over the top of mine in a gesture that's so intimate it shocks me. 'Ever since I heard Nigella say she never cuts carrots into rounds, I always cut them into little batons.'

'Oh,' I say, 'OK.'

'She says she finds round carrots depressing, and I'm inclined to agree with her.'

'Well, could the domestic goddess ever be wrong?' I say, trying to shake off the intense heat left behind by Ivy's touch.

'So true,' says Ivy, who appears to be experiencing absolutely no feelings at all. Other than sworn allegiance to Nigella Lawson.

'I was on vegetable duty with my brother at Christmas, if only I had known about this then.'

'How *is* your brother?! I had completely forgotten about him!' Ivy says, delighted.

'He's . . . well, he's Andrew!'

'Still uptight then?' Her throaty laugh takes me by surprise and it's all I can do not to smile.

'Just a bit,' I say, rolling my eyes. I remember Ivy always found him hard work, judgemental even as a teenager, always on at her about why she would possibly want to study a dead culture, dead languages at all, let alone at university level, when she *clearly had the aptitude* for maths and statistics, which he thought of as real subjects. 'He's got *three* kids now.'

'Three?!' Ivy says, disbelieving.

'And that's not all, there's another one appearing in a few months.'

'But if you have more than three kids you have to get a special kind of car to fit them in!'

'Look, you don't have to tell *me* that. I don't even want one, let alone four.'

'What are they called?' she asks, pushing a lock of hair out of her face with the back of her wrist in a gesture that I find annoyingly appealing.

'Erin is the oldest, then Maisie, then Matilda's the baby.'

'Three girls? Wow, we love a matriarchy.'

'Right? I hope the fourth is a girl too.'

'Or a boy so they can treat him like a little dolly when he's tiny and then teach him how to live with women as he grows up.'

'I suppose that wouldn't be so bad.'

'I find children's names really funny now,' she says, smiling.

'Do you know what . . . I did think of you when the trend for old people names started a few years ago,' I grudgingly admit.

'I was born at precisely the wrong time. Too young to be an actual old lady called Ivy, much too young to be a child with a reclaimed old lady name.'

'I'm always curious to see what the limit is,' I say, sliding my elegant carrot batons down the work surface to her. She was right – well, Nigella was right – they do look less depressing. 'Like, eventually will people run out of, you know, *nice* old people names and then they'll have to move on to the more niche ones.'

'You mean, will we see a boom in babies called Norman in a year or two?'

'Exactly.'

'You could suggest it to your brother. Norman for a boy, Norma for a girl.'

I clap my hands together in glee. 'Can you imagine?' I say, before wondering if all this is feeling too cosy and chummy and how I feel about that.

One thing I *do* feel good about is the delicious dinner we make. We eat it from enamel plates using vintage cutlery with brightly coloured plastic handles at her small gateleg table.

'Can you believe this flat has a dishwasher?' Ivy says, neatly stacking the machine. 'Best day of my life when I discovered it wasn't a fake cupboard.'

'The dream!'

'What's the time?' Ivy asks from over her shoulder.

'Ten to nine,' I tell her.

'God! I'm nervous, aren't you?'

'Of course I am!' I burst out, incredulous. 'I've been veritably shitting myself since the day we filmed it! I look so stupid!'

'Ohhh, I bet you don't,' Ivy says, frowning at me. 'I saw a Facebook ad for it yesterday using one of those photos Tilly took of us with the fake flowers. It actually looked quite cute, you know?'

She's got her back to me, closing the dishwasher. I don't know what to say to her. By the time she turns around again, the moment has passed.

Finally, it is nine o'clock. We sit side by side on her sofa and open the on-demand service for the channel showing *The Meet-Cute*. Of course Ivy doesn't have a TV. Her laptop is old and it keeps buffering, but finally it creaks into action.

A jaunty theme tune and the title card appear, followed by short clips of lots of people talking about their friend or family member that they're putting forward for a date. And then . . . Mum.

'I'm Janice!' Mum looks very groomed, very chic in a brilliant white shirt and big pearl earrings. 'And I'm Fran's mum! I want Fran to find true love because she's so . . . well, she's so full of life and I want her to find someone to share that with!' Oh, God, is my mum really going to make me cry? When I think of storming into the shop and continuing my meltdown at her . . . well, it doesn't feel good. All she wants is for me to be happy.

'God, your mum was always such an angel, wasn't she?' Ivy says, not taking her eyes off the screen, but her voice soft with nostalgia.

Then a sharply dressed skinny guy with grey hair and thick-rimmed glasses smiles a gleaming grin at the camera. 'I'm Marco,' he says in a strong Italian accent, 'and I work with Ivy. She's permanently single and, yes, she seems pretty happy, but I love the idea of her *finally* meeting someone great. I put her forward because she *never* goes on dates and doesn't use dating apps. How is she ever going to meet someone that way?!'

Ivy gestures to the laptop, laughing. 'Marco is always trying to set me up with his friends! Most people want to cut out the middle man, but Marco clearly thought he would have more luck in this quest by introducing one. He feels terrible about it now, of course, knowing we got paired up . . .' she mumbles. Even though I could have said exactly the same thing, I feel irrationally wounded by this, like she should be happy we were paired up, happy we were brought back together. And then I feel sick that I feel that way, that my emotions, my inclination towards the romantic, the dreamy, the optimistic, is already taking over me.

I'm about to ask her about what he said, about her being permanently single, but before I can, Mum is back on the screen. 'I would like Fran to meet someone who's calm . . .

you know, to balance her out because she can be quite, well, all over the place . . . impulsive, I suppose is the word . . . and . . .' Mum thinks for a moment, pulling a face I've seen her make a thousand times but I'm sure she didn't realize she made until she watched this, 'someone *tall* because I know she likes tall people . . . someone not boring! I can't bear the thought of Fran with someone boring!'

I can't help but laugh at that.

Cut to Marco: 'I think Ivy worries she's boring because people think classicists are old men that are, how do you say, dusty,' he says, smiling. 'But Ivy proves that's not true. I would love to see her with someone vibrant who brings out her more playful side . . . someone confident and fun.'

Oh look, it's me again! 'I used to be a serial monogamist, but . . . not so much these days. Now I'm in an exploratory phase . . . that's a euphemism for sleeping around. I guess you could say I'm just sleeping around right now.' I suppose that's proof I'm 'confident and fun' and able to bring out Ivy's 'more playful side'. Evidence that, on paper, we are a great match!

'God!' I say, clutching a pillow on Ivy's sofa in sheer mortification. 'Why, why, and *why* did I ever say that?'

She doesn't take her eyes off the screen but reaches out and reassuringly rubs the back of my neck for a few seconds. 'It's all right,' she murmurs, and it's as if for a moment we've forgotten there's no closeness here, no intimacy, that we, essentially, don't know each other. It's like she's reached through time.

The screen switches from me to Ivy, her watchful eyes focused on Tilly, who is sitting off-camera. 'Yeah, you know what? I think my friends are right. I do need to make time for some love in my life. Or at least . . . some romance. Or at least . . .' she laughs and shakes her head. 'Something other than work and listening to true crime podcasts!'

And then there's a shot of me: I'm walking across the square to the restaurant in my blue dress. I'm so full of hope! No idea what's around the corner! I watch myself be shown to the table, where I sit down and wait. And then . . . Ivy, slinking in, wearing that cool black blazer, her mass of hair framing that pale face, the strong nose, the heavy eyebrows, her fluid way of moving that hasn't changed since we were teenagers.

To see myself see her again for the first time in years makes my breath catch in my throat. No wonder I had a meltdown. And the meltdown is, of course, inevitable. It is coming! The horror!

The scene is cut so it's immediately obvious to the audience that we knew each other and that this is an unwelcome surprise, so me storming off and crying in the toilets (unsurprisingly *without* a producer offering me a grand) makes perfect sense.

'This is so mortifying I literally can't cope,' I say, holding a green velvet cushion over my face even though I can still hear the stilted conversation of our 'date' on the screen.

'It's not so bad,' Ivy says, still trying to reassure me. 'If anything, it makes *me* look like the villain!'

'You *are* the villain!' I wail, throwing the cushion at her.

'No way!' she says, throwing it back at me. 'I was minding my own business, going on a date on national TV and then . . . this!'

'God! I can't believe I'm watching!' I say, staring open-mouthed in horror at the laptop.

215

'At least it'll be over soon and then we don't have to worry about it anymore,' she says, very sensibly, her eyes still fixed on the screen. She's right – the black cloud hanging over my head will be gone, turned to very embarrassing raindrops.

Finally, the meal is over and it's time for our post-date verdict. There we are, sitting side by side against the *The Meet-Cute* backdrop: yet another location of me showing myself up.

'I can't watch this!' I say, covering my eyes with one hand, the other gripping the sofa cushion in between me and Ivy. And then I feel her hand on mine, a light, warm touch, the brush of her thumb across the back of my hand. As suddenly as I felt it, it's gone again. Did I imagine it?

'Well!' she says, as soon as our segment is over.

'Well . . .' I say.

Ivy jumps to her feet and slams the laptop shut. 'I don't think we need to watch any more of *that* now, do we?'

'No,' I say. I sigh heavily. 'That was horrible but . . . in a way it wasn't as bad as I expected.'

She chews her lip pensively. 'I know what you mean. I feel like I'd built it up in my mind for months. I'd probably inflated a lot of it in my brain anyway.'

'You didn't really have anything to be scared of,' I say, laughing a little bitterly.

'Why?'

'You weren't the one having a meltdown! You retained your dignity! You got to be the cool cucumber!'

'It's still very out of my comfort zone to be on TV!' Ivy protests.

'I guess so,' I concede. I look at the clock on the wall and it's already after ten and I'm on the complete opposite side of

216

London but, more than anything, I want to be the one that leaves rather than Ivy deciding I've outstayed my welcome. 'I should get going.'

'Are you sure?' she says, and she almost sounds disappointed. But I am sure.

'Yeah, got to get back home. All the way in Honor Oak at the moment. Got to cruise down the orange line . . .' I say, doing an awkward cruising motion with my hand.

'All right.' She nods and smiles at me, and I wonder if this is the last time I'll see her, since we have no reason to see each other anymore, or rather, as it feels now, no *excuse* to.

I pick up my coat and open the door, and she pulls me into a tight hug for the first time since we were eighteen. She smells the same. I always wondered if it was some product she used, a shampoo, a detergent, but now I realize it's . . . her. Ivy.

'I'm glad we suffered through this together,' she says, leaning her head against mine for a moment too long as we hug.

'Mmm, me too,' I say, my heart fluttering a little, against my better judgement.

As I walk down the many flights of stairs from her garret, I feel a twin sense of relief and loss. Relief that the show is out and it's not hanging over me anymore, no matter how embarrassing it was for me. And loss? Well, maybe I'd got used to the idea of knowing Ivy again.

When I tap my phone on the scanner at the station I see the screen is already filled with notifications from people who've seen my little performance. Oh God. I don't think I'm enjoying my fifteen minutes of fame. I take a seat at the back of the bottom deck and grudgingly open my texts.

Marie: OK so I get why you were stressed but I don't think the super injunction was really necessary!!! Obviously you had your little meltdown but I think in general you came across well? And Ivy has truly grown into her Patti Smith vibes hasn't she??? Don't remember her being this hot at school, just saying xx

Mum: Can't bloody believe I went on TV with that tuft of hair sticking up! Silly me!

Vic: I still can't get over the fact they paired you up with her! That's so insane! What are the odds! Was weird to see you on TV!

And it doesn't stop there. The messages keep coming all the way home. There's even one from George, not known for getting in touch unless he wants to sleep with me.

Jameel's girlfriend said she saw you on TV, sorry it was a bit of a car crash haha

But, amid all of the sweet and excited messages from friends and acquaintances, there are also . . . the other ones. An edited selection from my Instagram inbox:

How can one person be so fat

The only reason your date didn't get up and walk out at the sight of you is because she already knew you. Disgusting whale.

Fran, I saw you on The Meet-Cute and I wanted to say that I'm worried about you and want to help. You're such a pretty girl but it's really not healthy to be as big as you are. I used to be a big girl myself and I know how unhappy I was, but now I'm a group leader at The Wellness System. You should come to one of our meetings and get started on a path to a happier, healthier you.

I'm all for body positivity but you're taking the piss 😒

Hi Fran! I hope this message finds you well! I wanted to drop you a message as I saw you on The Meet-Cute and thought you might be interested in our product. Invigaron is a new holistic wellness brand that uses supplements derived from berries to help you lose weight fast!

Always nice to have a reminder that however joyful and delectable a life you manage to create for yourself in this shitty world, there are always going to be tragic losers who want to drag you back into their pathetic mindset of self-flagellation.

21

I got changed about six times before tonight's date. Obviously, I always want to look hot and cool and babely, but there's something about going out with another stylish fat woman that makes me want to bring my A-game.

It doesn't help that this March has brought especially wintery weather that is definitely *not* conducive to me looking my best (baby needs flirty sundresses and little jumpsuits!) but eventually I settle on a seventies-inspired kind of Western-looking shirt tucked into high-waisted jeans and my favourite pair of saddle shoes.

I'm extremely blessed that I'm flat-sitting for Davide, my photographer friend, once again while he's on assignment in South Africa. One of his biggest clients is a chain of game reserves and they've opened a new safari lodge that they want him to photograph, and are willing to fly him out to do so. Lucky for some. The flat is *delightful*, all high ceilings and period features, and although I definitely could property-catfish my date into believing it's mine, I am going to be a good girl and admit it's not even vaguely my flat. But I'm getting ahead of myself. Who says tonight's date is even going to lead to such a thing?

The first words out of my date's mouth are, 'I have that top.'

'What great taste you have,' I say, flashing her a smile.

'Tell me about it.'

I take a seat next to her on the emerald velvet bench. The room is arranged with all the seating looking out facing the bar.

'This is nice, I've never been here before, have you?'

'Yeah, a few times,' she says. 'Don't judge me, but you do develop some particular *haunts* when you end up going on loads of dates.'

'No judgement here,' I say, casting my eyes over the cocktail list. 'I sexually identify as a fat slag.'

'I cannot tell you how happy that makes me,' she says. I'm about to ask Nicole about her dating life, since it does seem to be nearly as prolific as mine, when she catches sight of my hand resting on the table.

'Is that . . . ?' She squints at the colour of my nails. 'Can I touch your hand?'

'Sure!' I say. She picks it up and looks intently.

'OPI Miami Beet?'

'The very same.'

'A classic!' she says. 'I love that colour.'

'I hate it when I have to do nails as part of my make-up jobs, but sometimes I get asked to when it's a . . . well, a cheaper client that doesn't have the budget to hire a manicurist. Those days, I just have to cross myself and pray for a steady hand.'

'I feel like make-up artists have pretty steady hands as it is, right?'

'Yeah, I guess. But nails are not my strong point!'

'I bet being a make-up artist is amazing,' she says, pouring us glasses of water from the big, heavy jug on the round marble table in front of us.

'I don't want to oversell myself! I'm not like . . . Lisa Eldridge or anything.'

She shrugs. 'Oversell yourself. No one else is going to, right?'

'I guess not,' I say, smiling. 'But yeah, it's a fun job. I've been lucky recently, I'm getting more and more work. Bridal and e-commerce mostly.'

Nicole nods thoughtfully. 'Your make-up looks banging, I've got to say.'

'Well, thank you,' I say. I feel a little disarmed at being confronted with someone as confident as I am. 'So, what do you do?'

Nicole sighs. 'I work in sales at a jewellery brand, but me and some friends are working on launching a clothing line. But it's expensive and hard work and a lot to figure out so . . .'

'The world needs more cool clothes for fat women. Assuming that's what you're doing?'

'Yeah, which is adding to the strrrress,' she says, elongating her r dramatically. 'It's actually amazing how backwards fashion stuff is about bodies. It properly blows my mind and it's my own fucking *life*, you know? Like I should have surely experienced all the various ways that people and companies can be arseholes to me because I'm fat, but every day brings a new discovery.'

'Tragically, it doesn't surprise me,' I say. 'I used to be a beauty journalist and the absolute shit I had to listen to from my colleagues on a daily basis was enough to make me want to curl up under my desk and fucking die. I mean, there were a few normal people there too, but the culture . . . absolute bullshit.'

'Is that how you got into make-up?'

'Yeah, I think a lot of people actually go the other way – start out as make-up artists then use their expertise to start writing about it, but I found I was so sick of either churning out the same old shit or having to really *reach* to find new stuff to cover. Like beauty tech – how many people do you actually know who have one of those weird blue light face mask things that make you look like a robot?'

'Precisely zero.'

'Exactly! And there I was writing about these £500 contraptions like it was normal!'

The waiter comes and takes our orders before floating away again.

'Your skin looks amazing,' I say to Nicole. 'Maybe you should be a make-up artist.'

'Nah,' she says, shaking her head. 'I know how to do my own make-up. I've got my own mad little methods. But I wouldn't want to be responsible for someone else's face. Plus, who can be bothered to wash their brushes as often as make-up artists have to?'

'Genuinely, not even lying, it is the worst part of the job. And you can't skip it! It must be done!'

'Even trying to clean my foundation sponge makes me want to die.'

'You can't imagine how many brushes I use in an average shoot,' I say, shaking my head.

'Well, play your cards right and once we're ready to launch the brand, I'll put in a good word for your services.'

'You haven't seen my work yet; it might look like absolute shit and then you'll have to backtrack.'

'Nah, you've got a good vibe. Plus I naturally trust other fat babes,' she says.

I smile. 'Me too.'

The waiter returns with our drinks and Nicole and I clink our glasses together. As she's taking a sip of her short, strong cocktail, I let my eyes pass over her. She's so different from Ivy that it strikes me she was probably the perfect person for me to meet right now. Cute, pretty, doll-features with big lips and perfectly done Instagram make-up and bouncy blond hair. She's absolutely beautiful.

'Dating as a fat girl is kind of an interesting thing, I've found. Like . . . it's not as bad as I expected it to be?'

Nicole thinks for a moment. 'Yeah, I think it depends how you approach it. Like I have a mate who took absolutely *no* fucking agency at all with the whole thing and ended up meeting loads of losers, so I think it's definitely possible to have a terrible time of it. But in general, yeah, I agree, you know. I mean, I get fucking bullshit sexist messages as much as the next woman, and there's often a little sprinkling of fatphobia in there for good measure, but it's not like it's impossible to meet good people.'

'You know what I love? When some rando messages you with something sexual about how *hot you are, baby* and you don't reply because it's a rando, and then they message you again because they don't know how to read your very obvious signals, and then you reply to say *thanks but no thanks, Mr Rando,* and then they reply like—'

'*Fuck you, fat bitch, I wouldn't sleep with you in a million years, you disgusting sack of fat?*' Nicole interjects.

'Precisely!' I say, bursting out laughing.

'It's a wild ride,' she says, widening her eyes. 'Full of contradictions.' She takes a delicate sip of her cocktail. 'You know how you know you're actually fat?'

'How?' I ask, curious.

'When you call yourself fat, no one tells you you're not fat.'

'Interesting theory . . .' I narrow my eyes and try to cast my mind back, wondering if she's on to something.

'They might say, *Don't call yourself fat!* Or, *You're not fat, you're beautiful*, because they can't fathom the idea that you see yourself as both. But they never straight up disagree with the categorisation.'

'God, that's such a classic! I get messages from random men all the time telling me off for using the word fat in my dating profile! Can you imagine having the audacity?' I say, shaking my head.

Nicole laughs. 'Babe, I'm pretty audacious, but not *that* audacious.' It's when she calls me *babe*, which sounds so gentle and affectionate coming out of her mouth, that I realize that while I'm having the best time with her, I'm already second-guessing myself. Are we too similar? Or am I only looking at her through that lens because she's fat and fun and confident? If she was exactly the same person but in a thin body, would I be questioning this at all? She reaches out and touches the fringing on my top. 'This looks good on you.'

'Thanks,' I say, blushing.

'Obviously I'm kind of obsessed with fashion in general, but I was in a charity shop the other week and I found this copy of that fucking . . . you know that Trinny and Susannah book from the early noughties, like 2001 or 2002 or whatever – I'm pretty sure my mum actually owned a copy at the time – and ever since then I've been obsessed with looking at everyone's outfits through the lens of *will this look absolutely fucking grotesque in twenty years?* I literally can't stop thinking about it! It's like I'm turning my razor-sharp fashion eyeballs on everyone, all the time!'

'I mean . . . yeah, I feel like a lot of stuff will!' I laugh. 'Even if it looks perfectly reasonable now! Because that's how trends work!'

'It's tough, man,' she says, shaking her head. 'Wanting to know what's going to last and what's fashion nonsense we'll laugh about in a decade.'

'The thing is, a lot of the trends of the past few years were a rehash of really nineties-looking stuff. All the chunky trainers and those little sunglasses. And even a year before that popped off, I would have said no way could it make a comeback because it's objectively too ugly. And there it was! A trend! I had to accept that I didn't know shit anymore and that I was glad I wasn't a teenager who had to actually be invested in this stuff.'

'Dark times, being a teenager. But *unfortunately*,' Nicole says, taking an elegant sip of her second cocktail, 'I do have to be interested in this stuff. I've been working on this brand with my mates Serena and Lola, though Lola mostly helps us in a sort of advisory capacity because she works in fashion. It's mostly me and Serena's thing. Cool clothes for fat chicks.'

Nicole is so pretty it's like looking at someone through a beautifying filter on Instagram. Maybe I should tell her that. But not right now. Too soon. Would it kill you to play it a little bit cool, Fran? It would not.

I sip from my third cocktail, the smoky taste working its

way up the straw. 'Obviously, you're really hot,' I begin, realizing that yes it may well kill me to play it cool.

'Obviously,' she says, flicking her long, blond hair over her shoulder.

'But I felt from your profile and your messages that you were also really funny and then I got all up in my head about what my laugh sounds like . . . as in, how do I laugh? It's not something I'd thought about before and then I couldn't stop thinking about it? But then I concluded that if I had a weird laugh then I would probably know about it by now because people love pointing shit like that out to you, don't they?'

'Give us a laugh,' she says, winking roguishly at me like an old man in a pub.

'What, now?'

'Yeah, go on, practise,' Nicole says, taking the straw out of her cocktail and drinking it from the rim.

'Ha-ha-ha,' I say with a joyous expression on my face.

'No! Do it properly!'

'I can't remember how to laugh!' I protest.

'Just laugh! Like this!' And she lets out a charming, resonant laugh. I try to copy her, and in copying her I feel so silly that I actually start laughing.

'See!' she says. 'Now do an evil laugh like you're a Bond villain and you've pushed the big red button to blow up the world.'

I pause for a moment, wondering how cartoonish to go. 'Mwa-ha-ha!'

'More evil!'

I furrow my brow in an approximation of real seriousness. 'MWA-HA-HA!'

Nicole joins in and before long we're both really, properly, hysterically laughing.

'This is fun,' she says. 'Are you having a good time?'

'People don't often ask you that.'

'I think people should ask each other that *more*,' she says emphatically.

'I am having a good time. Are you having a good time?' I ask, smiling, because I know the answer.

'I am having a good time,' she says, and I feel her hand slide along the seat towards mine. I don't move mine away. Why would I? I feel like she's done enough in terms of stating her interest, so I lean in and kiss her. She kisses me back and I realize she's the first fat girl I've ever kissed in my life and I'm almost distracted from the kiss by thinking about how completely wild that is.

'Where do you live?' I ask.

'Stratford, you?'

I have to think about it for a moment, which is *maybe* a sign that I need to find somewhere more permanent. 'I'm house-sitting in Clapton at the moment,' I say, looking at her face up close, its beautiful smoothness, the thickness of her eyelashes, the smell of her perfume.

'Before this goes any further,' she says, which makes my stomach drop because it's, let's face it, the kind of thing that generally precedes something I don't want to hear.

'Yes?'

'I'm really not looking for anything serious at the moment.'

Phew. Phew! Extreme phew!

'I'm really busy with this project, and in general, I feel like I've hit capacity with the number of people I'm seeing right now . . . but you're really hot so I didn't want to miss the opportunity to meet you.'

'Oh, great,' I say, putting my hand against my chest in relief. 'I thought you were going to say something, you know, *bad*. Like your vagina is haunted.'

'OK so I'm glad that was your first thought, but no.'

'It's all good,' I shrug. 'I'm not either. But you're hot. And fun.'

'I feel like *friend you have sex with* is a category that more people should take advantage of.'

'I completely agree,' I say, before summoning an Uber.

If tonight has taught me anything, it's that there most definitely *is* life after the cringe-inducing misery of a TV date. Coming face to face with Ivy has not been able to *completely* throw me off my game.

The post-sex chat with Nicole is almost as interesting as the sex itself. I guess because I'm very chill about my body I hadn't considered how fun it could be to have a fat ally in my bed. Someone to talk to about body stuff who'll understand rather than listen politely.

'Your mum is fat too, right?' she asks me when we're lazing in bed. 'You mentioned she had that plus-size bridal shop?'

'Yeah, and she never gave me shit about my weight. Let me be. I think that saved me a lot of angst, you know?'

'For sure,' she says. 'Me and my sister have always been fat, ever since we were kids. It's like it was meant to be.'

'Written in the stars,' I say faux-dreamily, and we both giggle.

'It's funny,' she says, propping herself up on one arm and lying on her side so she can look at me while we talk. 'You know the narrative is very much *inside every fat person is a thin person trying to get out*?'

'I am unfortunately familiar with this concept, yes.'

'Well,' Nicole says, furrowing her brow in thought. 'Don't you think it's the opposite?'

'How do you mean?'

'Like don't you think it seems as if a lot of thin people spend their lives punishing themselves and restricting themselves and denying them things to stop the fat person inside them getting out?'

'Huh,' I say. 'I guess you're right.'

She shrugs. 'Something I've noticed.'

'Hey . . .' I smile. 'I'm glad we met. It's cool to have a fat babe on the scene. Therapeutic or something.'

'Yeah, and fucking hot,' she says, reaching over and pulling me towards her for another kiss.

Hanging out in bed with Nicole is good for the body, the soul and the mind. When she leaves, I feel like my spirits have been raised without me even having to do anything. I convert the good vibes into a much-needed cleaning session.

Despite all my dates, despite all the babes and the fun, I can't help but feeling Ivy rattle around my brain. Nicole has infused me with an optimism . . . a joie de vivre or whatever. I pick up my phone, then put it down, then pick it up again, second-guessing and third-guessing whether or not I should text her. I shouldn't. But I want to. I shouldn't. But I feel my fingers typing out a message to her.

Hey you! Want to get a drink sometime?

22

'As you're the only person I know who has any opinions on fashion, I wanted to run this by you,' Ivy says as her opening gambit when we slide into a booth in the pub with our pints. 'I'm thinking of getting Crocs.'

'Whoa.'

'Is it a very terrible idea?'

'No, I'm taken aback that the only reason you've come tonight is so you can ask me about Crocs,' I say, taking a sip.

'Not only that. I thought it would be fun to see you. But I do want to know about the shoes. If it's the end of March now it'll be good to be ahead of the summer footwear game, you know?'

'I'm saying . . . no.'

'What about for pottering?'

'Not even then.'

'They would be my private shoes that only I would know about.'

'I'm sorry, but you have to have some kind of limit on this stuff. I refuse to accept they're a *thing*. There are comfy shoes that are less ugly, can't you buy those?'

'I suppose so,' she says reluctantly. 'I thought you might be into them for avant-garde reasons, like those cool weird eye earrings you have.'

'My antiques!' I say, delighted she's noticed them.

'So, are you finding everyone you've ever known is crawling out of the woodwork to tell you they saw you on TV, or is that just me?'

'Not just you,' I say, laughing. 'I've also been flavour of the month on my dating apps.'

'I bet you have,' she says with a smile. She holds my gaze with her dark eyes until I have to look away, feeling my cheeks flush.

'So,' I say, wanting to dispel my awkwardness. 'How was work today? Tedious enough to make you want to turn to drink?'

'You got it,' she says. 'How about you?'

'Well,' I begin, about to mention my various dates, maybe even meeting Nicole because she's so cool, but then I second-guess myself and hold back.

'What?' Ivy frowns at me.

'Nothing. It's just I was going to tell you about some dates I went on and then I was like *is it weird to talk about this with her?* So I stopped myself, but here we are anyway.'

She shrugs. 'You can talk to me about whatever you want.'

'I know that. It's a question of whether I want to.'

'Because . . . ?'

'Because it's weird, I guess? Because I'm only now getting my head round the idea of knowing you again, and having uncomfortable feelings to go with it,' I say, in as neutral a voice as I can. Because the truth is that I do feel uncomfortable with the little fizzing of attraction I've been feeling for Ivy. The push and pull of wanting to spend time with her, wanting her to like me, wanting *something* from her, against the knowledge that it didn't work out last time so why would it work out now, and the reality that I don't know what it *means* for me to want something from Ivy.

'I understand,' she says gently. 'I feel like it must be asking a lot for you to have a friendship with me. But I'm enjoying it, aren't you?'

It's the way my head swims a bit at the word 'friendship' that makes me 100 per cent sure my feelings for Ivy are back with an absolute vengeance.

'Or are you not?' Ivy says, her eyes wide and cautious when I don't answer straight away.

'Of course I am,' I say, giving her a reassuring smile.

She reaches her hand across the table and squeezes mine. 'Good.' Do my other friends touch me like this? I guess I spend so much time with dates that I forget what the boundaries of normal friendship are. I can't imagine feeling emboldened to reach out and touch her – it wouldn't occur to me. What would it feel like to lean forward and . . .

'Excuse me?' A tentative voice cuts through my thoughts. A young woman with a blond bob and a tartan dress is leaning on our table.

'Hello?' Ivy says in a mock-seductive voice.

'Me and my flatmates over there,' she says, nodding towards a table populated by similarly young women on the other side of the pub who are looking over at us expectantly. 'We saw you on *The Meet-Cute,* well, we *thought* we saw you on *The Meet-Cute* and they sent me over to check if it was really you, because they were like *why would they be hanging out?* I mean, if it was actually you two, you know?'

'Oh!' I say, laughing a little.

'Well, times change, what can I say,' Ivy says.

'So, are you two—' the girl begins, but I cut her off.

'No, no,' I shake my head. 'We're hanging out.'

'Oh! Cool!' she says perkily. 'We thought you would make such a cute couple, you know? Like when it was on, we were sort of rooting for you to have, like, some sort of breakthrough.'

'Instead it was more break*down*,' I say.

'Either way, we were rooting for you! Maybe we still are!' she says before turning on her heels and heading back to her table of friends.

'Fascinating,' Ivy says, shaking her head. 'Fascinating. I feel like a celebrity. What was that magazine you used to read in the sixth-form common room?'

'*Heat*.'

'I feel like I'm in *Heat* magazine.'

'Weird. Very weird indeed.'

'They're not wrong, though.' She shrugs and gets to her feet before I can reply. 'Another drink?'

I watch her as she walks to the bar, watch her move confidently, easily through the pub. I watch her as she leans languidly on the bar, raking her fingers through her hair absent-mindedly and know for sure that even if I'd never seen her before in my life, she would have caught my eye in this moment.

'So,' I say, taking a sip when she presents me with my pint. 'I was wondering.'

'Ye-e-e-s?' she asks, raising one dark eyebrow. She can do that. Many talents.

236

'Were you, you know, joking or exaggerating or whatever when you said you'd never been out with anyone else since me? You mentioned it when I was at your flat to watch the show, but I didn't want to, like, *grill you* then.'

'But you want to grill me now, huh?' she says with a wolfish smile.

I shrug. 'So what if I do?'

She lets out a whistle. 'Well, in answer to your question, no I was not joking. It's true.'

'Wow . . .' I am, understandably, taken aback by this.

'It's not like I've been a nun since then. Far from it. But I've not really found it easy to connect with people on some other level. A level that would make me want to have a relationship. I like being on my own, you know? It's not a great tragedy. I love my single life, I feel very fulfilled by it.'

'You don't have to sell the perks of being single to *me* of all people,' I tell her. 'It's like we went in very different directions . . . me going from one relationship to another to another, and you going off them altogether.'

'But now we've ended up in the same place.'

'I guess we have,' I say, feeling my face flush.

We drink and chat and I try to stay present in the moment while so many thoughts are whirring around in my head, but my feelings for Ivy are flooding through my body, the raw attraction to her, the nostalgia mixed with feeling magnetically drawn to the person she's become. I know I need to stop seeing Ivy. I know I won't stop seeing Ivy.

23

'Mum, this is vile.'

'You would be surprised how many people want a proper princess dress,' she says, as she attempts to zip me into a *very* meringue-looking number. She eventually decides she's not going to be able to zip me up and instead fixes the back of the dress to my bra strap with one of her trusty bulldog clips. 'Looks nice on you, Franny.'

'No, it doesn't,' I say, frowning at my reflection in the full-length mirror. 'I look like one of those doll things that went on toilet rolls back in the day. You could probably fit a twenty-four-pack of loo roll under here, no trouble.'

'Now, look happy to be in the dress,' she instructs me as she picks up the camera from the counter.

'Fine,' I mumble and flash a smile.

'You know, Franny, the photos on our social media that have you in them always do better than ones that don't.' She snaps away at me and I vary my pose very slightly each time.

'Then you should pay me more,' I say, through a cheerful grin.

'I pay you quite enough.' It's true. She does.

'I'm glad I'm helping you. I still feel bad about how I was after the filming. Do you promise you've forgiven me?'

'You were in shock, that's all. And anyway, it didn't kill you, did it?'

'No,' I concede. 'But it *was* horrible.'

'Ooooh I know, I wish I'd had a hairbrush with me!'

'I don't think anyone's going to remember your hair sticking up, Mum.'

'That's what Alan said too, but they might! Anyway, I'm sorry it was a wasted opportunity. I really thought you might meet someone nice.'

'I know you did,' I say fondly. I wonder if I should ask who Alan is, but I decide she'll tell me about him if she wants to tell me.

'I worry about you, you know? Out there meeting God knows who, and before you know it you'll be old and your whole bloody life will be gone. Over!'

'But this *is* my life, and I like it!' I protest.

'Do you though?' She looks at me imploringly.

'I promise you that I do. It's really, really lovely of you that you want me to, *meet someone*, but I need you to know that I'm happy, that whether I meet someone or not, I'll be happy. I feel so free at the moment and that . . . well, that means a lot to me. Life feels full of potential. So yeah, I wish the TV date had been good, but it's not like that was my last and only chance of happiness.'

'Just the only one *I* was involved in.'

'Exactly.'

'If you say you're happy, baba, I'll have to believe you, won't I?'

240

'You will.'

'Now, next dress.'

I change into a satin bias-cut number in a very chic oyster colour. Absolutely beautiful, but the ultra-light fabric has creased horribly around the hem from being delivered to the shop. 'I can see someone wearing this with a big fur stole. Fake, obviously.'

'Shame we don't have one of those to hand,' says Mum. She holds the little hand steamer against the bottom of the dress. 'Tell me if I'm burning you, Franny.'

'You'll know if you're burning me because I'll be screaming.'

I'm quiet for a moment, wondering if I want to tell her or not, and then wondering why I wouldn't tell her, and then deciding to tell her. 'I've actually ended up spending a bit of time with . . .' I say, before realizing that I'm smiling involuntarily. 'With Ivy.'

She screws her face up. 'Ivy? The one who made you cry and storm in here and accuse me of trying to sabotage your life? Are you two friends now?'

'Sort of. We're on our way there. Maybe. I don't know. I saw her again when we had to take some silly photos to promote the show, and we ended up watching the broadcast together. For solidarity or something.'

'Hmm,' Mum says tightly.

'What?'

'You've changed your tune, that's all.'

'Am I not allowed to change my tune?'

'You can do whatever you want, my darling,' she says. A slight frost has descended on the shop.

We stand in awkward silence. 'Mum,' I say tentatively. 'What did you think of her? Of me and her, I mean?'

'I don't know if I thought anything.'

'I guess . . . I guess I always felt like you didn't take our relationship seriously . . .'

'You were so young, weren't you? You were only a teenager! What were you? Sixteen?'

'Yeah, when we got together.' I pause. 'I guess I wondered if you didn't take our relationship seriously because she was a girl.'

'I don't know what would give you that impression,' she says, standing up and switching the steamer off.

'It was something I wondered about.'

'I've never had a problem with whoever you want to be with. Not at all.'

'As long as I'm with *someone*,' I say, smiling, trying to lighten the mood.

'I want you to be happy.' She shrugs. 'I know it's no fun being on your own.'

I don't know how to explain to her my feelings on this without patronizing her. Should I ask her if she's lonely? And how do I explain that I'm not *looking for a relationship* because *a relationship* is not inherently good or worthy of my time? That there are worse things to be than single, especially when you find being single very fun indeed?

I feel a lump in my throat. 'I don't think it's good to be with the wrong person, either. I don't think being single is worse than that,' I tell her.

'Maybe not now,' she says. 'But when you're older you might.'

24

It's Saturday evening and I'm out with Ivy. Didn't I tell you I wouldn't be able to stay away from her?

'So you're still on your mad dating tear?' Ivy asks across the top of our third drink.

'Yeah, still riding that particular pony,' I say. Not sure why.

'No interest in a relationship?'

'I don't know . . .' Would it really be the worst thing to have a romantic relationship again? And if I was going to, would it really be the worst thing to have one with Ivy? So I continue, 'I'm trying to live in the *now*. It's not like I don't have *relationships* with the people I date or people I sleep with. You have *relationships* with everyone you come into contact with, but we've squeezed and narrowed what constitutes a relationship down into this quite specific box. It has to be romantic, it has to be sexual, it has to be exclusive, it has to be long-term. But maybe that's not what life's about. I don't know.' I can tell I'm doing some pub pontification right now but also: I'm right.

'No, you're right,' she says, picking up a peanut and putting it in her mouth, chewing thoughtfully. 'The way I see it is that you're like Dennis Rodman at the height of his fame and you need a lot of Phil Jacksons around to be your coach.'

'I don't know what any of that means.'

'Dennis Rodman, the basketball player?'

'Was he the one with, like, the *look*? Really hot? Went out with Madonna?' I shake a distant memory out of my brain.

'Yeah, that guy. And he was a super, super talented defensive player, but kind of wild and liked going off and partying and doing his own thing and it would sometimes drive the other players completely mad because he would miss practice and was generally . . . an erratic presence.'

'So that's me, right, got it,' I say, nodding. An erratic presence. 'And the other guy?'

'Phil Jackson was the coach of the Chicago Bulls, an actual legendary coach, when Dennis Rodman was on their team, and instead of trying to, like, tame him or punish him, he would kind of . . . let him go and blow off steam and then come back and play when he was ready. Because he knew that the way to get the best performance out of Rodman was to let him be himself, rather than trying to make him behave more like everyone else.'

'Huh,' I say. 'Maybe I am a bit Dennis Rodman. There are worse people to be, right?'

'Oh, definitely,' Ivy says before gulping down the remnants of her pint. 'At least he had the talent to back it up.'

'Which means I do too, right?' I say, winking at her, roguishly. Or at least that's what I'm going for and then I feel instantly embarrassed about the whole thing because that's not the vibe here! This is a friends thing! We can be friends!

'Yes, you do,' Ivy says, looking at me a little hazily.

I look at her and I'm seized with the urge to lean forward and kiss her, just to see what would happen. I want to do it so much but the thought of finding out what happens next makes me nauseous.

'I should probably get going,' I say, smushing down all thoughts of kissing Ivy.

I've got a party to attend — or rather, because it's Marie's, I should say call it a *soirée*.

'Let's do that,' she says with a slight smile.

We leave the pub and pass a bus stop with a big poster featuring a slim curvy white woman in a bikini, advertising a fast fashion brand. *YOU ARE ENOUGH* the copy reads above the name of the brand.

'Don't you miss the days when brands just wanted to make us feel like shit so we would buy stuff?' I sigh.

'You know what,' says Ivy, looking up at the model's air-brushed body. 'I do. A simpler time. Now I feel patronized.'

'I wish I could go back in time and stop body positivity from ever happening,' I mutter. 'A fucking blight on the mental landscape of the world.'

'It's funny because I think people would expect that you would be, you know, all for it,' she says, looking amused.

'Yeah, well, I don't believe it has any actual real-world impact on . . . anything at all. Like, anything. Every day I open Instagram and it's like . . . oh look, there's a throwback photo where someone *has* to acknowledge how fat and gross they used to be, oh look, there's a caption about how this person I barely know is now *four stone lighter! Happy and healthy!* and it reminds me that I truly do live on this weird fucking cloud trying not to fall into the pit of bullshit below me. If I believed in any way it had any impact on women who look like me rather than women who look like her,' I say, nodding at the poster, 'then maybe I would be a little less cynical.'

'I don't associate you with cynicism!' Ivy says, shaking her head and laughing as we start walking again. 'You're normally much too happy for that.'

'Well, we've found my limit.' I nudge her playfully, and as we walk on, I feel her hand brush against the back of my hand. Instinctively, I move mine away, like an electric shock, like she must have done it by accident. Surely she didn't do it on purpose? I look at her out of the corner of my eye and try to read her body language, try to learn something from the way she's walking, the way she's holding herself, but there's something defiantly sphinx-like in her pose.

'I think that was one of the things I liked about you,' she says. 'You were never self-conscious about your body.'

'I guess I never have been,' I say thoughtfully. 'I think it has a lot to do with my mum. She never let me worry about it. I was lucky that way. But you already know that.' Suddenly I feel embarrassed, talking about my life to Ivy. I don't know why, exactly. A little exposed, somehow.

'How is she, by the way?'

'My mum? Same as always. Always busy, always at the shop, always trying to get me to meet someone nice. I explain to her that I meet nice people all the time, but she doesn't quite go for it.'

'Ha,' says Ivy drily.

'Are your parents still kind of weird about it?'

She sighs, thinking about her answer. 'Yes and no. Yes in that they wish I was straight, no in that they've come to accept that I'm not. I think it's easier for them to accept because they don't have to see it, like I'm not bringing girls home to them. So it's not like a constant struggle with them, more this sort of . . . low-level disappointment.' She smiles, but I'm not sure if she really means it.

'I see,' I say. I always suspected that her parents had something to do with her not wanting to stay with me once she went to university. I almost want to ask her if I'm right. Maybe I should ask her? Or would it be weird for me to be asking questions about things that happened years ago? I already had a meltdown at the sight of her, so fuck it. 'I was wondering . . . did they have anything to do with us breaking up?'

She sighs in that weary way Ivy does. 'I reckon they were worried that trying to keep up a relationship with you would distract me from university. And . . . I think they were right,' she says, shrugging. 'But that doesn't mean—' She cuts herself off.

'What?' I say, curious.

'Nothing.' She shakes her head, and I know she won't tell me. 'Hey,' she says, with the enthusiasm of someone who wants to change the subject. 'This was nice. I'm glad you said yes to a little afternoon stroll.'

'You sure you don't want to come to Marie's party with me?' I ask, and I'm not sure if I want her to say yes or not. I mean, of course I want her to say yes, otherwise I wouldn't ask. But these Big Feelings for Ivy are getting in the way of my plan to spend the year being as single as humanly possible, my bachelorette lifestyle, the slag era *if you will*.

'I'm sure. For starters she didn't invite me.'

'She would be delighted to see you again!' I protest.

'Well, who wouldn't? But no. I want you to have fun and not have to babysit me.'

'If you insist,' I say, shrugging.

'I'll walk you to your bus stop, though? It's round the corner.'

'How gallant of you,' I say, fluttering my eyelashes. Out of the corner of my eye I spot a magpie hovering malevolently in a tree. I give it the tiniest, most subtle salute to ward off bad luck, trying to make it look like I'm brushing my hair off my face.

'Did you?' Ivy's face instantly lights up, her eyes flicking between me and the lone harbinger of doom, a single magpie. 'Do you still do that?!'

I sigh. 'Yes, I still do that. Just in case.'

'Just in case what?!'

'You know, *just in case*,' I say, my voice laden with cosmic meaning.

She claps her hands together in delight. 'You're so funny! I can't believe it! After all this time, you're still saluting magpies.'

'I am guided by fate,' I say serenely.

All that separates us from the bus stop is a little parade of shops, all shut up for the night except for the convenience store, emitting a piercing beep every time someone enters or leaves. We pass a cafe, a fancy haberdashery where Ivy tells me she bought one single ball of eye-wateringly expensive wool to knit a hat with, and then before the bus stop, a charity shop.

'This is a really good one,' Ivy says, nodding at the charity shop. 'I get all my best stuff from there. It's where I got my blazer.'

As we pass, in the window of the darkened shop, something catches my eye. 'Isn't that . . . ?' I say haltingly, stepping away

248

from Ivy and moving towards the window. 'That bowl there
. . .' I point at it, looking over my shoulder at her. I turn back
to look in the window. And it is. It definitely is.

On my eighteenth birthday, Ivy gave me a vase. Black, with
brightly coloured flamenco dancers painted onto it, with round,
undulating curves and a handle on either side. *Like an amphora!* Ivy
enthusiastically said, before explaining an amphora was an ancient
Greek-style vase. She'd bought it in a charity shop somewhere on
the Kent coast where she'd been with her parents, who questioned
whether this was a particularly good gift for an eighteen-year-old
girl but Ivy had told them it was completely perfect for me. And
she was right. It became my first Homely Trinket, and came with
me to every home I had, until the last one.

'What is it?' she asks, peering through the glass. 'Oh!' So it
is. So she remembers it too.

'It's the same pattern as the vase you gave me. The flamenco
dancing ladies,' I say. 'I've never seen another one, or anything
else in the same design.'

'How funny,' Ivy says quietly. 'Do you still have it? The
vase?'

I almost feel my eyes prickling when I have to say, 'No. It
got broken. A few years ago now . . . but I kept it. I always
had it out. It almost always had flowers in it.' But I don't say
*at some point it became so much part of the scenery that I managed to
forget it came from you, until every so often I would remember and my
whole body would feel flooded with nostalgia and the loss of the person
I was, the person that thought we were going to be together forever.*
'It didn't survive a party. Someone kicked it over. I'm sorry.'
But I don't say, *And then I locked myself in the bathroom and cried
about it because I felt so powerless all over again.*

'Oh,' she says, her eyebrows contracting, 'That's OK! You don't need to apologize to me! It was so long ago anyway. It's nice it lasted as long as it did. The bowl is cute, though, isn't it?'

'The vase is nicer. It was actually the nicest vase I've ever had,' I say, with a small smile.

'You should come back and get the bowl!' Ivy says reassuringly.

I shake my head. 'Nah, I don't know what I would do with it. And it would be sitting there, reminding me that it's not as good as the vase.' I give a little laugh, and we take the last few steps towards the bus stop. The indicator board says it'll be four minutes until my bus.

'Four?!' I protest, to no one in particular. 'I'm more a *due* or a one-minute kind of gal.'

'Well, at least you have me to entertain you, right?' She smiles and we sit down next to each other on the red plastic seat that only accommodates quarter of a buttock *at best*.

'You don't have to wait,' I say.

'But I want to,' she says gently.

'I accept.'

We sit in silence for a moment. At first by accident and then it feels intentional. Ivy takes a breath, turns her head towards me as if she's going to say something. But she doesn't. At first. And then.

'You know you asked about me not having had another partner since you? Well, I think it did fuck me up a lot. I mean, I know our break-up fucked you up. But it did the same to me, too. It scared me a lot, that I could do that to a person,' she says, looking out at the passing cars, not looking at me. 'It

250

made me scared of myself and of the impact I could have on someone. It feels like such a huge, heavy responsibility and I've never felt quite . . . ready to take it on again. I've preferred to, you know, stay out of it. Never hurt anyone again. So . . . if you think that what happened didn't affect me too, then I want you to know you're wrong.'

'Oh . . .' is all I can say.

'So I guess I'll see you when I'm back from my trip?'

'What trip?' I ask, taken aback.

'I . . . thought I mentioned it,' she says, running her fingers through her curls. 'Maybe I didn't . . . um, it's not like I'll be gone long . . .'

'How long?' I ask, already knowing by the look on her face she isn't off to Marbella for a week.

'Two months,' she says, not looking in my eyes. 'Eight weeks. Whichever sounds . . . shorter.'

'Right,' I say, as brightly as I can manage.

'Duke University has these Greek inscriptions it would be good for me to be able to see in real life. For my research.'

'Sure! I assume Duke University is not down the road?'

'It's in North Carolina.'

'Oh, wow,' I say, forcing a smile. 'Hope it's not . . . too hot . . . while you're there!'

Before I can figure out what I want to say beyond those inane thoughts our four minutes are up and my bus arrives.

'Well,' I say, my heart beating hard and fast. 'I'll see you . . .'

'Yeah,' she says, still not looking me in the eyes, 'see you.'

There's something about her that almost makes me wonder if she's going to change her mind at the last minute and come with me, but she doesn't.

What a strange way to end the day. It's not like I'll never see her again, but I can't help feeling that's possible. She has this hold on my brain like she's a finite resource, a precious commodity and maybe one day she will be gone for good. I've got a scarcity mindset specifically for Ivy Shifford. I suppose it's not like she hasn't done it to me before. Disappear in the blink of an eye, that is. God, I really shouldn't be putting so much energy into her. I need to devote less brain time to Ivy and more to . . . everything that isn't Ivy. I hope Marie's soirée snaps me out of it.

It's Marie's girlfriend Carly's birthday so they've invited various friends and acquaintances over to Marie's flat, which is much nicer than Carly's and doesn't come complete with flatmates. I'm deep in conversation with Carly's friend Ben, who is extremely good-looking – exactly what I need right now – and opened with the line, 'Oh, Fran, you're the famous one right? The one from TV?' Which is not a bad way to endear someone to you. We chatted about the weird experience of filming something for TV, finding out how things work behind the scenes when you're only used to seeing the finished product. Yes, this is exactly what I need to distract me from Ivy going away.

'I would have *loved* to work in TV,' he says, shaking his head. 'When I was a kid I sat about five centimetres away from the television and watched cartoons back to back, like I was trying to soak them up by osmosis. I was always too creative for banking to be bearable for any amount of time. Can I get you another drink?'

'Yes please, whatever you're having,' I say, perhaps too

breathlessly, but he is truly a babe and I am not known for my poker face. He stands up and heads to the kitchen.

'You're really hitting it off with Ben!' Carly whispers to me as she passes with a bottle of wine, precisely as I'm thinking *Oooh, I'm really hitting it off with Ben!*

'I suppose I am,' I say, a little primly.

'He's kind of fascinating, actually, he's really into—'

'Carly! I'm gasping here, babe!' Marie interrupts from across the room where she's talking to Edward, who's studiously avoiding me, and Carly dashes off to Marie with the wine, leaving me none the wiser.

Really into what? Really into *what*?

When Ben returns with the drink, he's also accompanied by Heather, another of Carly's friends, who Marie has often complained about for getting *way* too drunk on every possible occasion.

'Hi Heather,' I say, a little wearily, knowing my cosy alone time with Ben is now decidedly over. He hands me the drink as Heather plonks unceremoniously down next to me on the sofa in what was previously his seat.

'Oh, hi Fran,' she says, her eyes sliding in and out of focus.

'How are you?' I've met her once before but I can't say I know a thing about her beyond the fact she's Drunk Heather.

'Oh, you know, getting by,' she says, taking a sip. We sit in silence for a moment, me, wondering what to say next, her, apparently trying to focus on not sliding off the sofa. 'Men are *aresholes* aren't they?' she bursts out, finally. Clearly she has a bee in her bonnet.

'Many, many, many of them are. What's up? Someone wronged you?'

'Ha, you're funny,' she says, taking a large gulp of wine. 'I got *ghosted*. Again.'

'I'm sorry,' I say, pouting sympathetically. 'Did you like him a lot?'

'Yeah,' she sighs. 'I thought he was different, you know, the one?'

'How long had you been seeing each other?'

'Two weeks!'

'But you thought he was the one?'

'When you know, you *know*, Fran. You *know*.'

'I suppose so,' I say, trying to placate her. I have no skin in this game, I need to get through this conversation so I can get out and recommence my efforts with Ben.

'Are you seeing anyone? Some arsehole man? Didn't you have a girlfriend?'

'I did, you're right. But not anymore. I'm very much single now, which is great fun. Er, for me at least. Sorry it's not so fun for you.'

'Well, it *would* be fun if I didn't have to date arsehole men. You're so *lucky*.'

'I'm bi. So I get the full, er, gamut of the human experience, arseholes and otherwise,' I reassure her.

'God, you know what, I just think that it's about *people*, you know? Love is love, right?'

'Mmmm,' I say, nodding very emphatically.

'Love is love,' she says again, 'that's all there is to it, love is—' before she turns and vomits into the bowl of crisps on the side table next to the sofa.

'Marie!' I shout, holding Heather's hair out of the way. 'We have a situation!'

Marie looks over and rolls her eyes, exasperated. 'Coming,' she sighs.

I rummage in my bag for a hairclip left over from the long hair days (what? You're telling me you clean out your bag more than once a year?) and clip her hair back while Marie whisks away the bowl and returns with a larger, empty bowl and a glass of water.

'God, I didn't know she was *that* fucked,' Marie says.

'Love is love!' Heather wails before she picks up a pillow, puts it under her head and promptly falls asleep on the arm of the sofa.

'Hey, how's stuff with you and Carly these days?' I ask Marie quietly, scanning the nearby bodies to make sure she's not within earshot.

'Tiring,' Marie says with a weak smile. 'Maybe we can chat later when it's chilled out a bit and Carly's passed out like this one.' She nods down at Heather, dead to the world.

I hope that Heather's digestive pyrotechnics don't alter the vibe too much, because Ben's caught my eye from across the room. He smiles at me, and I take that as an invitation to go over.

'Now you've seen Heather's party trick. Making her dinner reappear out of nowhere,' he says drily. 'Things . . . seem to be winding down.' He swallows. 'I was thinking, I don't live far from here . . .' He looks around the room, not meeting my eyes. 'We could have another drink at mine if you like? Unless that's too forward of me?'

Jackpot! 'Not too forward at all. I would definitely have . . .' I pause, smiling a little. 'Another drink with you.'

We subtly extricate ourselves from the party, but not so

subtly that Marie doesn't notice we're leaving at the same time. As I hug her goodbye, she whispers, 'Get in there, my son!' and I hiss at her to shut up. Ben did not lie, he doesn't live far from Marie. His flat is a tastefully decorated first-floor conversion where he lives on his own. Clearly working in banking wasn't *that* unbearable.

Before long we're making out on the sofa, as God intended. Maybe we won't even make it to the bedroom, although I do kind of need a wee . . .

'Where's your bathroom?' I ask, getting to my feet.

'The second door on the left out there,' he says, nodding in the direction of the hallway.

He can see me from the sofa and cranes his neck to direct me to the bathroom.

'Not that door!' he says suddenly, when I put my hand on the doorknob.

'Sorry!' I withdraw my hand from what is presumably the *wrong* doorknob.

My curiosity spikes. Memories of reading *Jane Eyre* in the sixth form flash through my head. Does the spare room contain his ex-girlfriend? I'm already wondering if I'm going to end up on a true crime podcast.

'The bathroom's the next door,' he says.

'Oh . . . OK,' I say, smiling weakly, wondering what's in that room.

'It's nothing weird,' he blurts out, his eyebrows jumping up his forehead. 'And it's not a . . . a sex thing.' Does he understand that all of this makes me more desperate to know what he's up to in there? I assume so.

'Look, it's fine, I totally respect your privacy,' I say breezily, deciding to reverse-psychologize him into thinking I'm not that interested.

He sighs, and I can already tell he's unable to resist giving me the details. Classic. 'It's . . . it's where I work. I'm a brick master.'

I cock my head inquisitively. Yes, I need a wee, but more than any bodily function I need to know what one of *those* is. 'A brick master, you say?'

'Lego bricks,' he says, with a casual shrug.

'Oh,' I widen my eyes, hoping he tells me more.

'Yeah, I quit my job, focus on that at the moment.'

I try to find a polite way to ask but fail. 'You . . . you quit your job to do Lego?'

'I make YouTube videos,' he says, looking at me very seriously. 'I have my channel, The Black Lego Guy. That's what I use the spare room for. My builds.'

'Well, can I see it? I want to check out your, uh, *builds*,' I raise my eyebrows suggestively.

He flashes me a smile. 'You can check out my channel. Like and subscribe!'

'So that's a no, is it?'

He exhales heavily, like I've asked if I can kick his mum. 'Think of it like an artist's studio where everything is a work in progress.' Ben holds his hands out in front of him like he's begging me to understand. 'I like to protect the energy in there so I can stay really grounded and centred when I'm in a build. It's kind of like my Brick Church, and you *have* to protect the sanctity of a space like that.'

I nod. 'OK, great, well, thanks for letting me know,' I say, wondering how this affects my innate sense of attraction to him. Positively or negatively?

Positively: cool that someone is doing their own thing, quitting their job to follow their passion and all that. Negatively: he calls himself a brick master and what am I meant to do with that?

'Well,' he says with a tight little cough, a clearing of the throat. 'Like I said, the bathroom's the other door.'

I call Marie from the toilet.

'Bloody hell, that was quick,' Marie says when she answers the phone. I can still hear a few people at hers in the background.

'No, no,' I whisper, 'we haven't done the deed yet. I just found out about his brick master status . . .'

'Oh yeah, that, Carly told me he quit his job a month ago to do that. What a life!'

'I don't know if I can have sex with a brick master!'

'You should be open-minded,' Marie says. 'What's wrong with a brick master anyway?'

'Doesn't it sound ridiculous?'

I can hear her roll her eyes. 'Well, yes, of course it does, but he's good at it. He's got, like, hundreds of thousands of subscribers! It would be worse if he'd quit his job to become a . . . a brick . . . master . . .' she says tentatively, 'but wasn't a master at all, wouldn't it?'

'But I don't know if that's a good enough reason for me to have sex with him.'

'He's really good-looking, though, isn't he? I mean, for a man.'

'Look, matey, this isn't time to chat, I'm hiding out in his toilet, I've resolved I'm going to have sex with the brick master, I've got to go.'

'Can't hang out in the toilet too long, he might think you're doing a poo. And everyone knows that ladies don't poo.'

'Bye!' I hang up.

'So . . . brick master,' I say, blushing a little upon my return to the living room. Not because I'm coy, but because of . . . well, the whole . . . thing.

'Ha, you sound like one of my subscribers.'

'Do you want to, er, subscribe . . . to . . . sex . . . with . . . me?' I ask.

He gets to his feet and leads me into the bedroom, which, *mercifully* is Lego-free and I am relieved to discover that his passion project has given him what I would describe as extremely good fine-motor skills.

'You're . . . so . . . hot . . .' he moans, breathless, as I grind down on top of him, feeling all of him inside me. He's holding me by my waist and gazing at me open-mouthed, a look of intense concentration on his face. My thigh muscles are getting a real workout but it feels so good I barely notice. To think I would have given this up out of anti-brick-master bias!

After we've basked in the post-coital glow for long enough, I make my excuses to get out of there and spring out of bed.

'Ow!' I shout, pain shooting through my foot, looking down at the floor. Of course. 'Fuck!' I bend down. Of course. Of fucking course. Underneath my foot? A small blue Lego brick. This is not sexy! Not sexy at all!

'Oh, sorry,' Ben says, rubbing his eyes absent-mindedly, like this is par for the course. 'I try and keep my equipment confined to the Brick Palace. But something must have escaped.'

'Try harder,' I growl. I thought this kind of lifestyle was confined to the likes of Andrew and his various children; I certainly did not anticipate treading on Lego as being a side-effect of my sexual activities.

'Huh,' he says, as I drop the brick into his hand. 'That's a perpendicular pin connector with an axle hole.' He holds it up and looks at it before putting it carefully on his bedside table.

I nearly went over on my ankle! Can you imagine! A broken ankle because you stood on some Lego because you were having sex with someone who called himself a BRICK MASTER? Some may say that would be exactly what I deserve for getting involved in something so blatantly ridiculous.

But do you know the annoying thing? The really annoying, frustrating thing? Amid all of this, the fun, the sex, the fucking LEGO BRICK, I can't stop myself from thinking about Ivy.

25

Absence has made the heart grow fonder and I do not care for it. I have a crush on Ivy. I'm choosing to refer to it as a *crush* because at least that way I can keep it in a trivial little box. Not a Big Feelings box.

I fear that letting her back into my life after all this time was possibly not my smartest move. The worst thing I could do right now is let her completely invade my brain while it's impossible to see her. So: I need distraction.

I go through my mental list of Everyone I Know and try to figure out who I haven't seen super recently that is fun enough to distract me from a case of Rapidly Encroaching Feelings.

Nicole? Gallivanting in Rome with her gentleman friend-who's-definitely-not-her-boyfriend Salvatore. Marie? Literally hung out with her last night. Jamie? Feels weird to ask him to hang out, given I see him most days at the cafe. Vic? Away for the weekend at some fancy hotel in the New Forest. George?

Well, he's not exactly *fun* but he is . . . a person, I suppose. George it is.

'Hey,' he says, when I appear on his doorstep.

I survey him with an appraising eye. It's funny, I do often forget what he looks like, since I see him so infrequently. 'Nice beard.'

'This? I stopped trimming it ages ago,' he says, smiling.

'I guess we don't see each other that often, do we?' I laugh.

'Oh, yeah, I suppose not,' he says.

The established order of things between me and George is *have sex first, hang out second*. So that's what we do.

I close my eyes when he goes down on me and I can't stop my brain from drifting to – No! Stop it! Bad! Stay in the moment! But . . . what if . . . is it really so bad for me to think about – to remember – fuck, no, come on, stay focused, you are *here now*. Not somewhere else with someone else. It's George's head that's between my thighs and I need to enjoy it. Ivy is not here! But I wonder what she's doing . . . is there some pretty girl in North Carolina . . . I concentrate very hard on not thinking about Ivy, which was pretty much the entire reason I wanted to meet up with someone, anyone, tonight, but it turns out that trying not to think about someone is a really good way to make yourself think about her. Am I thinking about her when I come? Maybe. Do I feel weird about it? Yeah. Maybe.

'So,' I say when we're in our post-sex chill state, both scrolling on our phones, the windows wide open bringing in a slight breeze against the heavy, sweaty London atmosphere. Summer has barely begun and we're in the first of what we already know will be several heatwaves. 'Are you seeing anyone cool?'

He looks shifty, like I'm trying to catch him out. 'Um, yeah, sort of,' he says finally. 'Nothing serious. You?'

'I've got this kind of situation with . . . well, actually with the woman from the TV show.'

'Yeah?' George says, glancing up from his phone.

'Yeah, I mean, obviously there's a lot of history there, but we started hanging out and—

'Right!' George jumps to his feet and claps his hands together decisively. Oh yeah. I forget. George doesn't *talk*.

I exhale loudly, sick of this shit. 'What?' George asks.

'You always do that.'

'What?' he asks innocently.

'Whenever I talk about *anything* from my life you get all prickly and weird.'

He scratches at the back of his neck in a pose of extreme casualness. 'Well, I thought this was meant to be casual.'

'Yeah, and?' I say, thinking of the many completely functional casual relationships past and present since my break-up with Miranda.

'If it's casual then maybe we don't talk about *this stuff*.'

'And what is this stuff exactly.'

'Feelings, yeah?'

'Just because it's casual doesn't mean there's a complete fucking *void* of, like, respect, does it?'

'I respect you, like, so much.'

'It's not like there's two options, you know? Zero feelings, only sex or alternatively a monogamous relationship. There are lots of things in between them.'

He looks shifty. 'It's a bit intense, you know?'

'Are you joking?' My mouth is gaping. 'I literally see you every two months!'

'What, is that not enough for you?'

'No, it's completely fine! But when I see you I want to feel like, you know, a *person*?'

'Fine,' he says. I've realized there's a category of men who do not want to resolve things, they just want the bad vibes to go away. George is very evidently one of them. 'You're a person, I'm a person. Are we cool? Do you want another beer? I assume you're staying.'

'Yeah, why not,' I say. I can't be bothered traipsing home at this hour so I might as well stay over, whatever his angle is.

When he returns with the beer we watch some peak era *30 Rock*, but the vibe is not the one.

The call time for my make-up job today is later than usual so I have time to go home and refresh myself and pick up my kit. I shower and then glamorize myself to a level befitting a professional make-up artist before grabbing my little suitcase and heading out to the studio in King's Cross.

'It's a shoot for a super inclusive athleisure brand, really body posi! There are two models, one plus-size, one not, but I suppose that doesn't make much difference to the make-up, does it!' the email said.

Well, the email lied.

'Hi Fran, this is Sandrine,' Erica, the harried-looking creative director says to me as I've almost finished unpacking my kit.

'Nice to meet you, Sandrine,' I say, unfurling my last brush roll. She's tall and slim but curvy with long, dark brown hair and sharp cheekbones.

'So we'll get Sandrine done first but Gemma's nearly done in hair so she'll be ready for you as soon as you finish with Sandrine,' says Erica, who disappears almost before the end of her sentence. I'm looking forward to meeting Gemma – fellow chubsters are not easy to come by in this industry.

'Great,' I say to the thin air that's left in her wake before turning to Sandrine. 'If you want to take a seat for me, we'll get going.'

'Sure!' she says brightly, and I get to work prepping her skin with various juicy hydrating things.

'That feels nice,' says Sandrine, her eyes closed.

'Good! That's what it's there for.' I scan the table for the foundation I think would be her perfect match but it looks a little dark so I mix it with one shade lighter on a little glass palette that I use for such wizardry. 'So, have you worked with these guys before?'

'No,' says Sandrine. 'But I'm hoping if they like me then I'll get more work with them.'

'That's the dream, isn't it? Nice, reliable clients.'

'It sure is,' she sighs. 'It's tough out there.'

'Anything where people are looking at you and *evaluating* you, that's got to feel quite hard.'

'It's like we're all fighting over scraps, all the time,' Sandrine says.

I stand back and check her foundation is blended in before working on the rest of her face. My instructions are for a super glowy face but with mascara and tinted lip balm rather than an elaborate eye look and super sharp lips, which means it's doubly important to get the base right.

'Looking good,' I say, picking up a pretty, coral-toned cream blusher and my favourite duo fibre brush. 'And yeah . . . I guess it's one of those industries where you're always made to feel lucky to be there.'

'Totally.' The coral looks perfect against her skin. Of course it does, I am a make-up genius. 'And it's even harder when you're a niche model.'

'Oh?' I say, buffing it into her skin so it's perfectly seamless, intrigued to find out what her niche is.

'Yeah, you see the same few curve models getting all the work and it makes you wonder how you're ever going to break through, you know?'

The brush in my hand clatters to the floor and I bend to pick it up, wondering if I heard her right. Some skinny legs in expensive-looking leggings appear in my eyeline and I stand up again to be faced with the other model.

'Hey, I'm Gemma! I'm going to grab a coffee and check some emails but let me know when you're ready and I'll come back!'

'Great,' I say weakly, surveying this very thin woman before me as I am forced to accept that Gemma isn't the plus-size model. Sandrine is.

Gemma strolls over to the catering table and pours herself a coffee. I am left with Sandrine.

'So . . .' I say, clearing my throat. 'You're a plus-size model?'

'Mmmhmm!' she says, checking her phone.

'Oh,' I say, figuring that since I don't have anything encouraging to say I shouldn't say anything at all. This woman is a 12, or a 14 *maximum*. I'm not naive, I know plus-size models are to plus-size women what regular models are to non–plus-size women, i.e., *smaller*. But to be told the brand is – what was the expression? – *really body posi*! It feels absurd. Rude, even!

'Well, actually, I prefer *curve*. *Plus-size* makes me sound, you know, fat,' she says, setting her phone down on her decidedly-not-fat thigh so I can continue my work.

I swallow hard. 'Heaven forbid.'

'No offence,' she says, her eyes darting to me and my actually-plus-size body.

'I want to be a positive role model, you know? For bigger girls? I want to show that you don't have to be thin to be happy and healthy.'

'Mmm. Hold your mouth still for me,' I say as I swipe on some tinted sheer lipstick but would be tempted to say anyway.

As soon as I retract the lipstick she starts up again. 'I do worry that things have gone too far, you know? You see some of these girls and you think, how can this be healthy, you know?'

I nod and wonder if I can charge extra for having to listen to this bollocks.

Gemma is a welcome respite, but not in the way I thought she would be. It turns out a thin model who doesn't say any nonsense is preferable to a 'curve model' with tedious opinions.

My phone illuminates on the table I'm using to spread out my kit, and as Gemma stands up to head over to the plates of chopped-up fruit and pastries provided as catering, I pick it up. George has texted me, and it looks kind of . . . wordy. Which is very strange, because George doesn't like to text me unless he's asking me to come over.

Hi Fran, I don't think we should see each other anymore as I get the feeling you want something serious and I'm not looking for that so I think it's better for you if we stop hanging out. I think you're cool but I think we want different things.

Wow. I read the message again. I laugh out loud. And then I re-read the message to check he actually said what he said. He did! He said what he said! He thinks we should stop seeing each other because I, Fran Baker, want him to be my boyfriend? When I have never given one shred of evidence that that would be the case? When I've never even *thought* such a thing?

Ugh! Men are such absolute *freaks*. Imagine cheating yourself out of perfectly good sex because you've taken it upon yourself to decide that the other person *wants something from you*. What a waste!

With a sigh, I type my response.

Yes, George, of course, you know me better than I know myself! You've got me there!

My message is SEEN almost immediately, but he doesn't reply.

I feel faintly discombobulated as I have to perform my duties for the rest of the shoot, keeping the models looking camera-ready. I don't feel so much *rejected* by George as indignant at his extreme audacity! I am completely and perfectly fine with the fact I won't sleep with him again. That is *totally fine with me*. But I am not completely and perfectly fine with him projecting all of this shit onto me! That in his freak brain I am cast as some desperate woman who wants *him* of all people as a boyfriend. But I can't protest this because it'll somehow only prove his hypothesis that I'm deeply wounded by the whole thing because I secretly want to marry him. Ugh! I think back to his tactics to get my attention that time months ago, pretending he texted me by accident, and decide that this new turn of events is actually not that surprising for someone who's clearly incapable of behaving like a normal person.

Marie wants to meet me for a drink tonight after she's been working late, and I frankly welcome the warm embrace of cocktails with my most beloved friend after the day I've had.

I check my phone on the walk over there and see a message from Nicole, which is always welcome.

How do you feel about doing the best work you've ever done for the least money you've ever earned?

Despite my cloudy mood, I can't help but smile as I look at the screen. She's mentioned before about the first photo shoot of the clothing brand that she's been working on with her friends Serena and Lola, and I told her I would be happy to help out in any way I can.

For you, anything, I reply.

26

'Shit day, mate,' are my first words to Marie as soon as I sit down in the bar in Dalston where we meet. It's like a lovely dark cave against the heatwave outside.

'Tell me about it?'

'Well, it started badly and got worse from there.'

'Baby,' she says, pawing at my hand and pouting.

'What do I hate more than anything else?'

'Liquorice?'

'Less specific.'

'Tell me.'

'Having to bite my tongue! And I fucking *had to* today. One of the models at work was driving me mad and I couldn't say *anything* because it's my workplace and I want more work where someone else is probably going to be a fatphobic nightmare too!'

'I'm sorry, mate.'

'I had to stand there and listen to it. Can you imagine! Me? And that's on top of some fucking nonsense from one of the guys I've been seeing. You know George? The one I met on my birthday?

'Best head you ever had?'

'That's the one. Why are straight men incapable of acting like normal people?'

'Mate, I'm the last person you should ask. Even my male friends are absolute weirdos – I mean, you know what Edward's like, and he's about as normal as I've ever managed to find,' she says, shouting a little over the noise of the bar. 'Ugh, I feel so *old* when places are too loud for me.' Marie looks around, extremely sceptically.

'We will never be old,' I tell her, grabbing both her hands and clasping onto them for dear life.

'You say that *now*. You're still in your twenties.'

'Not for much longer! Time gallops on.'

'So, what happened with this guy?'

'George fucking *projected* onto me.'

'Ew, gross,' she grimaces.

'Not like that! I mean, George doesn't want us to keep seeing each other because he's decided I'm too serious about it! Me!'

'You?!'

'Exactly! I mean, bloody hell, at least I'm not that bothered about him, so it's no great loss, but in a way that makes it worse! He's not even right!'

'Yeah, mate, I have no idea what's going on there. The male psyche is a mystery to me and I like it that way,' Marie says.

'The female psyche is also a mystery to me . . .' I sigh.

'What now?'

'The usual,' I laugh bitterly.

'Ivy Shifford, ruining lives since Year 12. You heard from her?'

I shake my head. It pains me to admit it but she hasn't contacted me since she's been in the US. I haven't contacted her either. It feels like she should make the first move.

'I don't get why she didn't tell me she was going away?'

'Maybe she thought it would seem presumptuous that you would care? Maybe she's trying to play it cool? Or maybe she really doesn't think you should be that bothered?' I'm about to protest that it couldn't be possible that Ivy thinks I wouldn't care when Marie glances over to the bar. 'Hey, I think those two are looking at us. Probably checking you out, hot stuff.'

'Or wondering if they saw me on TV,' I say, remembering the girl in the pub with Ivy. I turn around to see who she's talking about. Two women instantly turn away when I look in their direction, but I recognize them instantly. 'Oh! That's Ronnie and Avni. They're Miranda's friends. I didn't know them well.'

'I'm sure they're saying what a huge mistake it was for Miranda to break up with you, and wondering how they're going to break it to her that you've somehow got even hotter since the break-up.'

'You're too kind. I've been holding in a wee since we got here, too keen for the chat. Be right back,' I say, before disappearing to the toilet. I need to get an update on how things are going between Marie and Carly and don't want to be thinking about how much I need to wee. When I emerge from the stall, Ronnie is on her way in. Ugh. I cannot avoid acknowledging that we've met before.

'Fran!' she says, very happy to see me, which surprises me a little.

'Oh, hi Ronnie! I thought that was you at the bar.'

She nods, her very long, blond hair moving with her. 'I wanted to say, I always thought you were really cool. I really did. It's a shame we never got to spend more time together.'

If her tone of voice had been different, I might have wondered if she was maybe coming on to me. But there's something strained and sad about it that I can't quite interpret. Probably that now me and Miranda have broken up she'll never be allowed to. I always thought she was cool too, in a grown-up hippie sort of way.

'Thank you, that's so kind of you. I hope you're doing OK?'

'Oh, *I'm* doing fine,' she says, as if it's not her that anyone has to worry about.

'Well, best be off. See you around!' I say brightly, but I do actually want to get out of there and back to Marie, who is slightly less inscrutable. Scrutable Marie.

'See you,' Ronnie says, giving me another sad look.

'That was weird,' I say to Marie when I sit down again. 'I bumped into one of those women in the toilets, and the vibe was distinctly strange. Like she told me she always thought I was cool?'

'You are cool. But yeah, weird move,' Marie says, shrugging.

'Nothing queer as folk,' I intone solemnly.

'Miranda's moved on, you've moved on, you're both adults, it's all fine.'

'Yeah, I've been thinking about that. About moving on. It's not so much that I want the slag era to end,' I say thoughtfully. 'It's more that . . . I'm sort of . . . at peace with the idea of a relationship again.'

'But slag era is so fun!'

'I know. I'm saying . . . I'm open to it again. Like, in general.'

'In general . . . but also more specifically a relationship with Ivy?' she asks.

'The problem is . . . I have no idea what she's thinking beyond the fact I'm *quite* sure she could be interested in me in that way.'

'That's hot,' Marie says, in the style of Paris Hilton because she's decided what she needs right now is to get deep into a rewatch of *The Simple Life*. 'Yeah, look, for all I've felt quite cautious about you and Ivy hanging out, it does seem like you're in a good place about all this.'

'Mmm,' I nod. 'I feel like I'm maybe moving out of this mindset where relationships inherently feel like a trap. Or a place where people mess each other around and hurt each other and have different intentions or mismatched ideas about what's going on.'

'This feels healthy, my dude. I like it.'

'I'm not saying I'm 100 per cent going to get into a relationship imminently, but more that I feel like I'm not *actively running away* from the idea of a relationship. Does that make sense?'

She holds up her glass. 'To not running away,' she says with a slightly sad smile.

I clink my glass against hers. 'To not running away.'

27

A large part of the joy of being single is the prospect of having sex with someone new. And I've got pretty good at figuring out whether that's likely to happen based on app chat.

I feel like sex with Shane, tonight's date, is a distinct possibility.

When I arrive at the pub, Shane is already there. He's kind of cute, and at the bare minimum looks like his photos. I hide around a corner for a moment, cooling myself down with my beloved battery-operated hand fan. A fat bitch in a crowded pub on a hot July evening? You best believe I'm sweating. I check my face in my little compact mirror, delighted as always by the creepy Georgian eye earrings dangling against my jaw, and let the fan do its work until I look less . . . moist.

'Hey,' I say, taking a seat opposite him. 'I'm Fran.'

'Hi Fran, Shane,' he says, looking up at me. 'Nice to meet you.'

'Can I get you a drink?' I ask. On top of rent, I've realized all my money is going on make-up for my kit (good) and buying pints for people I meet on apps (good or bad, depending on the night).

'No, let me,' he says, standing.

'Could I have a glass of wine, please? White, any kind, I'm not fussed.'

'Nice and easy,' he says.

'That's me.'

When he returns, I ask him about his life. He tells me he lives up Pentonville Road between here and Angel, he tells me about the dates he's been on recently, he tells me about the trip he recently took to Paris, he tells me he works in a record shop in Soho but is writing a screenplay.

'Oh yeah?' I say, curious. 'What's it about?'

He sighs, like he's sick of people asking him, when I would have thought he should be grateful anyone's interested in it at all. 'Think *Midsommar* meets the *Social Network*. It's a metaphor for the monstrous imposition of social media on our everyday lives.'

I do my best vacant smile but manage to suppress the laughter that's desperate for a way out. 'Oh, wow, that's interesting,' I say, nodding like it's the first time I've ever heard such an idea from a random man.

'Enough about me,' he says, which surprises me because I didn't think he had any idea he was talking so much. 'What about you? What do you do?'

'I'm a make-up artist,' I say while taking a sip of wine.

'And you enjoy that?'

'Yeah, I love it. I used to be a beauty journalist but now I'm trying to get my career going as an artist.'

He smiles at my use of the word *artist*. 'Just playing devil's advocate here,' he says. *Here we bloody go.* 'But don't you think the beauty industry preys on the insecurities of women?'

'Oh, sure,' I say, shrugging. Of course I do. Creating

problems none of us knew we had so they can sell us the solution? Totally.

'And you don't feel bad about that? I mean, having a participatory role in that . . . *ecosystem*?'

'I've never told a single woman that she needs to wear make-up. Ever. I simply don't care whether people do or not. It's fun, a bit of expression, and yeah, maybe for some people it gives them extra confidence. Did the beauty industry *create* a lack of confidence? Maybe. But maybe it was some guy who pointed out some lines around her eyes or made fun of her as a teenager for having spots or whatever. The way I see it is, people wear make-up, you know? Get over it.'

'Well,' he says, laughing. 'That's me told.' I can't really get a handle on this guy. It's like he alternates between extremely good-natured and quite, what's the word . . . *curmudgeonly*.

I go to the bar for another round, and upon my return he proceeds to tell me why *Starship Troopers* is the greatest film ever made. He can barely believe me when I say I've never seen it, but something about his enthusiasm is quite sweet. He actually has a very nice smile, when he's not being extremely serious. We have a lengthy disagreement on the best Hitchcock films, followed by an enthusiastic conversation about why Walton Goggins isn't a huge star (*it's the teeth*, we decide).

Another round, his turn. In his absence I open Instagram and start scrolling through the usual weekend fare – brunches, rooftop drinks, summer holidays.

'Cheers,' I say, clinking my glass against his as he returns with the drinks. I look at him as I drink, trying to figure out if I fancy him or not. Or if I fancy him *enough*.

'You wouldn't catch me on there,' he says, grimacing at my

phone which is still open on Instagram. I pick it up and return it to the home screen before locking it.

'Well, I can imagine not, given your social media horror allegory screenplay,' I say, smiling.

'I take it you're a fan?'

'I don't know if *fan* is the right word, it's . . . there, isn't it?'

'Playing devil's advocate here, don't you think—' he begins, but I cut him off.

'Don't *you* think the literal devil is the last person who needs an advocate?' I say, smiling sweetly.

He looks suitably chastened. 'Look,' he says, 'you're more interesting than most of the women I meet on those apps. Do you want to come back to mine? Or would that be weird? Too forward?' He ruffles his hair awkwardly.

Shane isn't the worst guy I've ever met. But do I want to fuck the devil's advocate? Not really.

And yet I find myself saying, 'Sure,' swallowing down my last mouthful of wine and getting to my feet. I'm tired and far from home – I figure I might as well sleep with this guy.

In the hallway of his hot, stuffy flat, we kiss, and I can already feel the sweat trickling from my hair down the back of my neck. Very sexy. I'm about to suggest we take it to the bedroom when I feel a pull against my ear, where my earring had got caught on his watch strap.

'Just a second,' I say, taking out my earrings. 'That's better.'

He shows me into his bedroom. I lay the earrings down on the bedside table cluttered with books and bits of paper before we get down to business.

I'm almost home before I realize with horror that I've left my beloved creepy eye earrings at Shane's. I can't go back now, I'm miles from there and I want to go to sleep, but I feel panicked at the thought I've lost something so precious. I open the app and type a quick message:

Hey, just realized I left my earrings at yours, I can come pick them up whenever you're around, let me know! They're my faves so would be good to get them back ASAP!

He'll reply, won't he? He'd fucking better.

28

'You seem distracted,' Vic says from across the table in the sun-drenched pub garden as a fast-moving toddler dashes past the end of our table, screaming. Greg's buying our drinks at the bar inside like a true gentleman.

'Nope, I'm fine!' I say brightly. I am not going to open this hangout by complaining about the earring theft. 'I want to hear all about you. How's flat hunting?'

'Kind of mad, actually. We went to a viewing last night and the agent was like *if you want it you have to make an offer right now otherwise it'll be gone like that!* She snaps her fingers for emphasis.

'Ugh, it sounds like the Wild West out there.'

'It really is, I've seen some *very* dark things.' She shrugs, a serene smile on her face. 'But we'll get there in the end. I don't like the feeling of being bullied by some useless man in a cheap suit into making a snap decision about the most important purchase of my life.'

'Too bloody right. And yes, you'll get there. I'm excited for you two! Have you had any more . . . *discussions?*'

'Not for a while, but in my own sweet time I have come

to the conclusion that yes, I think I would very much like to be married to him.' A huge smile breaks out across her face, and I can't help but do the same.

'I think that would be a good decision. No pressure, though. It's about you two. No one else.'

At that moment, Greg sets a tray of drinks down on the table and Vic and I giggle like schoolgirls.

'I feel like I'm interrupting something . . .'

'Maybe you were,' I say, raising my eyebrows suggestively.

'So,' Greg says, taking a sip of his pint, 'what's new with you?'

Where to even start? I'm in denial about my feelings for Ivy so I definitely don't want to chat about that. I decide to narrow the focus of my woe onto the earrings. 'I got stealthily robbed of one of my most prized possessions.'

Vic gasps. 'Tell us everything.'

'I was wearing these earrings I like on a date and then I took them out when I went to bed with him, and then like a complete idiot I forgot to pick them up when I left in the morning.'

'And you have texted him to say you left them?'

'Yes!' I say indignantly. 'And he's ghosting me! An active ghosting! He's not just ignoring me but he's fucking *blocked me* on the app!'

Vic takes a sip of her wine. 'Which earrings were they?'

'My *favourites*!'

She gasps in horror. 'Not those creepy eye ones?'

'Yes! Exactly!'

'And I can't replace them! Marie bought me them off a market stall in Bath years ago!'

'This is bad,' Vic says, shaking her head darkly. I wonder if I need to enlist Marie instead, you know, use her top legal brain to write a letter to him or something.

'So it was a . . . a one-night stand?' Greg asks cautiously.

'Yes! You're a man. What do you think he's playing at?'

'Well, it could be that he thinks you did it deliberately?'

'Ah, to scam a second date out of him. Because all women want to tie men down in long-term relationships and don't just want their fucking earrings back.'

'What an arsehole! Now . . . how are we going to get these earrings back?' Vic's face is focused and determined. I've seen Vic look like this before, mostly at product launch events for her agency's most demanding clients.

'Could you not go over there and, you know, ask for them?' Greg suggests gently, because clearly his mind does not work in the same backwards way that Shane's does.

'I will not lower myself to such a thing!' I say. 'It was a one-night thing! I don't want him thinking he's, you know, *important*! If he thinks I left those earrings there as a fucking *ruse*, me turning up at his doorstep would only confirm it.'

'Men and their ruses.' Vic shakes her head.

'Men and their bloody ruses,' I chorus.

'I know!' says Vic, slamming her hand down on the table before turning to her boyfriend and grabbing him by the shoulder. 'Let's make Greg do it.'

'Me?' he says, blinking at her.

The buzzy summer afternoon is pierced by the sound of a siren on a police car speeding past the pub. Vic gasps with delight, looking around at the car. 'Now *that* is an idea.'

'What is?' I ask.

'Before I get too invested in my grand plan, you *do* remember where he lives, right?'

'Yeah, definitely,' I say, very curious about what's going on in that brain of hers.

'We'll get Greg dressed up as a policeman and he can knock on this guy's door and make him hand over the earrings.'

'What?!' Greg says in disbelief, unable to comprehend quite how he's been dragged into all of this.

'Yeah,' Vic says enthusiastically. 'Guaranteed success.'

'Where am I even going to get a police uniform from?!'

'Oh, there are loads of places one can acquire a police uniform. Yes, it's sorted. That's what we'll do.'

'Is it?' Greg says weakly, looking at her in a slightly horrified expression.

'Yeah, yeah, it'll be fine, say you've had a report of some stolen earrings and you're here to retrieve them, no, the lady doesn't want to pursue any charges she wants her property back.'

'Yes, to be clear: I don't even want to scare him or anything, I want my stuff back.'

'You understand I'm not a policeman so there's nothing I could do to this guy anyway?' It is possible that Greg is in over his head.

'Greg. You are a landscape gardener. I understand that, fear not,' I reassure him.

'OK good,' he says, apparently comforted.

'When shall we do this?' Vic asks, keen to get going on her master plan. I can't believe Marie ever tried to tell me that Vic was my *sensible friend*.

'Look, I'm barely involved at this point,' I say, holding my hands up in defeat. 'It's up to Greg. Also pending him securing the outfit.'

'There's a fancy dress shop down the road from us in Camden, we'll sort it out and have it ready to go . . . when do you think, babe?'

'S-sunday? Is that OK?'

'Perfect,' Vic says.

'And since we're going for the ridiculous fancy dress costume, then even if he doesn't believe you're a real cop, he'll be so weirded out by the whole escapade that he'll give the earrings back anyway,' I say, as if it's the most obvious thing in the world.

'Fine,' Greg says wearily.

'You're a good egg,' I say, pinching his cheek.

'Isn't he?' Vic says, flushing with pride at the idea of her boyfriend posing as a policeman to retrieve my earrings.

'Can you . . . can you let us know if he replies before then, though?' Greg asks, clearly hoping that he will be surplus to requirements.

'Of course! What, do you think I have some absolutely *burning* desire to see you dressed up as a cop? No! I just want my precious jewels!'

'Well . . .' Greg says, looking a little queasy. 'As long as they're precious, I suppose.'

'Operation Policeman is go,' Vic says as I approach her table in the pub around the corner from Shane's house on Sunday. 'Greg is getting changed. He's in the toilet. He's a little self-conscious about the outfit . . . the fancy dress shop didn't have one that exactly fitted him so . . .'

'Oh my God,' I say, putting my hand to my mouth at the sight of Greg, who at this very moment emerges from the bathroom looking extremely shifty. He looks like a schoolboy on his first day of secondary school, all too-long sleeves and too-big shoulders. The shields on his uniform read 'Official Police Inspector'.

'Don't say a word,' he says wearily. He hands the tote bag containing his clothes to Vic. 'Let's get this over and done with.'

'Oooh, Fran, do you have a notebook on you? A little one that Greg could pretend is one of those policeman notebooks like they had on *Line of Duty*?'

I peer into my handbag. 'The only thing I have is this,' I say, brandishing a spiral-bound Hello Kitty notebook that Jessie brought me back from Japan when she went there after our first or second date, along with about a year's supply of sheet masks.

'Well, that's not going to work, is it?' Greg says, while Vic takes it from me and opens it so you can't see the cover.

'There,' she says, handing it to him. 'Little *Line of Duty* policeman notebook.'

Greg snorts, unconvinced, but takes it anyway.

We walk round the corner to Shane's, desperately hoping we don't bump into him on our way. As luck would have it, we do not. But there's still no guarantee he'll be home . . .

'I hope this works, I don't think there's any way we could convince Greg to give it another shot . . .' Vic says with a giggle as we crouch behind a car outside Shane's flat, very much out of sight but not out of earshot if we don't shut up.

'Go on, Greg!' I say, waving him off as he looks uncomfortably over his shoulder at the two of us. I feel a *little* bit guilty at putting Greg through this, but not so guilty that it'll stop me from getting my earrings back.

Greg takes a deep breath before pressing the bell. He steps back from the door. He waits, no one answers. Vic and I lean over each other to get a better look. The way he's holding his body looks tense and full of anticipation. We don't know whether we want to squeal with joy or scream at the pressure of such high stakes.

Greg looks back over his shoulder again as if to ask us how long he's meant to stand there before giving up. But I'm in luck! Finally, Shane answers the door, looking sleepy, and crosses his arms across his chest at the sight of . . . well, the policeman on his doorstep.

Greg clears his throat. 'Hello, sir,' he says, looking down at the Hello Kitty notebook in his hand. 'Are you Shane Collins?'

'Uh . . . yeah,' he says, looking Greg over with suspicion, which frankly I don't blame him for because Greg looks completely ridiculous in his oversized policeman's fancy dress costume.

'I'm here because we've, er, had reports that you are in possession of some . . .' he pauses. 'Stolen goods.'

'Oh yeah?' Shane says. 'What would that be then?' I can't quite tell if Shane has an entirely healthy disdain for the police or he knows this is essentially a wind-up.

'A pair of earrings,' Greg says, pretending to consult his notebook again.

'Is this a joke?'

'I can assure you this is no laughing matter, sir.'

'Did . . . uh, Fran send you? All for that?' Shane replies,

very obviously feigning forgetting my name. The absolute scoundrel! I have to fight the urge to spring up from behind the car and remind him that if he had only replied to my text then I wouldn't have had to go to such *outrageous lengths* to retrieve my property!

Greg clears his throat again. 'Then you admit you are in possession of the stolen property?'

'I haven't stolen anything in my life! What are you talking about?'

'Can you please lower your voice?'

'All right!' Shane sighs wearily. 'I'll go and get the stupid earrings.' He disappears into the house and Greg doesn't even turn to try and look at us, holds his pose as me and Vic wait with bated breath. Finally, he returns! Greg holds out his hand stiffly and Shane drops the earrings into his waiting palm.

'Is that everything?'

'That'll be all . . . sir,' he adds as a final flourish.

Before Shane can close the door behind him, I jump out from behind the car. 'We wouldn't have had to go to all this trouble if you hadn't fucking *blocked me* and stolen my earrings!' I yell.

'You're crazy,' Shane says, shaking his head and closing the door behind him.

'Yeah? Maybe!' I say, shrugging, to no one in particular.

'I think I did quite well,' Greg says, relieved that the rigma-role has come to an end.

'You did *great*,' I say. I put the earrings in and feel the old familiar weight of them. Friends reunited! Me and my faves back together again! I pull him into a tight squeeze. 'Thank you soooo much, you're the best.'

'I would say *any time*, but I really don't want to do this again if you can help it,' Greg says, unbuttoning his uniform.

'I will keep much better track of my property in the future, I promise.'

'Pint?' Vic suggests, raising her eyebrows.

'Pint!' A celebratory pint never hurt anyone.

I buy a round in the pub, and as I feel the pearls of my earrings dangling against my jaw, I have to say, I feel pretty thankful for having friends like those two. Sex and dating occupy so much space in my life, but you know what? Friendship is deeply underrated.

29

What was it Nicole said? *The best work I've ever done for the least money I've ever earned.* Well, the day is here. I am the official make-up artist for the first photo shoot of Seloni, the brand that Nicole has been working on with Serena and Lola.

It certainly can't feel any worse than the last shoot. I've felt a little weary since then. A *little* bit self-conscious, which is not my vibe. It's extremely annoying to know, to be reminded how people are looking at you, judging you, evaluating you. To keep brushing up against it when you're trying *hard* to keep your life free of all that bullshit.

'Hello, darling!' Nicole says, throwing her arms around me as I enter the studio. It's a little ramshackle but the photographer is setting up a tidy white backdrop. 'God, it's fucking *hot*, isn't it? I'm not made for this.' She turns a surprisingly powerful hand fan towards my face and I close my eyes, letting the droplets of sweat evaporate from my warm face.

'Aaah, you must be Fran!' says a woman with a handful of safety pins who looks positively regal. 'I'm Lola!' She draws me into a hug. 'Nice to meet you. I'm helping out with styling!'

'And this is Serena,' says Nicole, leading over an anxious-looking fellow plus-size angel with a cascade of blond waves and an open, sweet face. 'The brains behind the operation.'

'My brain is broken!' Serena wails. 'But it's nice to meet you.'

'What's happened to your brain?'

'Serena's worked too hard recently getting all of this ready, sewing all the samples,' Nicole says, a little guiltily. 'She did it all herself.'

'You helped!' Serena nudges Nicole affectionately.

'Helped? I probably set us back about two weeks,' she mutters bitterly.

'Sewing not the one for you?' I ask.

'Fucking bollocks, mate, it's all ironing. No one ever tells you that. It's all ironing,' Nicole says, shaking her head.

'Right,' Lola claps her hands together authoritatively and looks over to a sofa where three people are sitting and chatting. I say people. What I mean is *true angels*.

Even the way they're sitting – sprawled, casually, not primly, elegantly, rigid, radiates a kind of comfort. They're laughing, unselfconsciously, one grabbing onto another's fleshy upper arm as they speak. These are my people!

'Fran, this is Louisa, Aaliyah and Scout,' Nicole says, introducing me to each one in turn. 'And this is our beautiful make-up artist, Fran.'

'Hi, Fran!' they all chorus, and I get the pleasure of surveying them up close. Louisa actually reminds me a little bit of Sandrine at the shoot that got me riled up – all high cheekbones and flowing dark hair, except she really *is* a plus-size model. No, wait, better than that: she's a plus-size woman. Aaliyah's gorgeous: her round cheeks are perfectly framed by her headscarf, and bob like cute apples when she smiles, which is often. Scout's look is tough, a septum ring, stompy lace-up shoes, a lot of tattoos, but a sweet face and a mess of short, sandy hair. All completely different, all completely perfect.

'Let's do pronouns quickly now everyone's here?' Lola says, and we all take it in turns to share our personal pronouns. A whole load of *she*-s plus a *he* from the photographer and a *they* from Scout.

'We wanted to show how the clothes look on a range of people,' Serena explains. 'We didn't want to, you know,' she nibbles her lip, 'decide for anyone *who* our customer should be or what they look like. We wanted them to speak for themselves.'

I nod. 'I think you've chosen beautifully. Today is going to go really well,' I tell her, because she looks so nervous.

'Thanks,' she says, smiling and shaking her head. 'We've worked so hard on it, you know? Nicole coming up with all these ideas and then me and her and Lola trying to figure out how to make them real, in the right fabric, in the right colour, that I can grade to the size range we want to achieve. I want this to work out.'

'It will.'

'Of course it bloody will!' Nicole says. 'But we need to get a wiggle on. Louisa, why don't you go with Fran first?'

'I'll need a second to set up!'

'Sorry, babe, I should have told you to get here before the models, shouldn't I?' Nicole winces as she shows me to my station on the other side of the small photography studio. 'There's so much to think of!'

'Ah, it's all right,' I reassure her. 'You'll know for next time.' I start unzipping my small suitcase and hauling things out.

'I hope there is a next time,' she grimaces. 'Serena's found this all so stressful that I don't know if she could go through it again!'

'It'll be worth it, I promise,' I say. 'So, what are you thinking, make-up wise?'

'Whatever these babes want,' Nicole says, shrugging. 'I want them to look like themselves, but so it all looks good under the lights and all that, you know?'

'Got it.'

'Do Aaliyah or Scout first so we can get them photographed in their individual looks before doing group shots after lunch, yeah?'

'Smart.'

'That's me,' she says, winking at me.

'Right! Aaliyah, what would you like to look like today?' I ask once I've unpacked the wild array of stuff I carry around in that mini suitcase of mine.

'Me but better?' she offers, smiling.

'Pretty, natural, all of that good stuff. Got it.'

Aaliyah takes a seat and then rummages about in her bag before handing me a bottle of foundation.

'Are you quite particular about what you use?'

'Not really — I mean, it's nothing special. I thought maybe you wouldn't have my shade.'

'Oh!' I say, frowning. 'No, I have your shade,' I say, gesturing to the long line of foundation bottles on the work surface. I pick one up and turn the bottle upside down to look at the label. 'Espresso would probably be best . . . or maybe Deep Chestnut. I might mix them together.'

'You came prepared,' she says, smiling.

'I always do.'

'I did a shoot last year where the make-up artist didn't have any shades darker than a paper bag.'

'So what did they use on you?'

She shrugs. 'Nothing. The whole thing was a mess anyway, clearly a brand trying to, you know, *do diversity*. I should have known better. But it's always flattering to be asked to do this, isn't it?'

'You mean getting paid for being extremely beautiful?'

Aaliyah laughs. 'Yeah.'

'I suppose so, but it's good to have boundaries. Next time someone doesn't have the shade for you, tell them to fuck off and ring me.'

'I will,' she says, grinning.

And she's still grinning when we finish her make-up. 'I think this foundation suits me even better than mine,' she says approvingly.

'I'm glad you like it!'

'Thank you,' she says, giving me a hug that I wasn't expecting.

'Oh, any time!' I can't help but smile.

'So, what are we thinking?' I ask Louisa once I've tidied up the products I used on Aaliyah.

'Full glam,' she says decisively, taking a seat in front of me.

'I love an excuse to do full glam!' I'm already mentally flipping through my various bronze eyeshadows to bring out her blue eyes.

'This chair is a fucking nightmare,' Louisa says after about ten seconds. I look at it, seeing its sharp arms and small seat. 'Can I get another one?'

'Oh, definitely,' I tell her. 'Sorry, Nicole?' I call across the room. She turns to me from where she's talking to the photographer, a heavy-set guy called Blake with a shaved head and lots of ear piercings. 'Can we get a nicer chair for over here, please?' I *thought* Aaliyah was a little bit wriggly, but equally she's smaller than Louisa so it might not have been as uncomfortable.

'One second!' she calls back, and scans the room for a suitable alternative before wheeling over a squishy-looking swivel chair and replacing the offending item.

'It's funny, I wouldn't ever mention something like that unless there were other fat people around to make me feel normal,' Louisa says thoughtfully, once she's installed in the seat.

'I know what you mean,' I say. 'Even though I don't give a shit about being fat you know other people have so much *baggage* about it that they make the whole thing feel extremely mortifying.'

'Precisely,' says Louisa.

I sigh, gently applying primer to her face. 'It's nice to be here. Nice to be in a room with, you know, fellow chubsters. And Lola.'

'For balance, you know?' says Lola, smiling.

I work away on her beautiful face, treating it like the perfect canvas it is. I step back and look at my handiwork.

'I think we've got it nailed,' I say, basking in the pleasure of seeing my make-up on a beautiful fat woman's face other than my own. Louisa turns to look in the mirror I've got propped next to her.

'Wow,' she says, picking up the mirror and surveying herself from every angle. 'Wow!'

'You like?'

'I love! Thank you *so* much,' she says, beaming and standing up from the chair just as Nicole passes.

'Gorgeous! Now, Scout, it's your turn,' says Nicole, squeezing Scout's shoulder.

'So, what can I do for you?' I ask.

'Well,' Scout says, looking unsure. 'I don't really wear make-up . . .'

'You have great skin, and I love the contrast between your eyebrows and your hair, so what if I do a bit of concealer to even things out, and then we can maybe go even darker and more intense with your brows?'

'That sounds great,' they say, visibly relaxing. 'I thought maybe you were going to get me to do, what was it Louisa called it? *Full glam.*'

'You don't strike me as much of a full glam kind of person,' I say, scanning my kit for my little concealer brush. 'Scout is a cool name.'

'Thanks, I gave it to myself.'

'A very good gift.'

I work in silence for a moment, until Scout asks, 'So are you friends with one of them?' They nod in the direction of where Nicole, Lola and Serena are huddled in discussion.

'Yeah, I'm dating Nicole, but I hadn't met Lola or Serena before. How about you? How did they get you three involved?'

'They put a callout on Instagram. I see a few brands do it every so often, and there's always something in the way they write that makes me feel like . . .' Scout looks around, their soft brown eyes scanning for the right words. 'Like, *you really don't get it, do you?* I don't know how else to explain it. It'll be a turn of phrase that makes me think, yeah, I'm not really going to have a good time here, am I? But this time, my girlfriend sent me a link to the post and I thought it seemed genuine. So I replied and then here we are.'

'I think you and Louisa and Aaliyah are *great* choices. It's such a *joy* to see actual fat bodies.'

'Amen,' Scout smiles. 'A-fucking-men.'

I brush their eyebrows up and out, making them fuller and fluffier. It looks great against their fair skin, a statement but still resolutely *them*. Exactly how Nicole and the gang wanted it.

'Happy?' I ask, showing Scout their gently make-up'd face in the mirror.

'I love it!' they say, touching their eyebrows.

'Hands off,' I tell them. 'But if you do mess them up I can retouch easily, no worries.'

'You all done here?' Nicole has reappeared. 'Let's get you in your first outfit!' she says to Scout.

I stroll over to where the photographer is snapping away at Louisa, who's a total natural, completely able to interpret his direction and change her poses or slightly tilt her head or body in the precise way he's telling her to.

'OK,' Lola says, 'we've got one more outfit for Louisa and then lunch break?'

'Sounds good,' says Blake from his laptop where he's uploading the files of Louisa in her current outfit, a chic, cute short-sleeved midi dress in white cotton with bright brushstrokes all over it.

Lola shows Louisa over to the rail with her outfits on and hands her some high-waisted nautical-inspired trousers and a ruffled off-the-shoulder top, which on her, combine to create a sultry vintage Miami look.

300

Serena keeps dashing in and fiddling with the clothes, making sure the seams are completely straight, making sure nothing is tucked in a way that doesn't showcase exactly what the product looks like.

'I think we're good, what do you think?' Blake asks, looking over at Lola, Serena and Nicole, who talk amongst themselves for a moment before agreeing we've got the individual shots nailed and that it's time for lunch.

As we're sitting around, enjoying our hard-earned break and some delicious rice bowls Lola ordered from a nearby Japanese restaurant, I can't help but bask in how great it feels to be here. Obviously, it's a high-stakes moment for Nicole and her friends, but even that can't take away from the positive, loving, warm atmosphere. Am I doing the best work I've ever done for the least money I've ever been paid? Probably, but I'd do it again for less.

Before long, we're back to work on the group shots, and for three people who didn't know each other before today, they do a great job of looking completely comfortable together.

'It's too quiet in here!' Blake says once we get started again after lunch. 'How am I meant to work like this?!' he laughs.

'Let me see if I can use my big brain to get Spotify working,' Lola says, turning to the computer on the desk next to her. She clicks around for a moment, and then . . .

The sound of 'Fantasy' by Mariah Carey fills the room, her slow, twinkly intro before the 'Genius of Love' sample kicks in.

'That's more like it!' Blake grins as Lola dances back over to where we're huddled on the other side of the camera.

A wide smile spreads across the models' faces at the sight of Lola dancing, and Blake can't resist having a wiggle while keeping tight hold on his expensive camera. I feel happy. The happiness makes me simultaneously *not* miss Ivy but also makes me want to contact her. To make the first move. She must be coming home soon. Maybe she's even back?

Hey you – it's been too long! Are you back yet?

When the typing dots appear, my heart leaps.

Good morning from my last day in Durham, NC! Your timing is unparalleled. Shall we do something when I'm home?

I don't reply, just let the promise of Ivy fill up my already-full heart.

There's something so infectious about the music that even Serena is looking relaxed, and Nicole nudges her and starts dancing herself. Aaliyah throws her arms around Louisa and Scout's necks and they all join in, and then Lola dances her way over to the models and gestures for the rest of us to come join them. In the space of twenty seconds, the spirit of Mariah Carey has filled the room and has got us all dancing, completely carefree, singing along and striking dramatic poses for Blake, who dances as he snaps away. Nicole spins me around and dips me like we're in an old-fashioned musical and I can't help but laugh and hug her. It's a feeling of complete freedom, of safety and love and fun and acceptance in a world created otherwise. We can't get enough of it. We're in heaven.

30

'Since doing the make-up on this photo shoot last week I've felt weirdly . . . alive.'

'Alive is good!' Vic nods enthusiastically.

'I walked out of there feeling sort of in love with the world. I wanted to throw my arms around the universe.'

'You're such a romantic!'

'I guess I am,' I say with a smile so big it's almost embarrassing. I suppose this is what having Feelings for someone does to you. And letting yourself accept that you have those feelings.

We're eating takeaway sushi at her tastefully decorated flat. I take a deep breath. 'I'm really into Ivy. I've missed her so much while she's been away. And even before that, I knew it had really developed into something for me. Like, every time I see her I'm excited to see her and I don't want to say goodbye to her and then when I'm not with her I feel really on edge if I don't have a plan to see her again.'

'So this has escalated somewhat?'

'It has.'

'Fran, you sly dog!' She swats at me with the back of her hand. 'What happens now?'

'Nothing happens now.' I shake my head resolutely.

'Come on.'

'Mate, I've talked such a big game about boning my way through London, and now I'm going to pivot to gooey romance? What will people say? They'll think I was secretly miserable and looking for love the whole time! Which I wasn't! This is not a backtrack! This is not a flip-flop!'

She sighs loudly. 'No one's going to think that. Anyway, who are all these *people* you think are thinking about you and your relationships?!'

'People,' I shrug. 'You know *people*.'

'Since when do you care about *people*? Anyway, everyone knows you can fuck around without it being a symptom of emotional distress. But one thing I will say is that doing this kind of very open and joyful fucking around means that you *also* have to be open to the idea that you want something different now. You know, listening to your intuition.'

My intuition is telling me that I want to be with Ivy. 'What if I can't trust my intuition? I mean, I am very happy being single, I'm happy trotting around town, meeting people, maybe having sex with them. Why mess with a winning formula?'

'Is it that you can't trust your intuition or that you're scared of opening yourself up to being hurt by Ivy again?'

I nibble my lip because she's right. 'I'm scared of opening myself up to being hurt by *anyone* again, to be honest. It's fun to be joyfully fucking around, why would I interfere?'

'Because people you feel this strongly about don't come along that often.'

'I don't like feeling strongly,' I pout.

'Look, I completely understand that you weren't looking

for *The One*,' she says, arching her eyebrows. 'But maybe you have to accept that you've found it? Or rather, The One found *you*. When fate offers you up your first love for a second time, who are you to push it away?'

'Well, quite.' I take a long sip of beer. 'You know how I know this is not the worst idea?'

'Tell me.'

'Because, finally, it doesn't feel like a trap.'

'Elaborate.'

'I've been resistant to getting into another relationship because the idea of it felt like a scam. A trap. Boring. Something I'd want to get out of as soon as I got into it. A bad decision I'd have to live with. But now . . . it doesn't feel like that. I guess I don't even mean *now*. I mean, *with Ivy*.'

'When things are right they don't feel boring.' A look of inspiration passes over her face. 'Maybe the best time to meet someone is precisely when you're happily single. That way you know you're in it because you want to be, you know there's something different about them, you know they fit into your life as it is, rather than filling a gap.'

I think about the *way* I missed her while she was away. I was getting on with my life. I was doing my own thing. But I knew I wanted her as well. 'You know what, you're right.'

Vic fixes me with a gleeful grin.

'I know I'm right! Look, you loved dating. It was fun. You kept saying yourself that it was an *exploratory phase*. Well, maybe you've done your exploration and now what you want is to be with Ivy? And it would be ridiculous to deny that.'

'Maybe . . .' I raise my eyebrows enigmatically.

'She's home from America now, isn't she? She lives sort of near here, right?'

The thought of it makes my heart race. 'In absolute terms, no, but in London terms, yes. Sort of.'

'You could get the 476 all the way there.' She grins. 'I'm just saying!' Vic raises her hands in mock surrender, but I can't help but feel this irresistible pull towards Ivy.

'A grand romantic gesture? Show up at her door with flowers?'

'Why not?'

'Because it's a step too far, even for me in my newly romantic headspace.'

She presses the side button on her phone and checks the time. 'It's not even that late. You could always ask her if she wants to get a drink on your way home?'

I can't help but smile. Again. A grinning fool. That's what Ivy's turned me into. 'It wouldn't be that weird if I asked her if she wanted to have a drink. Worst she can say is no, right?'

'Right.'

So I text her.

Hey! I'm having dinner with a friend kind of near your place! Want to get a drink on my way home?

I instantly feel sick. Why does every communication I have with Ivy make me feel a bit sick? Oh yes, it's because I really, really like her. As soon as I send it, I'm plunged into anxiety that she'll say no or, worse, ignore me for ages.

'Proud of you!' Vic claps her hands together joyfully.

I grimace at her for a second before my eyes are diverted to my phone illuminating. Could it be?

Just finished basketball in Holland Park! Could meet at the pub near mine in . . . a cool 90?

'Oh my God, she replied already?!' I look up from my phone, wide-eyed. 'It's on!'

'So are you going to declare your undying love for her?'

'I'll scope out the vibes,' I say, swallowing down my nerves.

'OK, I won't try to convince you further. I'm happy you're open to it. Rather than avoiding it for some kind of self-preservation.'

I nod. 'I do quite like preserving myself, though.'

31

'Heeeeey,' Ivy says, drawing me in for a hug. I try not to inhale the scent of her too deeply, try not to close my eyes and bury my face in her hair. Try not to hold her too close, like she could slip out of my grasp at any moment.

'How was basketball?'

'Boiling. But the bitch eating crackers wasn't there so I had a better time than usual. Of course she was off in her *holiday home* in the south of France,' Ivy says, rolling her eyes.

'Wait, crackers?'

'You know, the bitch eating crackers? It's a thing,' she shrugs.

'I am unfamiliar with this *thing*.' We take a seat on either side of a cosy booth.

'You know when there's someone and you find them *so* annoying that everything they do is annoying, whether or not it's *actually* annoying?'

'Yeah, of course, I exist in the world,' I say, remembering various colleagues and friends-of-friends of days gone by.

'So they could be sitting there, eating crackers, and you would find the way they eat crackers so annoying that it's like . . . *oh look at that bitch eating crackers like she owns the place?* That.'

'I see,' I say, nodding sagely. 'And you've got one of those on your team?'

'Yep,' Ivy says. 'She makes me feel crazy. Usually I'm very, you know, calm and chill and get on with everyone. But she really winds me up! Gah!'

'Are you sure you don't secretly fancy her?' I suggest, hoping the answer is *definitely not*.

'Ugh, no way, don't even say that! Anyway! What shall I get us?' she asks, standing up. She seems a little on edge, less calm and subdued than I think of her as being.

'Pint?' I say, eyebrows raised.

'Pint,' she nods decisively.

When she returns, she sets the drinks down and looks a little sheepish. 'I'm glad you texted me. I'd been feeling weird and silly for the last couple of weeks . . . like I'd done something wrong, somehow?'

I reach out and touch her hand. 'No, it's good. It's all good.' I have truly surrendered to my feelings, whatever they may be. 'I wonder if we were maybe both being a bit silly by not contacting each other while you were away?'

Ivy laughs. 'Silly? Me? Never.'

'So how was it?'

'Hot.'

'Aside from hot?'

'Useful! Definitely useful. And fun, too. I did a lot of travelling when I could. I figured I might as well. It's so bloody *big*, you know? I had this idea of going to Nashville for the weekend and then I found out that would involve being on Greyhounds for *fourteen hours*! Luckily my friend drove me and we had a great time, but still!'

310

The mention of the friend only serves to reinforce how fucking *wild* I am feeling at not knowing what's going on in her world. I decide it's time to bite the bullet. I feel like I'm standing on the top of a cliff and looking down. 'Ivy,' I begin, looking at her so she knows I'm serious. 'Are you seeing anyone at the moment?'

She looks a little taken aback, and who can blame her? Then she shakes her head. 'No, the TV show was actually the last time I went on a date.' Even though I am well aware we *technically went on a date*, I don't really think of us meeting on the TV show as a date at all, so it strikes me as sweet that Ivy sees it that way.

'Oh,' I say.

'Yeah,' she says, 'I'm fine on my own. I only went along with it because Marco put me forward for it. I fucking hate internet dating and at this point in human history I genuinely don't really know how else you're meant to meet people.'

'Why so anti-apps?'

'It all feels like work, you know? Like a lot of not particularly rewarding or enjoyable work.'

'Huh, I guess I must really enjoy it,' I say, smiling.

'It suits you, though. It makes sense. Besides, you're extremely photogenic, so you've got about a million photos to choose from.'

'You're not wrong there,' I say, thinking of the 72,715 photos on my camera roll, a good 60 per cent of which are selfies. (The other 40 per cent is roughly equal parts food and dogs I see on the tube.)

'I'm guessing that you don't use any of those wedding dress photos on your dating profiles?' Ivy says, swallowing down another mouthful of her pint.

I blink, a little surprised and taken aback by this. Clearly my mind is working faster than hers, because she doesn't seem to realize that she doesn't follow me on Instagram which means she must have been doing a social media deep dive on me at some point in the recent past, not just looking at *my* photos but scrolling through photos I've been tagged in. I clear my throat, not sure what to say to that, but I find that I can't suppress a smile at the thought of it.

'What?' Ivy says. 'Why are you smiling like that?'

'Oh, no reason,' I say breezily, which I know will infuriate her.

'Tell me!' she insists, banging her hand down on the table.

I sigh theatrically. 'Ivy Shifford, have you been creeping on me online? She won't deign to follow me but she *will* creep!'

Her pale cheeks redden. 'No, why?' she says, her eyes watchful and cautious.

'Well, I don't mean to embarrass you but you don't follow me so you must have been creeping on my Instagram to see those photos.'

Ivy stiffens in her seat, then a change comes over her face, and I can tell she's deciding to play it cool. 'And what if I did, eh?' She raises her glass to her mouth again, hiding a smile. 'What if I was poking around your Instagram while I was in the US of A? Is that such a crime, ma chérie?'

'Not a crime at all,' I say, holding my hands up. 'I can't blame you, I am very intriguing indeed,' I say.

Ivy props her elbow on the table and rests her cheek in the palm of her hand. She looks at me sideways. 'You are. You always were.' That makes me feel a bit funny inside.

'Shall I break the stalemate and follow you?' I ask, picking up my phone and opening Instagram.

'Oh, all right, but I promise you I'm very boring on there.'

But before I can follow her, I see a notification that I've been tagged in a new post.

I gasp with delight. There *is* more to life than Ivy, isn't there! 'The shoot is live!'

'Which shoot?'

'I did the make-up for the new collection by my, uh, friend Nicole and her mates. They have this brand . . .' I say, distracted by flicking through the photos. 'Fuck, they look so good!'

'Show me! I want to see what you get up to!'

I pass her the phone and she beams at the screen. 'Amazing. They all look incredible . . . hey, look at this comment!'

She passes the phone back to me and my eyes flit over the words, trying to find the one she means.

@ScoutIsOut – Thank you so much for casting me in this shoot. I look exactly like myself, and I love it. Thank you to everyone involved, but especially Fran ♥

'How nice is that?!' Ivy says. 'I'm proud of you!'

I feel a warm glow spread over me and I know I'm probably looking at her with a stupid, dreamy gaze.

No sooner do I put it back on the table than my phone illuminates with a call coming through from Marie, which is weird because she never calls me. Probably a butt dial.

'Ivy . . .' I say, blushing, and using turning over my phone as an excuse not to look at her. 'Stop being so nice to me, it's ruining my life.'

'Moi?' She eyes me with amusement.

'Yes, you.'

'Maybe I like seeing you blush.'

'Stop!' I protest feebly, shaking my head and grinning at the same time.

'Are you telling me you don't feel something? Really?'

My head is spinning with anticipation, nerves, everything. 'Of course I feel something! It's you! It's me and you! I always feel something! If I didn't feel anything I wouldn't have had a full fucking meltdown at the sight of you!'

'Well, I feel something too,' she says, shrugging.

'So if I came and sat there, next to you, and I kissed you now, you would be OK with that?'

'Fuck yeah,' she says, slamming her hand down on the table. 'Come here.'

So I do. I stand up and take a couple of steps to the other side of the booth and the second I sit down she puts her arm around me and draws me in and it's the most intoxicating blend of the familiar and the unknown, the smell of her skin, the feeling of her lips against mine, the years that have passed, the people we've become.

'Well,' I say as we pull apart. I can't help smiling. I can't suppress it. I am pure smile.

'Wasn't that something?' Ivy's looking at me like I'm the best thing in the world.

'It was,' I say, gazing into her dark eyes and reaching up to stroke her mass of curls.

'What are we like?' she says, smiling, but her voice sounds dreamy, romantic. I feel like I could swoon into her arms like a lady in a Victorian painting.

'Do you think . . . do you think this could work?' I ask tentatively.

'I hope so,' Ivy says.

'Me too.'

'Don't go anywhere,' she says, standing up. 'I'm going to the bathroom.'

'Oh my God,' I say, giggling as I stand to let her out, 'can you still not say *toilet*?'

'Ha!' Ivy claps her hands together, delighted at the memory deep-cut of our headmistress, an imposing woman permanently dressed in lavender who had an absolute horror of the word *toilet* and claimed it was *terribly uncouth, not the kind of word that her girls should be using.* 'Mrs Brooks poisoned my brain forever!'

'I can still hear her now! Such a prude!' I say, chuckling to myself as Ivy disappears to the *bathroom*.

I watch her walk to the ladies and my heart feels light and full and like whatever happens next will be good, like I believe in it, like I believe in my own ability to have a relationship, like I believe in Ivy wanting me, like I believe in all of it. I turn my phone over and see two more missed calls from Marie. What's going on? Surely this is more than a butt dial. Maybe she's broken up with Carly. I don't want to pierce the happy bubble of me and Ivy in the here and now, I don't want the outside world to creep in and distract me, but I need to be a good friend to Marie. I press the 'call' icon and hold the phone to my ear.

'Fuck, there you are. I was about to give up . . . chicken out . . . but now I can't.'

'Chicken out of what?' I ask, my heart suddenly speeding up, and not in a good way, not like the way Ivy makes my heart speed up.

'I was out at the Glory with Carly and some of her mates and I bumped into Gobby Bobbie again.'

'Yes? And?'

'Well, we got chatting because I couldn't be bothered talking to Drunk Heather anymore, and so, you know, there we were, talking away for ages.'

'And?'

'And then she was like, look, I know you're friends with Fran and maybe I shouldn't be telling you this, but it doesn't feel right that Fran doesn't know . . .'

'Know what?'

'That Fran doesn't know Miranda was cheating on her with Sarah, the woman she's with now.'

'What the fuck?' My head is spinning. I feel sick. 'Is this for real?'

'Look, we know that Bobbie loves a gossip as much as the next person, but I don't feel like she's ever given me bad information.'

'No . . .' I murmur. It's true. She may not be trustworthy but she is, at least, reliably untrustworthy. 'Did she say how long for?' I ask, trying to keep my voice calm, like it's nothing.

Marie pauses.

'Marie?' I urge her.

'Six months?' I can almost hear her wincing from here.

'Fuck! What the fuck! What the fuck! What am I meant to do with this? Fuck!'

'Look, I didn't want to tell you, I don't know what good it'll do you now, but I thought it would be worse for you to not know when other people do, like it would make you feel stupid or something.'

'No, you did the right thing,' I say breathlessly, my head spinning. 'I have to go.'

I hang up and put my phone in my bag and pick up my bag and stand up and scrape the chair against the floorboards and walk away from the table and oh look there's Ivy coming towards me.

'Are you OK?' She grabs me by the upper arms. She sees my pale, blank face, all the action going on inside my head.

'I got some weird news . . . I have to go now, I'm sorry,' I say, trying not to cry at the shame of being a person who got cheated on, the shame of being a person who didn't know they got cheated on, the fury at how this has completely crashed into a moment when I felt so, so happy.

Ivy staring at me bewildered, I walk out of the pub like a zombie, my brain feeling like a pinball machine, all these thoughts and feelings bouncing around, lighting up a new area every few seconds, all of them bad.

32

Yeah, like I said, all my life I wanted to be single. Hotties everywhere you turn, babes sliding into my DMs. But did I ever cheat? No I didn't. Not once. Because I *knew* how shit it felt, because of Daniel, because of how shameful it felt. I had the opportunity, of course I did. But I never took it because cheating is wrong, right? Well, it turns out Miranda didn't know that. Good, sweet, gentle Miranda who I thought would never hurt me, would never make me suffer. And now I have to walk around and exist in the world as a person who got cheated on, like an absolute idiot. I am a person who that can happen to. I always will be.

'I feel like shit,' I mumble from my position on Marie's armchair, a position that can best be described as a damp pretzel. 'The shock has worn off and I feel like shit.'

'Mate,' Marie says, reaching out an arm and squeezing my hand from where she's sprawled on the sofa. We're immobilized by excess KFC and a dusty bottle of Baileys left over from Christmas. 'I'm sorry. I feel like shit for making you feel like shit.'

'It's not *your* fault. *You* didn't cheat on me.'

'No, I bloody well didn't. I can't believe Miranda! Sweet, mild, decent Miranda.'

'There's me thinking *I'm* the troublemaker in that relationship. The disruptor. The bad girl. But no! It was her! And she would never have told me.'

'It's fucked, mate.'

'And the timing,' I wail, covering my face with my hands which smell of the sharp lemony scent of the KFC hand wipes. 'Me and Ivy had just had our first kiss. Well, our first kiss of what was meant to be the *new era*.'

'Mate! You didn't tell me that!'

'It's too horrible to contemplate.'

'So what happened?'

'We acknowledged how we felt about each other. Then we kissed. And then she went to the loo and you rang me. The end.'

'You left?'

'I wasn't going to stay after that!'

'So I *did* ruin everything,' Marie sulks.

'It's really not your fault. I appreciate you telling me. You're right, I would have been even more furious and mortified if other people knew and I didn't. Especially you!'

'OK, that makes me feel a tiny bit less bad.'

'Do you remember when we were in that loud bar in Dalston that was making you feel old?'

'Yeah, what about it?'

'Well, it kind of makes sense now, how weird Miranda's friend Ronnie was when I bumped into her. I couldn't figure it out at the time, but it's like she pitied me. Fuck, just saying it makes me feel *sick*. I am not someone to be pitied! I am me! Fran Baker!'

'Too fucking right.'

'But I must be. Fuck. This is the whole problem! It's fucking destabilized everything I thought I knew about myself and my relationships. It's scary. Actually horribly scary. Do I want to risk that again with Ivy, someone who has already hurt me?'

Marie gives me a kind look and a heavy sigh. 'I hear you. It's a huge leap of faith.'

'And I feel like I've very much *lost* faith in relationships. I don't want to be at the mercy of another person ever again. I don't want to put myself in a position where they could mean *that* much to me and hurt me again. I don't want to look like a fucking idiot.'

'Where are things with Ivy now?'

I shrug. 'Nowhere. She texted me to check if I was OK after I did a runner from the pub when you rang me. But it all feels messy now. The kiss, the interruption, the *implications* of the aforementioned interruption. It's not like I can go back to normal, pretend that whole thing didn't happen, pretend that it hasn't thrown a spanner in my mental works.'

'Noooo!'

'Look, it's fine. It's fine. I can live without Ivy. It clearly wasn't meant to be? This was the universe's way of telling me that relationships really *aren't* for me. Divine intervention or some shit. It's not like dating was so bad, anyway,' I say. Which is true. But it's not about that anymore. It's not about whether I'm enjoying dating too much to give it up. It's now transformed into something else, into the question of whether I feel safe, secure enough to commit to another relationship when it's clear to me that even when I'm *in* a relationship I can't always see what's going on.

Marie bites her lip. 'I wish it had worked out. It's not that I love seeing you in a relationship or like I'm trying to force you to *settle down* like your mum, it's that you seemed to really like Ivy.'

'I did. I do.'

'It's a shame to throw it all away because of what someone else did.'

'What can I say? It's really rattled me. I am *not* the kind of person who gets cheated on! How can you ever truly know someone? I never thought Ivy would have broken up with me either. I am cursed!'

She rolls her eyes and looks like she has something to say. 'You are not cursed. Take some time to decompress. I believe in the power of love.'

'I don't know if I do.'

Marie smiles sadly and shrugs. 'Me neither. But I might as well put on a brave face.'

I frown at her. 'What's up?'

I'm taken aback when she laughs bitterly and says, 'Carly and I broke up.'

'What?! When?'

'Like . . . two weeks ago,' she says, nibbling her lip.

'Why didn't you tell me?!'

'Look, I'm not doing this now,' she says sharply. 'Not while you're already down.'

'For fuck's sake, *what*?' My heart is pounding with the anticipation of knowing whatever she's about to say won't be anything good.

She looks at me wide-eyed and breathes the heaviest, most exasperated sigh I've ever heard. She closes her eyes and takes a deep breath. 'I don't know a nice way to say this, but I've sort of given up trying to talk to you about my shit.'

I feel like I've been punched in the face. 'What do you mean?'

'I love you. I always will. But recently . . .' she trails off.

'What?'

'Something that's so attractive and loveable about you is the feeling that you're very much the main character in your life. It's something I really admire about you and I know other people do, too. But with all the dating and the Ivy stuff, it's just . . . gone a bit far, I guess. I mean, I completely get that you've got your own stuff going on, and I know now is probably not the best time to bring it up, but I don't want to keep this bottled up anymore. Like, you just said, *I'm not the kind of person who gets cheated on*, like you're in some superhuman category of person who bad things can't happen to. They happen to *other* people, less important ones. Not you, the main character.'

It stings like a physical pain. Of course I'm the *main character*, it's *my* life?

'I've never stopped you from talking about anything? Ever?'

'No,' she says, not looking me in the eye, 'but it's not like you really seem that interested in it either.'

'Well, that's an incorrect assumption on your part,' I say, shrugging, and as I say it I can hear how defensive it sounds.

'OK,' Marie says, rolling her eyes. 'I'm completely deluded, you've never done a thing wrong in your life, whatever you want me to say.'

'Ugh, that's not what I'm saying. Tell me about you and Carly, then.'

She almost flinches. 'I don't . . . really want to now.' She exhales heavily. 'You know I'm not the only one who thinks this, right?' Marie stares at me, her eyebrows raised. 'Vic's noticed it too.'

'Great, thanks so much for that,' I say sarcastically, unable to stop myself.

'I'm not trying to hurt you, but I want you to know that this isn't something I'm making up in my head. It's like you're living your best life and that's amazing, but you forget other people are in your best life too.'

'Fine, I'll go then.' She doesn't try to stop me. I get to my feet and gather my things and I leave.

What the actual fuck.

I can't believe or make sense of anything I've just heard.

My head is swimming and the noise of the tube train hurtling through the tunnel feels like an assault on my entire being, all my thoughts so loud in my brain, most of which are *what the fuck?* Ivy . . . Marie . . . it's all a fucking mess. I snap out of it and realize I've been staring at the woman opposite me so intently that she looks a little scared, when actually I wasn't staring at her at all, I was running over everything in my mind, everything whirring away behind the scenes.

I make it home without even noticing I'm moving. It's like I'm on autopilot because I'm so lost in my thoughts. When I went over to Marie's I thought my big problem was that I'd missed my chance with Ivy. And when I left Marie's not only have I missed my chance with Ivy but I also had to listen to my best, oldest friend in the world tell me I'm a bad friend. It's too much.

I can't believe of the two situations, I find it more bearable to think about Ivy than Marie.

I retreat to my room and pick up my laptop. Then I stop. Then I open my laptop. Then I stop. I need to not think about Ivy. I need to accept we're not meant to be together. I need to get on with everything else. Whatever the hell *that* is.

But more than a small part of me wants to see what fate has to say about all this. So I go to eBay and type in *flamenco dancer vase*. I know it won't be there, but I want to look anyway. Just to be sure. I scroll through many, many iterations of the same ugly figurine-looking things, a couple of vases with ballerinas on rather than flamenco dancers, more ugly figurines . . . and nothing. Until.

RARE Vintage 1970s Flamenco Vase Height 35cm

I gasp. That's it. That's the one. And the auction closes tomorrow night. I move my finger over the trackpad to click on the listing, and then I stop myself. I do a lot of that at the moment. Stopping. Pausing. Second-guessing. I wonder if I want to get involved in this. If I really want to replace the vase. Maybe I should leave it in the hands of fate. I can't control everything, so let's surrender it to the universe. If I win the auction, me and Ivy are meant to be together. If I don't, then the universe doesn't want me to revisit that relationship, and we're not meant to be. It's like a coin toss. Except this way I might get a cool vase out of it.

There's currently only one bid, so I feel like I stand a pretty good chance of winning. I take a deep breath and type in a bid that's 50p higher. Would be nice to get it for a bargain as well, wouldn't it? My bid is in, and now I have to wait. And we know I hate waiting.

I open Tinder and do some swiping.

Why do all the men I fancy these days dress like Jerry Seinfeld? Why does everyone want to know if I think pineapple on pizza is a crime?

I'm free tomorrow night if you want to meet? says one of the people I'm messaging. I check out his profile again. A bit generic, but whatever. Photo of him with a dog, comment about his height, you know, the usual. I'm having dinner with Vic tomorrow night so I ask if he can do later in the week. Before I go to sleep, I check my emails and find I've *already* been outbid on the vase. Fuck. I grudgingly up my bid. I'm not going to lose this one.

33

'You're very much the main character in your life.' That line of Marie's keeps repeating.

As much as I can't stop thinking about Ivy, even more of my brain is taken up with thinking about Marie. And not only Marie, but Vic too. Does she *really* agree with Marie, or did Marie just say that to hurt me? I know the only way out is through, and the only way through is to ask Vic.

On the tube to our dinner together, I check my emails, hoping there isn't – damn. There is. Another email that I've been outbid on the Vase of Fate! I up my maximum price *again* – I'm up against some oligarch who keeps jumping £5 increments, so I go 50p higher each time. What? I'm concerned that even if I do win, I won't be able to afford to buy the bloody thing. But it'll be worth it in the end: because it will be the universe's very specific way of telling me that I'm meant to be with Ivy.

However, tonight is about the Marie situation. Talking about it is so painful and embarrassing I can't bring myself to do it. But I know I have to. So when we're sipping on limoncello spritzes, I take a deep breath and tell her about what happened between Marie and me.

Vic doesn't meet my eye when I ask her if she agrees. That's how I know it's true. She stares down at the marble tabletop of the pasta restaurant where we're dining.

'Well,' she says, furrowing her brow and wrinkling her nose at the same time. 'It's not so much that I think you're, you know, selfish . . . I didn't put it like that. I mean, I wouldn't put it like that.'

'But . . . ?' I prompt her. I stab at a juicy-looking bit of tomato in our shared panzanella.

'But you can be kind of . . . in your own world.'

'Right,' I say, waiting for her to elaborate.

'You know what I mean, don't you?' She looks at me so imploringly it's like she's begging me.

'Isn't everyone in their own world? What's so wrong about that? I like my world!' I protest.

'And that's why I love being your friend!' Vic says eagerly. 'I love how vibrant you are and how enthusiastic and fun. I love it. You're a wonderful person to have in my life.'

'But?'

'But I think sometimes you act like you're the only person in your world? Sometimes! Not all the time!'

'OK,' I say, still not really getting it. 'But what can I do about Marie?'

'Marie's having a hard time at the moment, maybe give her some space for a bit? The break-up with Carly has really shaken her, even though she knows it's for the best.' It feels like a knife twisting in my stomach to know that Marie has been speaking to Vic about this rather than me. They're not even that close. Or at least, I thought they weren't.

328

'But I want to talk to her about this,' I sigh. 'I hate it hanging over us.'

'I get that,' Vic says delicately, again not meeting my eyes. 'But I think something you have to accept in this situation is that it would be for the best if you didn't make this about you.'

I swallow hard. It *is* about me, though. I'm part of this as much as Marie.

'All right . . .' I say slowly, frowning. I twirl some pasta onto my fork.

'I really hate this,' Vic says, shaking her head. 'I'm sorry. I hate to see you two like this, but maybe it's a good thing?'

'How can it be a good thing?' I ask, incredulous.

'Not a good thing,' she says quickly. 'I don't mean that. I mean a necessary thing. To get stuff out in the open.'

'I think I preferred it behind closed doors,' I murmur.

We move on to other topics. Vic's interior design plans for her and Greg's house. Whether I've met anyone nice recently. The upcoming christening of Andrew and Kelly's new baby. But beneath the surface I'm never at rest. I'm always poking at the wound of my best friends thinking I'm the worst.

At six o'clock the next evening the auction ends. I'm doing my make-up for my date when I get an email from eBay. This is it, this is the deciding factor. My heart pounds in my chest, and I avoid looking at the subject line for a moment. Will we or won't we find our way back to each other this time?

I let my eyes flick onto the subject. A little red circle emoji. The word OUTBID. I sigh, feeling my whole spirit deflate in an instant. These objects that are more than objects. Things that become invested with some greater power, some higher significance.

I don't know why, but I open the email. *You can still get what you want* the message reads. No, I can't. *Find alternatives to your desired item.* I click, hoping by some miracle that another one has appeared in the meantime. But no, I'm directed to a page of ugly dancer-shaped figurines. I shut my laptop and slide it under the bed. I didn't think that losing would feel this bad. I didn't think that trying to put Ivy behind me again would feel this hard. But who am I kidding? I've been here before. I knew exactly how it would feel.

34

The thing about red flags is it doesn't matter how many red flags a person is waving and how big those red flags are or even if the red is hotter and brighter than the sun – we sometimes choose not to see them. We become red-flag blind.

Red Flag 1 – a last-minute change of plans
I get it, things happen. But it rarely bodes well for a good date when you get a message such as this:

> Hey been a hell day at work is it possible we do this nearer my end? I understand if you want to cancel

texts Jason, the guy I matched with the other night, with whom I made a date for central London tonight.

I am not a canceller. When I'm in, I'm in.

> Sure. Where do you live?

When it turns out he lives in Hampstead, I am suitably intrigued as it's not somewhere anyone I know lives.

Red Flag 2 – running late

It's bad form. Again, I get it! I have a chaotic life! I understand that things happen. But, like I said, it rarely bodes well. It's only when I get to the agreed-upon new venue (a cosy Hampstead village pub) that the next date amendment comes:

> I'm tied up in a thing with work. Here's an idea – do you want to come to my place? It's cool, you'll like it.

Come? To? My? Place? Well, I suppose I was going into this in pursuit of sex anyway so it's not completely audacious of him to shift the date into booty-call territory.

Who the hell lives in Hampstead anyway? It's for kajillionaires! So while the red flags are still being waved in my pretty face, curiosity spurs me onwards.

Red Flag 3 – House of Horrors

I put the address into Google Maps and let it guide me towards my destination. For all the unpromising vibes around this date, I also feel a bit like I'm going on an adventure. Every time I look up from the little moving blue dot on my phone screen, I see a cute little chocolate-box cottage or a less-cute, hyper-secure but undeniably luxurious Hampstead pile. Judging by the lack of remaining route ahead of me on the screen, I realize I've reached my destination as I cross the threshold of a huge metal gate. OK, so far so weird, but it could be the entrance to a luxurious stately home, yes?

His text just said follow the track down to the house. By this point night has fallen, and as I creep my way through the dark gardens, I realize my heart is fluttering like I'm watching a horror movie. I even look back over my shoulder at the gate and wonder if I should turn around and leave. It all sounded so delightful five minutes ago. Now it is very, very scary. But I'm being irrational! How scary can a house in Hampstead be? It's not like I'm in the middle of nowhere!

And then out of the darkness the house makes its presence known. It's a great lumbering thing – imagine an Edwardian suburban house on steroids. I'm standing in the forecourt wondering what I'm meant to do now and it's only then that I can make out a sign: *This building is protected by live-in guardians*. OK, this is starting to make a bit more sense.

All the lights are out. There is no sign of life. Jason hasn't emerged to escort me in. When I open my phone to text him asking where to go, I see he's sent me the door code with the extremely helpful instruction **Find me on the top floor**.

Once I'm in, it becomes very obvious very quickly that this house is a maze of corridors. In some areas, the only light comes from the glow of green fire exit signs. I pass occasional notices that suggest this was once some kind of care home, and it has a faded glamour that feels like something from a seaside town. It is both grand and dilapidated. In looking for stairs or a lift to the top floor, I end up in a high-ceilinged hall with a chandelier. It is set out with sofas that have been pushed aside on one end. The floor in the middle is being used for . . . what looks like maybe a sculpture (?) of a space-craft (?) or a spider (?). I wouldn't say I'm particularly scared of spiders but coming across a six-foot-tall sculpture in the dark of a haunted house is enough to tip me over the edge.

The only thing to do is keep moving. I head through the hall until I find the stairs. I feel breathless by the time I get to the top, which is only partly due to my own unfitness and largely due to the adrenaline and the fear. Why am I still here?

At the top of the stairs there is yet another corridor – this place is *made* of corridors. Aside from the grand hall with the spider, I haven't been in a room, just a series of transitional spaces. Music plays from behind a door. The first sign of life! I raise my fist to knock on the door. It cracks open. A man's face peeks out. He doesn't look like he did on the app, but hey ho, what can I do about that now?

'Jason?'

'Aaaaaaaaaaaaaaaagh!'

I feel something brush my shins – something furry.

A cat has darted from the room and the man runs after it. He is wearing a T-shirt and no bottoms, something that if I was less in fear of my life I would refer to as 'Winnie the Pooh-naked'. He chases the cat, his little penis jiggling haplessly around.

I glance into his room: there is a trestle table upon which there are multiple laptops. Upon its surface and all across the floor are what look like lots and lots and lots of scrunched-up tissues.

No, no, this is not the one. This cannot be the one!

As I take a deep breath and turn to leave, I all but bump into Winnie the Pooh and his jiggling appendage. Fortunately he has retrieved a writhing, hissing cat – but no, it's not a cat. He is holding a ferret. The man mutters, 'Jason's on the top floor.'

How am I not on the top floor? What kind of building is this? 'I thought this . . .'

He nods towards yet another fire door.

The quest for Jason goes on.

Red Flag 4 – 'I'm tired'

Truth be told, Jason has made his room in this ghoulish former hospital-care-home-asylum kind of nice. There are fabrics draped on the walls so it's less institutional, candles, some ambient instrumental hums in the background, and even, dare I say it, some homely trinkets. Could he have turned this whole thing around? Will I be waking up here in the morning chuckling to myself about what a fuss I made the night before? God willing! Yes, he could have turned it around. Had he not gone for that everlasting boner killer: banging on and on about how tired he is.

Never talk about being tired on a date! How can people not know this by now? A person wants to feel special and the recipient of your best attention. How dare these people bring such sub-par game to a first date! I, Fran Baker, protagonist of the universe, would never do such a thing.

Jason lists all the projects he has on at work at the moment and there are these weddings he has to attend and his mum is having a 'big birthday' and he's got terrible 'screen fatigue' – as being all the reasons he, uniquely, is feeling very tired at this moment. Great.

Red Flag 5 – expecting sex

'So . . . shall we?'

That is his overture to sex after doing . . . nothing. Unless a monologue about the difficulties of WFH – he kept referring to it by the initials – is supposed to constitute seduction technique, then this guy has done not a thing to entice, intrigue, entertain, or romance me.

Therefore to have the temerity to raise his eyebrows and

quasi-ironically mutter 'So shall we?' is the straw that breaks the camel's back: finally I have seen a red flag with my own eyeballs.

'That's the first question you've asked me all night,' I say drily.

'What do you mean?' Jason frowns at me.

'You haven't asked me a single thing about myself.' Saying it out loud makes the whole venture feel so deeply humiliating to me. I went through *all this* rigmarole for this guy?

'Well, huh, the night is still young?'

I might as well, mightn't I?

'I guess it is,' I say, even though I know I want to go home. More than that, I wish I had *stayed* home in the first place.

It's like I'm not even there. When I've slept with people in the past, even if the sex itself wasn't amazing, at least I felt *present*, like whoever I was sleeping with was definitely having sex with Fran Baker in particular. That my wishes and my desires were right there in the room with us. Not tonight. Tonight I get through it. And then I can leave. As I'm lying there with him on top of me, I wonder if *he* was out looking for a date tonight to take his mind off someone else, to try to cure a broken heart, to try to force himself to think about something different, to feel something.

'That was fun, we should do it again sometime,' I say mechanically, as I get dressed afterwards.

'Yeah,' he says, with a similar lack of enthusiasm. 'Were you planning on staying, or . . . ?' That's my cue to leave.

Jason doesn't accompany me out, and knowing there could be any number and manner of weirdos behind the doors that line the various corridors sends a fresh wave of fear through me. Back out of the labyrinth of the ghost house and back through the terrifying pitch-black garden path.

It's only when I'm back in the illuminated oligarch streets that I can breathe again. And with the relief that I'm safe along come the tears.

That was a terrible date. A terrible date I knew from the get-go was going to be terrible and yet I invested so much in it: time, effort and hope. That's the worst thing – the hope wasted that this might be anything other than a degrading waste of time. And I had sex with him, the thing that for so long was so fun and joyous.

Why am I even doing this anymore? I just want Ivy.

35

LATE LATE LATE, I AM RUNNING LATE. Amid all the other chaos of my life I do try to at least be good at timekeeping. But sometimes it's out of my control! Like today! I had to move house *again* and the Uber got stuck in traffic in Hackney for about a million hours and now I'm running late for my new niece's christening. Of course it was a niece, not a nephew – this is my brother we're talking about. Four girls! What a life!

Baby Nancy is being christened at the church round the corner from where Andrew and Mum live, and I am running *late*. I keep checking the train times app on my phone even though I am *literally on the train* to see if we've somehow managed to make up time between Victoria and Beckenham Junction, if by some chance the train has decided to skip some stations to make my life easier, but no. I am simply late.

By the time I get to the church, I am a sweaty mess. It's a sweltering August day and I've already done a house move and traversed the length of London to get here like an intrepid explorer, and instead of fame and glory to look forward to, I know I'm going to get an earful from my brother, which is very much the *last* thing I need right now.

I slip in at the back and hope no one notices, but obviously the second I open the door, my brother's head jerks around like a meerkat and he fixes me with a furious glare. 'Sorry!' I mouth, and sit in a pew at the back, hoping that my sweat will have dried by the time the service is finished. I attempt to fan myself with a Bible, but I am, literally, sweating like a sinner in church. I let the words wash over me and zone out, because I truly Did My Bit by showing up and at least my late arrival means my brother *knows* I showed up.

When the service ends, I make my way to the front where Mum was sitting. 'Hello, Mummy,' I say, hugging her. A hug from her makes everything feel that little bit better for a moment.

'Oh, so you decided to join us, did you?'

'I'm sorry!'

'Naughty girl,' she says, looking at me with great affection, which is more than can be said for Andrew.

'Mum, please *thank* Fran for gracing us with her presence,' he says flatly, bouncing Nancy in his arms, who doesn't look too perturbed to have been flicked with holy water or whatever happens at one of these things. Andrew, by contrast, *does* look perturbed and is refusing to make eye contact with me. I was on time to the *three* other christenings I've had to sit through on behalf of his children! How many christenings have I ever made him attend? Big fat zero, that's how many!

Mum rolls her eyes, 'Really, Andrew?'

'Really,' he says, glaring at her in lieu of glaring at me which would actually require him to look at me.

'I'm sorry! Today's been a nightmare! But I'm here now and Baby Nancy looks delicious,' I say, kissing her fat wrist.

It feels like she's only about ten minutes old, but apparently she's been alive for at least a month. Clearly Kelly is taking no chances with the Devil getting his gnarly hands on her baby and decided to get her christened ASAP.

'Can you please ask Fran if she's coming to your house after?' Andrew says to Mum. Ah, so he really is doing this.

'Yeah, bloody hell, I didn't traipse all this way for half an hour's entertainment in a church!' I say indignantly.

'Can you cool it with the swearing while we're in here, please?' he hisses at me. 'It's *inappropriate.*'

'Swearing? What swearing?'

'The *bloody hells*,' Mum whispers.

'All right, all right,' I say, and I'm about to ask him to stop riding my ass, but I realize that's also probably off limits. At least I've managed to get him to acknowledge my presence!

Mum has a granddaughter's hand in each of hers as we amble around to her house with assorted guests. These include Kelly's mum and dad, who are perfectly nice but Mum has a bee in her bonnet and believes they look down on her for being a single parent, and a few of their local friends, mostly people whose children are friends with The Girls.

I help Mum put out the food she's bought for lunch and Andrew finally deigns to talk to me, but only to boss me around. Classic older brother behaviour. I mill around, chatting to people I barely know, wondering when I'm allowed to go home, when I spot Mum through the window, in the little back garden. I open the back door.

'You all right?' I ask.

'Yeah, don't worry about me, sweetie, just needed some time away from everyone. I don't normally have so many people in the house!' she says, dabbing at her forehead with a scrap of kitchen roll. It's *hot* in this suburban sun-trap garden.

'It's a lot, isn't it? Let's hope this is the last one, right?' I sit down on the step and she joins me.

'You can say that again,' Mum says with a laugh. 'So,' she nudges me with her arm, 'how are things going with you?'

'You mean, have I met the love of my life yet?'

'No, I've decided to give up on that after last time, eh?'

I smile, knowing I sort of kept the whole thing to myself, all the times me and Ivy hung out after the TV show, the getting closer, the kiss, and now, the nothing. 'Actually, on balance that didn't turn out so badly.'

'Oh? Do tell.'

So I do tell her, everything.

'Miranda?! Did that?!' she gasps, horrified. 'The bloody cheek!'

'Yep. And I had no idea.'

'Why would you?! She was all sweetness and light!'

'Turns out she wasn't.'

'And you found out as you and Ivy were getting close?'

I nod. 'And after that I couldn't go through with it. It doesn't feel worth it. Not after how it ended with Ivy the first time round.'

Mum nods thoughtfully. 'But what about if the whole Miranda thing hadn't happened? How would you feel?'

'It feels so . . . scary? To let myself be vulnerable like that. I like dating! I enjoy it! So I might as well keep doing it rather than opening myself up to another relationship.'

'Darling, I don't doubt that you love going on dates – that makes perfect sense to me. But don't you think you're maybe

342

using it as a way to *avoid* having a relationship with someone you *know* you want to be with?' she asks, getting horribly directly to the heart of the matter.

'Well, even aside from all that,' I say, not wanting to dwell too much on the idea that I'm specifically avoiding a relationship I think would work, 'it always felt like a bit of a daydream. Too idealistic. Like it wasn't real.'

'Why not?' Mum frowns.

'Because people don't end up with their teenage girlfriends?'

'Would you say you're the same person now that you were when you were going out with her before?'

I think about all the years, all the places, all the people, all the experiences, all the pain and the difficulties and the happiness and the sadness of it all. 'No . . .' I answer.

'And she won't be either. That was so long ago it might as well have happened to someone else. Don't let *that* be the thing that holds you back.'

I sigh. 'All that is true, but it doesn't make any difference to me at this point, does it?'

'Well, that depends, doesn't it?'

'On what?'

'On you.'

We're silent for a moment, listening to the buzz of voices inside the house. 'Do you think I was wrong? To run away from it all?'

'I don't know if you were wrong, if that felt like what you had to do at the time. More that I don't agree with you that it's *completely impossible* for things to work between you now,' she pauses, and then she says the thing I've been scared to acknowledge all this time: 'Maybe what you needed was time apart, to grow up and live your lives and now is the right time for you to come back together. Maybe it's only a good thing that you went through it all before, not a bad thing.'

'Do you know what I keep thinking about?' I say, feeling a hard lump in my throat. 'She broke my heart before. It was the first time I ever had my heart broken so it was always going to feel like the *worst* thing that had ever happened to me, and maybe it was, I don't know. But I had no say in the matter, she had all the power and I had none, there was nothing I could do about it. I thought, *she must feel so good, so powerful, so in control*. Holding all the cards. And then here I am, this time, and I'm the one who said *no*. But I don't feel powerful at all. I feel sad.'

'Franny,' says Mum, leaning her head against my shoulder. 'The only thing I've ever wanted in my life is for you to be happy. Oh, and Andrew, let's not forget about him.'

'I know, Mum. I think you should be happy too,' I say.

'Oh, don't you worry about me,' she says, not meeting my eyes.

'I do, though. Not worry, I suppose, but I want you to be happy. You're always trying to get me set up with someone, but what about you?' I think about the long line of disastrous men she dated when I was in my mid-teens, when she had a bit more time than she does now with me and Andrew and the shop sucking up every atom of her energy and attention. Useless, the lot of them.

'Well,' she says, and I watch as a smile creeps across her face.

'Mum! What?!'

'Well, you know Alan? Nice Alan?'

'Who runs the jewellers?'

'Yes!'

'I thought he was married?'

'He was! But not anymore,' she says, holding her hands up. 'That was nothing to do with me, may I add. He asked me out for a drink.'

'When?'

She frowns, trying to remember. 'A couple of months ago.'

'And you didn't think to mention it to me?!'

'Well, you never asked!'

Another gut punch. I probably *didn't* ever ask, did I? The thought of Marie *and* Vic *and* my mum – three of the people I love most in the whole world – thinking the same thing about me makes me want to curl up in a ball and die. That's when reality crashes into me like a ten-ton truck. I can't avoid it any longer. I understand it now. Being happy and having a full, exciting, happy life isn't about swishing my way through London's dating scene. It isn't about chasing the highs of a good date, of good sex, of a fun story. Or rather, it isn't *just* about that. It's about existing alongside the people you love. It's about being part of a world that contains more than your-self and your stories and your woes and your desires. Yes, I love living my best life, bringing that main character energy to my own story, but when do you stop being the main character and start being the *only* character? I can't live like that. I don't want to live like that.

I take a deep breath. This time I won't get defensive. 'I'm sorry,' I say, squeezing her hand. 'And did you go for the drink? When he asked you out?'

'I most certainly did!' Mum says, and she's visibly beaming.

'How was it?'

'Never you mind!' she says, with a very naughty expression on her lovely face.

'Mum!' I say, experiencing the twin emotions of pure vom at the thought of my mum having sex with *anyone*, and delight at the obvious joy she's experiencing in the honeymoon phase. 'This is so great. I love this for you.'

'Maybe I'm entering my . . . what do you call it? My *slag era*,' she says drily.

'Mum!' I yell.

'What?' she says coquettishly. 'If it's good enough for you, it's good enough for me.'

'I might retire the slag era,' I murmur. 'Not sure it's so fun anymore.' And then it all hits me. 'Not sure *anything* is so fun anymore . . .'

That's when the floodgates open. Hot, salty tears mingle with the sweat that was already glistening on my face.

'Baby!' Mum says, throwing her arms around me. 'What's going on? It's not Ivy, is it?'

'It's not only that . . .' I say, between sobs. 'It's lots of things. It's me. It's everything. I'm sorry. I'm sorry for being a bad daughter and not paying enough attention to your life.'

'Don't be silly,' she says.

'No, I mean it. I get wrapped up in my own goings-on and I don't look around me enough and I'm sorry about it. I don't want you to feel like I don't care or don't notice you.'

'But you shouldn't be crying over that!'

'I've made a mess of a lot of things and I don't know how to un-mess them.'

Mum strokes the back of my hand. 'Telling the truth is always a good place to start,' she suggests.

And I want to. I desperately do. But Ivy and Marie feel so far away right now. I don't know how to get them back.

36

Another day, another totally random temporary sublet.

I have to say . . . this home is not the one. Of course, all I really need is a place to rest my weary head and all that, but I can't say this one feels like home. Not that I'm not grateful for it – one of Andrew's friends is only a bloody landlord and decided instead of doing the clearly very necessary sprucing up of the one-bedroom flat between tenants, he would rather make some money off me until the new long-term occupants move in. The only thing it really has going for it is that it's about three roads away from the cafe, so I don't have far to walk to work in the morning.

What it has against it? Well, something Andrew's mate neglected to mention was that although it's furnished (with Landlord Special furniture, of course: cheap, bleak objects), the mattress on the bed belonged to the previous tenant. Oddly enough, a mattress is not among the various bits of Life Junk I carry with me from one place to the next, so I'm sleeping on the sofa like a husband in the doghouse. On top of that, it's a bit . . . drab. Unloved. Crying out for that lick of paint Andrew's landlord mate is avoiding. And no amount of homely trinkets can make it feel more lively.

Sleeping on the sofa is not the key to a feeling of mental balance and well-being, I have to say. Maybe it's a sign that my non-committal home life needs to come to an end. But I'm not really in the mood to make big life decisions right now. I'm not really in the mood to do anything.

In the cafe with the morning rush over I take the opportunity to do some discreet swiping. No. No. No. No. Not in a million years. No. Maybe? I guess? No. No. Fuck, when did this all start feeling like a chore? When did my dating joy evaporate? Why am I still trying to make it work?

Enter Luke, who's been flirting with me semi-regularly since the day he and Ivy were in the cafe at the same time.

'Hi, Fran,' he says, gallantly removing his baseball cap.

'Hello, Luke,' I say, with as bright a smile as I can manage in my downbeat mood. 'The usual?'

'Am I that predictable?'

'No bad thing!'

Jamie's strolled off to wipe down some tables and gives me a cheeky wink over his shoulder as I prepare Luke's flat white.

'Up to anything fun today?' I ask Luke as I pour from the jug into his bamboo cup.

'Same old, same old, a bit of work today then out for dinner tonight with friends.'

'Oh, lovely!' I hand him his coffee, and he opens his mouth to say something then frowns and closes it again and thanks me, so I cheerily bid him farewell. 'Well, see you soon, I'm sure!'

'Yeah, have a good day, Fran!' He awkwardly turns towards the door, before turning back to me. He takes a deep breath. 'Actually, I was wondering if you wanted to get a drink sometime? Sorry if this is entirely unwelcome, I just thought I would give it a go.'

In that specific moment I realize that no, I don't fancy him. I don't think I do want to go on a date with him. I could say yes and accept a date with him because the idea of being the Hot Barista is fun, or because it would put even more emotional distance between me and Ivy, or for any number of reasons. But I know that I don't want to. And I know that it would be very, as Marie would say, *main character* of me to say yes and go out with this guy who clearly likes me so I can scratch another notch into my bedpost and have a story to tell.

'Um,' I say, furrowing my brow slightly. 'I . . .' I begin, wondering how to turn him down politely.

But I don't have to. He can sense it. A frozen smile descends on his face. 'Look, actually, forget I asked. It was rude of me – you're at work, I'm not. Let's pretend I didn't ask, and instead I paid you a compliment. Is that OK?'

I nod, enthusiastically. 'No, I mean, yes, it's very OK. I appreciate it. Thank you.'

'Well, best be off,' he says with an awkward grimace.

'I hope I haven't lost us a regular,' I say to Jamie once Luke has left.

'Don't be silly,' he says, nudging me affectionately. 'Never thought I'd see the day you'd turn down some frivolous fun.'

'Weird, init.'

On my walk home, I get a voice note from Vic.

HEY GIRL! I hope you're doing OK, not too down about Ivy . . . and Marie . . . any of that. What's the plan for your birthday?

Ugh! I was on such a high this time last year! I was at the top of my game! And now? Decidedly at the *bottom* of my game. I don't even feel like recording a voice note, trying to make myself sound *enthused*. I text her back:

> I'm not really feeling it, you know? I'm sorry, I know it's super boring!!! But yeah, not in the mood for a big party this year.

> What about a small party? Greg says he'll wear his cop outfit if it'll cheer you up?

She attaches the photo of Greg in the pub dressed as a cop, looking seriously put out after Operation Earring Retrieval. I smile.

> Nah, it's OK, I think for the first time in my life I'm going to have a quiet one.

> That doesn't sound like Fran tbh. But if you insist . . . Vic replies. I'll keep it free anyway in case you change your mind at the last minute.

The fact I have no plans for my thirtieth birthday hits me like a ton of bricks.

37

Today is my thirtieth birthday. I don't know how I envisaged turning thirty but it wasn't waking up, not only alone but achingly curled up on a sofa, in history's drabbest short-term let, with no plans. No party, no friends, no prospects of any fun on the horizon.

I would cry but in this moment I'm too miserable to cry. And in too much pain: this is no way to sleep, at thirty or any age. As I creak and bend myself out of the sofa and onto my feet, I think two words: Fuck it.

I do not want this for myself.

I am Fran Baker and I am not leaving things up to fate. Who needs fate? I am my own fate. Marie was right, I *do* have Main Character Syndrome, and now I have to use it for good.

What can I solve in my life *right now*? That is the question. I take a deep breath and ring my mum.

'Happy birthday, darling! I was about to call!'

'Thanks, Mum . . . how are you?' I ask, staring up at the horrible Artex ceiling in the living room which I'm using as a bedroom.

'Oh, I'm fine! But what about you? What are you up to today?'

'Nothing much,' I say, trying to keep my tone light, like I'm not that bothered I have zero plans on my birthday. 'But tell me about you – how's stuff with Alan?'

It's like I can hear her smiling all the way from South London. 'Wonderful, darling. I have nothing to complain about.'

'I'm so happy for you,' I say, and my heart aches a bit with how true it is. I pause for a moment. 'Mum . . .'

'Yes, baby?'

'I was wondering . . .'

'What?' she asks suspiciously.

'Would it be OK if I came to stay for a bit. Not permanently. But . . . semi-permanently?'

'I would love that, darling. But just so you know, Alan comes to stay every once in a while and—'

'Say no more! We will cross that bridge when we come to it!' I say. The last thing I need is to be thinking about *that* on my birthday. 'So you're OK with me coming back?'

'I can't wait, sweetie.'

Right! We have duly established that I am a person who makes things happen. So let's keep making them happen. Let's give myself a birthday gift. What would a main character do? A romantic gesture. That's what.

I spring off of the sofa that I'm using as a bed, hastily getting dressed, swiping on some mascara and lipstick. I grab my handbag and dash to the tube station, walking so fast I'm almost running, propelling myself forward into the future so I can be *there* rather than in the past, a place where I make bad decisions, where I focus on all the wrong things.

I stop at the florist's opposite the station, the shop that's always a gorgeous riot of colour and shapes, and I choose a perfect bouquet.

The whole journey, I feel sick, rehearsing what I want to say, anticipating all the different reactions I might be met with. Rejection, confusion, embarrassment, anger – anything could happen. I can't control it. All I can control is myself.

My heart is in my throat when the tube pulls into the station and before I know it, before I'm really ready, I'm spat out into a back street between the Strand and the Thames and it's like I can hear the blood pulsing in my ears as I walk up towards the street, away from the river and I feel as if nothing has ever mattered more to me than this.

The day is warm – a different version of me is so happy for good weather on my birthday because I've got big plans for my thirtieth, but real me, actual me, is hot and sweaty and wishing everything had gone differently so I didn't have to be here, now, doing this.

I walk so fast that when I get there I catch a glimpse of myself in the huge shiny glass frontage and realize I look like a sweating madwoman with a huge bouquet of flowers and for a second I don't want to go in but I know *I have to do this*. I have to. I take a deep breath and push on the heavy glass door, my hands shaking.

The wait for her to come down to the lobby is interminable. I feel so full of nervous energy that I'm pacing around like a lion in a cage, holding this stupid huge bunch of flowers, and I'm looking at the door wondering if I should leave again when—

'Fran?'

I turn around, and there she is.

'Marie, I—' I begin. I look at her in her sharp solicitor suit and expensive brogues, her hair sleek but her face tired. I swallow. 'I wanted to say how sorry I am. I wanted to say thank you for showing me what I was doing . . . how I was behaving. And I'm sorry that I was a bad friend to you and that I hurt you. I know you went through something and I should have been there, that I should have been perceptive to, and I wasn't because I was too invested in my own shit. I'm sorry. For all of it.'

She looks at me in what seems like disbelief.

'Oh, and—' I say, holding out the flowers. 'I bought you these. To say sorry. Call it a . . . a main character romantic gesture.' I smile weakly.

Marie reaches out her hand and takes the flowers from me. The next thing I know I'm being crushed half to death in the tightest hug I've ever felt.

'I've missed you so much,' she whispers. 'It's been the worst time of my fucking life. No Carly, no you. What's even the point?'

I'm about to say I know how she feels, that having no Marie and no Ivy at the same time has been total bullshit, when I resist the urge. It's not about me. It's about her.

For a long time, she doesn't pull away and end the hug. She stays there. And then I realize my shoulder feels wet.

Finally she lifts her head and wipes at her eyes with the cuff of her suit jacket. 'I have to go back to work now but . . . do you want to get dinner later? I hated the idea of not having plans with you on your birthday . . .' she says ruefully.

My heart leaps. 'Yes. Let's,' I nod.

'Maybe you can ask Vic? A cosy little threesome? At that

Japanese place you like?' Marie smiles. 'You are the birthday girl, after all.'

'I bet I can get Vic involved,' I grin. Maybe my birthday won't be such a washout after all. I'm about to push open the heavy glass door when I turn back to her. 'I love you, you know.'

'I love you too,' she says, holding her flowers in her arms like a baby.

Before I exit onto the pavement, I text Vic that she was right to keep tonight free after all, that I've changed my mind and that the three of us are going to have dinner together. The fact I have birthday plans seems to have rebalanced the universe a little.

When I step out onto the Strand, the world looks a bit more beautiful. The traffic looks beautiful. The busker looks beautiful. The group of Spanish school kids with matching backpacks look beautiful. I close my eyes and take a deep breath, basking in the warm glow of this moment. My moment of calm is interrupted by a fast-moving person bumping into me. I open my eyes in irritation to see . . . Ivy?

Her hair is wilder than usual, her big eyes wider, her dark brow set more seriously. She grabs defensively at her bag, a beaten-up old tote bag with the name of a queer bookshop in New York on it.

'Oh,' I say, blinking, my heart racing.

'*Oh*,' she says, completely taken aback. 'Why are you here?!'

I flinch at that. 'It's a free country, isn't it? The Strand is hardly private property.'

'No, no,' she shakes her head, her curls bouncing. 'I mean,

I was on my way to look for *you*. I had to teach a class first thing and all I could think about was getting out of there and tracking you down. That's where I work,' she says, nodding back over her shoulder towards King's.

'Of course,' I say, shaking my head. 'I knew that. This is Marie's office.'

'Neighbours,' she smiles.

I swallow, not sure what to say now she's here in front of me.

'God, sorry,' she says, shaking her head. 'This is too much, isn't it? I shouldn't have . . .' She turns to walk away, swinging the tote bag behind her.

'Wait . . .' I say. I can't let her go again. I can't. I won't. 'Why did you go looking for me?'

She turns back to me and takes a deep breath. 'I kept my distance long enough. I respected the fact that you weren't . . . weren't ready for whatever we were trying to do. Or thinking of trying to do. But it . . . didn't feel right. It didn't feel right to have you back in my life and then lose you again.'

'I know what you mean . . .' I say, but it only comes out as a whisper.

'And I wanted to do what I should have done back when we were eighteen. I shouldn't have given up so easily then and I shouldn't have given up so easily now. I . . .' she pauses. 'I understand why you might be cautious. I know that I hurt you. And I know that hurt has stayed with you. But if you think I'm going to break your heart again, if you think I'm not committed to you or my heart isn't really in it, then I need to tell you that you're wrong. I need to tell you that.'

I feel dizzy.

'I think about you all the time. And over these past few months I've found I think about you more than I think about anyone else. I go to a gallery and I see a painting and I think *Fran would like that*, or I eat in a restaurant and think *Fran would like it here*, or . . . well,' she says. She sighs and gently lowers her tote bag to the floor before lifting something big and red and sort of lumpy out of it. 'I wanted to give you a birthday present. I understand if you don't want to keep it, though. Sorry about the wrapping. And I only had Christmas wrapping paper. Sorry. I mean . . . happy birthday, Foxy.'

She hands it to me and watches nervously as I unwrap it, her nostrils flared with concentration. 'Be careful!' she advises. As I pull off the ridiculous red wrapping paper with white snowflakes, I see . . . black. A splash of colour.

'Fuck!' I shout, laughing. The vase. The fucking vase.

'What?' Ivy says, her eyes wide.

'It was you! I was bidding against *you*?'

'Oh my God! I thought you were going to bankrupt me!' she says, and now she's laughing, too. 'You very nearly did! But I was . . . well, I was determined. To get it back.'

'So was I . . . it's so—' I'm about to say *it's so cringe*, but I realize there is no place for that anymore. There's no room for worrying what someone thinks of you, worrying about being embarrassed, worrying about showing all your cards. 'I told myself that if I won the vase then we were meant to be together and if I lost then we weren't. I left it up to the universe or something.'

Ivy smiles tentatively. 'And what does this mean, then? For . . . the universe. Or . . . I guess, for us?'

'It means that the universe has done enough to get us this far and we have to kick it over the finish line.'

'Is that what you want?'

'The thing is, I could keep dating forever and I would be perfectly happy *if* I didn't know you existed. You are the spanner in the works. It doesn't feel worth it to *protect myself* from the feelings I have for you. It doesn't feel like protection anymore. It feels like a waste,' I say. 'I want to be with you. The you that you are now. The us that we are now.'

'Come here,' she says, holding her arms out to me. I gently slide the vase back into the tote bag and for a second I'm convinced that when I look up again she'll be gone, that none of this will have ever happened. But she's there.

When we kiss it's like nothing's changed and everything's changed. It's like the years never melted away and like we're bringing our real, new, different selves to this moment. It's the past, it's the present, it's the future.

What a year it's been.

Epilogue

'It's on!' Alan calls from the living room, his loud, jovial voice booming through the house.

'Coming!' Mum says as she drains a wine bottle into a glass and I carry two back into the living room.

'I was just telling Ivy about the Mohs scale of mineral hardness, how you assess different stones that are used in jewellery. Boring her, I imagine,' Alan says, a twinkle in his eye.

'No, it's very interesting!' Ivy says, and I can tell she really means it.

'For you,' I say, handing a drink to Kelly.

'Where's mine?' Andrew asks.

'You have legs, if you wanted one you could have gone and got yourself one.'

'Fine,' he huffs.

'Shut up, you two!' Mum says as she appears with drinks for Alan and Ivy.

Tilly told us we were on at the beginning, a recap on the 'success stories' of last season before this season starts. Obviously Mum decided *this* one had to be a group viewing event. The Girls are having a sleepover at Kelly's parents', and the rest of us are here. Mum, Alan, Andrew, Kelly, me, and Ivy.

361

'Some viewers will remember the explosive reunion of Fran and Ivy who hadn't seen each other since their break-up twelve years ago!' The voice-over artist says, a little too enthusiastically for my liking, before it cuts to a clip of me storming off to the toilets. 'But it turned out they weren't such a bad match after all!'

'Hi,' we say in sync, which took about six goes to get right when we were filming it on my phone last month.

'We wanted to say thank you for accidentally getting us back together!' I say, before turning to Ivy.

'Yeah, a lot has happened behind the scenes since the show but getting back with Fran has been the best thing that's ever happened to me and I don't know how it would have happened without you guys!'

'Thanks, *The Meet-Cute*!' we say, extremely cheesily, before it cuts to the next couple.

'How lovely!' says Alan.

'Better than our last TV appearance, anyway,' Ivy says drily. 'But!' she holds up a hand. 'I wouldn't change that for anything.'

'Aaaah,' Mum says, beaming at Ivy.

'We got there in the end, didn't we?' I say, leaning my head on Ivy's shoulder.

'Yeah,' Andrew says characteristically grumpily, 'took you long enough. Anyway, I can't believe you got us all over here for *that*. It was about twenty seconds long!'

'Oh, stop complaining,' Mum says, waving him away. 'I thought it would be nice to have all of us in one place! It doesn't happen often.'

'I know,' I say, 'I'm sorry. Since I moved into Ivy's we've been . . . nesting, you know?'

'I'm not complaining! I was only saying, it doesn't happen often.'

'We should come over more,' Ivy says, smiling. 'After all, we couldn't have done it without you, could we?'

'I suppose not!' Mum says, drawing herself up in her chair, full of pride. 'I was right all along! I wanted you to meet someone nice and I got you to go on that TV programme and look what happened!'

'You're always right,' Alan says fondly.

I reach over and squeeze Mum's hand, because it's easier than saying *No, it's more complicated than that. I wasn't looking for a relationship. I wasn't looking for anything. I wanted to live, and explore, and have fun. Ivy isn't an admission of defeat, that all of that was wrong, that it wasn't what I really wanted. She's proof that even after twelve years and long relationships and sleeping around and trying things out, what I want is her. Not a relationship. Her. Only her. Always her.*

Acknowledgements

Thank you as always to my wonderful, amazing agent Rachel Mann for the continued practical and emotional support. Thank you to Natasha Bardon for her essential and rigorous editorial work, and to Lucy Stewart for ushering *Big Date Energy* into the world. Thank you to Sophie Davidson for her invaluable insights into what it's actually like to film a TV dating show. Thank you to my sweet circle of friends, Beth John, Alice Slater, Jenny Tighe, Alex Smyrliadi and Jo Bromilow for the endless chat, cheerleading and good humour. Thank you to the authors Emma Hughes, Laura Kay and Lily Lindon: meeting you has been a very gorgeous upside to writing romcoms. Thank you to the entire Rutter family. Thank you to everyone I went on a date with during my prolific dating era, 2010–2015, for leaving me with such varied memories and feelings and experiences that I can continue to mine in my writing for years to come. Thank you to Paul Haworth for rudely interrupting my prolific dating era.

**If you loved *Big Date Energy*, make sure you read
Bethany's debut romcom . . .**

Serena Mills should be at her wedding.

Instead, she's eating an ice cream sundae and drinking an
obscenely large glass of wine in a Harvester off the M25.

She's left the man everyone told her she was 'so lucky' to find
– because she's realised that she wants to find love. Real love.

So she sets herself a challenge: 52 weeks. 52 dates. 52 chances
to find real love.

But sometimes even the best laid plans don't work out. And
it's the people that take you most by surprise who can really
sweep you off your feet . . .

Read on for a sneak peek . . .

1

Hiding out in a branch of Harvester on a roundabout, a huge glass of wine in one hand and one of those long ice-cream spoons in the other, is *not* how I thought I would be spending my wedding day. But today hasn't really gone the way I planned at all. The problem isn't the wine or the ice cream — those are fine — the problem is that it's 12:15 p.m. and the ceremony is meant to start in fifteen minutes. Not only am I not there right now, I'm not *going* to be there.

I fear I am fucking up very badly. I just don't do this sort of thing. It's so not Serena Mills.

The dream I had last night was probably the start of it. Or at least, the start of it *today*. I dreamed I was in a car with my fiancé Alistair and the car had crashed off a bridge and it was flying through the air in slow-motion. I had time to open the door and jump out, but Alistair was holding my hand and telling me not to, that it would all be okay if I just waited it out. So I stayed in the car and braced for impact, and just as we hit the water I woke up. On my wedding day.

I'm not really one for reading too much into dreams. They're just the subconscious' way of working things out. I know that. I tried to tell myself when I woke up in that hotel room that the water didn't symbolize our marriage – that it symbolized liberation. Or maybe it symbolized *nothing* and it was just water. It was just a bad dream. I gave myself a few minutes to recover, just staring around the hotel room, basking in the warm late summer light coming through the blinds, the way it hit the silky, blush-pink dress hanging on the back of the door. My wedding dress.

9:05

'I'm getting married today,' I said out loud to the empty room. But it still didn't sound real to me. It felt so improbable. But a lot of things felt improbable – it felt improbable that Alistair and I had been together for ten years. It felt improbable how handsome he was, how tall and gently muscular, how sharp his jawline was, how green his eyes were. It felt improbable that he was so reliable when the girls at work all complain about flaky men ghosting them on dating apps. It felt improbable that I'd managed to fall into such a stable, secure life with him, without really trying.

A text came through from my sister.

Are you SURE you don't want me to do your make up?

Melanie kept trying to find excuses to do *wedding things* with me – she thought I wasn't being wedding-y enough, but I thought I was being just the right amount. I quite like doing my own makeup – so there was no need to interrupt her morning routine with my sweet little niece. And my sister always manages to wind me up; I love her, but she's uniquely gifted at getting on my nerves. Always overstepping. And besides, my sister and the rest of my family are staying in a completely different hotel, marginally less fancy than here.

I started wondering what Alistair was doing right then, at home a few miles away. I could picture him perfectly, the way he combs his silky, voluminous hair in front of the mirror, the way he angles his face to shave. I didn't need to be there to know exactly what he was doing. I know him too well. Absolutely no mystery there after ten years. But that's to be expected, right?

I had a couple of hours until I needed to be at the venue – this beautiful old stately home outside a nearby village – but I knew that time would slip away from me if I didn't get a move on with my various grooming tasks. I rang down to reception to order a room service breakfast. Since today was . . . was meant to be . . . a special day, I decided it was allowed. Before I hung up, I remembered to book a taxi to get to the venue for twelve, which, let's be honest, was probably a request I should have put in last night. God, the idea of ringing my parents or Melanie and asking if they could come and pick me up was too mortifying. It was enough to contend with their disapproval that I hadn't booked some extravagant vintage car with a ribbon tied to the front.

10:20

After a shower and a hair-wash, I put on a sheet mask and watched a member of a girl band making meringues on a cooking show until my breakfast arrived. I should probably have interrogated more deeply the thought which went some-thing like, 'Ah, this is so nice. I wish I could do this all day.' But I didn't. I ate my eggs Benedict with great joy, before realizing I had made a mistake with the black coffee which was undoubtedly going to stress me out even more. Not that I was stressed. I wasn't stressed at all. I was fine, I told myself. But even if I *wasn't*, maybe it was okay that I was feeling a little, let's say, highly strung. You're not meant to be relaxed on your wedding day.

> OMG Serena are you even awake?????

Another text from Melanie, which, alas, I couldn't avoid replying to.

> YES I'm awake! I'm doing my own makeup so please don't worry about coming all the way over here with Coco, I'll see you at the venue.

I instantly worried that I hadn't been sufficiently festive so followed it up with a bride emoji and turned my phone face-down on the bedside table. *Everything is fine*, I told myself. *And I am getting married today.* Which meant I needed to get on with my makeup.

The wedding has been a great excuse for buying a ton of nice makeup. As I buffed the blusher into my cheeks and shaded my eyes with varying degrees of taupe and brown, I felt pretty satisfied with my ability to make myself look nice. The thought of someone flapping around me this morning was unbearable, even if they would have been able to apply false eyelashes for me – truly the pinnacle of event makeup (and well beyond my skillset). Until the ceremony, I just wanted to be on my own. I wonder if that was some sort of warning sign.

11:15

It was time. I decided I must put it on. The Dress. My wedding dress. The dress in which I was going to marry Alistair. It's a really fucking nice dress. I struggled to find something I liked, something that felt right, something that wasn't too depressing among the few plus-size bridal options. Then my friend – well, my and Alistair's friend – Irina sent me a link to the pattern for this one. And I put all my dressmaking knowledge, all my time and energy and brain power and fine motor skills into making it.

It's a floaty-sleeved maxi dress with a deep, plunging V-front and I really do look (at least) a million dollars in it. It's blush, rather than white, which, according to my family isn't 'very bridal', but it's the twenty-first century and what can I say – I'm an evolved modern woman.

I slipped it on carefully, making sure not to drag it over my makeup, and looked at myself in the wardrobe mirror. Yes. This was indubitably a look. My blonde waves had air-dried in the most perfect way and rested elegantly against the fine georgette fabric. My makeup had come together beautifully, down to the rosy pink lipstick. And the dress.

The controversial thing about the dress is not just that it's pink. It's that it fits me. It fits the body I really have, not the body my family (more specifically my sister) assumed I would have by this specific date. My decision not to do a mad wedding diet was . . . well, let's just say it was *noted*. Not just because I was opting out of a great bridal tradition, but because, to their minds, I'm refusing to confront the fact I've gained weight in the, God, decade that I've been with Alistair. As if I don't know that. Newsflash: I'm not a teenager any more. Am I aware I could lose weight? Yes. Did I do it? No. If I'm honest, it's more that I left it too late for it to make a difference than that I made a conscious choice not to diet. My body image is . . . well, it's a mysterious, ever-shifting beast. I wish more than anything that I could say I feel amazing and hot and sexy a hundred per cent of the time, but I don't. It's not like I lie awake at night worrying about it but, equally, it's *there*. This little bee buzzing around my brain and sometimes the buzzing is deafening. But today? I look fantastic.

As I was gathering up my lipstick and room key and phone and cash to pay the taxi driver (realistically I probably don't need my Boots Advantage card at my wedding but, you know, just in case), I caught another glimpse of myself in the mirror and realized that between the tumbling blonde hair, the muted lipstick and the slightly nineties-cut dress, I looked like a fat Sarah Jessica Parker circa *Sex and the City*. Like I said, a look.

11:59

The hotel phone ringing snapped me out of my trance. I walked round the bed, nearly tripping on the hem of my dress which would have been absolutely the last thing I needed.

'Hello?'

'Miss Mills? Your cab is here.'

'Thanks so much, I'll be down in a second.'

I hung up, my hand still on the receiver. I breathed in, held it, breathed out. I'd been doing that a lot lately. Feeling kind of dazed and with a sensation that all of this was happening to someone else rather than me, I picked up my clutch bag and headed downstairs.

This is it. It's go time, I remember thinking.

Before I could leave the room, I heard my phone vibrate which made me jump, which then made me realize I was maybe more nervous than I thought. It was, of course, another text from Melanie.

Are you en route?

I replied saying I was just leaving, which was plenty of time. It was like she thought I wasn't going to turn up, like she needed to hold my hand through the whole thing because I couldn't manage it myself. Turns out she was right.

So I made my way down and nodded politely at the receptionist, and I went out to the front of the hotel and there was a ruddy-cheeked, stocky middle-aged man in a grey polo shirt leaning against the car, checking his phone.

'Are you here for me? Serena?'

'Serena Mills to Audley Hall,' he said cheerily, looking up from his phone and slipping it into his pocket.

Ever so carefully, I got in the car, making sure I didn't trap the bottom of my dress in the door. And away we went.

I think this was when things started to go really, really wrong.

We sat in silence for a moment, which was nice. But then the driver noticed the silence and turned the radio on. It had just passed the half-hour and the tail end of the news blared out. The weather reporter said it was going to be a beautiful day – twenty degrees in early September. I couldn't in my wildest dreams have expected a more perfect day for my wedding.

'Off to a wedding?' He looked back at me in the rear-view mirror.

'Yes,' I said, with a cheeriness I didn't really feel, without adding that it was actually my own wedding. I should have been jumping at the chance to talk about it, bask in the glory of my 'Special Day'.

'Feel like I spent half the summer driving people to and from weddings there! Audley Hall's beautiful, especially on a sunny day like today. It could still be summer now. Your mates have got great taste in venues. Some of them around here are a bit expensive for what you get but that's a really lovely spot.'

'Mmm,' I said. He seemed like a nice man, but I just couldn't relax. I worried he thought I was being cold. 'I'm looking forward to it,' I added, as cheerfully as I could manage.

'You should have a walk around the lake if you get a chance,' he paused. 'Beautiful.'

I nodded, weakly, wondering why I hadn't outed myself as The Bride, why I wasn't saying that I knew the lake well, having been there on at least two occasions for viewing and planning meetings. 'It sounds lovely.'

A moment of quiet. 'I love a wedding, me,' he said warmly, which broke through my nervousness a bit and made me smile.

'Are you an old romantic at heart?' I asked.

'Old? Me? Never!' he scoffed. 'But yeah, you could say that. I've been married to my wife for forty-one years. Barely spent a night away from her in all that time.'

'Wow!' I said. 'Forty-one years. That's . . . incredible.'

'We were pretty young when we got married, but I just knew. I just did. And turns out I was right.'

'How . . .' I began, my mouth dry. 'How did you know?'

'You just do, you know? You'll know it when the time's right. You'll know what I mean.' He paused for a second, staring straight ahead with his hands on the steering wheel. 'I suppose it was because I was always excited to see her, you know? But like I could count on her. Safe, you know? And nothing's changed. I still feel excited to see her.'

'That's important, isn't it?'

'What?'

'The excitement?'

'Well, yeah,' he said, furrowing his brow. 'It's not about big romantic gestures, though. That's not what I mean. What I mean is that when I come home after driving people around all day, I'm excited at the thought she'll be at home in her slippers watching *The One Show* and I'll get to make her a cuppa and chat to her. It might not be, you know, *exciting* all the time but having that feeling that you are *excited*. I think that's one of the best things about being married.'

Ten years is a long time to spend with someone, especially someone you met when you were a teenager. Relationships grow and change with time, I know that. It would be stupid to think it would feel the same now as it did ten years ago. But all of a sudden it felt like I couldn't breathe. Because I knew this man I'd only just met was right and I knew more than anything that I hadn't felt like this about Alistair in years. *Whole years.*

But what if I never meet anyone else? What if I never again meet someone who loves me, who wants to spend the rest of *their* life with *me?* What right do I have to be ungrateful for Alistair? And do I really want to face the fucking *brutal* world of dating as a fat woman?

Jesus. That is *not* a good enough reason to get married!